POLISHED

• RUSTY KNOB • BOOK FOUR •

Copyright ©2018 Erica Chilson

Wicked Reads
PO Box 29
Nelson, PA 16940

www.ericachilson.com/wicked-reads

Printed in the United States of America

First Printing, 2018

ISBN-13: **978-0-9979899-8-4**
ISBN-10: **0-9979899-8-X**

When you're a divorce lawyer, nothing is more terrifying than marital problems, especially when they involve your husband thinking the ability to mind-read translates into unconditional love.

Daniel Bishop calls his old roommate for help– Kaden Marx loves nothing more than running to someone's rescue after a decade of always being the one in distress. Neither guy realizes their husbands have been conspiring for months– Uriah Crane has already confided in Wynn Gillette, and then some.

After being lied to his entire life, Wynn will never allow his nearest and dearest to lie to one another or to themselves. Determined, this time, the truths that need to be revealed match up with fantasies Wynn hungers to live out in reality.

Dan's at his wits' end.

Uriah is lost.

Kade is in denial.

Wynn is in charge.

Rusty Knob visits Pittsburgh in the present, but Polished revisits another Pennsylvania town, in another era– State College, back to where all the secrets and lies began for Dan, Kade, and Uriah at Penn State University.

POLISHED

• RUSTY KNOB • BOOK FOUR •

· NINE YEARS AGO ·

· STATE COLLEGE, PA ·

EONS AGO- FIRST DAY AT PENN STATE

Kaden Marx

"Are you all good, son?" My foster dad is such a manly man, no one in their right mind would comment on the sheen of tears glistening in his eyes. Royce Kennedy makes crying look masculine, while I just look like a whiny baby. Barely thirty, not even tall enough to reach my shoulder, Royce is my rock.

Like the baby I am, I want Royce to hug me, but not in goodbye. I need him to demand I get back in the truck with him because Rusty Knob needs me as much as it does him– I need him more, but there's no competition.

Rusty Knob comes first.

"Kaden," Royce murmurs softly, hand squeezing my shoulder affectionately, no doubt to take the sting out of whatever may come out of his mouth next. My foster dad knows what I'm thinking– always does, always will.

"This is what *you* wanted," Royce reminds me when I wish he wouldn't.

Looking away from his all-too-knowing gaze, I stare at the floor in shame. My great-granddaddy settled in Rusty Knob. My granddaddy is an ignorant rat-bastard who calls me a worthless faggot who won't amount to shit.

My daddy is dead– he can't leave Rusty Knob.

My foster dad fancies himself the town's savior– he ain't *ever* leaving Rusty Knob.

Rusty Knob is like a black hole– if you don't leave after high school graduation, you ain't ever leaving. I wouldn't even be a townie, just a pretender hillbilly who lives in a town he thinks himself better than.

The perverted gay kid whose granddaddy abused him. The gangly idiot who tried to off himself with a blade meant to gut dead deer. The faggot who is surrounded by manly men with hard-working jobs that require coordination, calloused hands, and strength, none of which I possess. The kids who Child Protective Services had to take away and hand off to Rusty Knob's Good Samaritan.

Kaden Marx is a worthless nobody.

To prove everybody wrong, I had to get the fuck out of Rusty Knob and be the first Marx to go to college. Not only go to college, Penn State. Not only go to Penn State, I'ma graduate too.

With a degree in hand, I'm going to wave it in their ignorant, hillbilly faces, then I'ma tell 'em to fuck off.

"Kaden?" Royce squeezes my shoulder again to gain my attention. "Wherever your head's at, don't go there, son." Pulling me into his embrace, you'd think hugging someone so much smaller than you wouldn't be such a comfort, but Royce bleeds safety and security. "Is it because Miriam picked out your classes for you?"

"No," I murmur, face seeking the side of Royce's neck while my mind flashes to my distant kin. Miriam wanted to take me in, even before my granddaddy got into trouble for doing the damage my clumsiness actually did.

Just after my daddy died, I grew more than a foot in height, and my equilibrium was shit. When I told Child Protective Services I walked into a door, tripped down the stairs, or wobbled to the side, they didn't believe me. Miriam Ross was not only my daddy's best friend from elementary school, she was my dead momma's second cousin. She was contacted by CPS, but I didn't know her, not really.

The irony was, I was too terrified to leave Rusty Knob, so Miriam contacted Royce to take me in. My mouth stopped protesting my granddaddy's innocence when he started calling me a no-good faggot whose only future was selling my mouth and ass in dank alleys.

Granddaddy wanted another son like the one he lost, but I'm no Darien Marx.

Since I moved in with Royce, Miriam has taken to mothering me from afar. Between my baby foster brother's nonstop privacy violations, Royce's smothering, and Miriam mapping out my life, I haven't had a chance to be up to no good…

Like stalk my best buddy's baby brother or indulge in my fascination with sharp and pointy objects.

"This is Miriam's alma mater, so she knew what you'd need to take." Royce is babbling as if I didn't already know this shit. "Even though she's in administration, she knows what courses you need to take to become a teacher."

I want to become a guidance counselor to help kids like me– kids who are gay, or awkward, or fearing they're a pervert, or dealing with dead parents abandoning them, or family who thinks they're the scum of the earth because they aren't society's so-called normal. But Miriam suggested I do elementary education as a major, knowing I was too stupid for an advanced degree. Sure, she didn't come right out and say it, using the fact that Kentwood Area School District will be having the majority of its teachers retiring in the next decade, so there will be a position for me no matter what as long as I go the teacher route. No guarantees for me to be a counselor.

No guarantees I can get a teaching degree, either.

Pulling from our embrace, I'm held out at arm's length, kind brown eyes tracking every emotion crossing my features. "Son." Royce sighs as if I exhaust him, and I know I do, which makes me love and respect him all the more.

Royce passes every test I give.

Endless trips to therapists, putting up with my tantrums and tests, buying me whatever my heart desires– including the brand-new Durango that had to stay in Rusty Knob because I'm a mere out-of-state freshman required to board in the dorm with no transportation, like I'm a goddamn two-year-old. It's not as if I'm not old enough to vote, get married, own property, or die in a war.

Back in Rusty Knob, folks my age are grown men, with grown men responsibilities. Here, at Penn State, I'm a child, which is why I want to be here, since I'm too stupid to be an adult yet.

"You don't have to do anything you don't want to do." Royce reassures me, but I know the tough-love bullshit is coming next. It always does with Royce, with a concerned delivery to soften the blow. "But this is good for you– you need to stand on your own two feet for a bit, get used to walking in your own shoes."

Asshole that I am, "Stop talking in clichés."

Snorting, Royce shakes his head at me, knowing I get prickly when I'm uncomfortable. "I'll never let anything happen to you, son. You know that. Never, *ever*. I'm four hours away– that's it. Call me, and I'll be here. If you don't like college, I'll come get you, no questions asked or judgments passed. But the only thing I ask of you is to at least try, because this is for *you*."

"I promise," flows before I can stop it, because Royce Kennedy is too reasonable, too nice, too amazing of a human being to let down and disappoint. "I will graduate from here," I vow with great determination, causing what was once glistening to spring into real tears from my foster dad's eyes.

"I know you will," Royce says with great pride, as if he sees something in me that no one else does. When I look in the mirror, all I see is a zitty, awkward asshole. "Gimme one last hug, then let your brother back into the room."

Snickering evilly over the fact that I locked Bren out in the hallway, because I wanted uninterrupted Royce time, I pull my foster dad into a tight hug, with both of us ignoring the tears flowing from our eyes.

As I said, Royce looks manly all teary-eyed, whereas I look like a sniveling baby.

Still reeling from being left behind, I don't even react when Royce pulls away to let his mini-me spawn into my dorm room. "Ugh!" is forced out of me when chubby arms wrap around my hips.

Bren's a cool dude for a twelve-year-old– a little bit chubby and hella short for his age. Bren's a naughty, bratty baby brother who won't give me a moment's peace. But, right now, I want nothing more than to go back home with him.

I'm gonna miss you, Bren.

"Stop bawling, ya little baby," I growl, trying to detach Bren from my hips.

I love you, Brennan.

"You're crying too, asshole!" Bren snarls, but he grips me tighter, fingers twisting in the back of my t-shirt.

I love you too, Kaden.

"I have allergies– what's your excuse?" Snotty, both literally and figuratively, I manage to pull the kid off me.

"Likely excuse," Bren gives me attitude. "Do you want me to make up your bed?" The kid knows I'm a lazy asshole, or maybe he has just given up and will do my chores without manipulation from here on out.

"No," Royce intervenes, knowing how I force Bren to do my chores at home. "This is a rite of passage Kade has to walk alone. You'll be doing it someday soon, too."

Cries turning to sobs, thankfully Bren runs out of the room before he has me breaking down too– he never said goodbye.

Secure in his masculinity, Royce has tears streaming down his cheeks, but he's smiling through them. "I'm gonna miss the hell outta you, son– you must know that." Yanking me into the tightest hug of my life, "I love you," is said without the fanfare Bren and I used.

"Proud of you," is the last thing I hear as the door closes behind my foster dad, totally wrecking me.

They left me here– left without me.

As I contemplate unpacking, my mind spins in a circle.

They left me.

Abandoned me.

Royce and Bren are happy to be rid of me.

Bed first, I grab for the box marked in Sharpie with Bren's scrawl: **Bedclothes**. I'm laughing elatedly the instant I open the box. **Knock your shit off, Kaden. You know damn well we love you. You're our family, blood be damned.** That was written in Royce's precise lettering.

Feeling lighter, laughing to myself, I manage to get the bottom sheet on my tiny bed before my roommate arrives. The knock on the door has me startling, but the anticipation is killing me. Miriam picked my roommate for me, knowing the guy's mom somehow, thinking we'd be a good fit.

"Hi, Danny," I'm muttering like an idiot as I open the door with a goofy grin on my face– we've been emailing back and forth for the past six weeks to get to know one another. "Do you need any help with your stuff?"

Taken aback, the guy standing in the doorway is a jock. Huge, dark hair with darker eyes, with his thick arms folded over his chest. Something about him screams bigot. I can already hear the word faggot on the tip of his tongue before he even speaks.

Horrified, what the fuck was Miriam thinking?

Words mirroring mine, "What the fuck is a hillbilly doing here?" Lips twisted in a sneer, the shorter guy backs me up. I may be nearly six and a half feet tall, but I don't feel it. Inside or out. "That accent– a fucking flannel? What are you, a lumberjack? My dad was way into grunge– the early nineties are calling, and they want you to stop giving them a bad name."

"Please tell me you're not Danny," I beg anyone who will listen in a squeaky voice that is too high-pitched for my size.

"Oh, a faggot too. Just fucking lovely." The asshole sneers again, thoroughly disgusted. "I'm looking for Dan, but instead I found you. Must be your family bought your inbred ass an in. There's no way you actually qualified to go here."

The guy departs as quickly as he arrived, leaving me shaking from the tips of my toes to the top of my head. Fingers wrenching my hair out of the way, I'd grown it to cover my zitty face, with the added benefit of pissing off my granddaddy.

My new friend and my granddaddy would get along great.

Did Royce buy my way into Penn State? He has more than enough money and the will to do it. Royce would do anything to keep sharp objects out of my fingertips.

Miriam? Did she mess with my Rusty Knob High School transcripts?

I doubt I was smart enough to get into Penn State on my own.

Crying, hating myself, I curl up on my tiny bed, feet hanging off the edge even in the fetal position. Between sobs, I whisper all the things I should and shouldn't do. "Think before you speak. Don't say ain't, gonna, I'ma, daddy. Lose the accent. Eat until you almost puke. Use the face shit the doctor prescribed. Weight train and drink protein shakes…"

Hiding the side of my face against my pillow, it keeps spewing and spewing. "Don't be you, Kaden Marx. Study hard. Learn to walk on your own two feet– literally. Grow up and fill out. Be smart. Graduate. Don't act like a faggot."

Shivering, sobbing, feeling more down on myself than ever without Royce and Bren keeping me in check, I fall asleep muttering all the things I should and shouldn't do.

Sometime later, I'm woken up by fingers carding through my hair. "It's okay," a soft voice is murmuring like a mom would to their upset child. "I've got you, Kaden. I don't know what happened, but it won't happen ever again– not on my watch."

Warm– taken care of and safe and secure, I recognize Danny as soon as I become cognizant, because his presence in person is as welcoming as it was in our emails, only more so. I still have no idea what he looks like, but Danny reminds me of Royce.

I didn't think I could do this without Royce, and I panicked.

I can do this– I'm not alone with Danny having my back.

• PRESENT •
• PITTSBURGH, PENNSYLVANIA •

PRESENT DAY WOES
Daniel Bishop

"You look worried," is the first thing out of Uriah's mouth as I walk into our apartment. After tugging his literal apron strings, my husband ditches the *Kiss the Cook* apron. Revealed is a see-through blouse flashing pale skin and slightly puffy nipples. "Did something happen at work?"

No doubt my frazzled appearance is a dead giveaway. "Nine hours of mediation, with my client being berated by his furious wife, without even a piss break…" I trail off, headed straight toward the bar situated in the far corner of our living room.

"That bad, huh?" Uriah is hovering, but I don't mind his usual frenetic energy, as it seems to suck up and devour the mood the Burgesses put me in. "Go sit on the sofa. I'll make you a drink."

"Scotch– neat," I mutter without hesitation as my ass sinks into the cushion. Sighing in exhaustion, the back of my head is cradled perfectly. I never want to move from this spot, except the delicious scent wafting from the kitchen is calling my name.

If only Uriah would bring me my supper, but I won't act like my clueless, thoughtless clients. We do have clearly defined, classic gender roles in this relationship, which is fine by the both of us, but I won't take advantage of it. Uriah was nice enough to cook me a meal– the least I should do is eat it at the table while conversing with him. But I'll go a step further by cleaning up the table and the dishes, because my husband worked all day too.

"Salvageable?" A glass is dangled in front of my face. "You only get this upset if the marriage is fixable, but they won't give in."

"All relationships are salvageable." I take an eager pull on my drink, smacking my lips to enjoy the lingering smoky flavor of the scotch. "If people would just get over themselves, give in a little bit, forget their pride, and be willing to evolve, every relationship is salvageable as long as there is love present."

Sighing dramatically, Uriah steps behind the sofa so he can reach my neck and shoulders. Fingers biting in with brutal accuracy, he tries to rub the stress from my muscles.

This is pretty much a weekly conversation for us– we both know the drill.

Lawyers get a bad rap, when some of us are actually altruistic. The Bishop Legal Group is not a cutthroat money bleeder. Our clients more often than not stay together, instead of how other firms break them apart to get a hefty commission and billable hours during marital warfare.

Outside of criminal activity, such as abuse of all kinds, generally every marriage is worth saving, all coming down to a lack of communication. Our clients would rather pay us a commission for keeping their marriage intact, instead of splitting their lives in half, losing time with their children, and dissolving a loving yet clueless marriage.

I earn every penny I make, and I do it because I believe in what I do.

Some days, I'm more therapist than attorney.

"My client's wife is so goddamn bitter, she won't communicate outside of screaming his faults. Meanwhile, she's just proving why he wants to get the fuck away from her, with her derogatory, emasculating rhetoric. I see too many wives treating their husbands like children, then bitching they aren't man enough to step up."

"You sure it's worth saving?" Uriah moves to sit next to me, plucking a gin and tonic off the coffee table.

Everything is worth saving.

The loudest voice among the public is how if one spouse cheats, the marriage should end to preserve self-respect. Even with adultery, there are underlying issues that need to be dealt with by both sides. If they divorce, they'd take their baggage with them and continue to taint every relationship they have, and I don't just mean romantic entanglements.

"Yes," I say without hesitation. "I may be sick of the know-it-all attitude, which seems to infect every marriage that comes my way, but there is always love there."

After taking another sip, I place my glass on a coaster on the coffee table. "My client ate his crow and saw the error of his ways. Now I'm just waiting for his wife to see that it takes two assholes to fuck up a marriage. One not hearing, one saying too much but never anything of importance, then expecting mind-reading. Emotional immaturity, at every age. Ted has grown up in the six months we've been mediating. Now it's time for Carol to let the anger go, and realize she's not perfect."

Always intrigued with the dirty details, "What has the wife been doing?" Uriah shifts on the sofa, his shirt pulling across his nipples. If I wasn't so tired, I'd be enticed. My husband tries hard to keep my attention, and I appreciate it. But sometimes it's exhausting to continually feed the sexual validation Uriah needs.

"Ted's no saint, not by a long shot, but he's a good guy. Who gives a fuck if Ted forgot to pick up the dry cleaning, or picked up the wrong type of ground meat at the market? Intent should matter. Meanwhile, Carol forgot his birthday *on purpose* to be spiteful and teach him a lesson, but Ted never brings that up during battle. He called her a bitch, and she'll never let him live it down... but he called her a bitch after she slapped him for looking at another woman's ass, even though he said he wasn't– a woman hitting a man is still abuse. Ted never mentions how Carol reads smut, has book boyfriends, and is active in a shit-ton of man-candy Facebook groups. He doesn't care, wanting Carol to enjoy herself. But she is vicious about it, saying Ted doesn't love her if he looks in the general direction of where a woman is standing– my personal assistant wasn't allowed in mediation because she looks younger than Carol. None of it matters, and it's ruining their marriage. Insecure hypocrite– if you put misery into the atmosphere, expect to receive it back."

Turning slightly, my words dry up the instant my eyes connect with my husband's.

Blind.

Insecurity is the number one factor in all communication problems.

Carol needs to tell Ted she's insecure in how he feels about her, but she pushes him away with her childish behavior instead. At the root of it, Ted can't fix *her* issues– only she can. But he's trying anyway, trying to reassure her, but I think it's negative reinforcement for horrific behavior.

I have my own Carol on my hands, only I'm smarter than Ted. *Now* I am, anyway.

A few months ago, I thought everything between us was perfect. Uriah and I had come to terms with why we wanted to mess around with Kaden and Wynn. I've known Kade since we were freshmen at Penn State, three years before I ever laid eyes on Uriah, so our husbands understood. But it took Wynn a few minutes of conversation to get out what I'd been too blind to see in my own marriage.

Uriah and I have issues we're working on, and I realized every relationship continually changes, and a lack of communication is what murders it. I wasn't listening to the things that weren't being said, and Uriah was saying everything but what was important.

I'd love to say having Wynn convince me, while tutoring Uriah how to work my ass, was a positive turning point in our relationship, but it wasn't. What truly brought Wynn and Kaden closer together has been slowly forcing Uriah and me apart, and it's not sexual in nature.

Trust.

Trust in our love, in our relationship, in our communication.

I'm willing to meet every need of Uriah's, even if it makes me uncomfortable, or find someone who can and will. It's impossible for both parties in a relationship to be on the same wavelength at all times, to want the same things. Only compromise and communication will get us through the tough times.

Uriah is his own person, with his own thoughts and feelings, and I won't stifle him by dictating how he should feel in fear of hurting my feelings, or worry over whether or not I'd be ashamed of him. I expect this same courtesy in return.

As I say to my clients, on a daily basis, relationships are a partnership, no different than a contractual partnership. The same tenets apply. You never *own* your partner, and their say in your relationship is just important as yours.

Meet in the middle.

Uriah broke my trust by evading his needs and wants since he was nineteen, while I've been an open book, even if it hurt to voice what I wanted aloud. Hurt me. Hurt Uriah.

That's what Wynn and Kade have– unflinching respect with no judgment. I thought Uriah and I had that too, but I was wrong.

"Ri?" I croak out, having no idea how to fix my own marriage when it's what I do for a living. Maybe I'm too close to the issue and need to look at it from a different perspective. What would I tell my clients to do?

"Dinner's ready," Uriah whispers, voice as raw with pain as mine. Cupping my cheek, he leans in to press his lips to mine. Desperate, I meet him halfway, but he pulls away all too soon. "I made your favorite."

Uriah's trying.

I'm trying.

Failing or not, we're both still trying. Eventually, we have to succeed.

▪▪▪ ▪▪ ▪▪

After a pleasant dinner, with Uriah and me trying to ignore our issues by going about our daily lives without the added stress, I find myself in need of advice as I wash up the kitchen. But I don't know who to turn to. My dad and grandfather would know best, but the last thing I want to do is draw them into our problems.

That's a huge no-no I give to my clients– don't bitch to your parents about your spouse, then get angry when they don't like your spouse after it blows over. Your parents aren't there for the make-up sex, apologies, or flowers, and their resentment and protective streak runs deep when it comes to their hurt children.

Besides, when it comes to personal matters, Grandpa and Dad hand over the responsibility to their wives. Since I was born, with three grown females lording over me, the two grown males have hammered into my head how the woman is always right– just agree with her and go about your business. Give her what she wants, and she'll leave you alone. She's right, you're wrong– grovel and beg and say yes. How an unnecessary apology will save hours' worth of lectures, even if she is wrong, even if there is no reason to apologize.

Dad and Grandpa would be no help on two fronts: Uriah is a guy, and I refuse to prescribe to emasculation, not after that toxic attitude harmed me for my formative years, and still affects me today.

Uriah is finishing up the layout of this month's issue of *Under the Rainbow,* while I use mindless chores to clear my head before we meet up in our bedroom.

Looking over my shoulder to make sure I'm out of earshot, feeling guilty for not only calling Kade, but talking about Uriah, I step out onto our balcony overlooking the river.

"Hey," Kade whispers, like he can sense why I'm calling. "You doing okay?"

"No," I answer without hesitation, never once holding anything back from Kade. "Are you free to talk?"

"Yep." A loud bang echoes through the speaker on my phone, reverberating my ear. "Even if I wasn't, I'd make sure I was for you. Wynn's taking an online course at the kitchen table, and I'm cleaning out the basement."

"You? Cleaning the basement?" I chuckle with wry amusement. "We roomed together for four years, you filthy fucking hog."

"Wanting to get laid ever again will have a man doing the damnedest things." Laughing sinisterly, another loud bang sounds in the background. "All kidding aside, we need a home office, and my need to foster kids took ours from the first floor. Compromise– I clean out the basement, and Wynn will renovate it for a shared office, especially with him trying to pick up credits for an industrial arts degree."

"Win-win," I mutter with appreciation. "Can't really concentrate at the kitchen table. I have to admit, that makes me jealous."

"What does?" Silence rings, Kade must have stopped moving. "You have seven years of higher education, so I know it's not the online courses."

"How you and Wynn work through your shit." I answer after a few moments.

"You mean by fighting and fucking?" Kade jests. I know they fight and fuck constantly, but when it matters, they get right to the heart of the matter and fix it immediately. "We just accept that we're going to hurt the other's feelings by telling the truth. But it goes both ways, until his pain is mine. It's almost punishing, until we're thinking of each other more than our own needs."

"Yeah, but–"

"I'm a selfish bastard, Daniel." Kade calls me by my birth name, so I know I'm in for it. "The more selfless I become, the more selfish Wynn gets, until we're balancing each other out… Wynn told me the other day how he either had to go to Bren's, or he was going to punch me in the nuts."

"What were *you* doing?"

"Annoying the piss outta him." Kade chuckles darkly. "I learned a lesson on how to control myself, or else it will either emotionally hurt when Wynn runs away from me, or physically hurt when he punches me."

"I… Uriah and I can't be like that," I mutter in mystification, never once resorting to violence or manipulation in our relationship. We rarely argue, never have I yelled at Uriah. "What works for you guys, most definitely won't work for us."

"How about you tell me what's going on, and I'll try to fix it?" Kade's voice is coaxing, a tone he mastered way after we roomed together.

Kade's a grown man now, strong enough to shoulder many burdens– a part of me is sad Kade doesn't need me anymore, but a larger part is thrilled we're finally equal in power within our friendship.

I'll admit it to myself, but never aloud– the confidence in Kade's voice goes straight to my dick, even if it has guilt suffocating me.

Sighing, I lean against the railing, eyes cast downward to the river below and all the chaos in Pittsburgh. All those people with lives just as fucked up as mine.

"Listen, Dan," Kade orders, when it's usually me in charge, with Wynn doing his damnedest to out alpha dog me, which I allow with great relief. "It's always been you taking care of me. Let me return the favor. It's what I was trained to do. Lay it on me."

"I need your help." I admit at great length.

"'Bout time."

• NINE YEARS AGO •
• PENN STATE •

EONS AGO- FIRST DAY AT PENN STATE
Daniel Bishop

I'm more than mildly curious to meet my new roommate, after getting a call from Mom's college friend. After I agreed, Miriam gave me the lowdown on the guy. Some seriously heavy shit.

My upbringing made me the perfect candidate to deal with Kaden Marx. With conservative values bred right into the folks of Rusty Knob, and with it warring with the guy's natural persuasion, Miriam was terrified the wrong roommate would cause Kaden to end it all. Again.

We Bishops are conservative Christians with strong political ties to the Republican party, with many of my family members in high positions, reaching every branch of government.

I loathe politics and have no political leanings, refusing to vote on principle.

I am conservative in nature, having absolutely nothing to do with politics, meaning I was raised to work hard and live within my means. My childhood was filled with mowing lawns and shoveling snow for my neighbors in their larger houses, babysitting, and my teen years were filled with unpaid internships and volunteering.

After being bullied, spit on, and had trash thrown in my face at boarding school because of my family's political ties, I was warned to keep my trap shut at this liberal university, because they would see me as inherently evil.

My surname is too obvious, plus I'm too close to home to escape the legacy. I've prepared myself for the influx of people wishing me to do for them, and those who wish to punish me because of my familial ties.

This left me in the perfect position to understand Kaden– the values of my upbringing not necessarily representing my true self, or sometimes completely conflicting with who I am, mixed with bullying attacks.

The only thing people think when they hear my name is republican.

We Bishops reside in a murky gray area, but our conservative nature pigeonholes us as the *R*-word that earns shocked gasps of horror– *Republican* –when we wish there was a better alternative not at the expense of our value system, economic standing, and global location.

Free-thinkers.

Hard-workers.

Bishops will teach you to do for yourself, only helping if you cannot. We believe if you do for those who are capable of doing for themselves, you're part of the problem. An enabler, stunting growth while taking from those who truly need help and education, while losing those who always slip through the cracks.

Conservative by definition doesn't mean pro-life, anti-LGBTQ rights, racist, uneducated and ignorant, selfish, evil, believe women are second-class citizens, or are religious fanatics. All it means is how we live a conservative lifestyle, within our means, and without excess.

We worked hard to earn our money, and we think we should get a say in how it's spent. We have what we need and nothing more, with the rest going to charities that fit within our belief system.

Bishops are about family without condition, which means if my third cousin-twice removed lost his job due to cutbacks, the family rallies to take care of him. With so many of us, giving a small amount we won't even miss, it's better than expecting the United States government to take away from families who are struggling to survive, believing that it's better used for those with the misfortune of not having a supportive family.

If that makes Bishops assholes, with the rest of the conservative folks, so be it. Most of my bullies have been loud-mouths who haven't given a penny or lent a helping hand, but are more than willing to be the squeaky wheel to make others feel like shit for not giving their time and money. The hypocrisy would be hilarious if it wasn't so sickening.

Above is the rhetoric I've been bred on, the same as Kaden has, which is why I loathe politics and its need to divide, and refuse to vote within a corrupt power structure.

Miriam said Kaden needed stability.

I spent my senior year at boarding school, where I was tormented for my family's political roots, but I didn't care how they got it all wrong, choosing to believe I was someone I am not. Evil. Selfish. *Wrong*. Not giving a fuck has bullies fleeing quicker than shit, and that was what Miriam said Kaden needed the most.

Confidence and conviction.

Structure and stability.

Boundaries and rules, without a gray area to get lost in.

A friend.

Like a clan, my grandparents, parents, my big sister, me, and my nephew all live in the same home. Bishop values only allow us to move on once we begin our careers or marry… but not far. While that sounds stifling, it's not like my grandfather and father have mapped out my life– independence was bred into me from birth.

My new roommate is gay, and while times are changing, becoming more sympathetic, bigotry still exists. Yet again, Miriam knew I was the man for the job.

When I was a little guy, my fourteen-year-old, big sister got pregnant by a kid her age. Accidents and mistakes happen, and my family never made Ainsley feel ashamed or guilty. It was just sex, driven by hormones and human nature, and not a big deal, no matter what our neighbors said.

We knew my nephew was gay from the moment he could walk and talk, and Ransom never had to come out. It wasn't a big deal to any of us. We just asked if Ransom had crushes on boys, instead of asking about girls. At four years older, the only difference was how I chaperoned all of Ransom's sleepovers.

Ransom is my favorite person in the whole wide world, and after seeing me with Ransom and her son, Tyler, Miriam decided I could handle Kade's fragile state and keep him safe from bigots. Because, unlike Ransom and Tyler, Kade hasn't had a stable, loving, unconditional upbringing where you have an entire family at your back to do battle should someone try to hurt you.

Ransom's gay. My sister is an unwed, young mother. My family is republican. I'm going to be a lawyer. None of that makes us who we are– it's just a facet. Miriam said Kade takes this shit to heart, and hasn't totally accepted that his gay identity is no different than being straight, and it plagues him.

"Hey, Dan!" A jackass from boarding school collars me in the hallway, when all I want to do is get back to my dorm room. The Bishop father/son team is mediating a high-profile case in court today, so we moved my stuff in last night, because I had to watch the action instead of meeting my roommate this morning.

"Kyle, what's up?" I keep walking– the universal sign of *I'm busy, so leave me alone*. "Did you get moved in okay?"

"Yeah… yeah." Kyle's acting all shady while walking a step behind me. "Listen, Matt was looking for you earlier."

"Christ," is torn out of me. "What did that asshole want?"

"Um… so," Kyle stammers, causing my heartrate to jack up. "Matt met your roommate."

"Motherfuck," is flowing from my mouth way after my feet start taking the steps at a dizzying rate. My key is in the door, hand twisting the knob, way before my mind checks in. I enter our room silently, terrified of what I'm about to find.

Miriam said Kaden tried to kill himself almost two years ago, and still cuts himself on a daily basis. Kade's foster dad shelters him from bullies, terrified it will cause Kaden to try to take his life. Again. Knowing Matt from high school, now I'm terrified.

With a deep breath of relief, I close the door behind me as softly as possible. Kade's curled up on his bed, knees cradled to his chest, with his feet still managing to hang off the edge. The guy is massive.

"Don't let anyone know you're a faggot," Kade stammers in his sleep, tear tracks staining his cheeks. Wincing as I walk forward, because no one should use that word, especially when speaking of self. Ransom just uses gay, because there should be no negative connotations to being a guy who likes other guys.

Not sure what to do, I gingerly sit on the edge of Kade's bed, wondering if I can survive four years of this if this is Kade's natural state of being. He seemed witty, intelligent, and confident yet self-deprecating in our emails. I thought he was a pretty cool guy and connected with him immediately.

My dad and grandfather would tell me to snap out of it, then put me to work. My mom would pat my back and brush my hair with her fingertips to comfort me. Gazing down at Kaden, he's too distraught for the tough-love approach, so I go the way of mothering.

"You have great hair," I mutter with some surprise, as Kade had described his hair as unruly and wiry. "Jesus, it's like silk." Deciding this will be no hardship, I pet Kade's hair to comfort him. Half asleep, he shifts so I can reach him better.

Pulling the hair away from his cheek, I notice his clear skin, when Kade had said he had really bad acne. The hair, the clear skin, it makes me check out the rest of him. The boy is huge in all ways– tall and strong, a nice amount of meat on his bones, when he'd said he was scary skinny.

"Hey, it's gonna be okay. I promise no one will ever harm you." Continuing to comb Kade's wicked hair, I murmur soft reassurances to draw him out. "I have no idea what happened, but it will never happen again."

"Danny?" Kade moves slightly, giving me a full view of his face. With a gasp, I can't look at him long– Kade's too pretty. I've never felt so protective of another person, especially one who looks like he should take care of everyone else. Nor have I ever felt a stirring of lust when looking at a guy, all because his features are more beautiful than the prettiest girl I've ever laid eyes upon.

"Hey, you're gonna be okay," I mutter my reassurance. "I'll make sure."

Visibly relaxing, I realize Miriam didn't pick me because I was sympathetic to Kaden being gay, or able to understand how he was raised back in West Virginia, or how he needs a sense of family. Miriam picked me because there's something about me that will comfort Kade, make him feel safe.

"Let's get you unpacked, okay?" Sliding to my feet, I give Kade room to crawl off his bed. "Let's put down some roots."

It's easy to sort out which box to open first, because someone wrote the contents in giant letters on each box. Finding the one marked **HOME**, I do the first task of many, by making Kaden feel welcome.

I'm not an alpha male, but I'll pretend to be one as long as it helps Kaden survive. This omega enjoys an independent life, intersecting many groups while never conforming to one. Today, I start a new group, with Kade as my sole member.

"Let's see what we have here." Kade stares at me as I rifle through his personal stuff. Huffing a laugh, I think of the bear-trap in Mom's purse, and how it's a privacy violation just to get a piece of gum. But here is this guy, letting me do whatever I want to his shit, and he looks comforted by it.

"Grab the tape out of the first drawer in the desk. Over there–" I point in the general direction while sorting through a handful of pictures I found in the box marked **HOME**. "I'll help you put down some roots, then you can help me put down some. We're going to be here for four years– might as well make ourselves at home."

Kade does as he was asked without complaint and no communication, but then he does take the stack of photos out of my hand, sorting through them.

"My mom and dad and me." Voice sheepish, I can tell Kade feels ashamed of his behavior, but is willing to ignore it as long as I do. Fine by me. "Darien and Lydia Marx." Kade's father is a huge, burly man with a shaved head, and his mother is a tiny, beautiful woman, and I can see Kaden in both of them.

Taking the picture from Kade's hands, I tape it on the cinderblock wall next to his bed, so he can look at it while lying down. "You and me, we're always going to be blunt with one another. I know you're gay, an orphan, and living with a foster family. Miriam is a relative of yours, but she's been a family friend of mine since before I was born."

"You know Miriam better than I do," Kade mutters reluctantly, ducking his head to appear shorter. "My grandfather wasn't a fan of people sticking their nose in our business, so after Momma died, her friends and family weren't allowed around anymore."

"How'd they die?" is said with compassion, but bluntly. I'm a tear the Band-Aid off type of guy.

"Accidents. When I was three, my momma was riding her bike and died from a hit and run. Alcoholism is rampant where I'm from, so we assumed the person was drunk and thought they hit a deer."

The non-emotional way Kaden says this hurts my heart, but then I realize it's his coping mechanism.

Taping the photo while wincing, it appears Kaden can barely look at his father and keep his shit together. "Almost two years ago, my daddy died in a logging accident. Hazard of being a logger. While felling a tree, it kicked back and landed on him, crushing him instantly."

"My family is perfect in their imperfect way– I just thought I'd throw that out there." I grab for the next picture in Kaden's hand. "Who's this?" I have a sneaking suspicion, as the guy reminds me of me, only with brown eyes. Same body type, same personality glowing from the image. "Who's the kid? That's definitely you– or, I should say, how you see yourself *now*."

"My foster dad– Royce Kennedy." No wonder Miriam picked me. The guy looks like he could be my father, we look so much alike. "That ugly, gangly kid is me, obviously," Kade says with disgust. "The chubby shit is my baby brother– Brennan."

"Cute kid– looks cuddly. Bet he gives good hugs." Smirking to myself, I tape the picture closer to Kade's line of sight.

"Bren does," Kade mutters wistfully, obviously missing the kid already. Shuffling through the pictures, he hands me one, then puts the rest in a box. Blushing, Kade really turns sheepish now.

The picture was obviously taken a bit ago, as Kade is still awkward looking. Four kids are hanging all over each other, with Kade the dark spot in the middle of three blond-haired, blue-eyed stunning siblings. A stocky blond is smiling at the camera like the cat who ate the canary, arm slung over his taller buddy. On the far left, with an arm around the blond fellow's waist, a beautiful blonde girl is glaring openly with defiance at the camera. On the right, a kid almost as tall as Kade is hugging close and staring openly at Kaden instead of the camera.

"Best friend, annoying little sister, and the kid who has a crush on you?" I guess. "Their father must be beside himself, keeping those kids from being up to no good."

If I live to be one-hundred, I'll never forget the sound of Kaden's uninhibited laughter. Tossing his head back, all traces of fear, shame, and sadness disappear as peals of humor spill from his large lips.

"They're past no good," Kaden mutters wryly. "Their daddy is a piece of shit. Warren– my buddy –he's the biggest slut you'll ever meet, screwing every girl who isn't a blood relation. But now War's obsessed with a little redhead, so that may change. Willa, she's already married off to my foster dad's brother, and has a pair of twins… twins that belong to my foster dad."

"Shit," I utter in amazement, wanting to hear more. "This is soap opera worthy. The Life & Times of Rusty Knob's Hillbillies. What about the youngest?" Kade's already given me the lowdown during our emails, but purposefully must have left out the good shit until we met in person.

Kaden turns a shade that can only be described as beet-red, then turns to face the door, like he's imagining running out on me. I wait a few heartbeats, readying to force Kaden to explain his reaction, but he puts me out of my misery.

"That's my little shit– *Wynn*." Kade breathes the kid's name so softly, I have to strain to hear it. "I'm not a pervert!" He whips around to face me, expression filled with shame. "I want to protect Wynn– wait for him. Whether we end up together doesn't matter, because Wynn deserves more than anyone I know."

"That's sweet." I gaze at the picture of the kid. Wynn's going to be a heart-breaker. "I've never really given a shit about a girl– it's just sex. My family is my world, and until I want to add someone to it, it's going to stay just sex."

"I can't–" Kade stalks away from me. "I can't have sex," is his admission. "I want to, but I'm not a pervert."

"Being gay doesn't make you a pervert." I get a clue. Virgin. "My nephew is a young teenager, and he's already experimenting. My family doesn't like us screwing around, but they get it."

"I'm not a pervert because I'm gay." Kade draws a knife from his back pocket, unfolding it, and alarm bells ring in my head. I was told Kade wasn't allowed to have sharp objects. The sound of tape being sliced to open a box has me shivering. "I don't operate like you do. I have to love the person, and the person I want isn't ready, so I'll wait."

"That's admirable." Leaving Kade to unpack, I decide to do the same on my side of the dorm room. "Just don't pressure yourself, okay?" I look over my shoulder to make sure Kade's listening, and actually hearing me. "If you end up having sex with someone other than this Wynn kid, it's not the end of the world. Okay?"

"Um… sure," Kade mumbles, not agreeing with me, but doesn't have the balls to say it out loud. "Thanks for making me feel better earlier– I feel like a fucking idiot."

"No worries," I mutter lightly. "I knew what I was signing on for." My voice holds no resentment, only the need to help. "It's in my nature to take care of people. All lawyers aren't smarmy assholes– some actually want to make a difference in their clients' lives."

"Someday I'll repay the favor," Kaden promises, and I don't doubt it for a second.

• PRESENT •
• PITTSBURGH, PENNSYLVANIA •

PRESENT - HELP ARRIVES
Daniel Bishop

"You didn't have to come all the way up here," I whisper in Kade's ear as I welcome him and Wynn into our home. "Where are the pups?" I ask, eyes flicking between both of them.

Wynn, always knowing more than he should, flashes me a pointed look because he heard what I initially said to his husband. After ushering them into our apartment, I shut the door, then lean on it with a heavy sigh.

"Tater and Tot are with their uncles, because Willa's a goddamn dog thief." Kade's anger only amuses Wynn, blue eyes glinting with naughtiness.

"We see Perty no less than three times a day." With an impatient eye roll, Wynn turns to me. "Kade said it was an emergency, so here we are."

Blushing to his hairline, Kade pretends to take intense interest in their weekender bag. Mumbling underneath his breath, "You've helped me so much, I needed to return the favor."

"Ah," I grunt, slapping an embarrassed Kade on the back. "You're welcome here– both of you. Anytime. And thank you, because we do need your help."

Wynn gives me a bro-hug, then shoulders their bag. "Hi, Uriah." Leaving me in an instant, Wynn finds the source of the issues. Uriah's ghosting by the entrance to the hallway, eyes wide with fright. "Don't hate me by the time the weekend is over."

Suddenly terrified of Wynn, I understand Kade's moods better. Wynn is the sweetest, most caring person I've ever met, but it's also his way or the highway. Tugging Kade into a hug, I whisper in his ear. "Your husband is up to no good."

"Wynn's always up to good," Kade mutters wryly in return, hugging me tighter than most men ever would. After a decade of trying to ignore how warm and inviting Kaden feels in my arms, my body reacts on autopilot. The first time I got hard for Kaden, my world tilted on its axis.

Pulling away, both Kade and I look to our husbands, trying to pretend we don't feel guilty. Can't explain it– it is what it is. But Wynn looks back at me with a challenge in his eyes, a level of calculation I've only ever seen by opposing council.

"Get it over with and kiss already," Wynn demands, managing to stare down Kaden and me at the same time. I don't know what bullshit Wynn has up his sleeve, but it's terrifying. In the past few months, since their wedding, we've spent a few weekends together, all of them platonic, no more than a hug. But Wynn just lies in wait, and hell if I know why.

"*Wynn,*" Kade and I admonish together, never daring to kiss with good reason.

"This weekend is about truth and trust, and I'm sick of playing pretend." Wynn issues me a challenging look while silently ordering Kaden.

"Fine," Kade bites out, sounding none too pleased, then he leans down to peck a quick kiss on my lips. It's over before I even registered it happened.

"Try it like you mean it," Wynn sounds put out, like we exhaust him.

"Daniel," Uriah murmurs my name, asking me to comply for some unknown reason, so I do this for him, even if we all know this is Pandora's Box opening, and we may not like what we find inside.

"Don't act like we didn't warn you," I issue to our husbands, but then say to Kaden, "Don't cry this time."

Leaning up while Kaden leans down, I initiate the kiss we've avoided for a decade. Even the kiss meant to distract me during Wynn's tutorial on the joys of anal play wasn't like this one.

This kiss is real, even if we're both straining to hold the worst of the intensity back.

Lips merging, tongues seeking entrance, it's our bodies' reactions that are most terrifying. Kade pulls me into a full-body embrace, every inch of our flesh trying to connect. A strong chest presses against mine, a hard bulge rubs at my belly while mine grinds against a thick thigh. Fingers clench and grip anything they can reach. But when we part, the passion has abated and turned to intimacy. Lips pull apart, but hands still cup faces.

"Uriah." Wynn's voice has Kade and me stepping away from each other as if we'll burn the other. "That's what truth looks like." Faster than my eyes can track, the possessive streak of an alpha male erupts, and Kade's bulge is being cupped in Wynn's large palm, fingers biting. "God, I can't believe you're this hard so soon."

"Why?" Kade whispers, looking betrayed because Wynn's playing a game with us when he promised to always be truthful.

"Look at how fucking huge Dan's bulge is right now," Wynn orders, and all eyes, including my own, ogle my privates. Shame. All I feel is shame and guilt.

"Your husband just kissed the fuck outta me, so explain why *you're* sporting wood." I turn surly, hating this type of bullshit. "You put us in this position, now you're calling us out for it. We warned you."

"Admit it," Wynn challenges me.

"Admit what?" Kade looks around, seeming lost, and his eyes connect with my sad husband.

"Stop it!" I demand of Wynn. "This can't work if you're playing this nasty game. I thought you were here for Uriah and me, not to tear us apart."

"I'm hard because I love the way Kaden looks free when he comes apart beneath me, and he had a similar expression on his face when you were kissing him. I'm not playing a game– I promise. I'm making a point that has to be made. So admit you want to fuck my husband."

"I don't," I mutter the truth, causing both Kade and Uriah to relax.

"No, you don't." Wynn's tone is calculating, almost angry. "But you want to make love to him, don't you?"

"Fuck," I snarl. "Fine! Yes, I want to make love to Kaden. Are you happy now?" I glare at Wynn, refusing to make eye-contact with Uriah. "But we're never going to go there, no matter how hard you push for it."

"The truth hurts for a reason," Wynn mutters with satisfaction. "But it doesn't hurt as much as living a lie, believing a lie, or feeling betrayed when you realize someone has lied to you. My life from birth was a goddamn lie, and I refuse to allow the people I care about to live a lie anymore."

"Wynn." Kade reaches for his husband, but Wynn steps out of range.

"My relationship with Royce will never be what it was after he lied about the twins being Donny's kids. Daddy treating me like shit didn't hurt as bad as knowing I had a brother he kept from me. Every time I look at my niece and nephew, or look at Cain, I see the betrayal. Maybe we're better now that the truth is out– maybe not. But I refuse to live in la-la-land. Lies destroy lives, while the truth sets you free."

"Little shit," Kaden tries again, but Wynn's not having it.

Voice breaking with intense emotion, "I love Kaden, and we promised never to lie to one another, so I won't let anyone lie to him either. I also know he'd be devastated if anything made you upset, Dan, and that includes if you lose Uriah. Because evading the truth is a betrayal, even if the truth hurts."

"I can't do this." Exhausted, I slump to the sofa, elbows resting on my knees with my head in my hands. "I can't."

I need to know what's blocking Uriah from connecting with me, but not at the expense of letting things out that should remain buried. The brutality between Wynn and Kaden may work for them, but Uriah is a soft person, and so am I.

"You won't be," Wynn warns, informing me we'll all be doing this– I won't be going it alone. "Uriah, help me unpack my bag. I promise it won't hurt too much."

The longer I know Wynn, the stronger he becomes, and Kade tells me on a daily basis how Wynn terrifies him in a good way. Kade always needed a keeper, and somehow Wynn has tapped into that source of need. Not only is Wynn doing a good job, he's excelling at it.

Kade sits next to me on the sofa, looking amused yet proud of Wynn. A loud slap to my back has me jerking forward. Uriah and I share a look as he leads Wynn from the living room, a look screaming '*help me!*' Meanwhile, Wynn and Kade share a look, and there is no handbook to decipher it.

"How long have you wanted to have sex with me?" Kade is hesitant to ask, which makes me answer without hesitation.

This is a landmine we're navigating. We've always had firm boundary lines in place, and absolutely no kissing was the first rule.

I've always pretended I didn't want to have sex with Kaden– for his sake, for Wynn's, for Uriah's, but mostly for my own sanity.

"Since I met you– freaked the fuck out of me." Staring down at my hands, I can't believe I just admitted that. "It wasn't in a gay way, not that there is anything wrong with that. I just felt connected with you, and wanted to connect more."

"I just assumed…" Kade trails off, refusing to finish, and so much is said in the ensuing silence.

"Wynn's jealous," I whisper, hoping the guy is out of earshot. Our apartment isn't large, with all rooms branching off the living room.

"*Oh, yeah.*" Yet again, Kade only sounds amused. I can't look at him to learn if he looks amused too.

"When we discussed playing together, you said no jealousy was to be involved, because it hurts relationships." I remind Kaden of our first rule of engagement.

"Human nature cannot be erased." Kade's laughter draws me up short. "Wynn's jealousy isn't just about me, I don't think. I always said we had to be our own people, with no possessive bullshit. But Wynn's possessive and jealous, even if he won't admit it. It's a good thing I want to be his."

"His?" That is something Uriah and I have, but probably shouldn't because of the imbalance. Uriah always wanted to be mine, yet he wouldn't make me his.

"Wynn is trying to give us what we want, because he's just that fucking *good*. His attitude is because we're not doing as we're told, not because he's jealous. He would probably celebrate if we gave in and had sex, but would kill us if he wasn't in control of the when and where, and let him watch."

"I'm baffled," I express the only emotion filling me.

"C'mere." Kade pulls me off the sofa with a hand to my arm, then tugs me across the living room to our spare bedroom. "Listen."

"Kaden," I caution. "That's wrong."

Looking more amused by the second, "Are your ethics more important than your happiness?" Laughing silently while shaking his head, Kaden bugs his eyes out at me. "We're here to help. Wynn is helping you more than you could ever realize. *Listen.*"

Leaning against the wall on the left-hand side of the bedroom door, I slump in defeat. Kade flashes me a grin from his station on the right. It takes me a moment to realize the door is ajar, as if this was planned.

Snorting, Kade gives me a thumbs-up, making fun of me for being an idiot.

"We're going to tell each other the truth," Wynn demands in a soothing, coaxing tone. "If you value your relationship with Dan, you'll stop lying to yourself."

"That's not how it is," Uriah protests, and it takes everything in me not to charge into the bedroom and hold him, reassure him.

"Yeah, it is," Wynn says with great confidence. "You're upset about how Dan feels about Kaden."

"Aren't *you*?" Uriah sounds flabbergasted.

"Yeah, to the point I said I was going to tear you a new asshole before I ever laid eyes on you. I told Kaden I was going to fuck your brains out, and he laughed, knowing why I said it. So don't be a hypocrite."

"Hypocrite?"

"Yeah, hypocrite." Wynn's snort is so loud, it echoes in the living room from the bedroom. "You want me to fuck you. I know it. You know it. Dan and Kade know it. You probably look at other people too. You're a hypocrite."

"They're *in love* with each other, you fucking idiot." The real Uriah comes out– the one I first met selling his mouth for ten bucks a pop. Somewhere in the past few years, Uriah turned into a Stepford Wife, and neither of us recognizes him anymore. "We're just fucking with each other to make them bleed."

"Yeah, and which is worse? Us fucking for spite, or them fucking out of love? One is destructive, toxic, and negative. It can be positive when it's about pleasure, but you're making it nasty. What our husbands have is not nasty."

"I don't get you." Uriah's voice is stiff with suppressed anger. "How can you be this *good*?"

"Hypocrite!" Wynn charges. "We look at other people, lust after one another, but we don't offer Dan and Kade the same benefit. You feel like he doesn't love you because he loves Kade. He doesn't want you because he wants Kaden. Then explain to me how you feel about Dan? Especially after you asked to suck my dick in my bathroom last month."

Uriah makes a choking sound, and my heart sinks. I quickly look at Kaden to see if he knew about that, and he gives me a sympathetic look in return.

Shit.

I didn't know that.

"There's a difference between you and me, Uriah. I don't fuck to feel good about myself. I don't need someone else to say I'm hot. I'm confident, and you're not. Your insecurity is infecting your relationship with Dan. I've had to deal with Kade's bullshit. It's not how Dan feels about you– it's about how shitty you feel about yourself. That's a lack of trust."

"*Trust?!* My husband wants to make love to yours!" Uriah shouts in outrage, and I never realized he was that hurt by it. Tears of guilt prickle at the back of my eyes. If I could change how I feel, I would in a heartbeat.

"And you want me to fuck you..." Wynn trails off, the word *hypocrite* ringing in the silence. "Trust. You don't trust how Dan feels about you. You don't trust what he says when he says it. You disregard what he says, and then throw it in his face by not believing in him. Not believing he loves you, wants you. Not believing in your marriage."

"Shut up!" Uriah shouts, voice strained with discomfort. I don't intervene, simply because this has been my uphill battle since we met. Uriah always holds himself apart from me, never truly letting me in, and I don't know why.

"My husband is straight, and I have a dick. No matter how feminine I am, I will never have a vagina!"

"Uriah." Wynn sighs. "You're using that as an excuse– Dan's no more straight than I am... Dan has proven to want you every day you've been together. It must be exhausting for him to have to prove himself day in and day out. A lesser man would've left you by now."

"You are such an asshole, Wynn!"

"Nope, I just tell the truth."

"As you see it."

"No, this is the definitive truth. I'm here because your husband asked for help, and this shit came out of his mouth. Your insecurities will cause you to cheat at some point, should the opportunity present itself. Then you'll feel like shit and your marriage will fail. But with Kade and Dan, they can't cheat– they're incapable. They're not built the same way we are. They see sex as sacred, especially Dan."

"I'm not good enough for Dan," Uriah gasps, and it takes Kade holding me back to keep me from barging into the bedroom to comfort him.

"Why didn't you fuck Dan at my house?" Wynn demands an answer. "Why did you chicken out?"

Eyes held wide, I mouth to Kade, "That was out of left-field." A silent chuckle is his answer.

After Wynn and Kade went up to bed, Uriah stopped what he was doing to me, even though I was starting to enjoy it. I asked Uriah to penetrate me, but he refused, and I knew he wanted to. His confidence was rock-bottom that night, and hasn't risen since.

"I didn't know what I was doing!" Uriah protests. "So I'd rather not do it."

"Listen," Wynn whispers softly. "It's you and Dan, not some stranger. Do you think he cares if you're not perfect? He may be a top for life, and you a bottom– not all gay men penetrate, or are versatile. But it's shortchanging your sex lives if you don't experiment. Resentment will grow, cheating will happen, and Dan will be on my doorstep after my husband. I can't have that," Wynn demands.

"That makes me feel so much better, like Dan's sticking around, waiting for me to fail, then he'll go after the one he truly loves and wants."

"You're a goddamn fool," Wynn snarls. "They love us, and they don't need to prove that ever again. You should just fucking believe what Dan says, how he acts, and how he reacts. Knock your bullshit off."

"I can't!" Uriah gets defensive. "You don't understand what it's like to be me."

"And you sure as shit don't understand what I've been through, where this confidence has come from, and why I won't let anything get in my way of being happy. So I can't wrap my mind around you wanting to top your husband, yet refusing to do it. Maybe it's something you'll both enjoy– maybe not. You're going to be having sex with each other for the rest of your lives, and you'll need to change it up a bit."

"I wanted to, but I was scared." Uriah's voice gets more confident as he speaks, like he's channeling Wynn. "If you would've stayed down there with us, I would have tried it. But I was scared I'd fuck it up, and ruin it for life "

"I'll help you this weekend, if you want," Wynn offers, no doubt getting off on Uriah needing and accepting his help.

I squirm around, earning a silent laugh from Kaden, because I'm not sure I like where this is headed. I wanted to know what my husband's malfunction was, why he was acting like a hormone-addled teenage girl, but I'm getting more than I bargained for.

"Yeah, but…" Uriah hesitates. "I need to know I'm the one affecting Dan, so I can't have Kade touching him while we–"

"I'll help you get started, then leave you be. Kade won't even be in the room." Wynn sounds like he's saying, *"Better?"*

"Thanks," Uriah sounds relieved, and it makes me relax. I slide down the wall to sit on my behind, elbows on my knees.

"I know you're afraid of how Dan feels about Kade, but you shouldn't be. They knew each other for years before they met you. There is a lot of history there. If they wanted to be together, it would have happened before they chose us instead. But there's one thing you're not taking into account."

"What?" Uriah's calming, judging by the tone of his voice, sounding open to whatever Wynn has to say.

"I'll liken it to how it must have felt to come to terms with being genderfluid. Not all of us just know who we are sexually at puberty. I thought I was asexual because I was terrified of being gay. Kade closed himself off sexually, knowing he was gay, because he feared the fallout in town. Even if you're feeling more feminine or more masculine, you still know you want guys. So neither of us can imagine how terrified Dan must have felt as he was falling in love with you, but you should empathize instead of feeling insecure."

"I can't just shut it off," Uriah pleads.

"No, but you can hear me out, and see how it's not about you. Dan's feelings about Kade aren't about you. At. All. To go from wanting girls, to learning he's romantically but not sexually attracted to guys–"

"Dan likes dick," Uriah mutters gruffly, falling into Wynn's obvious trap.

"So glad you finally admitted that out loud." Wynn's laughter is so lust-fueled, poor Kade shudders next to me. I'd love to lie to myself and say I'm left unaffected– Wynn's another complication I hadn't expected I'd have to deal with.

"Yeah, Dan's lust can't grow without emotional connection first– so stop making it about *you*."

"But it affects me," Uriah blurts out, voice breaking.

"So what? That's like blaming the person who's handicapped for being handicapped. Dan loves your dick, so get over the fact he's not gay. It ain't about you."

"But Dan wants Kade's dick," Uriah reveals, when this has been an off-limits topic between us. "Your *husband's* dick."

"You're jealous," Wynn points out, no doubt feeling the same way. Who wouldn't? It's why Kade and I feel so goddamn guilty. "But you shouldn't be. Do you know how much Dan loves you? How much Kade loves me?" All rhetorical, but Wynn answers anyway. "Enough to never have a taste of something they so desperately want. I'm not that selfish, but I'm selfless enough to give Kade what he wants. It's not about if Dan loved you, he wouldn't look at Kade– meanwhile you're lusting after me –it's if you loved Dan enough, you'd want him to experience Kade."

"Shit!" I stalk away, toward the kitchen, where I'm going to hide out while Wynn continues his intervention.

But Kade follows me, then yanks my refrigerator door open to grab us each a bottle of beer. "This is Uriah's wakeup call, Dan." A heavy hand lands on my shoulder, while another hands me a beer. "But you need to hear what Uriah has to say, because it's your wakeup call too."

With a deep sigh, I charge back to the cracked bedroom door, only to catch the most disturbing revelation yet.

"Dan's unable to say no to me– to anyone, Wynn." Uriah pleads, and it breaks something pivotal within me. Brow beaded with sweat, fists curled, my stomach threatens to revolt. "I always make sure Dan comes to me... that's why I couldn't go through with it... I couldn't penetrate him. Whether Dan wanted it or not, he would let me do it. After what happened to Dan, that's too much like rape–"

Nothing could stop me from going to Uriah– nothing.

• SIX YEARS AGO •
• PSU- STATE COLLEGE,
PENNSYLVANIA •

SENIOR YEAR EXISTENTIAL CRISIS
Daniel Bishop

"Harder," the girl beneath me begs in a raspy voice, making my cock throb for release. Sweating, panting, my hips snap with near violence as I put on a show. With sexual intent, I remove my hands from Manda's hips, then slide them down my chest in a slow movement, wicking away sweat as I go.

Undulating my body in a wave, my voice is thick with lust. "Ya better cover your head with my pillow, Manda," I warn, knowing she's a screamer, but that's not why I do it.

Bent over at the waist, hands gripping the edge of my bed where it meets the wall, round ass in the air with her feet hanging off the other side of the bed, Manda is at my mercy.

Manda's movements should gain my undivided attention, seeing as how my dick is lodged deep in her pussy, but it's the slight shift across the room that has my eyes lasering in on the action. Kaden's eyes are slits, just a tiny bit of hazel peering out at me– they miss nothing, devouring my body that's on display.

Body moving on autopilot, seeking release, my eyes are focused on Kaden, yet my mind wanders to the disturbing perversion my life has become.

I assume I'm straight by definition, finding girls attractive since I figured out they weren't like me. I liked their softness to my roughness. I loved their curves compared to how I wasn't. They smelled good, not musky like me. Their voices were melodious, never failing to either make me feel soothed or horny. I loved looking at them, touching them, being inside them.

Even this instant, I crave everything Manda has to offer.

For twenty-one years, I was one way, then one day I realized I was another. I'm not gay. Something has gone haywire inside of me, and I don't know how to handle it, to the point I've fucked a girl every day for the past one thousand and forty-nine days.

Most are repeats– like Manda, whom I've screwed for nearly four months straight, with Carrie on the side. We're not dating. We just fuck. With Kade watching.

Even before I met Kaden Marx in person, I connected with him. Having him in my everyday life, in my dorm room, having him need me to survive, it's done bizarre things to my sexuality. Things I can't comprehend, let alone put into words.

At first, I didn't notice how I was hard when we hugged and joked around… until recently.

Realization hit last week, how all of the sudden Kaden didn't hide how he was jerking off in bed, no longer pretending to be asleep. It was at the same time I realized I was showing off for him, angling myself so Kade could look at me. It took coming while staring into Kaden's eyes, for the third time, before I figured out we were fucking each other through whatever girl I was inside.

To say I find this a disturbing trend is an understatement.

I don't have a fucking clue what's going on with my body, but it's taken over my life. Unable to help myself, I'm holding an intense staring contest with Kaden. Right now. While fucking Manda.

Manda's moans spur me on, hips jerking rapidly. The harder I pound, the louder she moans into the pillow. But the pillow wasn't for sound absorption. Walk down any hallway on this floor, and you'll hear sex pouring from behind thin doors.

The pillow was for Kaden, so Manda wouldn't see us sexually commune with one another.

Head hitching backward as I notice Kade's hand pick up speed beneath his sheet, I can almost see the outline of his huge cock. The most disturbing factor of my newfound confusion, for the past few months, I've craved making-out with Kaden– sucking his face while rubbing on each other. Nothing gay… until yesterday, when I was hit with the need to know what his cock looked like, felt like… tasted like.

"God, Dan!" Manda releases a guttural groan, ass rearing back to meet me halfway. "You're like a machine this morning." Reaching down, I grab her tit, flesh filling my palm, just to prove I still love it. Dick throbbing with pleasure as I knead Manda's tit– yeah, I still love everything girly about her.

What is wrong with me?

I feel straight.

Everything in me feels straight.

I love women, and no man has ever made my dick hard, except for Kaden. But I'd rather make-out with him, especially cuddle before, during, and after.

What the fuck?

Am I bi just because I want to make love to my roommate? Did three years of keeping Kaden alive while he had meltdowns somehow alter my sexuality? Is it because I've never felt the need to bring a girl home to my family, because my family is sacred, but Kaden has gone home with me for the last six months of weekends? Did it happen because Kaden's foster dad comes to see me once a month, where we have lunch and talk about Kaden's welfare? Did it happen around the time I made sure Kade actually went to his therapy appointments? Or was it because I stalked him in the shower, watching him scrub himself through the not nearly opaque enough shower curtain to make sure he wasn't cutting himself?

All I know, I can't find out what's making us tick, simply because we have another year left here at Penn State. I'll be going to Yale for law school in less than a year, and Kaden will be going back to Royce for safekeeping.

We can't fuck around to satisfy my curiosity because Kade's life depends on our stable friendship, and I truly love him– mental issues aside, which only adds to his appeal, Kaden is one of my favorite people. No one argues like Kaden Marx does, challenges me. A lawyer loves a good debate, and fuck if it doesn't make me hard when Kaden argues until he's blue in the face.

Mouth open on a silent moan, Kade's hazel eyes pop wide, then slide back into lusty slits. With a grunt, I yank from Manda's body, tear off my condom, and then pump into a hand towel I had stowed beneath my pillow.

I lost my virginity in a confusing wash of nonconsensual drunkenness with a much older woman– the wife to my uncle's rival during a cocktail party. She plied me with drinks when no one was looking, then stalked me to my bedroom, trapped me inside. I said no, but she didn't listen, ignoring my voice when I was too intoxicated to fight her off, instead listening to the fact that my dick got hard when she sucked on it. She rode me when everything but my dick was paralyzed.

That shit sticks with a person for life.

My sister got knocked up at fourteen– for the last seventeen years, Ainsley's been too terrified to marry my nephew's father, fearing Joel only wanted her because he's an upstanding fellow. After what Mrs. Turner did to me, the only person I'll ever come inside, even with a condom on, will be my spouse. Bishops marry for life, and my future kids will not face the same issues my nephew has.

"I wish you wouldn't pull out," Manda whines, but I ignore her. Too hyper-focused on Kaden, I jerk off into the rag, holding my roommate's panicked gaze while he comes for me. Body jerking violently, I'm too terrified to know what it would be like without a conduit. Just how fucking painful would it be?

The virgin blushes, hides his face in his pillow, and then yanks his sheet up over his head before Manda notices Kaden's awake.

Coward.

Rolling over, beautiful face scrunched up with bitter disappointment, Manda whines in a nasal voice. "If we're coming at the same time, and you pull out, I get interrupted and can't get off."

"You already came– I have plans, hun," I reply to Manda's complaint, finally giving her my undivided attention now that Kaden is playacting a turtle. "Plans that don't involve marriage until after law school. Condoms break. My moral, ethical code would require we marry. No one is going to know what it feels like for me to come until they have my ring on their finger."

"You're so romantic," Manda murmurs snottily, crawling off my bed.

The only times I've said no were due to self-preservation. Over the last seven years, Mrs. Turner tried to come back for seconds and thirds and tenths, but it only took once for me to learn that lesson– she found a boy who wouldn't be culled from the herd a second time. I may have only weighed a hundred pounds soaking wet, but I was still a baby Bishop. At thirteen, I was already smarter than the woman, knowing exactly what she wanted from me– I'm my uncle's heir, now Ransom is too.

Extortion from false rape allegations was the least of my concerns, when the woman was trying to grow the proof in her belly.

I never told a soul.

Pittsburgh may be a few hours from State College, but my fellow students know who the hell the Bishops are, which is why my bed is never empty, why I never fail to have a drink thrust into my hand, and why I have phony, network-seeking friends everywhere I go on campus.

Only Kade knows the real Bishops, how we don't live in a mansion or drive expensive cars, or use our money as a badge of honor. Our accomplishments speak for themselves, not the amount of zeros in our bank accounts.

My grandmother, mother, and sister taught me how you never say no to a woman. It's sacrilege. My grandfather and father have preached this to me, day in and day out, over the course of my lifetime. The woman is always right. Apologize and agree with her. Give her what she wants.

I learned this at an impressionable age with Mrs. Turner, how I had no autonomy when it came to a woman wishing to have sex with me. On the flip side, a man should never pursue a woman, or else they're a rapist– my women's rights lobbyist sister taught me that.

The only sex I've ever had is because a woman wanted me to fuck her, not because I wanted to have it. They asked, and I did as they bid, because I was taught I shouldn't say no.

A very large part of me loathes Manda and the rest of her ilk, seeing them as predators. Since I'm not allowed to say no when solicited for sex, because it will insult the girl or upset her, make her feel badly about herself to be rejected, I have rules used to protect myself– rules I refuse to break.

"We've had this conversation before, Manda," I warn her, praying this is the last time I have to suffer through this.

Usually, after they figure out I can't be hooked, they give up and go seek other prey. I'm not allowed to break up with them– as Uncle Edward's heir, it would reflect badly on him. Hell, I never asked them out to begin with– they always come on to me. When I try for an actual friendship, they bulldoze right over me, dragging me to the nearest flat surface.

"I have a future I will reach."

"Yeah, you don't trust me." Manda is pissed, tugging on her shirt, forgetting to put her bra on first, then comes the skinny jeans minus the underpants. "You won't even take a condom from me."

"Practice makes perfect," I mutter to myself, yanking on my clothing as quickly as possible. "It's not that I don't trust you–" I lie. "–just that it's *my* rules."

"Your rules?" Manda scoffs, seeking out her purse hiding near the foot of the bed. "What about *my* rules?"

"Yeah. You have NO rules, Manda. If you did, you wouldn't be overreacting right now. A mature woman would appreciate *my* rules and have her own set."

"Oh, you'll never get near my pussy again, Dan," Manda drawls, like it's a major loss. Instead of making herself unique by letting me know her, Manda is acting no different than the long string of women who turn on me, going from a fuck-buddy to a girl who tries to trap me into a relationship by hooking me with a kid.

I can say with one hundred percent accuracy that the condom handed to me earlier was poked full of holes, like the other twenty in the past from both Manda and others. Later tonight, Kade and I will take bets, then head to the bathroom sink for a test. The last condom could've been used as a sprinkler.

Like the philosophy from eons ago, Manda's at college to catch an educated man who might get a high-paying job in the future, not to get an education and begin a career of her own. Her parents know this, and are paying for the chance to get some poor schmuck as a son-in-law. I learned long ago how to spot them. At first they act like they want the same thing as me. No-strings-attached sex. But then they do the bait and switch act and shit gets shaky.

The sad thing is, Manda doesn't even realize this is what she's doing.

Manda looks ready to tear my dick off for calling her out on her own bullshit, like I'm the one who's not as advertised. I'm not slut-shaming Manda– I respect a woman who knows what she wants and has the courage to take it. We both wanted a hard fuck, and we both fucked hard and got off. It was what it was and nothing more. To expect more is called bait and switch, and makes Manda a fool while she plays the victim with her friends.

Ladies, the guy isn't playing games– *you are*. You're seeing shit that isn't there, so you won't feel ashamed for having casual sex. Sex is sex, and there's no shame in that. Stop making it about love and romance and calling the guy a player or a dog. You're getting what's being advertised– sex.

"*Your body, your right*– that's all that matters, right?" I mock, Mrs. Turner's face superimposed over the scene playing out before me. "I'm more than just a cock you ride when you want to get off."

I'm so sick of vapid women. Yeah, they seem to flock to me, but I wonder if this is fueling my odd attachment to Kaden now. Kade's blunt. Real. No mind-reading required. No game-playing.

"Just because I have a dick doesn't mean I'm not responsible, have goals and feelings, or have rights too."

Hands fisted on her hips, teeth bared, eyes narrowed, voice tight, Manda reminds me of every female in my family, going after the kill to get what she wants. "What rights?" Manda mocks me back, fury radiating from her pores.

"My body, my right not to have some money-hungry chick pricking holes in condoms, or risking an accidental broken condom. No seductive luring of '*just put the head in,*' where I end up with herpes and a lifetime of child support. No position other than doggie, because I refuse to be forced to come while inside a woman, with legs wrapped around my waist or a body holding me down. No sex mixed with drinking, where my inhibitions are lowered and there's a chance I forget my own rules. No drinking, so the chick can't say I took advantage of her. Where we're both plastered, but only *I'm* responsible because I was the one born with a dick. I'm never ruining my life for pussy, where I end up in jail and my family name is tarnished because the beer goggles faded and the girl doesn't want to take responsibility for *her* choices."

"So it's the girl's fault she was raped?" Manda is livid and being purposefully obtuse.

Rage no longer simmering in my blood, it takes everything in me to control my emotions. As a boy who was raped, knowing I'd be mocked or patted on the back if I ever admitted what happened, after growing up in a culture where male teachers touching female students was rape and female teachers touching male students meant they wanted it, Manda and the rest of her ilk make me physically sick.

"You know damn well there is a difference between what I'm talking about and date rape."

"There isn't– the guy is always in the wrong." Manda folds her arms over her breasts, glaring at me. "A girl can't rape herself– a dick has to be involved."

So ignorant. Educated ignorance.

"Yeah, because my honor code, where I refuse to have sex while intoxicated, or with an intoxicated person, I'm propagating rape-culture," I snarl, rolling my eyes. "There's date rape, and then there is regret and shame. On campus, more than three times a week, a chick is destroying some poor guy's life after they both got drunk, but only he's at fault for both *their* choices. Punished because he doesn't want to date exclusively now."

With a know-it-all glare, Manda sneers at me. "You can't rape a guy– he can't fuck unless he's hard. So if a girl rides him, he still had to want it enough to get hard."

All the oxygen is sucked out of my lungs, and it takes noticing Kaden readying to reach out to me before I regain my ability to breathe. No one knows, but the tortured look on Kade's face tells me he's reading more and more into this confrontation than what I want him to.

"You're the most ignorant person I've ever met." Eyes bugging out, all I can do is shake my head back and forth. Sensing I'm back in control, Kaden pretends he's not here again. "We are on a campus, where at least fifty percent of the population is drunk and fucking each other every night. That would mean all sex was nonconsensual. What about gay sex? A woman can't rape another woman?"

"How?" Aghast, Manda looks at me like *I'm* the idiot. "That's impossible. There's no dick. No dick– no rape. It's always a guy's fault. If it's two guys having sex while drunk, I doubt either one of them will say it's rape. Guys want sex nonstop. They got hard– no rape."

"Manda needs to go back to kindergarten," Kade mutters for only me to hear. "Along with most of the population on this campus."

"If a guy is accused of rape because a girl can't consent when drunk, shouldn't she be culpable for fucking a drunk guy too? It should cancel out who can or can't consent if they are both intoxicated. Whether a girl is stone-cold sober, or drunk, and fucks a drunk guy, no one bats an eyelash. The guy wanted it, right?" I twist out nastily, voice taking on a tone it never has before.

Manda takes a deep breath, gearing up to bitch me out, not processing a single word I'm uttering. She's right. Full stop. Never contemplating that she could possibly be wrong.

"Don't debate me on this hypocrisy, Manda– it's not going to make me change my mind on my belief system and ethical code, and it sure as fuck isn't going to make me take a condom from your hand or fuck you raw."

"Dan, you're why women hate men." Staring me down, Manda tries to cut me deep. "At their core, all men are rapists. You just raped me, because you didn't give me what I wanted."

"I wish sterilization wasn't frowned upon," Kade grumbles loudly, no doubt Manda heard him.

"And you're why men can't stand women," I volley back. "Manipulation and narcissism, crying foul when you don't get your way. There is real date rape, then there are girls like you, Manda– a predator wearing a victim's clothing, lessening what real survivors go through. I will pray you never suffer the life-changing experiences a real victim survives."

"What ethical code, you fucking maggot of a republican?" Manda sneers, going way too far, doing what is always done. When caught in their own bad behavior, they make it about the things I am not, simply because this is what bullies do. "You don't believe in women's rights, you sexist asshole. You're a bigot. Just listen to yourself right now. If a girl is drunk, it's rape. She can't consent. Even if the guy is drunker than she is, he raped her. It's his fault and responsibility."

"So ignorant– *you* are the reason I have rules. Ethics. No sex when drinking. No sex with someone who thinks it means anything but having a mutual orgasm. No coming inside, even with impenetrable latex. No pregnancy, where *I'm* responsible for life, while the girl plays the victim. No STDs, where I put my life at risk and every lover I ever have, including my future spouse."

"Jesus, why do you even fuck then?" Manda stomps across the room, waiting, expecting to be answered simply because she asked. Somehow that became one of those women's rights I don't believe in– getting an answer for shit that is none of her damn business, simply because she wants to know.

Why do I fuck? Because it was demanded of me, and I'd be an asshole if I said no. That's why.

As a soon-to-be third-generation attorney, I believe in the fifth amendment. It doesn't apply here, because I have a right to privacy, not having to be interrogated by some crazy chick, whom I owe nothing, and it's my right not to answer her.

I've learned what not to do by watching my parents fight. Dad suffers in silence as Mom interrogates him for hours on end, screeches at him. The whole time, I always wonder why Dad doesn't just stand up and walk away. Just because Mom has the right to be heard, doesn't mean Dad doesn't have the right not to have to sit there and listen to it.

I blame their modeling for what happened to me with Mrs. Turner. If only I'd know my body belonged to me, like the conversations Ainsley received, maybe I could have said no loud enough to have been heard.

The squeaky wheel always gets the grease. Not only was I taught not to be squeaky, I discovered I wasn't even the wheel– I was the one handed the grease.

Blinking out of my thoughts, I catch the tail-end of Manda's incensed ranting, which has me going into lecture-mode. Something I apparently inherited from my mother, compounded by my father's debate techniques.

"It's called being a responsible adult while having fun. I think you should appreciate the fact that I'm not taking advantage of you, enough so that you shouldn't try to take advantage of me by manipulation and guilt-mongering. This arguing act is just a tantrum because I called you out on the bullshit you were trying to pull on me. You were trying to trap me, and we both know it."

"You're an asshole, Daniel Bishop!" Manda storms from our dorm room, and I know I'll never hear from her again.

"Always the same," Kade mutters, head peeking out from beneath his blankets. "It takes a few months, then the bitching starts. Do you go by a script?" After shifting to sit up, Kade says his universal truth. "This is the first time I'm thankful I'm a gay virgin. I love women– some I'm good friends with. But the ignorant, irrational chicks you pick out… it'd turn me gay if I already wasn't." Shuddering, Kade's sheets rustle. "I doubt I'll be able to get hard again for the next week."

"They seem to be the only ones willing to screw me." Amused laughter turns to sadness, I just shake my head over and over as I finish getting dressed. "I know nothing of them, so how can I commit? I don't know who's teaching these girls this skewed way of life, but it's a fail unless all they want is a hard fuck."

"I have no idea what they're thinking." Kade shakes his head sadly, totally looking baffled.

"They think fucking me will make me want to date them. *Dating* them before *fucking* them would probably get me to commit. I won't miss Manda, because all pussy feels the same through a condom, and all I knew was Manda's pussy."

"You're a disgusting hog," Kade grumbles, always grumpy in the morning, even after getting off.

"I'm not," I say with utter conviction. "I treat them with dignity and respect, which they don't return to me. I give them exactly what I promised and nothing more. When I meet the person I'm meant to be with, I will love them without reservation– that is the person who I will marry, share a life with and have kids. They will join my family and me theirs. Until then, it's just mindless fucking."

"Why don't you ask them on a date first, then?" Kade looks at me like he's trying to figure me out, the ghost of his earlier revelation still riding his expression. I'm glad he's not bringing up what he no doubt discovered. "If all you're doing is screwing them, how will you get to know them enough to find out if they're the one?"

"Because they try to fuck me before we even get to the restaurant, that's why," I answer, thoroughly disgusted. "I like these girls at first– we talk a bit outside of class, and they instantly come onto me. But they don't want to get to know me. At all. They go straight for the kill-shot. Jesus, I'm a man. Grab my dick, and I'll be more than happy to use it, but that's all you're going to get from me after that."

Kade's eyes drift south, becoming heavily lidded, and it's my turn to bloom with a crimson kiss of embarrassment. He'll never do it, no matter the intent in his gaze. I fear ruining our relationship, but I fear his guilty conscience more. Royce says Kade's little shit doesn't exhibit any sexual interest in anyone, and I had worried

Wynn would be fucking around without knowing Kade was saving himself for the kid.

If Kade were to mess around with me, and I know he wants to, he'd probably feel so guilty the knife wouldn't be to release pain, but to release life. No amount of curiosity or lust will make me go there. I value Kaden too much.

"I may like girls, but I don't get them. They get pissy when all you do is fuck them, but they ignore all my attempts to get to know them first. For serious, they think the way to my heart is through my dick."

"Probably is for most guys." Kade won't leave his bed until after I leave the room, because he's too modest to show me the mess he made of himself. "And they think the way to your wallet is through your heart."

"Pessimist," I tease.

"You taught me that, bud." Kade's laughter is the most ironic thing I've ever heard. "I have class at ten," is his hint to get the fuck out of here. When I don't move, he hits me where it hurts. "What I just witnessed wasn't healthy."

Hand out, I issue a warning. "Stop!" Part of me wants to turn around and run out the door, and another part of me wants to glare Kaden down. "Don't analyze me."

"I've been watching you for years, Danny. *Years*. On campus and in Pittsburgh. Other than Tonya, you don't get along with women. Why is that? They're just people."

Eyes narrowed, I glare down at my roommate, feeling betrayed. "You're not my therapist."

Kaden shifts on his bed, folding his blankets beneath his arms. "Maybe you should– hold up!" He tries to get to me stand still long enough to listen. I don't like this shift in our relationship, where Kaden thinks he's in charge.

"Your grandmother and mom are the sweetest women– a little bit controlling, but sweet." Kaden chuckles at the death glare I issue him. "I get it– I'm just like them. How no one will tell me no. If I bitch loud enough, everyone gives in and does what I want. They're still good people."

Kaden doesn't get it. No one does. "I can't talk about this," I seethe, unable to go there with him. Kade's right– he treats me with the same level of disrespect. It's like being held emotionally hostage, relent or suffer. Just as I can't seem to get my feet to move as he decides to lecture me for the first time.

Boundaries are important, but women, especially Bishop women, allow no boundaries where I'm concerned. I'd love to man-up and do what I want in front of them, lecture be damned, but it's hard when every other Bishop man humors them instead. I can't be the squeaky wheel– that's not my familial role –so I swallow my pride and be a good boy.

"I can't."

"Grandma and Mom, their behavior rolls right off the rest of the men's backs, Grandpa and Dad thinking it hilarious, but it bothers you. Why is that?" Kade knows, maybe not the details, but he *knows*.

"Let it go!" I turn, unable to look at Kaden. Grabbing for our cum-rag, I try to distract Kaden from digging for the truth, but the intense, pity-filled look on his face has me dropping the rag back to my mattress.

"It's not mommy issues, but it's definitely not healthy– you need help." Kaden shifts again, trying to get my undivided attention. "You don't trust women, yet you let them use you."

What I don't say, and I need no therapist to explain it to me, is how I blame the women in my family for weakening me to the point I couldn't protect myself. I blame my dad and grandfather for hammering home how it's easier to grease the squeaky wheel versus set boundaries and fix the problem.

They need a therapist, not me.

"You're an arrogant fucker, aren't you?" Kaden challenges me, when normally he lets this shit go. "A know-it-all. We all have our faults, but you hold a grudge. You allow those girls to use you, then blame them for it. That's not fair to the girls– do I think Manda is a zit on humanity's ass? Yes, but she'll grow up eventually. But you helped turn Manda into that… The *no* starts with you, bud– start using it, because I never want to see what I just saw ever again in my life."

Understanding dawning, an apology is automatically prepared to spill from my lips, but I force it down. "Yeah, okay… I gotta hit the dining hall ASAP." Shouldering my bag, I backtrack to grab *our* jizz rag. "Put it back under my pillow when you're done with it."

Forgiving me in an instant, rare burst of alpha male poofing out of existence, Kaden's pupils are blown as his fingers curl around the rag damp with my fresh cum. The virgin refuses to date, refuses to find a mindless fuck, and is living like a monk. I'll do *anything* I can to make sure he's as happy as I can make him.

That's my nature, anything to not make a ripple in the waves. To appease. To make others feel good about themselves. I can't help it if it harms me as much as it fulfills me.

I'd love to think sharing a jizz rag with Kade is like when I was fourteen at summer camp, where we jerked off to see who could be the quickest and shoot the furthest. But that's a goddamn lie. That was chest-thumping, competitive idiots. This isn't. I get off just knowing Kade is getting off, more so than I do on actually getting off myself.

FORMING A QUEUE

My altercation with Manda and Kade's burgeoning take-charge attitude follow me across campus and affect my mood. My psyche is so raw, I swear my flesh should show welts. Five junior and senior PSU students are crowded around a table, all eyes lighting up as I enter the dining hall. "It's about time!" My gaggle of hangers-on are waiting for me at our usual table. As I said earlier, I'm an omega who everyone treats like an alpha. Everywhere I go, I have a bunch of people wanting my opinion, wanting to trail after me, and all I want to do is be alone without their responsibilities. I take care of my beta because I love Kade like family– everyone else can take care of themselves.

"Hey, guys!" I modulate my voice so it's chipper, when inside I dread what comes next. "Anybody need anything?" I hitch my finger over my shoulder, in the general direction of breakfast.

"I'll get you something." Josh hops up quickly, going to grab my breakfast for me, like I'm an invalid, when in reality it's to butter me up for my notes. Is this a study group, or a bunch of lazy assholes trying to use me?

Admitting defeat, I slide into my seat at the table next to Carrie, who I'm going to have to cut loose right now. No more revolving bedroom door. The more sex I have, the lonelier I feel.

Manda was the last straw. NO is now in my vocabulary when it comes to the female gender. My grandmother, mother, and sister's disappointment, be damned.

It's toxic, and most definitely not worth the stress of the inevitable tantrum like earlier. I think it would be more fulfilling to jerk off on our cum rag, toss it across the room, and catch it five minutes later when Kaden was finished with it.

They don't want to know the real me, and they won't let me get to know them, but they hope to use my name to get internships, jobs, or hold out for a Bishop kid to drain my family dry.

I'm done.

"Why were you late? Was your roomie having another meltdown?" Carrie shoulder bumps me while giggling nastily. "Kade's a total freak. I know damn well he watches us screw. I tried to get in his pants once, but he pushed me off. He so wanted it," she draws out, smirking at everyone around the table.

Mother figure's palm cupping my crotch, fingers tightening as my dick starts to fill, "Daniel, you know you want it." Mrs. Turner's voice invades my thoughts, and I struggle to push it away, concentrating on how I need a different circle of people in my life instead.

Ego much, Carrie?

Men are more than a *dick* that needs to jizz.

If a guy said *she wanted it*, he'd be part of the rape culture. Instead, I got to talk Kade down from cutting himself because he felt like he cheated on Wynn when Carrie grabbed his crotch– underneath his waistband but over his boxers. Kade sure as shit didn't ask for it, show Carrie any interest whatsoever, or *want* it.

Call a spade a spade. It was sexual harassment at the very least, even sexual assault. But it would have been laughed out of court, if the cops even filed the paperwork, because guys are sexual beasts no matter who is touching them. We should just be thankful a girl was willing enough to pleasure us.

I'd know. I tested the waters on a few of my older classmates just after Turner raped me, and the guys all hooted and slapped each other on the backs, laughing about how they wished a hot, older woman would molest them. That was the first and only time I tried to tell anyone what happened.

If Kade had called Carrie out on it, she would have shamed him by calling him a fag or told everyone how he had erectile dysfunction or a tiny cock, whatever would soothe her bruised ego. Not all men think women are just T&A. On the same token, some girls only see a guy for what he can do for them.

This shit ought to work both ways, and my analytical mind can't take the hypocrisy anymore. Equality should be about equality, not lowering a grouping of humans to raise another. Guys are assholes, but so are girls.

Asshattery is not gender exclusive.

There is no tally, where until a grouping of people commits the same number of atrocities on the group who abuses them, there is no such thing as equality. I was raped by a grown woman, and it counts dammit.

It counts.

I was born to be an attorney– I'm blind to who you are, what you look like, and where you came from, but not to how you behave. I judge actions, with compassion when dealing with difficult past events that were precipitous to the act at hand.

This is individualistic, because it's an individual committing the crime.

"Kade has someone back home," is the standard answer, because it's none of anyone's business, and the guy hasn't come out here at Penn State. The next lie is the easiest, because I don't want to hurt Carrie's feelings, even if I think she deserves it. "I can't mess around anymore, either. A girl I dated in high school came back into my life, and I don't want to fuck it up."

"What she doesn't know won't hurt her," Carrie purrs, and Tonya grimaces across the table from us, waiting for my reaction.

Not all girls are assholes– only the ones I fuck, apparently. Tonya's a real study partner and friend, and I wouldn't destroy that for anything.

Tonya and I met in class, and connected cerebrally. We talked, got to know one another, and it was a relief that she didn't ask me to fuck her in the first ten minutes of knowing each other.

Tonya earned an internship at Bishop last summer– and not on her knees. By her merits. I showed Tonya the ropes, and Ransom joined us for his first year of interning for his grandpas. My nephew thought Tonya was hilarious too. Win-win. Tonya's following me to law school next year, and we're rooming together.

This table is full of pre-law students, and it won't end well for humanity if they pass the bar, because ethics would be dead.

"*I'd know,*" I state firmly, removing Carrie's hand from my thigh, setting it on the table for all to see. "I don't need to study this morning, so I'm going to jet in a few."

"C'mon, Danny," Carrie whines, hand back on my thigh, way too high up for my liking. "Crans is being a pain in the ass. He wouldn't give me an extension!"

"Oh, the humanity," Tonya deadpans, eyes connecting with mine, holding great irony. "You could have just done the work when it was assigned."

"Novel idea," I mutter out the side of my mouth just as Josh drops a tray of food in front of me, but I've lost my appetite. "I can't help those who refuse to help themselves, Carrie."

If my father and grandfather ever met Carrie, they would go on a tangent over entitlement. Carrie is the perfect example of someone who doesn't deserve to be at a university. She sucked in high school, but we can't call her lazy, because she sure as shit isn't stupid. She dicks around, parties, uses her crotch to get guys to do her work for her, which is why she was screwing me. Manda wanted my babies for a free-ride, while Carrie wanted me to do her assignments.

Wouldn't it be easier to just do the work herself than to go to all the effort Carrie uses to not do it?

Asshattery is not a gender exclusive– there are three male equivalents of Carrie at the table, two of which targeted Tonya for help with sexual favors, and another who targeted me.

They didn't get anywhere, and never will.

My conservative nature hates these people, and Tonya's looking at me like what I'm thinking is playing out in stereo in her head too. We're here to study, to get job experience, and to excel, and we're literally paying for every second of it.

Don't bitch about student loans after not taking advantage of what you were purchasing in the first place.

Professor Crans isn't assigning work for shits 'n' giggles– he's teaching us. *Law*. Because we're the idiots who will be governing this country someday. No matter how much we pay for the lessons, if we refuse to learn them, we shouldn't be here.

I don't understand following a path in life because it sounds cool, versus having a real passion for it. All they're doing is filling the seats and taking away real one-on-one time we need with our professors. The professors spend way too much time on people who will never use this portion of their education, while those who need the insight struggle alone because we're passionate and driven enough to help ourselves.

I'm empathetic enough to understand not knowing what you want to do in life at age eighteen when you enter college, but don't go pre-anything if that's the case. Try a little of everything until something sticks.

Pre-law and pre-med courses should only be filled with those who truly know that's their life's work. LIVES are on the line, either medically or judiciously. People like Carrie are taking away valuable time where we learn from our professors to serve the public to the best of our abilities, because she thinks it would be ego-boosting to say *I'm a lawyer* someday.

"Ugh!" Josh slumps to the tabletop, head in hands. "I'm too fucking hungover to handle class today."

Tonya and I share a loaded look as everyone commiserates with Josh. Twenty-one-year-old toddlers, being loud and obnoxious, they don't even hear what I say next. "I think we'll just study together from now on, and let them deal with their own consequences."

"We can meet at my apartment." Tonya smirks, thinking it funny how I've had to endure dorm life because Kaden was comfortable there. "It's dinky, falling down around my ears, but it's clean… and quiet."

Both of us hitch our eyes to the side as Josh regales everyone about his exploits from last night. Arms flailing around dramatically, he knocks an entire tray of food off the table. With a sharp clatter, the tray bounces once, pancakes and eggs splattering across the floor in a wide arc.

Instead of looking contrite, the table erupts in obnoxious laughter, and Josh doesn't even have the decency to blush.

"Hey!" Carrie shouts. "Where's Pat?"

"Pat?" Looking around the bustling dining hall, I try to figure out what the hell she's talking about.

"The bitch who busses the tables–"

"I think he's a dude, actually," Carrie mutters in a condescending tone to Josh. "His name's Pat."

"*It is not!*" Tonya snarls, thoroughly disgusted. "Are you going to clean up your own goddamn mess?"

"Nope." Josh snags a sausage link from Tonya's tray, smirking around the piece of meat as his teeth sink into it. "And nobody's gonna make me– Pat better do the job he's paid to do."

"Fucking creep," I growl, lunging from my chair, only to flip back around to glare at an entire table of people who need to learn many hard lessons. "You have no idea what it means to be a work-study student, cleaning up after disgusting hogs like you."

"And I thank God every day I'll never find out." Carrie winks at me, thinking she's being cute.

Dropping into a crouch, I begin scooping up splattered food, flicking it back on the tray. Tonya chases down the plate, bowl, and missing flatware, then reaches for a handful of napkins.

"Uriah working his way through school says a lot about him." Tonya glares at our classmates. "You making his job harder than need be says a lot about you. The former earns my respect, while the latter shows your worthlessness."

"Condescending dyke," Josh snarls, jerking Tonya's tray off the table. Landing with a bang, the meal splatters both of us, oatmeal glopping on my chin.

With no anger riding my voice, I look up at Josh. After a few years in elementary school together, then senior year at boarding school, and now all the way to the start of our last year at PSU, Josh knows what I say next is gospel.

"You're done in this school," I promise, inflection calm. "Any pre-law classes you're in, be prepared to find a replacement. You won't be accepted into a law school in this country, or be able to practice on American soil. Are we clear?"

In a jerking motion, Josh is up out of his seat, foot kicking the tray halfway across the dining hall. Before anyone can react, he's already slamming through the outside doors.

In silence, with at least forty other students and faculty staring at us, Tonya and I continue to pick up the mess Josh made. After a few suspended moments, our table erupts in rancorous laughter.

"Oooo…" Bill, one of the quieter of the bunch, drawls out, face paling. "Now that's what I call power."

"It pays to have a granddaddy as a senator," Carrie chirps. "Or is it an uncle?"

"Uncle," Teri pipes in. "Danny's paternal side: aunt is a congresswoman, uncle is a senator, his grandfather and father are lawyers, and his sister is a women's rights activist. His maternal side: his grandmother is a mayor, his mother's brother is a judge or something or other, and his mother is the head of several prominent charities."

"I'm so glad you have my family tree memorized and can accurately state the Bishop and Randolph résumés." With narrowed eyes, I fist a bunch of napkins.

It's telling how they all know what branches of government houses which family members, missing a few while they're at it. My political ties run deep, not something I find as either a source of pride or shame, since all we share is a name. Their achievements belong solely to them, with me taking no ownership in them. What's telling is how the people only see me as an extension of my family, someone they can use to get them where they want to be in the future.

I'm done.

"Sorry," Tonya mouths at me weakly as we tackle the mess Josh made.

After spending all summer together with my family, Tonya gets how I don't let anyone in. I've never had a girlfriend, just a series of hard fucks. I've never had any true friends, just acquaintances trying to get close to me to use my family name. Tonya and I respect one another as colleagues, but it will take a long time to progress to friendship with her using my family to jumpstart her career.

I respect Tonya, and I believe in her, so I'm thrilled the Bishops are backing her, but this will forever be a wedge between us forging a real friendship.

The closest people to me are my nephew and the guy who shares a cum-rag with me, and I still don't trust them enough to share the dark secret I carry. I wish Mrs. Turner didn't know– hell, I wish it never happened.

"Allow me," a soft voice whispers, a tiny hand brushing mine away from the mess. "I'll mop it up– you go get another meal."

Head darting up, I take a quick look at the kid everyone called *Pat*, arguing gender. I can still hear them doing it in the background, trying to be sneaky by whispering. But if I can hear it, so can– Tonya said his or her name was Uriah.

"I'll help," I offer, intrigued.

Tonya snorts, smirking at me ironically, then she rises to her full height. "Meet me at my place at eight tonight, and we'll actually study. Okay?"

"Yeah, sure," I mutter absent-mindedly, trying to get a good look at Uriah's face. The navy PSU hoodie covers all but the sharp blade of a nose and the shadowy slope of a cheek. The eyelashes are inky black, hinting that the hair hidden beneath the hood is probably dark too.

Try as I might, the androgynous bagginess of a hoodie, Sharpie-covered Chucks, and loose jeans makes it impossible to know if Uriah is a boy or girl, not that it matters to me. Just, it's hard in my head not thinking without a pronoun.

Working quickly, as if I am making Uriah uncomfortable with my need to help, Uriah tries again. "The cashier saw what happened– she'll comp your breakfast, so hurry up and go get another meal."

"How about you mop while I toss the trash and take the dishes and trays to the pass." Stilling, I turn my head, trying to catch Uriah's eye. With a rough shake, pitch-black, silky hair escapes the loose confines of the hoodie, becoming an impenetrable shield between my gaze and Uriah's features. "Team-work?"

"Suit yourself," Uriah mutters none too kindly, voice soft and airy with a biting edge. Realizing how rude that sounded, Uriah tacks on a begrudging, "Thanks."

"No problem." Rising to my feet, two trays filled with trash balanced in my hands, I'm suddenly hesitant to leave, yet I can't think of anything else to say. Chuckling underneath my breath at myself, I stalk across the dining hall to the trash cans and the pass to the kitchen.

"You're such a good boy, Mr. Bishop." The elderly dishwasher lady pauses in her work to come over to chat me up as usual. Smile lines bracketing her mouth, missing an incisor, Mrs. Wilber has been a highlight of my mornings since the first day of my freshman year.

Chuckling with good humor, a wide smile pulls at my lips. "Mrs. Wilber, you do realize calling me Mr. Bishop and a good boy in the same sentence is an oxymoron, right?"

"Danny," the grandmotherly woman releases as tinkling laughter. "Thank you," she murmurs with all sincerity, and she's not talking about cleaning up Josh's mess, or being polite enough to scrape the dishes before stacking them in the rack.

I'd overheard Mrs. Wilber and her grandson fighting a few months back. The teenager was arrested for shoplifting, when he said he didn't do it. Dillon is one of those boys destined for a bad life because no one expects anything out of him– believes him. Believes *in* him.

Dad took on Dillon's case at my behest, proving the kid didn't shoplift and that the mall rent-a-cop had a beef with him and lied– the security footage backed Dillon up. It could have ruined the kid's life, that asshole's ego-trip. Instead, Dad sponsored Dillon at a high school in a better school district, and Dillon's brought his grades up from all Ds to a solid C-average in a matter of weeks.

Bill is wrong. Power isn't wielded like I did when I promised Josh would never become an attorney. Power is doing the right thing for those who are powerless, like Dad did for Mrs. Wilber and her grandson.

It's those same beliefs that had me getting on my hands and knees to clean up Josh's mess, instead of sitting at the table, watching with self-righteous indignation like the rest of my peers. It's that same drive that has me intrigued with Uriah, rather than being mocking and bullying of something I don't understand.

Catching sight of Uriah and one of PSU's newest football recruits headed into the men's room, my heart starts beating in overdrive. "I better go wash up after that mess." Self-deprecating laughter spills from my lips, and it's only half an act. "Then actually get something to eat."

"You have a good day, Danny." Mrs. Wilber reaches through the pass to pat my cheek in a grandmotherly gesture that will stand the test of time.

"I'll see you tomorrow morning." With a flash of a grin, I'm off to the restroom, with my table of ex-study-buddies jeering at me for being such a do-gooder. A magnetic pull has me arrowing toward Uriah, one I cannot deny or define.

Pausing to catch my breath, I rest my hand on the door, an unfathomable pull drawing me forward. After a minute, I get the balls to step forward, heart beating a rapid tattoo against my ribs.

At first, I don't hear anything as I enter, just noting this is one of the cleaner restrooms on campus, and I wonder if it's in part to Uriah being on duty. Doing as I said I was going to do, I plunge my hands into the sink after flicking the knob to the faucet.

Eyeing the mirror, looking through my own reflection to the stalls behind me, the only occupied stall gains my undivided attention. I don't know if it's a good thing or a bad thing how there is at least a three-inch gap between the stall and the door latch, giving me a bird's eye view of a footballer's back and a pair of tiny Chucks peeking out as Uriah squats in front of the other guy. Noticing how the body is swaying in a rhythmic motion, my mouth pops open wide in shock.

My raspy breath joins the labored breathing from the stall as I turn from watching the reflection to watching it from less than five feet away. Faster. Faster still. The breathing and the movement ratchets up several notches, causing adrenaline to punch through my veins in the same way it does when I look Kade in the eyes when I come.

The wet slurps and slight choking noises are unmistakable and have my imagination running wild. I've been on the receiving end of the action a few times to know what's happening inside that bathroom stall.

Jealousy– envy, maybe –I cannot recognize the emotion inundating me this instant, other than it's one of the first times I've felt the unmistakable stirrings of lust. Normally I see a hot girl, and it's not that I want what she has to offer, but more like I anticipate how rewarding it is for me to know I can work her body better than anyone who came before me. A conqueror.

Lust.

I want what the guy is getting in the bathroom, and I suddenly want it from the person who is giving it to him– someone I've never met, never seen their face, and have no idea if they are male or female.

That's why I'm so goddamn hot right now– Uriah sparks of forbidden.

Panting, my palm cups my bulge, squeezing tightly to stop myself from popping off in my jeans like I did at summer camp. My first year, during the masculine games, I had to forfeit for coming in my shorts before I got to take my turn. My last year at camp, I won for lasting the longest and shooting the farthest, but was middle of the road for length and girth.

I'm not that idiot kid anymore, but I suddenly feel like one, because this is uncharted territory, where a future member of the court witnesses a crime and is getting off on it.

After a series of porn-worthy grunts, which I nearly cream my shorts listening to, the footballer steps back until his ass bangs against the door, giving me a thin slice view of Uriah crouching in front of the toilet– small hands hanging loosely, forearms resting on knees. With the way the Chucks are scrunched, I can tell Uriah's toes are curled inside the sneakers.

"If you woulda let me go bare, I woulda tossed in another ten." The footballer's arm moves, then an unmistakable plop hits the toilet water. Bending, he flushes the toilet. "It was over too quick," he chastises, voice taking on an edge of anger.

"You know the rules," Uriah whispers succinctly, voice raspy from sucking the ungrateful fuck off. "Keep your hands to yourself– no touching. Blowjobs only. Condoms only. Ten bucks for ten minutes or less. You last longer, you pay more. Not my fault if you pop too quick or not quick enough."

"Yes, it is, you fucking freak–"

"No!" Uriah's tone is sharp yet quiet, lashing out in command. "I know what I'm doing. If you come too fast, that's on you for being too worked up. I don't deal in whiskey dick, which is why I have a dollar a minute rate, payable in ten-dollar increments, not exceeding thirty minutes. Your dick, not my problem."

"You were working it too hard, getting me off too quick," the footballer whines. "I'm not paying ten bucks for three minutes."

Refusing to argue or negotiate, "Not my problem," echoes from the stall. "We're not alone right now, so don't make it my problem or his problem," Uriah threatens, when I hadn't realized my presence was known.

"I'm not– you just lost my business!" The footballer pounds the stall door open. Eyes connecting with mine, he glares me down with fierce rage, until recognition hits. Cowering, shoulders curling, the freshman tucks tail and slinks out of the restroom.

"You're quite the cowboy 'round these here parts," Uriah taunts in a teasing tone, smirking at how I can't take my eyes off a face finally revealed without the cowl-like hood used as a shield.

Still crouched in the stall, Uriah's tiny hand lifts, a single fingertip smudging across a pouty, bottom lip. Uriah's gender is unmistakable now. The pale planes of his face too sharp, the blade of his nose, the edge of his jaw, the intensity of his whiskey flamed eyes.

The darkest black, thick silky hair hangs in a straight curtain, cut in a sharp edge along Uriah's harsh jawline. Gobsmacked, the most socially unacceptable, intolerant thing blurts out my mouth.

"Are you part Native American?" Shaking my head, kicking my own ass, I manage to make it worse. "You're so pale, though."

Chuckling, Uriah tilts his head to the side, sighting me in his hawk-like eyes. "Ah, my cowboy joke went right over your head, I take it." One finger rises, curling, beckoning me forth. "C'mere and latch the door– I can kneel for hours, but realize I may get arthritis in my old age."

Blinking out of a daze, I find myself already in the stall with the door closed at my back. Uriah's palms flow up and down my thighs in what should be a soothing rhythm but is anything but.

"I didn't stick around for this," stammering, I have to swallow a few times. "I'm not–"

"And here I thought you were forming a queue over by the sinks," Uriah taunts, voice raspy and soft with suppressed laughter– so quiet I find myself leaning forward to hear him better.

Those eyes– I can't tear myself away from them.

Whimpering, a shudder rolls down my spine as a sneaky fingertip nears where my sack is resting snugly in my jeans, then the palms roam downward, taking the exhilarating sensation along with it.

When I'm a politician someday, will there be a news broadcast about how I was caught getting a blowjob from a male prostitute in a PSU bathroom stall?

Last year, last week, a minute ago, the only skeleton in my closet was Mrs. Turner. I fear I'll be adding another one if I don't get my libido under control. Never before... never felt this level of insanity before.

Hunger.

"I'm not gay," blurts out my numb lips. "Nothing wrong with being gay– I'm just not..." I trail off, sounding foolish yet even more confused to my own ears.

"Tell that to ninety-percent of my clientele," Uriah murmurs wryly, breath wafting in a hot wave against my jittering fingers. "My androgyny is a bit of a mind-fuck for guys and girls. Straight guys and gay girls want me because I'm effeminate. Gay guys, not so much– bit of a conundrum for me, don't you think?" The palms rise again, headed farther north with every pass.

"Ugh!" My sack is grazed, and it's a close call that I don't cream my pants. Making sure he never actually touches *me*, a prostitute shows more respect for my autonomy than Mrs. Turner did when I was a boy, more than any of the women who have touched me has.

Uriah waits for me to say yes.

"I don't pay for it."

"And I don't expect you to." Uriah finally blinks, breaking the spell he's cast me under. Gaze roaming me from head to toe, making several passes, a jolt hits my bloodstream as his eyes light on my groin. "This is for me, something I never had the luxury of experiencing." Voice cracking, he seems startled by his own confession.

"I'm not letting you give me a blowjob," comes out all growly, because I want it... I really, *really* want Uriah's lips spread wide around my cock, tearing grunts from his throat. When it's all over, I want to witness how ruby red that mouth becomes, all swollen from working me roughly. That fingertip won't be used as a seductive tool, but will actually be wiping a bead of my cum away, where he'll lick it off his own fingertip, groaning as it melts on his tongue.

"One helluva fantasy you're spinning there, Mr. Man Around Campus," Uriah teases, voice getting raspier with every word. "I can see your bulge beating, and you're leaking through your jeans, so don't tell me you're not interested... what's the actual problem? Is it because I have a dick? 'Cuz I always keep it in my pants, especially around the straight guys."

That comment breaches the lust-fog Uriah's woven around me. Taken aback, I end up shaking my head over and over to clear it. "Aren't you gonna jerk yourself off too?"

"No." Face twisting in confusion, Uriah sounds flabbergasted. "A blowjob isn't about me– they pay me to get them off, not the other way around."

"But I'm not paying you–"

"My dick's not joining the fray, straight guy," Uriah interrupts, getting agitated.

"Well, I don't engage in one-sided sexual transactions." Stubborn, I cross my arms over my chest, peering down at Uriah, my own bulge taking up quite a bit of my view. Uriah glares back up at me, like I'm taking away his favorite toy. "You either get off too, or no sucking my dick."

"You're–" Uriah is rendered speechless, staring up at me like I'm a new species of animal he's come upon in an undiscovered, foreign land. "You're serious, aren't you?" Laughing to himself, Uriah rises to his feet, signaling how no one will be getting off in this stall now. "You're a rare breed, Daniel Bishop."

"And you're the first person I've met who doesn't want anything from me, Uriah…" I trail off, asking for his last name.

"Crane," Uriah practically breathes, as if it's a secret.

Standing in silence, I begin to wonder if my guess at Uriah's gender is wrong. Maybe there isn't a dick in his pants and that's why he doesn't want to find pleasure too. It doesn't matter to me either way, I just refuse to take from someone and not give anything back.

"Will you eat breakfast with me?" I blurt out quickly, before my mind catches up. "Are you on a break right now?"

"My shift's over." Eyeing me, obviously not trusting me, Uriah watches every muscle twitch in my face. "Why? Why do you want to eat breakfast with me?"

"Because the dining hall is filled with people who want something from me, and I'd rather spend a few minutes with someone who doesn't," I answer in all honesty.

"Alright." Voice cracking slightly, Uriah sounds shocked at his own easy acquiescence. "Since you're the first person I've met who actually wants to give me something, instead of take, I guess I'll share a meal with you."

Reaching past me in the tight confines of the bathroom stall, Uriah flips the lock on the door. Slipping past, his slim body rubs against mine– the hard press of a flat stomach against my bulge has a quiver running down my spine, but it's the obvious hardness that grazes my thigh that has my heart galloping out of control.

Intrigued, I follow Uriah back into the dining hall, having absolutely no idea where the fuck I'm headed with this insanity.

MARY KAY PINK GREMLIN

Uriah is eating his scrambled eggs and toast in contemplative silence, hood back in place on his head, covering all but the very tip of his nose. The fork enters and disappears within the shadowy darkness of the hood, and then returns missing the eggs it carried.

Not hungry myself, I fiddle with the wrapper on my Snapple bottle, gazing around the dining hall. A few stragglers are wandering around, with tables on the periphery filled with students camping out for the long haul, most likely avoiding annoying roommates and a packed dorm room.

After a bit of a squabble over me wanting to buy Uriah's breakfast, the guy hasn't said a word to me that carries. His lips move, but it's not audible. All that intriguing confidence the guy exhibited while on his knees evaporated the instant we left the stall, leaving shy awkwardness in its place.

"What year are you?" I try again to get Uriah to come out of his shell– that hoodie. An insane need to grab a butter knife and begin hacking away at the sweatshirt comes over me. If it wouldn't be deemed a physical assault, I'd just reach over the table and yank the shirt off Uriah's body.

"You're not going to eat?" Uriah eyes the empty space in front of me as if it personally offends him. "Why did you ask me to share breakfast?" Voice warped with annoyance, his head turns to check out all the corners in the dining hall, seeming suspicious or embarrassed to share a table with me.

Acting on impulse, I reach over and grab a slice of toast, then spoon half the eggs on it. After folding it into a half sandwich, I do the same with the partially eaten piece of toast and the rest of the eggs. Doing what I like, I squeeze grape jelly from a packet onto both sandwiches. Then I hand Uriah the one with the bite taken out of it, and take the other for myself.

"Let's walk and eat." After shoving the Snapple bottle into the back pocket of my jeans, I hold my sandwich in one hand and grab

Uriah's tray with the other. He ghosts behind me in silence while I take care of the tray, then dutifully follows me outside.

I can't get heads or tails of Uriah Crane, but no matter how shy and silent he becomes, I'm determined to get to know him.

"So…" I drawl out slowly, chewing a big bite of my egg sandwich. "Let's try this again, shall we?"

Instead of answering, Uriah jerks his head slightly in a practiced move, and the hood falls away to reveal his intriguing face. Taking a bite of sandwich, his eyes narrow in contemplation. "Wasn't sure about the grape jelly," he muses, then takes another bite. "But it's growing on me."

"Better with cherry preserves, but we have to make due." I'm not going to put on airs, and I'm not going to pretend I'm something I'm not. I could lie and say Welch's is on the Bishop's table, but I won't. Our pantry is stocked with goods from the farmer's market. "Ransom prefers strawberry jam, and Ainsley loves ketchup– the rest of my family calls us heathens for putting condiments on our eggs."

"Ransom?" Uriah's voice pitches high with interest. I'm not surprised, though.

"My nephew. Odd name, right?" Chuckling to myself, I hear my sister telling me why she named my nephew that. "Ainsley– my sister –she has a dark sense of humor, even when she was fifteen. When she was pregnant, our family and Joel's family fought nonstop– Joel is Ransom's dad. Anyway, Ainsley said she felt like the negotiations were actually ransom attempts on who got their way. *If you do this, we won't do that…* A family of lawyers versus a family of religious leaders. When the kid popped out, she named him Ransom."

Feet stilling, sandwich poised before his luscious mouth, the guy is floored by my laughter. "And your family was okay with this?"

Uriah seems shocked, no doubt believing all the propaganda he's heard about the Bishops and Randolphs. Talbot– the other half of Ransom's family is powerful in religious circles, adding another layer to the right-wing religious fanatic pile of bullshit suffocating me with every social interaction I have.

Yeah, people hate us sight unseen, and I wouldn't blame them if it wasn't for the fact that it's all untrue generalizations. Being born deep into politics, I know firsthand how it's just two sides of the same corrupt coin.

Taking pity on Uriah, I tug on his hoodie to get his feet moving, then plop down on the nearest bench. "My dad thought it was hilarious. Joel's family was enraged, but Joel was secretly amused– poor guy has always been in love with my sister. Seventeen years later, and Joel's still trying to woo Ainsley instead of moving on."

"When I heard about your sister…" Uriah stumbles over his words, the shyness overcoming him. "I assumed she was married forever and had a bunch of kids."

"Lemme guess," I mutter sharply, the cross I bear getting the better of me. "Ainsley Bishop lives in a big house, drives expensive cars, wears designer brands, has a wealthy husband and three perfect kids, and only playacts at being an activist?"

"I–"

"I don't want to get off on the wrong foot with you, and I know I sound like a rotten asshole right now, but that pisses me off." Taking a deep breath, I try to get my emotions in check.

"Ainsley got pregnant by our pastor's son when she was fourteen, popped a kid out at fifteen, finished high school and went to college, and is married to her job. She's always been in my life, but she's fought to raise her own son as my mom and grandmother tried their damnedest to mother him instead. We're not rich. We're not perfect. We're just trying our best to eradicate the false narrative that conservatives are selfish scum, religion is oppressive, and having a core belief system means you're trying to control everyone else's lives. All. Bullshit."

"I didn't think that about you," Uriah mumbles, but his gaze quickly flashes away, calling him out as being a liar.

This quiet routine– the reason he didn't want to be seen with me in a near empty dining hall is because my family's reputation precedes itself. Clearly this guy, who is definitely a member of the LGBTQ community, is terrified they will take his membership away for sharing breakfast with a card-carrying conservative pre-law student.

"I could make false assumptions about you too," I admit without hesitation. "But I won't, not after having to live with my peers spitting on me–"

"You've been spit on?" Uriah's voice pitches higher than his eyebrows are raised, and if I wasn't so frustrated, I'd be amused. "I've heard people talk, but I didn't think they'd act on it."

"It didn't take long for people to figure out who I was. Most want to use me for my connections, but others see me as evil incarnate, even though none of this has anything to do with me."

"What do you mean, nothing to do with you?" The accusation is loud and clear in Uriah's tone, as is the disgust for everything my family stands for, when he has absolutely no idea what our beliefs are.

Yeah, Uriah thinks like the majority of everyone who meets me do. I hope this won't be a wedge between us, but it always is. There's a reason my nephew is my best friend and my roommate is the only person I have on campus that I can talk to without a dozen filters from my mind to my mouth.

"I was born into my family– I didn't choose it. I don't get to dictate what they do when they are seventy and younger and I'm only twenty. Same as my sister getting pregnant was on her and Joel, their choices are not mine. I get sick of classmates blaming me for what my family does or doesn't do, not realizing I'm going to school to get an education, so when I finally speak, my voice is not only heard, but respected."

Not allowing Uriah to speak, all the frustration and rage bubbles out of me. "My sister is shamed by women everywhere she goes– shamed for being an unwed mother, shamed because she was so young, by members of our own party who don't believe in abortion. Shamed by women who hate where Ainsley comes from, when they have the same goal. But the disgusting thing is how she is fighting for equality every waking moment of her life, being dragged down by the very women she's fighting for. So that fact that you already had preconceived notions about one of the best human beings I know, that makes me sick…

"We didn't choose to be born into politics, nor does it mean we agree with their stances, but we have to love them anyway… Every time there is a controversial bill put up for a vote, people come out of the woodwork. Ainsley had her car tagged with slurs. Ransom gets bullied– the gay kid gets bullied over LGBTQ legislation by people in his own community... I've been *beaten* by a gang of *pacifists*," I twist out, voice heavy with irony. "The last time someone took offense to how one of my distant relatives voted, they spit in my face in the middle of a lecture hall and called me a bigot... fun times."

"To be honest..." Uriah sighs heavily, and all the sudden it's like the atmosphere changes, and whatever mood that had descended since we left the bathroom stall dissipates. "Okay, I was nervous and freaking out– not gonna lie. I'm a queer, poor as dirt, Native American kid, who grew up in a trailer, living on welfare. I've been known to pull on a dress as often as a pair of jeans– I don't believe in assigning gender to clothing and cosmetics and emotions and boats and cars and toys... going to school on a work-study program with a shitload of grants and scholarships because of my mother's culture, the handout meaning I'll never pay a cent myself... so I assumed you'd be an asshole, judging and hating me for all that, Daniel– I apologize."

"I'm not my family," I hammer home hard. "My immediate family is nothing as you'd expect. We aren't what you assume." Sighing, body losing all its fight, I slump to fall back against the bench. "Now that that's settled, how about we get to know each other, instead of making assumptions based on political leanings."

"You know what they say about assumptions," Uriah teases. Chuckling, we sing the *Makes an ass out of you and me* song together. "No talking politics, though," he negotiates. "Because that's a landmine field we're not going to navigate without blowing us to smithereens. Agree to disagree, because there's no way in hell we'd ever agree."

"No politics," I mutter in relief, relaxing– most people never give me a chance to get to know me once they hear my name, automatically going into antichrist mode. Reaching back, I tug the Snapple bottle out of my back pocket, since it was digging into my ass, and then take a hearty pull. "You have no idea how relieved I am to not talk about it– I live, breathe, eat, sleep, and shit politics. Inescapably imprisoned by politics."

"My mom escaped a similar upbringing." Uriah's face twists, as if he's shocked with whatever he's just discovered. "What's your favorite color?"

The swift change in our conversation makes my head spin. Laughing, I answer without hesitation. "Navy blue. You?"

"I'm totally shameless and unashamed by mine." Uriah winks— it happens so quickly, I wonder if I imagined it. Something tells me Uriah is a shameless flirt too. "Pink."

Laughing freely, I cannot help but imagine the guy wearing a pink, frilly dress, and I'm shocked to discover I'm curious to know what it would look like in reality. "Pink— it suits you."

"And navy suits you." Smirking, Uriah plucks at his PSU sweatshirt. "Your room was probably covered in blue growing up. Your daddy had your college picked out before you were conceived— alumni, no doubt."

Blushing profusely, my skin feels tight as a swarm of buzz-saw wielding butterflies assault my belly. "Not gonna lie, blue's my color, through and through... I'll be the fourth generation Bishop to attended both Penn State and Yale."

"Your kid will be the fifth," is said without a doubt. Uriah suddenly sounds sad, or maybe he thinks the legacy I'm so proud to call my own is disgustingly entitled. Either way, I hate seeing the vibrant light go out in his eyes.

"Nope." I pop the P, trying to lighten the mood. "Ainsley beat me to it with Ransom. My nephew will be haunting this campus next fall. We're four years apart, so he'll arrive just after I enter Yale, and four years later he'll follow my footsteps there."

"So sure of yourselves." Turning to the side, I fear the incrimination I'll witness on Uriah's face, but I'm surprised to see curiosity instead. "It must be so comforting to know what you want to do, and know there's nothing that's going to stop you." Pausing, Uriah keeps staring at me like he can see inside my mind.

"Unless..." Teeth sinking into his bottom lip, I can tell Uriah is filtering himself, and I can't have that.

"I have a thick skin— you won't offend me. Say whatever."

"Is this even the life you want to lead? What are the odds that every generation bears a kid who wants to be a lawyer? Seems like an impossible standard to live up to."

"It can be," I murmur softly, understanding exactly what Uriah's saying since it plagued Ainsley. "You know how a kindergartener will say they want to be a fireman, a ten-year-old will say a rock star, and a sixteen-year-old will say they don't know what they want to do so stop asking? Well, my answer never changed, and neither has Ransom's. We want it for different reasons, and my family is good with that."

"What's your reason?" Uriah actually sounds curious about how my mind ticks, instead of buttering me up to ask me to do something for him.

Blushing brighter, I fight the satisfied smile from breaking across my face. This is a high from making a friend– Uriah is my complete and total opposite in all the ways that matter, but exactly what I need to understand how the other half lives.

"My father calls me an idealist. My grandma calls me a romantic dreamer." Shrugging, I whisper the truth, "To make a difference in just one person's life." Embarrassed, I trudge on before Uriah can reply. "Ransom toyed with becoming an activist like his mother, but for the LGBTQ community. I'm not gonna lie, our family name means we can do anything we want, go anywhere we want, and be accepted wherever we set foot. But it's not a legacy we take for granted. Ransom decided he'd be better going into law, wanting to help people who are like him– be the voice the powerless have not."

Uriah stares at me gape-mouthed, flush slowly working a way up his pale cheeks, eyes darkening. "I can see... I can see where your grandma is coming from," Uriah stammers, words breaking as his flush deepens. "Romantic creamer is an accurate description– and completely unexpected."

Laughing at himself, or maybe me, Uriah shakes his head back and forth, inky hair flying. "Idealistic too, just like your daddy said."

"Enough about boring me– all I know about you is your name, your love of pink, and how you don't believe in boy toys and girl toys." Pulling off a fake shamed face, I blurt out something I've never admitted to anyone else. "Add another reason to the list on why you can't like me... but I did name my car a girl name."

"Oh, yeah?" Laughing at me, Uriah rewards me by taking off his sweatshirt. Unveiling himself slowly, face disappearing as he pulls the shirt over his head, a silky blouse is revealed. I try to wrap my mind around a guy wearing a blouse, but I realize it doesn't matter. Then I feel guilty and shitty for even having it enter my mind. It's hard to break out of conditioning.

"That suits you too." I try, and probably fail, to compliment Uriah. "Pink is your color."

"Shameless, remember?" Uriah arches a brow at me, readying to call me out. "Tell me what you named your car and why, and I'll tell you why I have balls big enough to wear a satin top to class."

Chuckling, I blurt out, "Sybil, because my car has multiple personalities– never know if she's gonna start."

"*You*– a Bishop –have an unreliable car?" Uriah's reaction is priceless, and I cannot wait to see what happens when I tell him the rest.

"It's a classic," I manage to say with a straight face. "Time-warped out of the 1970s. My grandfather almost had a coronary when I brought it home on a rollback and said I was going to restore it to its former glory. I was sixteen, and it was my first and only car."

"What kind of car?" Uriah leans forward, seeming enthralled. "I'm not a car whore or anything… I drive my godmother's hand-me-down Subaru, because I drive her kids all over the place."

Swallowing my own laughter, I continue to set the scene. "My sister ran out of the house, laughing her ass off, then she had the audacity to ask if I was making a joke or trying to be ironic. Only Ransom got me, having to one-up me on his sixteenth birthday. Ransom's car is called Jack– Jack from The Shining."

"C'mon, what kind of car is it?!" Frustrated, Uriah slaps my thigh, and I love how comfortable he is with me. It feels natural. Real.

"Jack is a metallic gold Pinto," I admit, trying my damnedest not to laugh. Uriah gives me a look, thinking I'm bullshitting him. "We have trust funds, obviously, but Grandpa and Dad, and even Ransom's family, have always hammered home how we have to work. So when I worked my ass off mowing our neighbors' yards, I only saved up so much money. Like always, Ransom followed in my footsteps."

"Bet refurbishing the car didn't come out of your lawn-mowing money," Uriah says with confidence, and he'd be right. "So Sybil's a Pinto too? I'm guessing in metallic blue?"

Unable to keep a straight face, the laughter spills unbiddenly from my chest. "Wrong! Sybil is a Mary Kay Pink Gremlin."

"No!" Uriah gets slap-happy, swatting at my chest, and it's hard to ignore that I'm positive he's feeling me up a bit with the brief touches. "You're lying, you douche-noodle!"

Still laughing, I grab for the hand just before it makes contact with my chest again, then tug Uriah behind me to where I parked Sybil. It's not until I notice people are giving us sidelong looks as we pass that I realize we're holding hands. Not thinking too deeply about it, I don't let go since Uriah seems okay with it too.

Turning abruptly, I stand between Uriah and the parking lot. "Wait for it," I murmur softly, placing my hand over his eyes. "Sybil deserves to be unveiled slowly." Stepping to the side, I shuffle until I'm standing behind Uriah, with my palm still covering his eyes.

"I don't believe a word you say, just so we're clear." Voice serious, I can tell Uriah is amused by my antics. "Get it over with, the foreplay is getting tedious."

"Prepare yourself," I whisper into Uriah's ear, surprisingly delighted by how he shivers when my breath hits his neck. "But I think our meeting is kismet–"

Breath rushing out of me with the force of a comet to the chest, I realize how true my words are. Ignoring the gravity of the situation, I soldier on, keeping my voice light and teasing.

"Five years ago, when I saw the ad on Craigslist, clearly the universe knew I'd meet you one day. I wasn't trying to be ironic. I wasn't trying to be amusing. Hell, I had no idea why I bought the car, or why I picked such a ghastly color. The only thing I know for sure, is I'm pretty sure Sybil has finally found her owner."

"What are you talking about?" Struggling slightly, but somehow Uriah doesn't dislodge my hand, "I can't take your car."

"I'm not giving her to you." *Yet.* "Are you ready?" Eyelashes tickle my palm, as no doubt Uriah rolls his eyes at me. "On three. One… Two." I drop my hand before I get to three. A second later, my arm is wrapping around Uriah's waist because his knees go weak.

"Oh!" Uriah whispers breathlessly, feet moving before his mind catches up. "She's perfect."

Following with a giant grin on my face, I can't explain the emotions I'm feeling as I watch this stranger stare at my car, completely enthralled by the monstrosity. "I thought inanimate objects didn't have a gender."

"Look at her–" Uriah pets the hood. "She's a girl, no doubt about it. Gorgeous," is mouthed inaudibly. "Can we ride in her?"

Every date I've ever had was embarrassed to ride in Sybil, which is probably why all those girls just found their way to my bed instead of a restaurant or movie. My sister found it hilarious just to be near the car. Kade refuses to get within ten feet of the car, spending all of freshman and sophomore year bitching about how hard it was to get a parking permit for campus when he had a beautiful SUV at home he couldn't drive. As soon as the Durango made it to State College, Kade stopped going everywhere on foot and we started going places together. Ransom was the only one who understood the power of Sybil... until Uriah.

"Hop in– but it's your turn to tell me about yourself."

"Keys," Uriah demands, the confident guy from the bathroom stall makes a reappearance. "If I'm going to talk, then I need to distract myself with driving."

WE'RE DOING A DRIVE-BY

With confidence, Uriah pulls out of the parking lot and heads in a direction as if he has a destination in mind. With the windows rolled down, the scent of crisp autumn leaves assaulting our senses, Uriah flicks the radio on to see what station I was listening to last.

"Rap?" Uriah looks at me sideways, then flicks his gaze back to the road. Lips curling, Uriah's mouth ensnares me in its unescapable trap. "I figured you for country or Christian rock."

"Hey!" Thoroughly insulted, it's my turn to tap Uriah on the chest, but I pull my hit. Flat as a pancake, the silky blouse caressing my skin has conflicting thoughts warring with my body's intense reaction. "Stereotype, much? Nothing wrong with country or Christian rock, but I have a thing for the rhythmic beat of rap."

"You're full of surprises, aren't you?" Those lips curl more, making me feel as if it's my life's mission to never let them draw into a flat line. Confused, I'm feeling a bit insane with the bizarre thoughts thundering through my mind. "I listen to classical."

"What?!" I shout, causing Uriah to release a sadistic giggle. "Bullshitter, what do you listen to?"

"Tribal music, actually–" readying to call Uriah out on his bullshit again, he stops me. "No, really. I do. It's a beat thing. It's like my heart slows or speeds up until it marries with the music." Voice sounding faraway, Uriah's finally showing me a part of himself. "My godmother says it's in my blood– no denying it."

"I know nothing about your culture, so I'm terrified to ask any questions, fearing I'll come off as insensitive," I admit without hesitation. "I know nothing about Native Americans that I didn't learn in elementary school."

"And I don't expect you to know." Voice light, words heavy, Uriah is matter-of-fact. "Ask whatever, and I'll answer if I feel like it. But I'm not a walking source of knowledge, so don't pester me about it. There's more to me than just that, same with don't act like I'm an endless fountain of information about gender or sexuality."

"Okay, so we're not allowed to talk about politics, Native American culture, gender, or sexuality. 'Kay, how about those Cubs?"

"What?" flows out on a laugh as Uriah drives Sybil down interstate 99. "What the hell does that even mean?"

"Ainsley was a shoe-in to win prom queen–" Uriah's obvious confusion has me chuckling sadistically. "Mom and Grandma were helping decorate for prom. Ainsley had a rival, and her mother just so happened to be the vice principal of the high school, and one of my sister's teachers too. The vice principal and her daughter were discussing how she and her boyfriend were going to be crowned prom king and queen, not realizing Mom and Grandma could overhear. When they were crowned, the crowd was silent, could hear a pin drop, because no one voted for them… they voted for Ainsley."

"You're shitting me– what cunts!" Uriah's outrage amuses me, because this is a story we pop out about the power of having dignity and ethics while sticking to your convictions. Even if you get fucked over, never allow it to change who you truly are.

"Ainsley's classmates started chanting recount. *Recount! Recount!* Calling the girl out as a liar. They all knew the vice principle counted the votes, sad but true. With complete dignity, as if she wore the crown she deserved on her head, Ainsley shouted above everyone else… *How about those Cubs?*"

Smiling to myself, "I wish I had been there, but I was only seven and Ransom was three. Grandma woke everyone up in the house when they got home, bitching up a storm."

"I think I like this grandma of yours," Uriah murmurs with wry amusement. "What would you have done if you were in your sister's place?"

"Stayed silent, I guess." I mull that over for a few minutes, unsure what would have been the best course of action. "Everyone just let it go. Dad said the girl knew she rightfully lost and wore a stolen crown, and that feeling was punishment enough, because she had to live with it for a lifetime. Too bad it was her mother who was to blame, a vice principal and teacher willing to screw over her own students and to teach them cheating was the answer."

"What would your nephew have done?" Uriah drives on autopilot, as if this is a route he takes every day.

"Oh, Ransom would have torn the crown off her head and plopped it on his own, then grabbed the prom king and did the dance– my nephew is the epitome of flamboyant. Daring as all get out too. Sometimes I wish I was as brave as he is."

Uriah chuckling brings me up short. "What? What'd I say?"

"Nothing." That infuriating smile curls deeper. "You surprise me is all."

"Where are we going?" I grasp at straws to change the subject, because I'm beyond uncomfortable. For a guy who promised to talk about himself, he sure is turning me into a chatty Cathy, when normally I'm the listener.

"We're doing a drive-by–"

"A drive-by?" I squawk in a panic, heart equalizing with the insane beat of the music. "What the fuck, Uriah?"

Jarring peals of laughter flow from the devious fuck driving my car– Sybil and Uriah are the perfect partners in crime. "Dude, just because we're listening to rap music doesn't mean we're going to go hit some bitches." Snickering, Uriah keeps shaking his head left and right, hair flying around his jawline. "There's no Native American tribal mafia in Bellefonte, Pennsylvania. Drive-by, as in you wanted to know about me, so I'm driving you through my town, dumbass."

Hands outstretched to grip the dashboard, "Oh, thank God!"

"Could you imagine, though… imagine doing an actual drive-by in a pink Gremlin?" Uriah's laughter is infectious. "*In Bellefonte?* You're priceless, Daniel Bishop– priceless."

"Maybe hit up Main Street with a rainbow of paintballs," I mutter wryly about the small town that is no doubt not known for its tolerance, causing Uriah to lose his shit. "Ever been paintballing?"

"Have you?" Face serious, Uriah is trying to figure out if I'm fucking with him or not.

"Registered republican, remember? We've got guns tucked in every crevice– nothing is more fun than shooting your entire family with paintballs on the weekend–"

"You're lying… I can never tell if you're telling the truth."

Expression serious, palm pressed to my chest, "Hand to God, we paintball." We do, Ransom and I do, but not the rest of the family– they've never touched a gun in their lives. It's the truth and a lie all rolled into one. "It's the perfect quality to have in a lawyer or politician, the inability to tell when they are or aren't lying. It's inborn in the Bishops."

"You asshole," Uriah snarls, fingers gripping my steering wheel. "I truly have no fucking clue if you're lying or not, dammit!"

Sitting at a stoplight with no traffic in any direction, I pull out my cellphone and bring up a recent picture of Ransom and me after a major shootout. We're covered in splotches of paint, showing off the bruises blooming on our chests. We're the winners, so Ransom's buddies are lying down near our feet, reenacting the pose hunters use with their trophy buck.

Ransom's many friends hero-worship me, so I love going home to Pittsburgh.

"Jesus, there are two of you." Uriah hisses a pained sound, then speeds through the light before it turns green. "You look just alike. You sure he's not your kid–"

"Well, since I was four when Ransom popped out of my sister's body– I don't think I was fertile at the tender age of three to make a viable contribution –so I know for sure Ransom's mom is Ainsley and not my mother's kid."

"Well, that answers my question, since I was asking if he was your kid *brother*," Uriah stresses, simultaneously pissed yet amused that I cut him off. "So... this is home for me."

"Color me shocked that you're a local." Not a tease, I truly am shocked. It's hard to believe someone as colorful as Uriah came from a small town.

"Yeah..." I can hear the eye-roll in Uriah's tone. "Because I look like someone who has enough money to go to Penn State if I wasn't a local?" Hand gesturing to the right. "I grew up here, as the only Native American in my school until my godmother popped out a few more kids."

So many questions on the tip of my tongue, but Uriah and I have a landmine field between us, so I keep my trap shut on those and go for the safer topics. "You've mentioned your godmother a few times, but not your mother..." I trail off, coaxing.

"Long story short, because I hate my story, and it ties into politics we will not be discussing." I can hear the clamor of a door smashing shut, and I have the feeling it's locked for everyone on the planet, not just this right-wing asshole.

"Summer Crane is from the Cayuga Nation of New York– don't ask, because I'm not giving you a Native American Culture lesson." Uriah sighs, realizes he sounds bitter and baiting, and then puts me out of my misery instead.

"Cayuga is one of six nations of Iroquois who lived in New York. If you know anything about both of our histories, you'd know what all went down there… I'm from Seneca Falls, New York– at least that's where I was conceived and where I've spent all my summers and mini-trips throughout my childhood, because my godmother took me back there to make sure my roots were strong– my mom never comes with us.

"But forget all that… anyway, my mother is a real piece of shit, to be honest. Not gonna lie, dear ol' Mom and me are oil and water. She's lazy. Worthless. A product of the system. I'm sure we'd agree on those political points–"

"Actually, I believe in social programs," I quickly interject, hating yet another one of those stereotypical judgments used against me. "It's the abuse of the system that we struggle against, calling for reform in–"

"Jesus, don't make me fall in love with you," Uriah murmurs underneath his breath as he puts Sybil in park on the side of the road, just outside of the gravel entrance to a rundown trailer park.

"When my mom was growing up, my people were still fighting for the rights to their land, buying up parcels since the government refused to give back what was taken from us. My mom's entire childhood was a court battle, lawsuits and politics, and bitterness. So when I said politics ruined my mom's life, I meant it.

"She was flighty, immature, and impulsive. My grandfather wasn't as chill as he is today, not during the height of their battle with the government. My mom was fucking around with a bunch of pale-faced assholes–" Uriah points at his complexion, several shades lighter than my own. "My grandfather was none too pleased when his daughter got pregnant. Now, Mom says grandpa kicked her out, so she took off with her best friend– my godmother. Summer Crane, forever the victim, and pity is her currency," Uriah mutters snidely. "My grandfather, my godmother, and every single Cayuga I've met, all told me to take a long look at my mother and allow what I see to be the answer. She's a deadbeat, so I believed it when they told me she took off, not that she was thrown out."

"How old was your mom?" Voice breaking, I envision a young girl, like Ainsley looks in her pregnancy pictures. I can't imagine how terrified Uriah's mom must have been.

"Oh, don't go pitying the woman," Uriah mutters harshly. "She was twenty-three, never worked a day in her life. A drunk. Wasting oxygen. Quit school at fifteen because she refused to go, and her parents didn't know what to do with her. I know I sound like an asshole, and when I've shared this story with people at school, they asked me what caused my mother to be like this, as if I'm being insensitive. But she was born a goddamn horrific human being, not made that way, and I'm the byproduct of her behavior, so if anyone can bitch and complain about her, it's me."

The bitter loathing wafting from Uriah is toxic, to the point I roll my window down more. I never thought this intriguing creature could feel such darkness.

"About those social programs I was counting on you hating…" Uriah murmurs wryly, flashing me a wink. "It's a double-edged sword. I'm using them to the best of my ability now that I'm an adult, but I hated it when I was a child. There hasn't been a day in my life that I wasn't treated as other because of it. Only Native American kid, so bullied here, but also bullied in Seneca Falls because I'm so pale. I never fit in anywhere I go.

"The free lunch at school was a source of taunting, but I was happy to put food in my empty gut. This is where I tell you I loathe the hand that fed me, because it was the same hand that enabled my mother to never evolve. She had the same advantages I did. From Head Start on, I was groomed to reach for the stars, but torn down by my peers because I was using the very programs my case worker diligently made sure I took advantage of. By my sophomore year in high school, I was taking free courses at the community college, and my friends were pissed because they weren't allowed. I was poor and Native American, so I deserved it and they didn't, even though they earned it and felt I didn't."

"Don't, Uriah." I reach out unbiddenly, my only thought to comfort. The shame and guilt in Uriah's voice has tears springing to my eyes. To think how disgusting Uriah must find me because of my political leanings, as if I'd begrudge him of an education and happiness.

"I had no friends because of this– my teachers loved me. The better my education, the worse my home life became, and the less people were willing to hang out with me. At the same time, I was hit with a double-whammy of being a queer kid who didn't understand that I shouldn't wear a dress to school just because I thought it was pretty. So I was just fucked all around, wasn't I?"

"I kind of want to know what you look like in a dress, to be honest," I say to get Uriah to laugh, and it works but only for a few seconds.

"I love my education, even though when I transferred from community college to Penn State, they only partially accepted my credits– so I started as a sophomore instead of a Junior. I didn't want to be like my mom, so I did the opposite. I took advantage of everything I was offered."

"You are a success story, Uriah– your humble beginnings do not lessen the pride you should feel but accentuates it."

"My mother is a failure story, the negatives of a flawed system," Uriah mutters in a hollow voice. "She's the poster woman for the republican party. She's the person they love to use as an example as to why social programs need to be cut from the budget."

The dig hits home, seizing the breath in my lungs, even though I wasn't meant as the target. I fully understand Uriah, which is why I loathe politics, with its smoke and mirrors used to hide propaganda.

"Buying expensive cuts of meat with an EBT card, then selling them at a deep discount to neighbors for cash, so she could buy drugs and alcohol and cigarettes. I then needed the breakfast and lunch program, or else I'd starve, because even though the government provided my mother with a way to feed me, she refused to do it. I needed the school supply drive, and the sneaker drive, and the winter coat drive, and the pity Christmas presents, even though my mother was given enough money to afford all of that but refused to spend it on me, taking it away from the kids whose parents truly couldn't afford it... by the way, she'd take my shit from me, then sell it, so I never got to keep it anyway."

A choked sob is torn from my throat, sound filled with pain and rage for Uriah.

"I've spent twenty years mulling over how I want to switch to the enemy camp on this issue– *seething*, as I watched men come and go into our trailer, after trying to touch the kid who they couldn't tell if he was a boy or girl until their hand was in his underpants. As I opened cupboards and found mouse shit left behind. As I cleaned up beer cans and liter bottles with a shovel into a trash bag to make a pathway in the living room to my bedroom. As I flipped on light switches, only to still be terrified in the dark. To be filthy and turn the knob but no water flows out of the faucet… to know Mom was given enough money for the rent, for the utilities, and for our food, but I didn't receive any of those things because they didn't make sure the money went where it should have gone. I took advantage of the education because it was given directly to me, and it wasn't something Mom could steal from my mind. But I blamed the hand that fed me, because they created Mom as much as they created me– the enabled failure and the educated success, a social experiment."

"Jesus fucking Christ, Uriah," I gasp in shock, heart breaking into a million pieces as I envision how he must be warring within himself.

"I kept the hood up during breakfast, not because of who you are, Daniel." Uriah turns to me, tears shining in his eyes. "But because of who I am." Pointing to a dilapidated trailer at the head of the trailer park. "This is where I grew up, but not where I came from. This isn't who I am, but I can still feel the filth and stench of it in my sleep, even though I haven't slept in there in over a decade. When we moved in, that trailer was *brand new*, and my mother destroyed it quicker than I could maintain it."

Like a switch is flipped, Uriah reaches forward and turns over Sybil's ignition, then he backs out of the gravel driveway to the trailer park. In silence, he traverses through town, into a nice section of neighborhood.

"You said you wanted to know me, so I'm not going to gild the lily, so to speak." Uriah parks at the curb in front of a quaint two-story house with mums lining the front walkway to a cozy sitting porch. "This is where I came from– this is where I live."

In awe, I stare at the house, spotting a few bikes resting against the side of the garage, near a rack for kayaks. There are five plump pumpkins waiting to be carved in a few weeks, and a waving skeleton hanging on the front door.

"This is nice– it feels like a real home, Uriah... and I'm not saying that because it's not a trailer. It's the feeling of welcome instead of chaos."

"Trust me, I know." Uriah stares at his house, fingers strumming a rhythm on the steering wheel, refusing to look at me. "It's the mentality– my mom versus my godmother's views on the world... I don't have many friends, so I'm showing you this. Adults like me, even the ones who think I'm a freak. Everyone else, I'm not white enough to fit in here, yet not Native American enough to fit in with my people. I'm too queer for my peers, yet my gender fluidness freaks gay guys out."

Uriah turns to me, finally looking me in the eyes, and the intensity of his gaze catches the breath in my lungs. "I wasn't going to beat around the bush with the getting-to-know-you friendship stage, since you seemed so eager to befriend me," he mutters wryly. "So we're getting the nastiness out of the way first."

"Yeah, especially since the first time I saw you, I was cleaning up spilled food as my class-leeches mocked you... and the second time I saw you, you had a guy's dick lodged in your throat, and he was pissed because your blow job skills were far superior to his longevity abilities. Mad props on not backing down during the payment negotiations, though."

Sharp guffaws fill the interior of Sybil, reverberating off the ceiling. "Yeah, and then I offered to blow you."

"That was my favorite part of the story actually," I murmur, voice sluggish. A second later, I realize how flirty and lusty I sound, and notice Uriah is eyeballing me in confusion because of it.

"Story to tell our future grandkids someday, eh?" is a self-deprecating tease. "Mom ran away from Seneca Falls with me in her gut, riding in a car stolen from my grandfather, with her sixteen-year-old best friend in the passenger seat. Wanna know how they ended up in Bellefonte? The car died, that's how."

"You're shitting me, right?"

"Nope, true story." Uriah points up at the house. "Rain McDonald, formerly Rain Woods. The best friend my mother committed crimes against by taking across state lines at the tender age of sixteen, when Mom was twenty-three. The same girl who grew up into a woman in the same trailer as me, taking advantage of the same programs as I did, by getting her high school diploma, then an associate's degree in accounting. The same woman who my mother leeched off for years, draining whatever money Rain earned on side jobs while going to school, and conning her out of whatever money the government gave her. The same woman who fled after one of my mom's many boyfriends tried to rape her in her own bed… then came back two years later to steal me from mine."

"Your mother–"

"Is a waste of oxygen," Uriah snarls. "Mom cut Rain off, refused to speak to her, blamed her for the boyfriend wanting her. Those two years, Mom bitched and complained about how Rain was looking for an older man to take care of her, and all this other horseshit about how Rain always thought she was better than everyone else, while Mom was fucking anyone who would have her and had all the same advantages but refused to use any of them. I didn't understand it at the time, but now that I do, it's sickening. Mom and Rain haven't spoken since that happened. Rain came back after she got married, and tried to get legal custody of me, hoping to use our Cayuga tribal connection since we weren't biologically related."

"That didn't work," I say with complete confidence.

"And you'd be correct… Mom wouldn't speak to Rain, only would go through Bob– Rain's husband. Mom hit on Bob every chance she got, right in front of Rain, even in front of the judge. The court wouldn't give them custody of me, since Mom cleans up real nice and is a consummate liar. But Mom didn't want me, she only wanted the benefits the state was giving for my care. They compromised on the courthouse's front steps after the judge's decision– Rain and Bob got me, and Mom got the funding, only needing me to make appearances when a case worker scheduled a visit."

"You're shitting me, right?"

"Nope. Sorry, but I'm not." Sighing, Uriah stares up at the house. "I know the flaws of the system, because I am the system. I used to hate it, hate myself, but shit happened and it changed my way of thinking, until I appreciated what it offered, not just the education I'm receiving."

Sitting in silence, Uriah and I watch as little kids travel in pairs and threes down the sidewalk, holding their mommies' hands– the littlest ones are being pushed in strollers, all waiting until their older siblings get home from school and their daddies from work.

Uriah's home is situated in an idyllic neighborhood, not much different from my own, but worlds apart from our first stop earlier. Summer Crane's trailer stuck out among the others, as if they were trying to purge it from the park. No doubt, as Summer's neighbors try so hard to carve a nice life, Summer is marring it as quickly as they try to polish it.

"Rain and Bob took me in when I was nine years old, and raised me as their own. They wanted me, even without the benefit of a monthly payout. They wanted me enough to make sacrifices and go without just so they could support me.

"I've lived in this house for more than half my life. Bob was a widower, fifteen years older than Rain, with two children at the time who needed a mother. RJ and Fiona are my brother and sister, close to my age, so they were my allies in school. But I couldn't let them be my friends, because I was ashamed to let them *know me* know me."

Sucking in a deep breath, Uriah's words hit me harder than expected, having lived a life exactly like that. Ransom is my nephew, the one I call best friend, but I keep shit from him, too ashamed to voice it. Sometimes the words almost spew out to Kade, but I swallow them back down.

"Then came Sunny and Winter– they're seven and five, and I'm envious of them, even as I try to help them navigate a school devoid of Native American children. They are dark-skinned, despite their father– a white father they know, when I don't even know mine's name –and when we visit Seneca Falls, our relatives are comfortable around them, while they treat me the same as they do RJ and Fiona. An outsider. They are simultaneously accepted into the tribe, yet born into a more diverse world where they are seen as exotic instead of different, as I was in school."

"Let me guess… you adore them but feel like shit because you resent them?"

"Nail meets head," Uriah mutters flatly. "I'm bitter and resentful, and I know I'm allowed to feel that way, but I'm also not ungrateful. I resent the hand that feeds me, but I won't bite it, not after I've seen the good it can do."

"What do you mean?" The bitter cynic so far has sounded like he'd fit in with some of the politicians I've met, ones even my grandfather can't stomach to be around. It bothers me how the intriguing guy I met doesn't match up with this enraged version driving my car.

"The negative side to social programs is my mother, because she refused to learn to live life instead of just exist. The positive side is Rain and me. But the necessary side was when Bob had a heart attack and a triple bypass. He couldn't go back to work for a few months as he recovered, so he was laid off. It takes months to get on disability, and since he would recover they said no. Unemployment offers no medical benefits, and since he was laid off from his job, they had to cut his medical insurance. After living through all that bullshit with my mom, I felt powerless as this family was being torn apart because of a heart attack."

"They're okay though, right?" I beg, unable to sit here while staring at the house I'm praying they are currently in, and hoping this isn't the second stop on a three-stop horror story of a nightmare.

"Oh, yeah– they're fine." Uriah finds my concern amusing for some reason. "It was a terrifying year, where us kids tried to get jobs and help pay the bills. RJ and Fiona tried to get Rain to cash in their college funds– the small life insurance claim left by their mother. Rain got a second job. Bob was prideful and didn't want any help, but finally gave in when Rain convinced him this was the exact situation why the programs were put into place. So he gave in, when otherwise he would have lost the house and been forced to cash in those college funds."

"Everyone's good now, right?" So quickly I've become emotionally invested in these strangers' lives. It's ridiculous, because I'm the idiot who has a hard time reading books and watching movies and shows because it's too real for me, always turning into an emotional wreck.

"Rain's down to only working during tax season– *with Bob*," Uriah stresses, and I guess that's how they met in the first place. "Bob's back at the same accounting firm, and is the proud owner of a shiny gym membership. RJ graduated from NYU last spring, and

Fiona is taking courses at the same community college Rain and I attended. The kids are enrolled in every sport and camp and music and dance class you can think of–"

I cut Uriah off before he skips over himself, sensing he will never feel a part of this family, no matter how long he's in it. "And you're…" I coax.

"A sophomore at Penn State University, majoring in communications, with big dreams of founding an LGBTQ online magazine and writing life-changing articles… and has mommy issues bigger than any other issues he may have."

"I swear to God." Chuckling without humor, I reach over to swat Uriah in the chest, similar to how he did so with me earlier, because it reminds me of the camaraderie I share with Ransom and Kade. "Up and down. Up and down. Pro and con. Pro and con. We could use your story as a PSA on the benefits of social programs and/or why they need to be reformed… and I swear to God, you did it on purpose just to fuck with me."

"Maybe." Uriah smirks, just a slight curl to those devastating lips. He pinches the tip of his thumb and forefinger together. "Maybe just a little bit for your benefit, but unlike you, I'm not a liar. Every word was the truth… and you asked."

"You said it was the long story made short," I remind him.

"Who said that wasn't the short version?" Uriah volleys back, arching a wicked brow. Reaching forward, he turns over Sybil's ignition, then pulls away from the curb. "It'd take a lifetime to cover the first twenty years of my existence."

"Jesus fucking Christ," I hiss, terrified to know what else could possibly be in the longer version. "What didn't we cover?"

"I said politics, Native American culture, gender and sexuality were off limits, yet we've pretty much covered all those but one."

"Ah, but we really haven't covered the gender fluid business, which I'm confused about, to be quite honest, but terrified to offend you if I ask insensitive questions." I take a deep breath and release it on a sigh, relieved to notice we're headed back toward State College. For once, I can't wait to be back on campus, where I know Uriah has no scary skeletons he'll add to his personal memoir of a conversation.

"You didn't ask me about prostitution," Uriah murmurs in a flirty, teasing tone, so I know it's a sexy story, not a tortuous one.

"Oh, God!" is an involuntary moan on my part, and I truly don't understand why. "Tell me," I demand.

"Nope." This time, Uriah pops the P, imitating me from earlier. "I have class in fifteen minutes, and it's a short story, but longer than that. We'll save it for later."

The sound of there being a later has butterflies doing assaulting summersault in my belly, their saws tearing up my guts. "Gimme your phone, you tease."

Chuckling sinisterly, Uriah points at the hoodie tucked on my dashboard. I dig through the marsupial pouch for the phone, then input my info, quickly texting myself to make sure I have Uriah's digits too.

"If we're giving this friendship thing a try, just know I can be clingy." Smirking, I think of Kade.

Kade thinks I'm this stoic rock as he clings to me for support. But I randomly make drives home– not so random as they coincide with when Kade is busy in study groups at night, or visiting home, or when Royce and Brennan are in town –just so I can be clingy to Ransom, and on the off-chance Ainsley isn't in Harrisburg, after Kade wrung me emotionally dry.

"We'll be discussing prostitution on our next visit, which better happen in the next forty-eight hours."

"You have no idea how eager you looked when we met." Uriah's tone sounds pleased yet amused by how obvious I was being. "So I expect I'll be hearing from you sooner rather than later, since you're the sucker I hooked with my sob story."

"You were telling the truth, right?" I ask, wondering if I've just been played, knowing I truly am a sucker for someone who needs me.

I'm the collector of tortured souls, because Kade's and my party of two is pretty lonely, and Ransom is too perfect and happy to join our little gang of misfits. Uriah, on the other hand, would fit in perfectly flawed.

"I don't know… your entire family goes paintballing, right?
"Shit!"

IT'S NORMAL TO RANDOMLY START CRAVING DICK ONE DAY, RIGHT?

After a quick hello to Kaden's visiting family, I made tracks to give them some privacy. Royce and Brennan come up from Rusty Knob like clockwork, sometimes as much as once a week. Then Royce randomly sneaks up to visit with just me, curious as to how Kaden is truly doing. A welfare check, Royce calls it. In the in between times– and let's face it, there isn't much in between time with the Kennedys –Miriam Ross drops in unexpectedly to check on her cousin. Royce and Miriam have always tag-teamed Kaden since CPS got involved when he was a teenager. I'd feel smothered as fuck, and I grew up in a household with three mothers and two fathers, but I know Kade well, and the guy needs all that smothering to keep his shit together.

I do what I always do, unable to be alone inside a space where a bed is located– I find somewhere else to be. Yes, I admit I have a problem, and I know I can't get better until I acknowledge said problem– I share a dorm room with a guy who has no less than four therapists, and is majoring in education with a minor in psychology. I get it, which is why Kaden knows nothing of my early childhood trauma. Since that night, I can't be in our dorm room during the dark hours without another person in there, which is one of the reasons I've had a revolving door on my dick. Same with my shared bedroom with Ransom– my nephew sensed my terror, so our room was always filled with his buddies on the weekends, because he never had sleepovers at their homes.

When Royce comes to visit, without fail, I get into Sybil and find myself headed to Pittsburgh. Last year, the Kennedy family was torn apart. I have no idea what happened, but Kaden was gone for over a month. I wanted to be supportive for him, but I was also losing my own shit– there's only so much fucking a guy can do, but the girls always wanted to go back to their dorm rooms afterward.

I managed to convince Ransom to have the college experience during his junior year in high school, forcing him to take Kaden's empty bed for that month. My parents and grandparents threw a fit, but Ainsley immediately stepped up and contacted Ransom's school for permission. My sister and nephew know what happened to me, or at least surmised it in the aftermath, but we've never spoken a word about it– they protect me the way I protect Kaden.

Earlier, I thought my neighborhood wasn't much different than the one Uriah lives in now, but that's true if you don't look at the size of the houses and the lots they rest upon. Our house is four times larger than Uriah's, but tiny by comparison to the homes flanking it. The same welcoming sensation clenches the heart, with its tree-lined streets, bordered with sidewalks neighbors are strolling along as they take their pups out for a potty break. Pumpkins. Mums. Halloween decorations as far as the eye can see.

Sybil's engine is loud enough to announce my arrival as I pull up to the garage doors, but I'm banking on everyone being too busy with their own shit to pester me when I get inside the house. I'm here for advice, not smothering. Royce and Brennan are only here for a few hours, taking Kaden for dinner, so I want to get back to State College to sleep. But, if the mother hens of the house spot me, that ain't happening until tomorrow.

Smirking at Joel's car as I get out of Sybil, I'm wondering at what point the guy will finally give up. Sneaking in the kitchen door from the garage, I tip-toe silently, ears tuned into whatever activity surrounds me. I just need to get to my bedroom unnoticed, and I slam right into a hard chest.

"*Oomph!*" is torn from my throat. "*Shit– goddamnit!*" is just the beginning of a string of curses that would make a drunk sailor proud. The chest is too flat to be Grandma's or Mom's, and I'm praying to God it's not Grandpa. I can tell Dad why I'm here and he'll laugh at me, but Grandpa will take me into the study and not let me out until hours later.

"It's a bit early to be sneaking *into* the house, don't you think?" Joel's dry voice draws me up short. "I know the women of the household treat everyone as children… but, Daniel, you're twenty-one, for shit's sake."

"Shh…" with my fingertip pressed over my lips, I flash my would-be brother-in-law a gigantic grin. "Trying to go undetected– you know there's no such thing as a quick visit."

"True," Joel muses, nodding his head. The guy is drier than a popcorn fart, with this bizarre sense of humor I've never understood. He's a bit of a whipped pup, never standing up for himself, or at least not when it comes to a Bishop. Joel is firm with his own family, just not mine. The guy has been Ainsley's doormat since he knocked her up at age fourteen.

"I've been here for four hours, and I just came to see my son for a few minutes." Folding his arms over his narrow chest, Joel looks down his nose at me. He's not arrogant, just insanely tall and willowy compared to the compact nature of a Bishop. We're built like old-timey boxers, whereas Joel looks like a runner– Ransom took after the Bishops, thank goodness.

"I take it Ainsley is in Harrisburg?" Peering around the doorframe from the kitchen into the hallway, I listen with one ear for my family members.

"Yeah, isn't she always?" Poor guy sounds put out, which makes me wonder if my sister ever puts out. I know Joel has never had another girlfriend, probably never bedded anyone else. So my sister must randomly throw the dude a bone, or he'd eventually lose interest.

We have a theory– both the Bishops *and* Talbots– that Ainsley is holding out until Ransom graduates to accept lucky proposal number seven, that way she knows for sure Joel wants her and isn't trying to be an upstanding guy by marrying the mother of his son. Ainsley wants to know Joel loves her for her, not because of Ransom. That's our theory, at least, and we hope we're correct, because this angsty love affair is starting to get tedious after eighteen years.

"What are you doing here, Daniel?" The arms cross tighter over his chest as blue eyes peer down with suspicion. "It's not like you to be sneaky."

"Because I normally don't get caught," pops out before I can stop it. "Okay, so I sneak in here a few times a month, not having the energy to deal with a billion people.... I– I came here for the same reason you did. Ransom around?"

"After dinner, Ransom and I sat on the patio for a few hours, but he had to take a phone call." Joel fits in with the rest of the family, totally detail-oriented, and always holding out until the very last second with the detail we want most.

"*And...*" I coax.

"Your mother and grandmother are at the neighbor's next door, planning some type of event. Your grandfather is sawing logs in his recliner with the news ten decibels too loud in his bedroom. I was just about to join your father in the family room for some Netflix and microbrew."

"And..." this time it comes out frustrated and annoyed. Joel and his goddamn, bizarre, dark and dry sense of humor, he's playing with me.

Joel pokes me in the forehead with a single fingertip, lips curling into a smirk. "In your bedroom, dumbass." Then the rat-bastard strides away on his too-long legs to avoid getting his nonexistent ass kicked by me.

I take the steps, two at a time, wishing for once I had Joel's stride, knowing there is a good chance I could meet Grandpa on the stairs. Grandpa is known to nap for five minutes at a time, then the hungry bear makes his way to the kitchen to scavenge around for unhealthy snacks hidden in the depths of the pantry. But there are no unhealthy snacks in the pantry, so Grandpa tries to sneak up to our room, bartering Ransom for a snack in the junk food stash.

I enter the bedroom, quickly spotting Ransom standing at the window with his back to me, cellphone pressed to his ear. Turning with a grin, "Didn't you bring me any takeout?"

"How did you–"

"I spotted you coming up the driveway." Ransom continues to listen to whomever is on the other end of the call, cellphone turned practically upside down so the mouth mic isn't anywhere near his lips. "What took you so long to get up here?"

"Your dad," I mutter dryly as I cross the room to land face-first on the ginormous king-sized bed dominating the space.

A few days after Mrs. Turner hurt me in this room, in which I'd spent the nights before cuddled up with Ransom in Ainsley's bed, I walked in here to find a king-sized bed with trundle beds on each side for Ransom's big posse of buddies. Somehow my sister convinced the entire household Ransom and I were too big for our twin beds, and everyone– including Ransom and myself –was confused as to why my sister thought us sharing a bed was more mature. After the first night, I realized my sister knew exactly what happened, even if I didn't tell her.

I've never slept alone, not once in twenty-one years. I spent the first four years of my life in my parents' bed because of co-sleeping. Ainsley wasn't having that practice, so when Ransom was given this room as his nursery, I asked for my own bed in here, and the rest they say is history.

At camp, we slept in a bunk house filled with little dudes. At home, I shared this room with Ransom. Boarding at prep school, I shared a dorm room with three other guys. At Penn State, I pretended the living arrangements were because Miriam thought Kaden needed it, but it was me who did. When I go to Yale, I've already made sure Tanya and I are sharing a one-bedroom, so she'll have to keep me sane at night.

After a series of *mmm... yeah... really?... tell me more...* Ransom yanks my hair. "No takeout?"

Rolling over on the bed, I squint up at my nephew. "Didn't you just eat dinner?"

Face twisting with hunger, "Yeah– but... Grandma's on a health kick again, and you know I hate vegetables, and Grandpa found my junk food stash last night." Realizing he forgot to shift the phone before speaking to me, Ransom jolts as whoever he's speaking to gives him the riot act. "Sorry, Danny just got home– I'll call you back after he leaves. Later."

"Who was that?" Eyeing my nephew as he pockets his phone in his skinny jeans, I contemplate whether or not he's finally seeing someone. "Ooo... do you have a boyfriend?"

"Jeesh," Ransom hisses dramatically, scowling down at me as if I've insulted him somehow. "The only way I'd have a boyfriend is if Mom finally gave in and let me go to boarding school like you did."

"Sorry, not sorry– no one sane would drop you into an all-boys school during senior year. It's the plot to a gay porn fantasy."

"Fucker." Ransom falls into his desk chair. "First you fail to deliver takeout, when I can smell that Quarter Pounder on your breath, you prick, then you take my erotic dreams away."

"Best avoid the fatty foods, or else you'll never reach stardom in the gay pornography industry, since I know for a fact you're not packing anything above average. Probably because your too-tight pants cut off circulation to your junk." I'm just razzing the kid, because no matter how stocky we Bishops are, Ransom inherited his father's Energizer Bunny metabolism. The kid eats eight or nine times a day.

"Why are you here?" Ransom folds his arms over his chest, looking exactly as his dad did earlier, if you ignore the dark hair and darker blue eyes, when Joel has WASP features. "Besides to pester me."

Shuffling on the bed, I scooch up to rest against the headboard, and then steal Ransom's pillow to hug to my chest. "Do you think pussy is gross?" pops out before I can stop it.

"What?!" Ransom shouts, aghast. "What the hell, Danny?"

Backtracking, "Kaden reads these M/M books nonstop– ya know, male/male fiction–"

"I know what M/M means, you flipping idiot," Ransom mutters dryly, sounding like Joel now too. The four-year age difference doesn't matter, because my nephew and I are equals when it comes to emotional maturity– he's a good decade older in street smarts, I suspect.

"Anyway, Kaden is always bitching about GFY, whatever the hell that means… but he also reads me passages about the guys hating on pussy. So I was curious whether or not you thought pussy was disgusting… because I don't think dicks are gross."

"I know you." Ransom points at me, eyes narrowed. "You're bullshitting your way around something here, I can sense it. As for you not hating on dick, it's because you have one– same as a straight girl not hating on pussy, because she has one."

"So gay guys loathe pussy?" The confusion ringing in my voice is beyond obvious.

"Something tells me we're focusing on pussy, but that's not the issue." Smarter than the average bear, my nephew eyes me for a few moments. "No, I don't hate pussy, you idiot. It gave me life, and it's the only way I'll ever have kids. I may not lust after it, but I respect it and appreciate it, more so than most body parts."

"You want kids?" No doubt, Ransom finds the shock in my voice insulting. "I don't know if I do or not."

"Just because I'm gay doesn't mean I don't want kids." Now Ransom's furious with me.

"I didn't mean it like that, dummy." I toss Ransom's pillow at him, hitting him upside the head. "I meant it's a shock, that at seventeen, you're contemplating something that should be a decade from now."

"I'm gay– nothing's going to change it." Sadness wars with rage in Ransom's voice. "If I ever get a partner, we don't have the luxury to have kids like most straight couples do. The advanced planning is necessary."

"You were talking on the phone to a girl, weren't you?" It dawns on me, most guys don't talk to people the way the person on the other end of the line was. Uriah's gender-fluidness pops into my head, but some things are inborn for the most part. Call me sexist, but that nagging conversation could only be from a girl.

"Claude," Ransom answers without hesitation. Claudia has been my nephew's best friend forever, to the point I've been jealous of her. She was the only girl who attended all the sleepovers in this room. The boys' mothers threw a fit until they met her in person, then it was an every weekend thing for years. "She likes girls."

"Color me not surprised," I tease. "That's a *no shit, Sherlock*, same as it was with you."

"Well, Claude's in the same boat as me, ya know? Two girls can't make kids together, same as two guys. We're getting ready to graduate, go to college, and in a few years, we might want to start families, whether we have a partner or not."

"You're not..." I trail off, shocked beyond belief, and it only makes me even more confused about my situation.

"Best to figure it out now versus when it really fucking matters, Danny." Angry at the world, my nephew glares down at the pillow he's twisting in his hands. "So your question about whether or not I loathe pussy hits a bit too close to home tonight."

"Holy shit, Ransom. Were you negotiating sex with Claudia just now?"

"Yeah," Ransom breathes, refusing to look at me. "We're both just lonely, pitiful virgins in a straight-dominated high school."

"Yeah, but–"

"It's better to try it out now, Danny," Ransom barks sharply. "We're best friends, so there won't be any fighting over the kids. We'll co-parent like my mom and dad do. We don't have anyone right now– won't feel like we're cheating. If it doesn't work out, we'll use a turkey baster in the future. If it does, we'll know we won't fuck it up when it comes time to make a kid."

"Yeah, but you're both gay," I point out the vital flaw in his plan.

"So?" Ransom's really insulted now. "As long as I stay hard, I'm sure it will feel good enough to keep me there, seeing as I know how much you get off on being inside a long string of chicks."

"But I'm straight–"

"Are you? *Are you really?*" Ransom challenges me hardcore. "Because I'm sure you weren't actually asking about me and pussy… more like you and dick. Am I right?"

My head jerks backward into the headboard. "You don't think I'm straight?"

"Since we're being so open and honest tonight…" Ransom trails off, unsure if he should continue on. Nodding once, he wounds me deeply. "Pretty sure you've been rage-fucking Gayle Turner lookalikes, so I don't think we can label you based on your bad behavior."

Gasping, my guts ache as if Ransom delivered a swift blow below the belt. "You know?"

"Danny." Ransom unfurls from the chair, then slips onto the bed. "I may have been only nine when Mom and I found you, but we both cannot deny Mom knew what happened. Watching how she treated you, and how you started acting, and how you acted around a certain person, I put two and two together."

Fisting the blanket at my sides, "I don't want to talk about it," I mutter petulantly, outright refusing to go there.

"We've never said a word about it to anyone– not even to each other. Mom and I have kept your secret. But you had to have realized every girl you fuck looks like a baby version of Gayle. Blonde. Blue-eyed. Bubbly personality. Flirty and sexualized. Vapid and vain."

"I didn't, actually." Yanking the pillow from behind my back, I bear hug it to my chest, drawing my knees up tightly too. "But now that you mention it… so you don't think I'm straight?"

"I don't know what you are– sorry it's not as easy for you as it was for the rest of the straight people," Ransom mutters wryly, sounding just like his father. I know he's secretly laughing at me right now.

"Says the kid who knew he was gay since birth– Claudia knew too. Everyone else in this house just *knew*. I don't know what I am, nothing's ever fit right with me. But I know it's not normal to start craving my roommate's dick after twenty-one years of wanting pussy."

Loud peals of laughter echo around our shared bedroom, the bed vibrating from the force of Ransom's amusement. "You have no idea, you idiot. As soon as you started chatting with Kaden online, it was *'Kade said this, Kade said that'*. You were like a hyper tween during their first crush. Mom and I have been taking bets on when one of you would slip into the other's bed."

"Kade's in love with Wynn Gillette back in Rusty Knob," I remind Ransom. Kade's spent many weekends in this bedroom with the both of us over the years, so he has no secrets from my nephew. "He feels guilty just jerking off, like he's cheating on the kid."

"That's seriously messed up– that fucked up ideal that you have to save yourself for the love of your life." Ransom plops down on the bed next to me, bouncing me a bit. "It's why Claude and I are practicing now, because who wants to suck at sex when you finally find the person you really want? Nothing like crashing and burning to ruin a good thing."

"That makes sense, actually." Self-deprecating laughter spills from my lips. "My first attempt was with my prom date– you remember Meghan?"

"The only brunette," Ransom teases me. "The only actual friend."

"Yeah, it was a total clusterfuck. I had a hard time staying stiff, Meghan was in pain, and neither of us finished– I never really got in there. So I get what you're saying about this unobtainable fantasy world Kade's living in. The first time is going to suck if you've never experimented before."

"Just because we're guys doesn't mean we were born with carnal knowledge," Ransom mutters wryly, finding himself far too amusing. "Claude and I may or may not have already done the deed."

The tone in Ransom's voice is the same one I used on Uriah during the paintball story, so I have no fucking clue if my nephew is bullshitting me. "Details," I demand, knowing I can catch him in a lie that way.

Ransom rolls until he's lying on his stomach, then props his head up with a palm. "You came for advice, clearly freaking out. Is it Kade? Did you finally figure out you want his dick?"

"Idiot!" Roughly palming the kid's head, I nearly shove him off the bed.

Scrambling to right himself, Ransom's laughter fades into the comforter. "So I've been studying you for a few years, and I have a label for you, but I'm not telling you until you do a few things for me."

"Explain," I demand.

"First, what freaked you out?" Ransom negotiates like the Bishop he is.

"Fine. A few days ago, I realized I was showing off for Kade's benefit. I figured out I liked the way he looked at me, liked how he got off on watching me. I get off on taking care of him. I'm not in love with him, so get that out of your thick skull– Kade is Wynn Gillette's through and through. But none of that is the problem per se…"

Embarrassed, I roll over and hide my head underneath a pillow. Voice muffled, "I met a guy today, and I fucking want him hardcore."

"Oh, my God!" Ransom squeals, weight disappearing off the bed. I peek out at him from beneath the pillow, spying him grabbing his tablet off the desk. Then the mattress shifts beneath his weight as he sits back next to me, smashing my thigh under his heavy butt. "I have a list of questions I've been waiting to ask."

"Are you fucking serious?" Shifting, I toss the pillow onto the floor and scramble to sit upright. "What the hell?"

"I said I had a label for you, and I meant it. I just need you to answer these questions for me, so I can be sure. Then I'm going to send you back to State College with homework to prove my hypothesis."

"You're a freak–"

"Was that ever up for debate, Uncle?" Ransom is satisfied with himself, the little puke. "Okay, do you feel sexual attraction when looking at a stranger?"

"Of course," is my standard answer, but the look Ransom levels at me has me truly mulling it over.

"I don't mean where you look at a girl and think she is really pretty, or think a guy is strong and healthy... or whatever your mind conjures up. That's not attraction or lust, just finding someone pleasing to the eye. I mean, do you ever just look at someone and feel this undeniable urge to bend them over the nearest surface and listen to them moan your name."

"Jesus fucking Christ, Ransom– you need to get laid," I snarl, freaking out because his voice just dropped an octave, and the last thing I want to know is what my nephew sounds like when he's aroused.

"I'm just setting the scene," he mutters sheepishly, blushing. "If this law gig fails, I could always fallback on my storytelling abilities."

"Word," is my blunt reply. "Okay, so... usually when I see a girl, it's me who was scoped out first. When she comes up to me, I want to get to know her, but she doesn't seem interested in anything but getting fucked."

"Just guessing here, but maybe that's a self-fulfilling prophesy. You're picking out specific girls who you know only want to fuck, and I bet you've never deviated from the same scenario with them, have you?"

Eyes shifting to the side, it's my turn to feel sheepish and ridiculous. "No comment."

"I'll take that as a no, you don't lust after strangers?"

"Yeah, but... this guy today, I wanted him immediately."

Ransom stares at me for a few suspended seconds, seeming confused, then his eyes light up as his brain fires an answer. "What happened before you met him? Did you have foreknowledge, which wouldn't make him a stranger at all?"

"He's... he's genderfluid– and fuck if I even know what that means –but my class-leeches were making fun of him. Calling him Pat, and it made me sick."

"Oh, my precious bleeding-heart, right-winger," Ransom murmurs with mock pity, reaching out to caress my forehead.

"That's an oxymoron," I deadpan, and Ransom cracks up, enjoying nothing more than making jokes at our own expense.

"So that's a no for insta-lust with strangers." Ransom clicks a few times on his tablet. "I don't even need to ask about your insane need to make friends, yet never truly making any. Not that that's what the question is asking. It says, *'Do you prefer to befriend versus flirt?'* and the answer is befriend, hands down."

"True," I agree without hesitation. "I like people. I like being around people, and talking to people, and helping people."

"Not real big on fucking people, are you?" Eyebrow hitching high, Ransom sees right through to the core of me. "Besides the doggie-style, rage-fucking of Turner lookalikes. I doubt you've ever done another position– missionary is my favorite. You failed at fooling around with your brunette friend, you're sexually attracted to your male roommate, and you're freaking out over this new revelation that you're in insta-lust with a genderfluid dude… FYI: I know what genderfluid means– Googling that shit is your first homework assignment tonight."

"Did you… did you just say missionary is your favorite?" stammering, I really take a look at my nephew, but he's doing a good job at deflection tonight. "You tucked that right in there, running off at the mouth to cover that shit up."

Ransom ignores me, but the blush and voice warble are telling.

"When you're sexually attracted to someone, you either feel confused or single-minded? Double-check the hell out of that question." Ransom finds great amusement and enjoyment in my discomfort. *"You've been called old-fashioned or prudish?* Jesus, can we check that off about a bazillion times, Mr. Traditional Man?"

"Stop making fun of me," I pout, sounding pitiful. "What are you reading, anyway?"

"None of your business." Ransom snaps the cover shut on his iPad. "I'm not going to tell you the label you most fit, because I don't want you to wedge yourself into it out of comfort. I need you to figure your shit out on your own, then I will explain– tell me about this genderfluid fella."

"I spent a few hours with him today… even let him drive Sybil–"

"Oh, Lord! Please save Daniel Justice Bishop from himself." Ransom utters dramatically, forearm draped across his forehead like a damsel in distress. "You're textbook when it comes to your label.

Sure as shit, you spent the day buddying up to the object of your infatuation, getting to know–"

"He took me to his hometown–"

"Of course, he did." Ransom rolls his eyes at me. "And he has a gut-wrenching sob story to match, I bet. You are such a sucker, Danny."

"You think he's lying to me?" Heart beating uncontrollably, sweat beading on my forehead, my mind spins and my emotions boil over.

"Jesus, you're an easy mark." Ransom swats me upside the head. "Simmer down. Seriously, I don't know how you were born in this family. I see your future as a public defender in a bad section of neighborhood, doing all you can do for the little guy."

"You're a prick, a self-righteous asswipe."

"I'm teasing you, you idiot." Ransom glares at me. "I'm sure the guy wants to be your friend too, and he's not lying to you. I'm just saying you are predictable. You're not attracted to a tight, hot bod– you have a savior complex. You get off on saving people, getting to know them– I bet all those girls, you felt like a god when they got off, and you didn't give two shits if you did too. Just like I bet you get off on Kade getting off on you more than anything else."

"Now you're just being mean." Whimpering, I crawl off the side of the bed to fetch my pillow, then bear hug the bitch as tightly as possible. "What's my homework? Aside from a long Google session, because I'm done with this conversation."

Standing from the bed, Ransom gestures to the doorway. "I'll walk you out." As if I'm a visiting guest and this isn't my fucking bedroom too. Noticing how livid his comment made me, he backtracks. "I have considerable skill when it comes to sneaking in and out of this house undetected, dipshit."

"Yeah, that makes more sense than your sudden elitist attitude on social decorum." All a good-natured ribbing between uncle and nephew.

I lied– the trundle beds weren't for when Ransom's buddies slept over. It was for when we were fighting and out for blood. We'd sleep with the massive bed between us, each on a trundle bed.

Ghosting through the house, pausing with every noise, it's obvious my dad and Ransom's dad are still Netflix 'n' drinking, judging by the intense discussion about a true crime documentary they're watching. My grandparents' bedroom is on the first floor, just off the family room, and we can hear Grandpa snoring over the volume of two warring television shows.

A few seconds later, I'm standing in the dark kitchen, and a new fear enters my mind. "What time do the hens usually return to the coop?"

"Thank your lucky stars they're at the Sexton's place." Ransom is now talking at an audible volume, with half the house between us and the roosters. "Sheryl always brings out wine– we're good. Safe."

"Why are you sneaking out with me?" Eyeing my nephew sideways, it's like I don't know him inside and out anymore.

"Interrupted negotiations, remember?" Nose-to-nose, we stand frozen in the doorway to the garage. "I've got my own problems too, Danny."

"You're not actually screwing Claudia, are you?"

"Homework– you're going to have sex with Kade." It's a demand and a challenge all rolled into one. Before I can beat the shit out of my nephew for even suggesting it, he explains. "This new guy. If you get in bed with him and reach for his dick, only to discover it was a myth that you were okay with dick, wouldn't that injure you both for life?"

"Shit!" I hiss, terrified. "I never thought of that. I never thought past spending time with him."

"Don't be a cock-tease, Danny," Ransom chastises me. "Eventually the guy will think you're dating, and he'll develop feelings, and he'll want to get off with you."

"Fair enough," I concede.

"Kade is as fucked up as you are. He shouldn't go near Wynn without any carnal knowledge. It's a recipe for disaster. Do it before you're in too deep with this new guy– it's not cheating right now, but it could be if you wait too long. Just see if dick does or doesn't do it for you, that's all I ask."

"And hit up Google," I remind myself as I head toward Sybil. After slipping into the seat and shutting the door, I crank the window down.

"I'm curious to meet this guy." Ransom leans into the window, smirking at me. "I wish I could tell Mom—"

"Don't you dare," I threaten in a caustic tone, causing Ransom to lock his lips and toss away the key. "I'm scared, and freaking out, but all I want to do is go seek Uriah out and talk to him for hours on end. Am I nuts?"

"No, you have a crush." Ransom's smile turns from a snide smirk to a genuine grin. "It's sweet, Danny. So much healthier than your rage-fucking."

"Quit bringing that up, and no matter what label you give me, what happened will never be common knowledge."

"Fine," Ransom sighs dramatically. "Be that way, why don't ya? We'll just say you're straight when it comes to women, and this other label when it comes to men. It will throw off suspicion about Gayle Turner, but will open you up to a lot of people in the community calling you on your bullshit, but whatevs."

"How do I… what do I do?" Whimpering, I'm at a loss, having no idea what I'm doing.

"How the hell should I know, Danny?" Now Ransom is really getting irritated. "You've been around more dick than I have. My best fantasies are the stories you told me from camp and your cum rag… but I get told no when it comes to boarding school. You've had latent homosexual urges your whole life, while I'm forever a gay virgin when it comes to guys. I have no advice for you when it comes to this, but I'm hoping you'll give me some soon."

"I find it hard to believe you've never gotten any, when it falls into my lap." Ransom narrows his eyes at me, not understanding what I meant. "We look just alike, dumbass."

"Oh," Ransom whispers, mollified. "We do, don't we? That gives me hope that I won't die without ever tasting dick."

"Eww…"

"You say that now," Ransom taunts me, stepping back from my open window. "I've got to go see a girl before she tears my nuts off."

"You're not screwing Claudia, are you?" I ask for the umpteenth time.

"I don't know, Danny…" Ransom keeps stepping further and further away, toward Jack the golden Pinto. "What do you think?"

For a good half hour, I mull that over, realizing I can't get a read on my nephew anymore. Then I feel sympathy for what I pulled on Uriah this afternoon with the paintball story, realizing Ransom just pulled the same bullshit with me.

LITE BRIGHT IN THE CLOSET

I'm a social creature, but not a fan of huge crowds. I love having two or three people shoved up my ass and keeping me company at all times. After about a half hour of listening to the radio, I start feeling lonely and needy, missing a handful of important people. The biggest problem my clingy ass faces, when travelling back and forth to Pittsburgh a few times a week, is how I have two and a half hours, one-way, of complete silence.

My usual checklist goes as follows: Kade, but I don't want to interrupt his family time. Ransom, but I'm skeeved out thinking he may be banging his best friend turned future baby momma. There's Tonya if I'm desperate, but I already called off our study session, saying my parents called me home.

The phone is ringing before I even think to press **call** on the contact. Just as I'm about to beat myself up for calling too soon, Uriah answers.

"Eager, are we?"

Chuckling, I'm feeling a little bit high. "What was your favorite toy as a child?"

"You first," is an intimate purr in the dark of my car, but there's an underlying challenge in Uriah's tone.

"Hey! You're the master at deflection, always getting me talking about myself and we never circle back to you."

"A mailbox," flows from my cellphone, voice dry.

"What? A mailbox?"

"Yep, a mailbox. There were a lot of kids in the trailer park, and we had to be creative. I would use the drop-off mailbox as a gas pump. The kids would drive their bikes and Big Wheels up to me, and I'd pretend to fill their tanks from a broken section of garden hose. We found a broken ice scraper-brush combo, and I used that to clean imaginary windshields."

"Mad props on originality." Laughing in surprise, I cannot imagine what it must be like to be deep inside Uriah's mind. "But why didn't you ever get to drive up and get serviced?"

"Didn't have a bike." Uriah's voice wavers, and then shifts. "Your turn."

"Ransom," I answer without hesitation.

"Your nephew? Let me get this straight, your nephew was your favorite toy?"

"Yeah, I was four when he was born, and Ransom was a nonstop source of entertainment. He made friends much quicker than I did, and those friends would look up to me in awe and idolize me. It was great– still is."

"Oh, Daniel Bishop, how you surprise me." Uriah's laughter has a grin tugging at my lips, and makes the miles between me and him go by so much quicker. "Give me an inanimate object. Instead of a rattle, you rich fucks probably had a gavel instead."

"Ha-ha!" I mock laugh, but it was pretty fucking funny. "I could return that volley, but I won't. Lite Bright."

"Lite Bright? This isn't another instance of bullshitting like with the family paintball carnage."

"Not a total lie– Ransom and I paintball all the time, even purchased our own equipment."

"No shit, Dan, I saw the photographic evidence worthy of a wet dream. But I didn't buy grandma and grandpa out on the course, being hunted by a high society matron and a divorce lawyer." Uriah doesn't have a sense of humor when it comes to my bullshit. "Why a Lite Bright?"

"Well, I'd take it into the closet–"

Uriah's laughter is so loud and high-pitched, I startle so badly I end up riding the rumble strip. He continues to assault my hearing for what feels like several mile markers.

"What? I don't get it." The laughter continues, trailing off into sadistic giggles because of my confusion. "Oh! Just stop. I get it, you ass."

"You set yourself up for that one, Dan. Sorry. Not sorry. What are you doing anyway? You sound like you're under water."

"Driving back from Pittsburgh."

"Why? Something wrong?" Startled, Uriah's concern over my family's wellbeing makes me feel good.

"I needed advice."

"And you couldn't call?"

"Advice that ties into why it was so funny about me taking my Lite Bright into the closet… which, I have to tell you, was because it was prettier the darker the surroundings. In the closet," I grumble, annoyed.

"You really did set yourself up for that, you know? So what did you figure out?"

"I have no idea– I'm more confused than ever. Ransom says he knows what I am, but he's not going to tell me until I figure it out for myself. Shithead. He told me… I can't say. It was probably bad advice."

"Tell me," Uriah whispers through the darkened car. "I'm lying in bed, staring at the ceiling, and you're probably careening down the highway as fast as the Gremlin will go. Explain."

"What'd you do tonight?"

"See how ya are? Picking up my tactics. I'll tell you, but you immediately have to explain when I'm finished."

"Deal. You're an excellent negotiator, by the way."

"Ha! Thanks. After class, I came home and watched the little ones for a few hours. I ran a few errands, and then came back in time to help Rain measure them for their Halloween costumes. Then I ran out and met with two of my longtime clients."

"You gave two blowjobs tonight." Guts churning with anxiety, I'm not sure how I feel about it.

"That topic is off-limits until we're face-to-face… but, just know, I respect both of the men, and leave it at that."

"Okay," whispers faintly from my lips, and I fear the sound didn't carry.

"Tell me what advice you received, and why you think it was bad advice."

Since Uriah is passing out blowjobs, I guess admitting it won't feel like I'm cheating on something we aren't. *Yet.* "Ransom told me to have sex with my virgin roommate, who is saving himself until the kid he's in love with grows up enough that it's no longer a crime."

"Lot of story jam-packed in there." Uriah chuckles, an infectious sound I cannot deny. I end up joining him, releasing a bunch of stress with the carefree sound. It feels good to be the one dumping my shit at someone else's feet. I'm usually the one with the listening ear, with Ransom and me equally bugging the piss out of the other.

"My roommate has it in his head that he needs to save himself for this kid, who may or may not want him back. Ransom knows Kade almost as well as I do, spending a lot of time with him. Ransom thinks waiting is a horrible idea."

"It's romantic, but stupid as fuck."

"So you agree? I need to try to have sex with Kade?"

"Whoa… back that pony cart up, mister." Uriah laughs harder, finding me endlessly amusing tonight for some reason. "I need a bit more background, and I think it matters on whether or not you and your roommate want each other."

"Kade's almost twenty-one, from a really small town in West Virginia." It all spews out, and it is cathartic to release it to the universe, but also comforting to know it's hitting Uriah's ears.

"Kade's best friend back home has a little brother. The kid is fifteen right now– huge, motherfucking, disgustingly gorgeous. Like hurt your eyes beautiful. So I get why Kaden wouldn't want to do anything to jeopardize it."

"If there's no pics, it's not true." Uriah and Ransom would get along famously. "Show me this boy tomorrow… Why does your nephew think Kade shouldn't wait?"

"Could you imagine waiting until you're twenty-four to lose your virginity?" Uriah's odd choking cough draws me up short, but then it keeps tumbling out. "But Kade is almost religious about it, fanatical to an unhealthy degree. He thinks he's cheating on a kid who doesn't know they are together. It's a fantasy right now, and it could blow up in his face. Kade's already too fragile because of his other problems."

"I think I understand where your nephew is coming from. Imagine…" Uriah breathes, voice sounding scratchy with static. "Imagine the pressure for it to be perfect. Building the moment up for– shit, gotta be a decade with their age-gap. The stress, the pressure to make it perfect. First times are gonna suck, and going into it blindly is only going to make it worse."

"That's what Ransom said. He said…" I stumble over how Ransom was talking about me, *not Kaden.* "He said, what if something uncomfortable happens and it ruins it forever? It's best to know for sure."

"Yeah, save that messy shit with someone who doesn't matter– and I mean with a friend who isn't going to judge you. I know how the anticipation of waiting for someone you truly want crashes and burns. It's mortifying and painful, and it matters, never truly leaving you."

"Wanna talk about it?"

"Ties in with another talk we're going to have eventually." Uriah is the master of evasion. "Does Kade want you?"

"Yeah," is a meek admission into the comforting darkness. Face-to-face, no way in hell could I have admitted it. "I'm starting to think it might be mutual, and my head is just now getting out of my ass. I trust Kaden, and he trusts me, and both of us know we're not the other's one and only. It'll mean something, but not what it will mean when Kade's finally with Wynn."

"The pressure is freaking me out, and I'm not even involved. If you're too scared or worried that you don't like dick, I'll do your roommate. Same rules, not a trick. Something tells me if you want him, and he's got some child god waiting in West Virginia, he's probably something to behold."

"You'd do that? You'd blow Kade, sight unseen?" Shock is overpowered as lust descends out of nowhere. It's perverted, yet intriguing.

"What's Kaden look like?" Uriah's voice takes on a seductive edge, like he's getting off on this conversation. The thought that Uriah is enjoying himself has me getting hard in reaction.

"A lumberjack."

"A lumberjack?" Uriah pauses, waiting for me to laugh or say just kidding. "You bullshitting?"

Laughing, loving how the miles are flying by and I'm more entertained than I've ever been. "My hand to God, Kaden Marx is built like a goddamn lumberjack– his daddy was one. He's six-four and two hundred pounds of pure muscle. His dark, curly hair is like silk– wears it in a man-bun."

"Is his dick proportionate to the outside package?"

Feeling weird, amused, but also natural, I snicker at the hunger in Uriah's voice. "Wouldn't you like to know?"

"I would," Uriah mutters gruffly, clearing his throat. "By profession, I deal in dick. I can't help myself but wonder."

"Kade's shy. For serious, the dude is modest. Never seen him fully naked, but he makes a mean impression against his sheet when he's hard. That help?"

"If it looks big on his ginormous body, it's big." Silence descends for a few minutes, barely able to hear the other breathing. "This should feel like a weird conversation, but it's not… in a few years, when the kid is finally legal, I want to see Wynn and Kade side-by-side."

"You'll probably faint," I tease.

"Swoon, baby. Swoon's more like it."

"When can I see you again?" Not giving a shit how eager I sound, desperate even, I'm prepared to beg. "Can I buy you lunch?"

"You don't need to woo me or buy me, Dan. If you wanna hang out, we'll hang out. Let's keep it honest."

"I wasn't suggesting we go to a fancy French restaurant, Uriah. I was thinking we'd pick up Subway and eat it outside somewhere, get to know each other better. I know you probably think I'm a pretentious asshat, but I've never dated anyone before."

"Are we dating?" The shock and pleasure in Uriah's voice has sweat beading on my forehead. Part of me is freaking out, but a stronger part is giddy.

"This is all new to me, and I'm running off pure instinct, but I'm willing if you are," I mutter without hesitation and absolutely no guilt or shame. "I was thinking something fun, where it's easy to get to know one another– trivia night at one of the coffee houses, or sitting around and making fun of drunken PSU students singing karaoke."

"You surprise me at every turn, Daniel Bishop–" a commotion sounds from his end of the line, kids screaming bloody murder at each other. *"I have class until three, and two appointments here at home after eight. Sorry!"*

A second later, Uriah's voice shifts, pitching higher, holding more authority. "Winter, stop pestering your sister!" A fist pounds on a wall loudly. *"I'm on the phone!"*

"Having trouble?"

"Yeah, dang kids have been wound up all night. I'm going to have to let you go and go beat their asses into submission– can't wait to get my own place. Fiona and I have been thinking of joining forces and escaping this insanity." It all tumbles out in a rush. "Four o'clock tomorrow afternoon, I'll meet you at Subway, and you best give me roommate details, or no prostitution details for you."

Uriah's anticipatory laughter rings in my ears for the rest of the drive home.

KISS ME

It's super late when I get in, and I'm going to get hardly any sleep if I plan on making my first class early in the morning. It might be the first time in my academic career that I blow off class– for some reason, it just doesn't seem important right now.

I'm paranoid about having an unlocked bedroom, or being locked in a bedroom with someone I don't trust, and a dorm room is essentially just a bedroom. Kade and I lock the door, no matter what. We've never had to deal with the sock on the doorknob bullshit, since I've never fucked anyone who didn't get off on my roommate walking in on us or blatantly watching from his bed. At just past two in the morning, adrenaline surges when I find our door unlocked.

Terrified of what I may find on the other side of the door, I swing it open slowly, the hinges adding an eerie soundtrack to my fear. Finding Kade in the fetal position, with his back to me and a book in his hand, I let out the breath I'd been holding in a big gust of relief.

"Door was unlocked," is both a reminder and a chastisement. "Lot of assholes roaming this hall."

"Sorry," is muttered lamely, followed by a soft sniffle. "Bren probably left the room last– he forgets shit sometimes." Another sniffle, which I ignore for now. Kade likes to keep his dignity, modest and prideful, so I'll wait until I can't wait anymore.

"How was dinner?" Going about my nightly routine, I engage Kaden to pull him out of his post-family-visit funk. He's worse tonight than usual, but nothing I haven't seen before.

"Royce took us to Carnegie." Another sniffle.

I don't care about putting on airs, but Kaden does for some reason. Royce is a family man first, and a man from the hills second, but he has more money than every Bishop combined, thanks to a settlement with Ford Motor Company that killed three members of the Kennedy family– Royce's daddy, wife, and unborn daughter. Royce is meat and potatoes, and Brennan is burger and fries. Kaden loves the finer things in life. Royce finds this hilarious, and he coddles and caters to Kaden, giving him anything his heart desires.

In Royce's defense, sometimes it hurts to not give in and make Kaden happy, no matter the cost. Here Uriah's worried I'll pay for his Five-Dollar Foot-Long, and Kaden doesn't think twice when I buy him concert tickets or pay for a steak dinner. In Kaden's defense, I want him to have anything he wants– making him happy makes me happy.

"What'd you order?" Stripping out of my shirt and jeans, I catch Kade watching me and pretending he's not. I chuck the clothing into the corner we've dubbed *the hamper*, and I'll pick up the mountain on laundry day next week.

Rolling over to face me, Kade's feet hang off the foot of the bed. Wearing only a pair of dark-colored boxer briefs, he must be out of it to let me see him nearly naked. Hundreds of razor blade marks create a morbid landscape along the sides of his torso, dipping beneath the waistband of his boxers. But it's the thick wrist scars the tell a deeper, more painful story.

Kaden Marx was gifted several more years of life since he was fully committed to ending his existence, and I pray every day he makes it to a ripe old age. *That* is why we give Kade anything he wants, when he wants it, no matter what.

Catching the direction of my gaze, Kade's chest flushes crimson. "The venison." Ah, one of the most expensive things on the menu.

"I'm surprised you didn't get that giant steak like usual." Buck-naked, I root around in my dresser for a pair of loose boxers, getting ready for bed.

"I wasn't too hungry– wanted something light." Kade murmurs absentmindedly as he reaches over to pull his blankets to cover his torso. Modest? Yes. Self-conscious? Hell yes. Hiding an impressive erection? Fuck yes! "Bren bitched the whole time, so Royce was gonna stop at Arby's for him on the way home."

"I had Arby's as a keep-my-ass-awake snack." Crouching next to the desk, I reach underneath to the mini-fridge, and grab a couple cold bottles of water.

"Mozzarella sticks and jalapeno poppers?" Kade guesses, amusement heavy in his voice. Kade was born in the wrong family– the Bishops love him, and he loves coming home with me. He's not a fan of cocktail parties and politics, but he loves the fare.

"Our suppers were complete opposites." Chuckling underneath my breath, I wedge my ass in the six inches of space Kaden isn't occupying on his bed, then hand him a bottle of water. "I had a Double Quarter Pounder, a large fry, and a vanilla milkshake first."

"You went home tonight?" The shock etched across Kaden's face is humorous, but it reminds me of Ransom asking *where's the takeout*. It'd be freeing to do whatever I wanted, no expectations or demands. "That's five hours– no way did you stay there that long."

Royce makes that drive, and then some, a few times a month, and he only stays here for a few hours at a clip, and I don't hear Kaden complaining about it.

"Probably less than an hour, to be honest," I muse, realizing how idiotic it was to make the drive. "I needed to see my nephew– Ransom's like a touchstone for me sometimes... why were you crying?"

"Don't worry about it." Kade tries to roll over to face the wall, but I'm taking up too much space for him to maneuver his big body. He settles for cocooning himself in his blankets instead– that's his *I'm embarrassed* turtle tactic.

Eyes flicking to the desk, I spot two coloring book pages. "Do you miss the twins?"

Kade is Royce's foster son, Brennan is his foster brother, but there are a pair of five-year-old twins connecting Kade's foster family to Wynn's family. Their father is Royce and their mother is Wynn's big sister. As an orphaned, only child, I know Kaden misses everyone back home, because he sees them all as his family. The twins aren't just Kade's foster siblings– they're his future niece and nephew.

"Royce showed you pictures, didn't he?"

"Bren," is whispered from the depths of his blanket cave. "He's been trying to befriend Wynn, even joined the basketball team to get closer to him. Bren's lost fifteen pounds of baby fat, and actually looks good. Bren's getting popular– has a girlfriend now, and came out as bi. Bren's bisexual, Danny... and he's getting near Wynn."

Jealous. So jealous.

For some reason, the negative emotions Kaden displays are cute instead of annoying.

"My baby brother isn't a virgin anymore, Danny," is snarled from the blankets. "Royce sat there as Bren bragged about it, and he was thrilled. Then I get lectured about being careful, when the only cock I've touched is my own."

"Excuse me?" I don't mean for it to sound snotty, but that doesn't make any sense. Doesn't sound like the Royce Kennedy I know.

"Boys fucking girls is natural, ya know?" Bursting out of the blankets, Kade is so enraged, he doesn't give two shits that I'm seeing him in boxer briefs. Miles of tan skin and striated muscles, I'd have to be dead to not appreciate how well Kaden is formed.

"Boys wanting to have sex with other boys ain't... *Don't come home, Kade. Wynn's sleeping in yer room on the weekends– only way I could get Corbin to lemme have visitation with the twins. I don't like the way yer lookin' at Wynn, Kaden– stay away,*" Kade twists out, his diction and accent matching that of the boy I first met, sounding exactly as Royce does when things get heated. "Jesus fucking Christ, I ain't gonna molest 'im– I just wanna have a conversation with Wynn."

"Explain," I order in a firm voice, getting Kade in hand before he loses his shit. "That doesn't sound like Royce. At. All."

"It does when it comes to gay sex." Lunging off the bed, Kade tosses a paperback at me. "You wanted to know why I was crying– read it!"

Sitting cross-legged on Kade's bed, I tuck my water bottle between my knees, and then open the paperback to the dog-eared page. I could tell by the cover it was a Young Adult novel– the profile of two young boys sitting on a dock while gazing into the water beyond.

"You're my best friend, Tom," Cody whispers, voice warbling with fear. "I don't want to ruin it."

Leaning forward, Cody's fingers twist into the fabric of Tom's t-shirt. With a jerking motion, Tom propels Cody against his chest. Shocked by the sudden movement, neither boy protests when their lips bang together. Giving in, letting go, they kiss.

It was far from Tom's first kiss. It was only Cody's second kiss ever. But it was their first kiss together– the only kiss that mattered.

Crying out for my friend, taking on his pain as my own, "Oh, Kade–"

"I'm so mad, I'm crying!" Kade *stomps* around our dorm room– being a large man, it really is stomping. "Brennan's a couple months younger than Wynn, but it's okay that he's getting his dick wet. But Wynn's not allowed to be talked to– not touched –*talked to*. By me, that is. Royce plays Wynn Gillette keep-away when I'm in town. Royce is terrified if we come face-to-face, Wynn will realize he likes boys too. Instead, he's happier to let the kid think he's broken."

Snatching the book out of my hands, Kaden tosses it onto the desk, knocking over a bunch of shit in the process.

"If Wynn suddenly realizes he's a sexual being, it's okay for him to fuck around, as long as it's not with me... Royce lectures me nonstop about the horrors of anal sex, and how it's the right thing to remain a virgin. When I finally find a guy, we shouldn't do penetration, because not all gay guys do... and I know Wynn's gonna get the same lecture as soon as he figures out he's gay. I get that Royce has valid fears about anal after what happened to him, but it's demoralizing to have the one thing you want more than anything vilified nonstop."

"Wow!" I mouth to myself, never seeing Kaden like this before. Usually his pain and anger are directed inward, self-inflicted. He's really hating on Royce. No doubt there was a lecture with that expensive meal tonight.

"I'm almost twenty-one, goddamnit!" Enraged, tan face crimson, Kaden leans down and shouts at me, "I've never been kissed!"

"Kiss me," is torn from my throat, in a voice I barely recognize. "Kiss me."

Stunned silent, we stare at each other from inches apart. Kaden is known for his epic temper tantrums, but not ones so candid. Never once in my life have I asked someone to kiss me– Kade has listened to me go off on tangents about how kissing is a necessary evil, one I don't enjoy. Too intimate, when all I want to do is get the girl off, then get her off me.

Voice softer, more open and honest than I've ever been, I need to give this to Kaden. "Kiss me... just trust me this once– kiss me."

"I–I–" swallowing audibly, I watch as Kade's throat muscles shift beneath his skin, Adam's apple bobbing. Intense eyes zeroed in on my lips. "I want to, but we shouldn't."

"I'm not going to initiate, Kade– you have to be the one to kiss me, because I refuse to be made to feel as if I took advantage of you. I get how you want some fairytale romance with Wynn, but it's not realistic. Think of that book you're reading– those boys have kissed other people, but the kiss between them is the only one that matters– it's brand-new. Do you really not want to know how to kiss when your lips finally touch Wynn's?"

A lawyer in the making, I have at least another dozen arguments on why this is the right thing to do, but that also means I have another hundred reasons on why this isn't a good idea. Before I can utter any of it, Kade is shutting me up in the ultimate of silencers as old as time.

Teeth knocking together, lips getting snagged, a bark of manic laughter is shared between us. Kaden pulls back, pupils blown, with an expression of pure embarrassment. "Sorry– I suck."

"That's why it's a romantic notion to expect a first kiss to be some magical, fireworks exploding event." Laughing with an edge of insanity, there's no judgment in the sound. "Let's give it another go– we're gonna get you so practiced up, Wynn will have that magical moment because he's following your lead."

"You don't like kissing," Kade reminds me, falling to land next to me on the bed. The single isn't big enough for the both of us, or strong enough to handle all of Kade's weight. It bucks beneath us, struggling to keep us from the floor.

"I have a feeling I'm going to like kissing you," I murmur as a confession, terrified it's the truth.

Terrified I'll crave the kissing, the holding, the pouring out of our souls, soothing Kade's hurts– it's not about the sex, but I won't be turning that away if it's offered. A part of me is going to hate Wynn if he takes that away from me. No matter how much I'm feeling Uriah right now, if he tries to take this away from me too, the resentment is going to kill whatever is budding.

Ransom is right– I was giddy, fluttering around like a crazy person in anticipation of meeting Kaden for the first time after sharing so many emotionally deep emails. It was a transcendental experience carding my fingers through Kaden's hair in comfort that first day.

As the days turned into months, and the months into years, sharing a life together has been the most intimate experience of my life, more so than the sex I've been having nonstop.

I finally admit to myself how Kaden Marx was my first crush, but knowing Wynn was waiting in the wings has kept me from getting too attached. Kade and I have had many talks, declaring we'll forever be in each other's lives, and our future spouses better deal with it or they aren't the ones for us.

It's not about sex, or the kissing– even though I have a feeling denying that urge is going to kill a big part of me, because I've never wanted to kiss anyone as badly as I have Kaden.

For me, this is a bigger deal than figuring out whether or not I can kiss a guy– fearing I'll fuck it all up and wound us for life when I go to touch Uriah –and I'd be lying if I said it was about teaching Kade how to kiss Wynn.

This kiss matters, because it's an intimate turning point between me and the best friend I've ever had. No more denial.

"Let's try again– slower this time," I warn, voice a whispery breath. Noses nearly touching, faces so close I can count Kaden's thick eyelashes, I pull away slightly. "Follow my lead." Coming closer, I whisper against Kade's lips. "Go slowly."

A breathy, "Yeah..." is all the permission I need.

Brushing my lips against Kaden's, just a whisper's breath, I pull away. Subconsciously adjusting the mechanics of it, I hope Kaden is following my lead and filing this away for later. Tilting my head more, since I'm used to smaller faces with button noses, I come in again for another taste.

Kissing for me was always a means to an end, where I made sure I knew exactly what was necessary to pull specific reactions out of my lovers. The soft or hard pressure of flesh against flesh. The swipe of a tongue against sensitive skin. The allure of hot breath casting over a swath of cooling saliva. Proving my mastery, I employ all these techniques on Kaden, not to get into his underpants but to teach.

It's the shuddery sigh flowing into my open mouth that changes kissing from mechanics to insanity. My mind shuts down, body running off instincts. The bed beneath us protests the shift in our weight as bodies collide.

Fingers sinking deep into Kade's hair, I adjust his head at a better angle, ensuring my tongue can delve deeper into his mouth. Annoyed the silky curls aren't crushed in my fists, I tear the band from his bun and toss the bitch to wherever it lands. Growling, the feel of hair cascading down my arms has another switch being flipped.

"*Jesus Christ!*" is cried out sharply, and it isn't until several minutes later that I realize it flowed from my lips.

Closer, needing closer still, my fingers twist in Kaden's hair, pressing our faces together so tightly we're locked. This is a new experience for me– not because it's a hairy, hard chest rubbing against mine… not because my chin is getting rubbed raw from whisker stubble… not because a hard cock is grinding against my thigh… the mechanics no longer matter, the gender of the parts I could give a shit less about.

It's because it's Kade.

The intimacy is staggering, and the more and more I feed it, the bigger and hungrier it grows. Grows to the point I realize I've been starving for it. The connection was what was missing.

Kaden pulls away, and I fear I've pushed too far. But he gazes down at me with eyes gone blurry to lust. "How do you know…" As he swallows his words, I watch the play of his neck muscles beneath his flesh. "You don't like kissing, so how will I know if I'm welcome? What if I kiss Wynn and he doesn't want it? How will I know to initiate without looking like a pervert?"

"Look at me," I order, knowing Kade will do exactly as I say. I pray to God this kid is strong enough to handle Kaden, because the guy needs a keeper. Part of me is sad, and a bigger part is jealous, because I truly get off on taking care of Kaden. "Really take a good look at me and see– does this look like someone who doesn't like kissing you?"

Releasing his patented, self-deprecating laugh, Kaden's thick eyelashes flutter shut and then pop right back open to capture me with intensity. "I've been watching you fuck girls for over three years, Danny… you always look furious as you bang them from behind, like you've got something to prove."

Ignoring the complexity of what Kaden revealed, "And how do I look now?"

Hazel eyes glued to my lips, "Like you want me to keep kissing you." Coy, Kaden's being coy, but he's also flirting with me. Never once have I seen the guy flirt, and it leaves me speechless. Ten minutes of making-out and a new Kaden Marx is revealed. I cannot wait to meet the man who's no longer innocent. "Body language– I'm guessing body language is how you know, right?"

Now it's my turn to swallow. "Yeah... body language." I'm terrified for Kade's future, yet equally intrigued. Instinct tells me Kaden's never going to have to worry about initiating or body language, because Royce answers every question I've ever lobed at him about Wynn.

The kid is going to drop Kaden to his knees.

"Going by body language," Kaden purrs– *purrs!* –against my cheek, already picking up impressive seduction skills... staring deep into my eyes, I'm captured to the point I don't realize what's happening until a manly hand cups my dick through my boxers.

Shuddering, my eyes snap shut, breaking our connection. "Fuck!" So absorbed by the kissing, the feeling of closeness with Kaden, I hadn't realized how turned on I was. A fingertip brushes over the head of my cock, where it escaped the confines of my boxers, dampness is smeared around, and it's the first time I appreciate being touched in return.

Sex was always about getting someone off, feeling like a man because I could do the impossible– satisfy my lovers. I never realized how I kept distance, never making it mutual.

"Do you like touching me?" whispers softly from my parted lips as I lift my gaze to connect with Kaden.

In answer, a hand sinks beneath the waistband of my boxers, fingers slide around my girth and grip. "No oral– no penetration," Kaden warns, suddenly deathly serious. "Don't worry that I'm going to feel guilty, okay? I want this– *need it*. But those are the two things I want to save for Wynn."

"Okay." Leaning back on my hands, I lift my hips slightly, wordlessly asking Kade to pull my boxers off.

Fingers immediately seeking the waistband of my boxers, Kaden lowers them, eyes always on the prize, all the while holding a serious conversation with me. "This ends when we graduate."

Kaden meets me on my level, going straight to negotiation-mode, which is why we are so compatible as best friends. "I'll try," I whisper, for once more concerned with how my dick is throbbing than with what we're discussing. Debate is my favorite hobby, yet I've suddenly turned into a horny guy only thinking with my dick– I'd agree to just about anything right now.

"I'm going to go home and wait for Wynn– to clear my conscience, I'll need to behave by avoiding you. Agree?" Kaden stops just short of gripping my dick again, eyes leveling on mine instead of the object of his affections. "No more of that unhealthy bullshit you've been doing in your bed– it creeps me out."

"I'm seeing someone," I blurt out before my mind catches up with me, stilling Kaden's hand just as it wraps around my dick.

"Just don't bring her around me," Kaden mutters brusquely, hand clenching my dick harder than pleasurable. "If you don't want her to know about us, then don't tell her. But if we're starting this, it doesn't end until graduation. But I can't watch– *I can't*. I'll admit just the thought of you caring about some chick makes me see red."

The desperation and starvation in Kaden's tone has my stomach tightening in knots. "I want this too," I mutter without hesitation. "Need it– Uriah's not a girl."

Floored, Kaden just stares at me in confusion, hand loosening on my dick. "What? *You're fucking a guy?*"

"No." I grab Kaden's wrist before he can pull away, and then wrap his fingers back around me. To hammer the point home, I rest my palm against the front of his boxer briefs, loathing how he's gone soft. "*Seeing* a guy– *dating him*."

"Holy shit!" Kade whispers, getting the gravity of what I'm saying– I've never dated anyone in my life. In reaction, Kade's eyes go large as his dick fills out beneath my palm. "You're serious? I doubt he's going to like what we're doing right now, Danny."

Laughing without humor, I blurt out the truth. "Uriah blew two guys tonight– for cash. Our first real interaction was me watching him suck a guy off in a bathroom stall. No way am I crossing that landmine field to ask Uriah to curb his career, so he'll have to deal with what we're doing."

"Okay, but you still need to tell him about us." Kaden tries to draw away, so I dip my fingers underneath the waistband of his boxers to take his dick in my hand. Both of us pause, confusion and lust warring.

Testing the waters, I drag a fingertip up and down Kaden's length, exploring the vein beneath my touch. Growing hotter and harder the longer I hold him, the erratic pulse and kick to the flesh is intriguing. Even though I know I'm holding a dick that's not my own, I wait for the ick-factor to kick in, but it never comes. It's never going to, because this isn't just a dick– it's Kaden.

"Yeah, I'm good with dick," I mutter underneath my breath to myself. If anything, I get harder, which has Kaden getting harder in an erotic chain-reaction. "Enough negotiating– I need to kiss you again… I didn't get enough of it."

"Wait!" Kaden may be the type of guy who wants someone to tell him what to do, but he's also one of the strongest men I've ever met. A hand on my forehead stops me from leaning in to steal a kiss. "Explain why all the sudden you're not straight?"

"I'm not straight… I'm not gay," I say with conviction, the truth settling deep in my bones. "When we were kissing… it had nothing to do with your dick, just that it's you. Ransom said I've been rage-fucking those girls who look like someone who hurt me once. He won't tell me what I am, thinking I'll wedge myself into the label instead of figuring out who I am for myself."

"Hints?" Looking on the verge of falling on me and ravaging me, Kade is struggling to talk.

"Said I was a romantic, whatever that means."

"Holy shit!" Kade's eyes grow motherfucking huge as he stares at me, grin tugging at his face. "I know! Jesus fucking Christ, Ransom's right. How did I not notice it before?"

"What?" Eyebrows furrowed, I glare at Kade. "Tell me."

"No." Kade's stumbles over the edge, revealing a sexed-up man who's going to get what he wants no matter what, and I always give Kaden Marx what he wants. "I'll tell you after we get off together, because that will be the last nail in that coffin, bud." Laughing in wonder. "Oh, my God– this is hilarious. Explains the cum rag sharing, the condom fetish, and the pulling out."

Annoyed, horniness evaporating, I try to get off the bed, but Kade has other ideas. "Ugh!" I'm flung back to the bed, landing on my back. Kade shifts, straddling my thighs, and then stares down at me with a huge smile on his face.

"You want to kiss me, I know it," Kade says with conviction, as if my wanting him feeds a hunger I didn't know he had. "That cum rag is telling, bud."

Kaden slowly lowers himself on top of me, as if sensing I have a real problem with anyone being on top.

Not once have I had sex in any position other than doggie-style. When I tried to lose my virginity to a friend from school after prom, it was a big fail, because it hurt going in from behind for her, and we stopped. The next girl I fucked was four years older and had a shit-ton of experience– I fucked her upright against a door, taking her like an animal in front of three of my schoolmates in our dorm room at boarding school. When we were done, she told everyone who would listen how I was the best fuck of her life. It's been a nonstop fuck-fest ever since. Never once have I had to hunt down a woman– they just bend over and beg me to screw them.

Mrs. Turner rode me, not needing to hold me down as I was paralyzed by too many non-virgin Shirley Temples and Sea Breezes. That terror sticks with a guy for life.

Kaden settles his full weight on top of me, expression soft and understanding. I'm amazed the anxiety doesn't punch me in the junk. I actually relax as a guy who has seventy pounds and half a foot on me lies on top.

"Let me show you how badly I want to kiss you," Kaden whispers against my cheek, then leans in for the kill. The low, starve-gutted sounds echoing around the room have a fever rushing over us both, and I realize those sounds are coming from me.

All inhibitions flee, Kaden no longer caring he's almost naked as my hands dive deep beneath his boxers to grab his ass. Thick and meaty, hairy and fleshy, so very different from the shapely curve of a woman's smooth behind– it doesn't matter either way for me. It's a new experience, but it's also Kade. I know the guy inside and out, literally not just figuratively as my tongue thrusts into his mouth and my fingers delve deep into his crack.

With every grab, the boxers shift south, hips thrusting upward and downward in a rhythm as old as time. Straining in pleasure, masculine groaning fills the room, as our bodies come in contact without a barrier between us.

All sex has been by my rules, rules I've never broken until now. Body fluids.

Kade's body fluids are marking me as mine are marking him. Saliva is drying on the side of my neck, mine slicking across his jaw. Combined pre-cum is smearing all over our dicks. Sweat is slickening between our bodies as we roll in a wave together. My fingertip sinks a fraction of an inch, *inside* Kade.

Before, it was too much. I didn't want them touching me softly. I didn't want them exploring my body. I'd explore them, touch them, but wouldn't even let them suck me off without a condom as a constant barrier from truly connecting with them.

We never got off together. Unless Kaden was watching, there were no guarantees I'd even get off at all, as that wasn't the purpose. The purpose was proving my worth by conquering them. Conquering a long string of baby Mrs. Turners, young women who will grow up to look and act exactly as my rapist.

Kade– this is Kade, and this is what he meant about coming together… and all over each other.

Sounds I've never made, sounds I've never heard, experiences all new, my world tilts on its axis as I lose my virginity for real this time.

Sweaty, sticky and spent, panting lips resting against one another, we laugh and laugh and laugh, as the bed is tested to its limits.

"So that's what it's like." Still laughing, Kaden slowly rises off me, reaching back to help me disengage the three fingers I have impaling his backside. "Just so you know, for future reference," he mutters wryly, glowing like the goddamn sun at me. "If you keep begging to fuck me, we're going to have a problem."

"Shit!" I hiss, then laugh at myself. "I kinda lost it there for a bit– I have no fucking clue what I said or did."

"The only problem would be me losing it enough to let you." Raising an eyebrow, Kaden does that thing he does, where he manages to twist his hair into a bun one-handed. I'm always in awe when I watch, but even more so right now. "Had a couple of close-calls there for a minute or two." Eyeing me like he's never seen me before, and he likes what he sees, "I shoved more of your fingers in me to keep your dick outta me. Let's use lube next time, though… gonna be sore, but I think I like the uncomfortable sensation."

"Oh." Mortified, I want to roll to the side and hide my head. How our positions have changed. Kaden has never looked more confident, relaxed, or satisfied, while I'm a bundle of nerves and insecurities. "Did you like it, though?"

Laughter rumbles from Kaden's broad chest, a sound of pure sex I've never heard from anyone in my entire life. "I was terrified of anal, but was having intense wet dreams about it in my sleep. I think… I think your fingers in me was the best part. How about you?"

Kaden swaggers across the room to his dresser, body sheened in sweat and covered in cum– normally he sulks and broods and lurks, curling into himself to look smaller.

"Kissing," I mutter meekly as I watch Kaden toss on a pair of sweats and a hoodie. He grabs for his toiletry bag, laughing that tauntingly insane sex laugh.

"I'm going to shower." Kaden smirks, knowing I fear he'll cut himself in there. "I don't feel guilty yet. Kinda high, actually. I'm sure I'll come up with a safer coping mechanism to handle it when the guilt finally pours in. Maybe I'll just go the denial route." Huffing another laugh, "I know I've rendered you immobile, but when you get a chance, gaze into a mirror."

"What?!" Shaking my head to-and-fro, I'm confused beyond belief. "What are you talking about?"

Kaden ignores me, headed to the door with his toiletry bag, then he smirks at me over his shoulder. "I've never seen my come-face, but I've seen yours, countless times… and I've never seen you look as you do now. You're not angry, begging me to leave so you can be alone. You're fused to my bed, looking fucked-out, like you want me to come back and join you. You'd probably even braid my hair if I asked."

Kaden leaves me reeling, exiting the door, but a second later he pops back in. Swaggering over to my dresser, he grabs my cellphone and then lobs it at me, with it landing on my belly with a grunt-inducing thud.

Laughter following in his wake, Kaden shuts the door behind him, then I hear shouted loudly from the hallway, "Demisexual– Google that shit after you call your nephew!"

DEMISEXUAL

"What does demisexual mean?" I ask in lieu of a greeting. Kicking impatiently, I fling Kade's dirty boxer briefs across the room near the *hamper*. "That better be the label you were teasing me with earlier, because I can't take being any more confused than I already am."

"Who told you that?" Ransom accuses, voice tight with bitchiness. "Did you just get laid?" Rustling sounds from his end, no doubt the sheets on our gorgeous bed. We need better beds in this dorm room. "Shit, Danny– it's four in the morning."

"Just answer the question," I demand, having little patience with this game Ransom's playing. "It's my life, and I deserve to understand it."

Sighing heavily, a telltale thud reverberates in my ear– no doubt Ransom just butted the back of his head into our headboard out of sheer frustration. Opposing trundle beds, remember? My head has hit the headboard many a time, with Ransom yanking my hair from behind, slamming my skull into it before I'd get the upper-hand. Nephews. Brothers. Best friends. We know what buttons to push to get optimum violence.

"A demisexual is a person who does not experience sexual attraction unless they form a strong emotional connection with someone. It's more commonly seen in, but by no means confined to, romantic relationships. The term demisexual comes from the orientation being halfway between sexual and asexual." Ransom recites dryly as if he's reading it from a textbook, sounding exactly like his father, that is if Joel were a lawyer. "Now answer my question– did you get laid? And was dick involved?"

"Are you a virgin?" I go on the defense, mind reeling with what Ransom just said. Is it true? Am I demisexual?

"You know I am," Ransom snaps.

"I meant with Claudia."

"Your previous straight orientation has society's definition of virginity stuck in your head." Ransom pauses, sounding guilty, which is his tell when it comes to lying. He's been with Claudia, and he's fighting with me because he's frustrated. "Us queers would be virgins for life, since the way we have sex doesn't fit into the heteronormative societal construct of a penis-in-vagina intercourse."

"Which, by society's standards, means neither one of us are virgins." I call Ransom out on his lie. "And I'm no longer a virgin by anyone's standards."

It takes a few heartbeats for the bomb I dropped to ignite. "Oh. My. Fucking. GOD!" My eardrum nearly explodes from the force of my nephew's enthusiasm. "Tell me everything... how was it? What did you do? Anal? Please tell me you did anal? Jesus, what was touching someone else's dick like?"

"Whoa... whoa... back up," I barely get out, I'm laughing so hard. "Tit-for-tat. You explain the shit with Claudia, and I promise I'll give the embarrassing details. You first– go!"

"I lost my Gold Star status," Ransom whispers, as if I have any fucking clue what that even means. "Having a baby Patterson-Talbot-Bishop was more important than pissing off some gay guy who won't touch my dick because it's been inside a pussy."

"You're talking a foreign language," rumbles out of my chest, sounding suspiciously like laughter. Snorting, I locate Kade's pillow, then shove it under my neck. "I hate these beds. Your kids are going to have three hyphenated surnames? Talk about elitist."

"Shut up," Ransom snarls, always so easily riled up. "Blame your sister for carrying my dad's balls around in her purse. Ransom James Joel Talbot-Bishop is a bit of a mouthful. No way is Claude not going to insist the kid takes her name. We're fucked if our partners want in on the action."

"Kid's name won't fit on any forms," I murmur with wry amusement.

"Shit, mine doesn't right now," Ransom whines. "Gold Star means a gay who's never fucked the opposite sex. Claude was dating a girl who broke up with her when she heard our plan, hating dick so much that she refused to touch Claude if Claude touched dick."

"That's insanity."

"Yeah, well… too late now." Ransom snorts, and he doesn't sound amused. "Talk about a month-long ordeal. You better offer up some good details, because I'm stressed the fuck out."

"Dump it on me, nephew– I'll listen."

"I found out I love getting blown, all fifteen seconds I experienced." The pain in Ransom's voice has me barking out a sharp laugh. "Claude's not a fan of dick– never doing that again. Checked oral off the list."

"You go down on her?" Propping an arm behind my head, this is more entertaining than television.

"Yeah, it was weird. Not like gross, like Claude thought my dick was, but interesting. I don't want to repeat it. *Never. Ever. Again.* But it was hilarious how jealous Claude got– like pissed at me jealous because I went down on a girl before she did. She was seriously jealous, when I was the one going down on *her*."

"You're shitting me, right?" Catching a chill, I grab Kade's plaid blanket off the floor and cocoon myself in it. The scent of Kade wafting up has my dick taking interest. "Are you sure you want someone so insane sharing DNA with yours?"

"Claude was just freaking out on me. But, yeah, I'm not lying– she was jealous."

"How'd the in and out action go?"

It's Ransom's turn to laugh like a hyena, and that's answer enough. "Nightmarish. But we learned two things. One, we're both definitely gay. Claude isn't a fan of dick, and the only feeling I have for pussy is respect. Two, we needed help for me to get off. Ended up watching porn together while I jerked off. Then I stuck it in, and lasted about forty-five seconds, because pussy does feel divine wrapped around a dick."

"Jesus, you're an idiot," I growl, trying hard not to laugh. "Only you would do this experiment a decade before you needed it."

"Well, at least we know now, right?" Ransom sounds so hopeful, innocent. I have no idea why he's worried about propagating the species. "When I finally get a guy, I'm pounding his ass nonstop. Penetration is a hard-limit for me– I need it."

"And I didn't need to know *that*," I chastise, because Ransom is going into TMI territory. "Fuck it." I give up on keeping any boundaries. "Yeah, that's my problem too, it seems. Any idea how I can keep my dick out of Kade, both his mouth and ass since he's saving that for Wynn."

"Holy shit, you *really* did have sex with Kade?!" The fact that my nephew sounds in awe has a shit-eating grin plastered on my face. "What's his dick like?"

Rolling my eyes, I murmur, "Big."

"Asshole!" Ransom's nonstop snarling is hilarious.

"Really big– big enough that I'm glad he has rules against using it... I thought it would be weird, but it's not." Shrugging to myself, "It was just Kade."

"Yeah, that's what Claude and I thought, but there was no *it was just Claude and Ransom*. Ick!" Ransom's shudder is obvious as his voice breaks. "You're definitely demisexual, and I'm fucking relieved I'm not, because I want nothing to do with pussy until absolutely necessary."

"Turkey baster?" I taunt, laughing too loudly for my dorm room accommodations. We gave the freshmen on the other side of the wall quite the education earlier.

"More like jerking off into my palm and shaking hands with Claude's partner, and letting the woman finger Claude with it... don't think we'll be doing any in and out action between us in the future."

"Well, that'll make Claudia's future partner feel like part of the conception, I guess." Baffled, I just shake my head. "Your insanity with procreation is skeeving me out. What's up with that?"

"It's exacerbated by two queer best friends with the same fear, I guess." More sheet rustling on Ransom's end. "No idea, actually. Just this biological drive to know the option is there when I need it. If you hook a guy instead of a girl, you'll see what I mean, Danny. Just another kick in the gut for being gay– no kids will be made in your marital bed, not between you and the person you love. No seeing both of you reflected in your children."

The pain and rage in Ransom's voice is undeniable. "I'm sorry you're worried about this, and that it's going to be a problem."

"Forget we talked about it... are you going after this Uriah dude now that you know you're not going to freak out in sexual situations?"

"Yeah," I admit without hesitation. "I want to get to know Uriah– there's something drawing me toward him, and it's like I can't help myself. I don't... my head's in knots."

"I'm going to die a virgin."

"You're not a virgin anymore."

"Asshat!" Ransom snarls. "I'm going to go out and pay for it. I want more than a fifteen-second spit-shine."

Heart beating erratically, I lunge upright in bed. "No!"

"What?" Ransom's beyond offended. "You don't think I should get any? That's cruel, Danny. Just because sex isn't your driving force, doesn't mean I don't think about it every three seconds out of five."

"Just meet a guy and fool around– don't pay for it," I beg, thinking of Uriah, and all the Ransoms he's serviced.

"Jeesh, I was just kidding." Chuckling, Ransom sounds uncomfortable. "I didn't actually think that was an option. But, let me tell ya, Miriam was over here last week, and Tyler's looking good. Got this 1990s grunge hotness going on– must be a West Virginia thing. Do you know who Kurt Cobain is? Because Tyler reminds me of that dead dude."

"HE'S FIFTEEN!" I shriek, thinking of Miriam's son, having double-loyalties because I've known him since he was born and he's also Kade's cousin. "Leave the boy alone. Miriam said Tyler has a serious boyfriend."

"See, even that kid is getting laid," Ransom grumbles, turning into a pouty brat. "I was only kidding. I'm a Bishop– laws are imprinted in my DNA. In a few months, if I touched Tyler, I'd have to register as a sex offender. His boyfriend better be his age."

"If all you want is to touch a dick, just go find one of your guy friends who's always blushed when you checked him out, and blatantly ask if he wants a blowjob. Just know, he's not going to reciprocate, but he won't beat the shit out of you for asking."

"Oooohhhh..." The glee in Ransom's voice freaks me out.

"I was kidding!" I shout, as if I can be heard before he hangs up on me.

"Gotta go!"

"Wait!"

"Gotta get ready for school."

"Right now?"

"Yeah, gotta find something hot– thinking my tightest skinny jeans. The red ones do magical things to my bulge. Later!"

"Ransom!"

Simultaneously terrified yet amused, I laugh up at the ceiling, only to discover another voice is joining mine. Eyes snapping to the open door, Kade is watching me closely, like he's waiting for me to lose my shit for once, when I'm always worried about him.

Smelling like coconut shampoo, with his damp ringlets wicking dry on his hoodie, Kaden flashes me a loaded look. "Should I warn Miriam? Or should you be warning your new guy he's got another client coming his way?"

"You heard?" I squeak out, still freaking.

"You've created a monster," Kaden deadpans, walking toward me after dropping his toiletry bag off on his dresser. Standing next to the bed, he stares down at me with the most serious expression on his face. A split-second later, the laughter comes.

Face glowing, joy at my discomfort spilling from his throat, Kaden draws all my frustration and annoyance away.

"Ran will call you tomorrow after school, so happy to have discovered that testosterone-filled jocks love their cocks sucked, not giving two shits what's attached to the mouth as long as it's got good suction. Bonus points for swallowing, they'll tell their friends. Ransom's gonna be popular by the end of the school week."

The horrorstruck revelation has my guts twisting. "God, I don't want Ransom used like that."

"Your nephew was born to be a slut," Kade teases me. "And I mean that as a compliment." For some reason, he's grabbing all the bedding off my bed, then he's flipping the mattress on the floor between the two frames. "Get up!" He hauls me off his bed, still buck-ass naked. Then does the same with his bed. "Ran's also a strong-willed, little bastard, so he'll feel empowered and rule all those horny boys."

After shoving the two mattresses together, then tossing the blankets on them both, Kade points down to the nest he's created. "Go to sleep– you have class in a few hours."

"I'm thinking of skipping," I admit, surprising myself, then I plop down on the mattresses, wiggling around until I find a comfy spot. "Everything's changed, and suddenly it doesn't seem important."

Gobsmacked, Kaden just stares down at me in loaded silence. After a minute or two, where I start to get the sweats, he reanimates himself. After tugging his hoodie off, Kaden dons a thermal, hooking his thumbs in strategic holes cut in the cuffs.

Kaden doesn't venture anywhere on campus but to class. He doesn't even go to the dining hall. With an unlimited source of money, via the Bank of Royce Kennedy, he orders takeout and delivery for all of his meals besides breakfast, which he has snack bars or Pop-Tarts instead.

Kade's introverted, yet extremely clingy and bossy to those he calls his own. The body dysmorphia is a mind-fuck he cannot escape. Summer or winter, it doesn't matter, Kaden wears a thermal with his thumbs hooked in the cuffs, no matter what. He just pulls a t-shirt or a dress shirt over top, depending on the situation.

The fact that Kade, not only let me see him without a shirt, but let me touch him, then allowed me to see him fully naked, that's a sign of the infinite amount of trust he's placed in me.

"Don't let the high of finally figuring out what your dick wants make you fail out of school, with only a semester and a half left."

"Semester and a half for you," I mutter, suddenly feeling grumpy, knowing there is a timetable for this thing we've got going on. I'm moving to Connecticut in May. "Law school will be three years of my life I will never get back, where it's study all the time, with no life whatsoever. No family, no friends, no lovers. Just Tonya and me keeping each other on task… don't be surprised if I do some erratic shit in the next few months, because I'm stressed just thinking about it."

"It's your funeral, just saying." Kade settles next to me on the mattresses, propping a pillow behind his neck. "Just because I'm going home to Rusty Knob, it doesn't mean I'm not continuing my education once I get there. There's a ton of bullshit I need to do in order to become a teacher. Plus, I'm really enjoying psychology– might want to explore a higher degree in it."

Kade has this odd belief that living in your hometown makes you a loser. If I've told him once, I've told him a hundred times, I'm not moving either. Once I'm done with school, I'm settling in Pittsburgh. Kade's comeback is that Pittsburgh isn't in West Virginia. My comeback is that a shit-ton of my classmates think staying in Pittsburgh makes them losers, and a bunch of kids who grew up elsewhere think moving to Pittsburgh is cool.

I think everyone has lost their ever-loving minds. What are we? Twelve, where we say cool and loser? Just live wherever the hell you want to live.

Kade's also stuck on degrees, as if it's important outside of landing a career. It's not a measure of your worth– a degree is paid for by the student to help them in a future profession, with the education tailored to that specific job.

We're not lesser because we all don't have PhDs. There are millions of types of jobs, and I'm only studying how to perform one. All those positions are equally important in the cog of life.

I'd say Kade's problems with his hometown and his level of education are almost as all-consuming as his issues with body dysmorphia.

"Are you saying you're so hot, I'll forget all about my family legacy at Yale, and all I'll do is fuck you nonstop?" I tease, snuggling into the blankets, smile curling my lips.

I expect Kade to tease me, instead I get a grumpy snarl. "No, that dude– Uriah. You'll get so wrapped up in him, you'll forget to go to class."

Kade's jealous– he heard me talking about Uriah to Ransom.

"Wanna cuddle?"

"No." Kade pouts, grabbing his paperback off the desk. "I'm going to finish my book, and you're going to go to sleep. I don't have class until the afternoon, but you have one at ten."

"I'll finger-comb your hair." I pretend Kaden never said anything, because I'm not making my first class. I'll go to the other two, though– I'm not a total idiot. "You can read your book and I'll try to go to sleep?"

I better give Ransom and Claudia the heads-up about never co-sleeping with their future kids, unless they want them to turn out like me– unable to sleep without being near someone. It didn't help that I was a chubby toddler in a house filled with a set of grandparents, parents, and an older sister. I was a novelty that loved to cuddle. By the time Ransom came along, I wasn't jealous. He became my playmate– hostage.

Kade's disappointed in me for not going to class, and jealous of a guy I met yesterday. Instead of answering me, he lifts his arm, so I can squeeze up against him while he reads.

Way too eager for attention, I curl up against Kaden, stealing his warmth. We've always had an affectionate relationship inside of this room, and I've soaked it up like a dying plant in need of water.

My eyelids slowly slip shut to the background soundtrack of fluttering pages, but just as I fall off the edge of sleep, Kaden wakes me. "Do you really think my dick is too big?"

My only reply is a sharp bark of a laugh against the side of Kade's neck. Allowing myself the luxury of touching him anyway I want, I grip his dick through his sweats, flexing my fingers until he grows to overflow my palm. Then I take my hand away, too tired to start something I don't have the energy to finish. I pat the blanket back over Kade's cock, like I'm telling it to take a nap.

"I get how that ought to be a compliment," Kade grumbles, embarrassed. "But… with Royce–"

"Hey!" I reach up to slap my hand over Kade's mouth. "Knock it off– it has nothing to do with me thinking you'll shred my asshole. It's just not something I've ever thought about. I'm curious, but it's not a driving force for me. Ya know?"

"You're a top– that was obvious earlier," Kaden mutters smugly. Must be whatever I was saying and doing in the throes of passion soaked into Kaden's ego and planted a seed of arrogance. He's acting like a different guy since he left to take a shower.

"And you're a bottom?" I guess. "I'm not too educated on the lingo, but I know what top and bottom means."

"Versatile." Kade's chuckle evolves into a sex-filled laugh. "I'm looking forward to all aspects of anal. Some guys don't do anal at all. Some top. Some bottom. Some do both. Some experiment once in a blue moon, but stick to what trips their trigger."

"I-I– um… we're going to have to do something to stop me from– ya know, breaking your rules. I respect your rules, but I have a feeling I'm going to lose my head when I'm around you."

"We're going to have to get your boyfriend in this room–"

"Uriah's not my boyfriend," I protest, butterflies swarming my stomach, this time wielding chainsaws.

"*Yet*," Kaden stresses, tugging me closer to his side. "Listen, Danny... we may have a problem, so I'm adding a few more rules. You and I can't kiss– *we can't*. I know you can't see your face right now, and you don't remember saying some heavy shit to me when we were having sex... but for sanity's sake, I'm going to have to put some emotional distance between us."

"I don't understand." Try as I might, I can't tug away to give Kade the distance he seeks, because he won't let me go.

"I want to meet Uriah– I want to look at you when you kiss him." Kade looks down at me, expression more serious than I've ever seen it. "I'm in love with Wynn, it's not some fantasy I'm spinning. I feel it in here." Kaden taps a fingertip on his chest, directly over his heart, then he taps his temple.

"I'm stuck in Rusty Knob, because that's where I belong. You're going back to Pittsburgh, because that's where you belong. That two-hour distance would be important, even if there wasn't a Wynn for me. So you need to explore whatever you've got going on with Uriah, and I need to not kiss you again."

"Why kissing?" is slurred with confusion.

"Because kissing means more to you than sex does, that's why... and maybe I'm feeling what you're feeling too. There's a reason I'm not freaking out right now, Danny." Kade sighs heavily, face twisting with indecision. "I'm taking psychology classes, you asshat. I know something major happened to you, and you've been fucking your demons with those girls. But you've also been watching me, looking at me how you're looking at me right now... for months, maybe years. That's why I'm not freaking out, because I was just waiting for you to make a move."

Eyes narrowed, I think of Ransom and Ainsley, and now Kaden. "How did everyone else notice and not me?"

"That's how denial works, Danny– it's how it works."

"I'm not in denial now, thank God." I don't know if I'm happy about that fact or not.

"Yes, you are– I was cognizant of what was being said and done, even when I was coming with you. I said the same terrifying things right back to you, but I can't go down that road with you, not until I know for sure about Wynn."

"You deserve Wynn."

Manic laughter rumbles against my ear. "Wynn is exacting, an old soul who refuses to budge– you must think I deserve punishment." More laughter, but it turns ironic. "A romantic would debate me, but a realist would agree with me– love is a choice. Intrigue. Infatuation. Lust. Those emotions are instant, and easy, and fade quickly. Love is a choice you make daily for the rest of your life, because loving someone shouldn't be easy. The longer I wait for Wynn, the more we deserve each other, and the more seriously I'll take that commitment when I finally get him… we'll have earned it."

"You're breaking up with me an hour after we made love on this mattress," I tease, but it does sting a bit. The clinginess I try to ignore on a continual basis has now attached itself to Kaden, and I don't want to give it up, but I do understand everything he's saying.

"The fact that you just used the turn of phrase *made love* is the problem." Laughing without humor, Kaden hugs me closer to his side. "We just won't kiss, and we need to figure out something to keep you outta my ass. Because I was pulling your fingers out of me so you could fuck me… but sanity returned for a split-second, so I shoved as many of your fingers in me as I could, to stop myself from riding your dick. You're not the only one struggling here, Danny– I'm confused too."

"Confusion isn't a strong enough word," I whisper beneath my breath. "Maybe I need to ask you some questions, since you're so informed," I tease, but there is an undercurrent of truth to my words. "It's like a whole new world, but I'm still me."

"I read a lot," Kade deadpans. "I have knowledge in theory, but not in practice. I'm just winging it– it's always bothered me how teenagers have to wade through this bullshit alone, with no support structures put into place with candid answers to their questions. Not some bullshit about abstinence, because parents would rather have confused kids, more worried about their kids getting laid… and they get shitty advice from their uncles."

"Hey!" I growl gruffly, barely keeping myself in check from throwing a punch. "Ransom's the one giving *me* advice, not the other way around… and we're both lost."

"Blind leading the blind, my point exactly," Kaden mutters wryly, a smile in his voice. "I've been talking to Miriam about starting up a Facebook group for the LGBTQ kids in my rural area–

maybe doing it through the school district. I've been researching nonstop outside of doing my schoolwork."

"What's a Gold Star?"

Now it's Kaden's turn to laugh at me. Chest rumbling beneath my cheek, he takes great enjoyment in taunting the hell out of me. "Something you'll never have to worry about, but something I'll be for the rest of my life, because I have zero interest in ever getting within several feet of a vagina."

"Can I give you some advice?"

"You're actually asking?"

"Okay, ya got me there." Suddenly I've picked up my own version of Kaden's self-deprecating laughter. The sex we had has a shift in our personalities. Kaden got bolder, more confident, and I seem to be feeling insecure and raw. Open and exposed.

"As a Bishop, I was born with an arsenal of cerebral weaponry I refuse to utilize."

"You have no idea how arrogant you can sound, do you?"

"Huh, and here I was feeling insecure," I muse to myself. "Anyway, let me help you. My mastery is in manipulation and extortion, but I feel guilty whenever I use it–"

"But this is for the greater good, right?" Kade taunts me, laughter thick in his voice.

"You're mad at Brennan for getting near Wynn, but you shouldn't be. He's your greatest ally. He reminds me of me. Needing pats on the back, needing hugs, needing a ton of validation. Just as Ransom is my favorite person, your Bren's… Anyway, Bren's getting near Wynn for good reasons. You guys share the twins, and maybe he wants to spend time with Wynn to feel closer to his baby brother and sister. They live half their time with Wynn and his family, and half their time with your family, with Wynn coming with them."

"Oh." Kaden sounds like he's feeling like an asshole right now.

"I know more about Wynn than you realize, because I just come right out and ask Royce–"

"Royce says Wynn is a non-topic with us." Kaden's resentment toward Royce is getting stronger. "I have to ask Warren how his brother is doing, and he gets pissed at me, acting like I'm a pervert. The entire Gillette family treats me like I'm a predator, and Royce is lighting their torches."

"Ask Bren–"

"Holy shit!" Kaden jumps up from the mattresses, tripping on the blankets, and grabs for his phone. "Bren just got up for school–"

"Why do you remind me of Ransom hanging up on me right now?"

"Because you give the best advice!" Giddy, Kaden starts tossing books into his backpack. "I'm going to demand Brennan tell Wynn all about me– the good only!"

"Oh, shit– if you ever decide you want to do drag, may I suggest the stage-name? Demanda."

Standing taller than ever, hazel eyes taking on an intoxicated edge, Kade fists his large hands on his hips. "I command you to bring me Uriah tonight."

With a roll of my eyes, "Yes, master."

SHOW ME YOUR FIVE-DOLLAR FOOT-LONG, I'LL SHOW YOU MINE

"Switch with me," I demand, reaching for Uriah's wrapped sub. The look Uriah flashes me across the table has me feeling a bit insane. While he's stunned, I make a grab for his sandwich, then toss mine in front of him.

"Never touch a man's food, unless you want a fork to the hand." Uriah's not joking, face a mask of fury, and I'm thankful we're sitting in the park with no fork to be found. "Is this because I refused to let you buy my food? Because switching with me, so I have to eat food you bought, doesn't really count when you're eating a sub I paid for. You're such a caveman, Daniel Bishop."

"And you're stubborn, Uriah Crane," I mutter with a wink. Opening Uriah's sub like it's a present on Christmas morning, "This is another exercise in getting to know one another, crazy– wanted to know what you like."

"You're not touching my fountain Coke." Uriah pulls his cup to the edge of the table, close to his chest, then creates a barrier with his arm to keep me away from his food. "Or the double chocolate cookie... and you can keep your Doritos– the Sun Chips are all mine."

"Just the subs." I smile down at Uriah's sandwich, feeling as if I'm learning a lot about him just by what toppings he picked. "Turkey. Swiss. Tomato. Lettuce. Red wine vinaigrette. Wheat roll. If it wasn't for the Coke and cookie, I'd think you were a health nut."

"An Italian sub." Uriah rolls his eyes at me, trying hard not to smirk. "Loaded with double meat, extra cheese, and every pepper on the menu. Why don't you weigh a billion pounds?"

"Luck." Popping the cap on my bottled Frappuccino, I drain half of it in a single gulp. "You should see my nephew eat. But I think the bad influence was Kaden. He's freakishly tall and large-framed. But he used to be too skinny, drinking protein shakes and eating all the calories he could to keep up with his metabolism. It wore off on me, I think."

"My body doesn't require much fuel." Uriah's eyeing his sandwich, wanting it back. "Maybe it was the lack of food as a kid, and the unhealthy shit the school pushed on me, but if I eat anything bad for me, I bloat up and gain five pounds."

"This is a really good combo." Biting into half of the sandwich, I smirk across the table at Uriah. He's losing his shit, fearing my choices will go straight to his hips.

It's a new experience being around a guy who is terrified to gain any weight. I'm not going to say he's being girly, or compare him to the girls I've been around, because they've always refused to share a meal with me.

The ladies in the Bishop family are hyper-focused on healthy food to keep their men healthy. Lots of late nights have been spent in my car, Ransom and me gobbling drive-thru junk food after a calorie-free meal left us starve-gutted. Sybil looks like a feeding trough on the weekends Kaden joins us.

Uriah's wearing his PSU hoodie again, thankfully with the hood down this time. Even with the bulky fabric, it's obvious a stiff breeze could knock the guy over he's so slim. I don't care what he looks like, I just don't want him going without because of it.

Reaching past the arm barricade, I grab half of my sandwich and then plunk half of Uriah's in front of him. "Just try mine– live a little. I'll work the calories off your skinny ass."

"I've got a great ass, I'll have you know."

Lips curling into a naughty smirk, my eyes cast down, trying to see through the top of the picnic table. "Why don't you show me?" is murmured in a sluggish voice gone husky with lust.

Since I met this guy, my little brain has been in charge. It's a miracle I heard a single word my professors said today, too busy thinking about getting off, when normally that's a nonissue for me.

Uriah rewards my shitty flirting skills by taking a tiny bite of the Italian sub. Inky eyelashes fluttering, a moan slips past his lips, and it punches me straight in the dick. "Okay, you win." Laughing, completely oblivious to the chaos he's wreaking, Uriah reaches over to nab the other half of the Italian. "I'm converted."

Leaning back, I let Uriah have all the food he wants, because watching him eat is one of the most erotic experiences of my entire existence. Shifting slightly, I try to alleviate some of the pressure going on inside my jeans, all the while repeating, "*Gorgeous*," inside my head.

Uriah freezes, whiskey eyes flicking up to my face, and I realize I'd spoken that word out loud. We continue to eat in silence, both of us wearing blushes. The most baffling thing is how Uriah seems surprised I'm flirting with him– complimenting him.

Uriah Crane is the most exotic creature I've ever seen, added on top of this insane need to know him inside and out. He intrigues the hell out of me, to the point I can't concentrate on anything else.

"You seem different today." Uriah eyes me over the top of his fountain drink. "There's this frenetic energy you're releasing– you're restless."

"Do you believe in energies?" I probably sound like a religious nutjob to Uriah, but I'm curious, not judgmental.

"If you open yourself up, you can sense the energies weaving around you. The more you're around someone, the easier it is to sense a change in them." Pushing the empty sandwich wrapper away until it's no longer in front of him, Uriah snatches up his cookie. "I don't know you well enough, but even I can sense you seem different."

"Can we talk about anything?" pops out before I can stop it.

"Now that's a loaded question if I've ever heard one." Uriah's toying with me, I can hear it in his voice. "I won't judge– you caught me sucking a guy off for ten bucks. I have no room to judge."

"World's oldest profession," I mutter with more admiration than expected. "Are you feeling this too?" I gesture between us. "Because I need to know that before I make a fool of myself."

Eyes slipping shut, Uriah gulps his drink as an excuse, so he doesn't have to answer me straight away. "We're not good for each other. You get that, right?"

"That's not what I asked–"

"I'm a walking skeleton-in-the-closet for a man with such potential–"

"I don't give a shit," I snarl, refusing to go down that path. "Answer what I asked."

"You're an all-in, intense dude, Daniel Bishop." Eyes held wide, Uriah gazes across the table at me, as if he's never met someone like me before. Voice a breathy whisper, "I feel it too."

"If we're going to get to know one another, I should probably warn you that there's some uncomfortable, embarrassing shit you'll need to learn about me."

Lips curling off his slightly crooked teeth, Uriah releases the most ironic laugh I've ever heard. "Trying hard not to judge you, Dan, especially after you lit into me over our political differences. You're not your family, I get it. But it's hard not to call you out as bullshit… hard to not see a pampered prince sitting across the table from me."

"It's not a competition on who's had it worse." Seething, my hands fist the wrappers into wads, and then jam them into the plastic takeout bag. "That's not what I want. This isn't a competition– I thought it was friendship. But I guess I was wrong, because that attitude reminds me of everyone I've met. I can't trust you not to judge the outside long enough to know the inside."

Blinking up at me, Uriah sits in silence as I attack our mess and shove it into the plastic bag. I toss his Sun Chips on his side of the table, my Doritos too. I lost my appetite and the bag of chips is now tainted with this bullshit interaction. Whatever I thought was happening between Uriah and me was a lie– it's not happening. Now or ever.

"Just forget it." Hopping up from the bench, I stride over to the garbage can and jab the trash with the force of a punching fist.

I make it a few yards from the table when something hits me in the back. Shocked, it takes a few seconds for my mind to catch up with what just happened. "You… you– you threw your drink at me?"

"Hit ya with it too." I turn to catch sight of Uriah still seated at the picnic table, his fountain Coke dripping down my back with the cup resting on my shoe– straw trying to climb inside my pantleg.

"Thought you needed to cool off." Uriah doesn't even blink, doesn't crack a smile, just keeps staring at me. "But for some reason, I think it only made you hotter." Lifting a single fingertip, he swirls it in the air, gesturing at my crotch. "Ice cubes sliding down the crack of your ass, your thing? You're popping a chub– that's not my kink, but…"

"Are you– are you being serious?" Frozen in shock, all I can do is return Uriah's stare.

"Cooled down yet?" Smirking smugly, Uriah whips his hoodie off his head. In the process, the purple silky t-shirt rides up to show off his slim, hairless torso. The expanse of pale skin has my mouth drying up, to the point I contemplate sucking the back of my t-shirt dry for a sip of Coke. "Take your shirt off and wear this." He wiggles his hoodie in his hand.

"Pretty sure your aim is good enough to hit me with it from there," I mutter begrudgingly, then take a slow walk of shame back to the table to fetch the sweatshirt. "Don't know if I want to invite you paintballing next time. It'd suck if you were on the opposing team, and paintball hits bruise like a bitch."

"I know." Uriah is still toying with me, fighting a smile. "I have a big brother and sister, you know? RJ, Fiona, and I used to paintball all the time. As for the throwing arm, Bob had to teach me to defend myself because of my ethnicity, sexuality, and lack of gender. Not trying to start a war with that comment, just explaining why my aim is so good."

"Why did you–" yanking my wet t-shirt over my head, I shudder as an ice cube wedges itself along my waistband. "Why did you douse me?" Reaching for Uriah's sweatshirt, I notice his eyes are fixated on my bare chest.

Showing off a bit, I flex and bend as I wiggle into Uriah's sweatshirt, not bothering to ask my question again since he's not paying attention to anything above my clavicles. About thirty seconds after I'm fully clothed, Uriah's brain comes back online, and I'm feeling pretty smug.

"Didn't think about it– just happened," Uriah stammers, pale skin blushing a pretty pink. "I couldn't have you walking away from me, and the next thing I knew, my drink was hitting you in the back. Sorry. Not sorry."

Cocking my head to the side, I breath, "Not sorry?" Annoyed, I stalk back over to the scene of the crime, and fetch the dropped cup, lid, and straw.

"Wait!" Uriah's latching onto my arm, thinking I'm blowing him off, when I just don't like littering. "Let's try this again, okay?"

"Not sorry?" I stress, voice warped with frustration, as I pitch the trash into the can. "Are you a psycho?"

Skin darkening with mortification, "I-I– um… I'm not sorry because I got to see you without your shirt on," Uriah stammers almost inaudibly, causing all the negative feelings I'm experiencing to evaporate in a heartbeat.

"I'm not sorry either." Reaching over, I tug down Uriah's shirt. He was so out of sorts, he didn't realize his silky t-shirt was still riding high above his hip, a hip that's bare because his jeans are cut so low the button is riding a scant inch above the base of his cock. Uriah's hairless, completely fucking hairless. "Those jeans you're wearing should be illegal."

Swallowing thickly, throat dry as fuck, I'm about to suck on my t-shirt clenched in my fist like it's a Capri Sun. "Let's walk." I start walking, not waiting to see if Uriah agrees, with the nearest store as my destination. "We're getting drinks– bottled drinks."

"Hmm… I don't know, Dan. That might be a bad idea." Uriah falls into step next to me. He's so slight, I expected him to be shorter. I'm not the tallest, not far from average, but Uriah is nearly the same height as I am. It's a surprising pleasure to realize we'll be eye to eye.

Lips to lips.

"Bad idea?" I detour across the street, toward the convenient mart. "Why's that?"

"If you piss me off, you might not just get wet when I throw my drink at you– a bottle is considered a weapon."

"I have a hard head– just aim for it." Chuckling, I make a mad-dash inside to grab a Gatorade and a Coke.

Smiling, Uriah gratefully takes the Coke, untwisting the cap, then takes a sip. "Thanks." He's being good, taking what I'm offering instead of fighting to buy his own drink, because he feels like an idiot. If the ass-end of my boxers and jeans weren't wet, I'd think Uriah was being cute.

"Wanna head back to the park?" This time Uriah doesn't wait for me to answer before he's striding back across the street. I slow my pace, so I can get a good look at his backside in those illegal jeans of his.

Tugging the sweatshirt down, I shove my unopened Gatorade bottle into the marsupial pouch to hide the effects Uriah's body has on mine. School's out for the day, so there are tons of little kids and high schoolers roaming the park, and I don't want to get arrested for looking like a pervert.

Uriah is a contradiction. When crouched before a client, he's in charge. When sitting in a crowded dining hall, he's shy, wishing to turn invisible. When in a park filled with kids, he has balls far too big to fit in his jeans.

"Can I borrow this?" Uriah bends down to grab a discarded basketball, picking it up before the kid can answer. "We'll be right over there." He points to the far end of the unoccupied area. "If you have to go, just come and get it from me. If not, I'll bring it back."

"Sure." The kid smirks at Uriah– he's probably twelve or thirteen, and he's eyeing Uriah's purple shimmery t-shirt. As Uriah dribbles the ball away, the kid continues to eye Uriah... until he notices his death in my stare. "Sorry," the little shit mumbles, running off to join his friends before I strangle his scrawny neck.

"I'm used to it." Uriah continues to dribble the ball, handling it as if it's second-nature. "Kid's just confused– can't figure me out. Am I gay? Am I a boy? Am I a girl? Does he find me hot, or does he think I'm a freak?" Turning, Uriah does a perfect jump-shot. "It's the adults I want to throat-punch, so save your anger for them."

Pausing, I watch Uriah for a few minutes, trying to see what others see. We all have these instinctive checkboxes in our heads on what belongs to a girl versus a boy. Grandmothers everywhere hack gorgeous hair off the heads of their grandsons, at the protests of the mothers and at the insistence of the fathers. Girls buy shimmery, silky purple t-shirts. Girls wear tiny jeans not big enough to cover their asses. Boys have an Adam's apple. Boys have flat nipples, and girls have boobies.

As Uriah takes shot after shot, hitting every basket, his hair swings around his jawline. His shirt catches sunlight. His nipples stick out enticingly like a woman's does, begging to be sucked. His jeans are so tight I can see the ridge running around the head of his small cock and the bulge of his sack. His sneakers are pink with black laces, feet finding a considerable amount of air with every jump-shot.

I understand that kid's confusion now– he wasn't judging, he was truly trying to figure out what gender Uriah is, when it shouldn't matter –and why Uriah said it's the adults that bother him the most. No doubt Uriah's heard countless times how he should just cut his hair and dress like a guy, but that wouldn't be Uriah.

Uriah is perfect the way he is.

Popping an eyebrow, "You play?" blurts out before I can stop it– just insulting Uriah left and right since we met.

Rolling his eyes, Uriah shoots again, and it sinks in with a swoosh. "Trailer park had a hoop, and we'd steal basketballs from gym class. By the time I moved in with Bob and Rain, I was pretty good at it. RJ was playing in junior high, so Bob put a hoop on the garage. I just shot around for fun, no interests in whatever bullshit would go down in the locker room."

"Self-preservation?" Swooping in, I steal the ball, using a sneak-attack to my advantage. I shoot. I score.

"Exactly." Uriah's out of breath now, trying to get the ball away from me. "At a risk of pissing you off again, I'm going to go ahead and guess you've played every sport, every instrument, and every hobby your parents could think of in the past twenty years?"

"At the risk of sounding like an elitist asshat…" pausing in speech, Uriah and I face-off, bent slightly as I dribble, and he tries to steal the ball from me. Offense versus defense. Pitching to the side, I try to flow around Uriah– his feet are fast, but his hands are faster. Before I can blink, the ball's out of my hand and swooshing through the net.

"At the risk of sounding like an elitist asshat?" Uriah taunts me as soon as he catches his own rebound. "Care to elaborate, rich boy?"

Blushing brightly, hoping the exertion covers it, "You'd be right."

Releasing taunting laughter, we go again, and Uriah earns the point. Again.

"Horse?" Uriah suggests, smirking smugly as he performs difficult tricks with the basketball. "Play for answers to uncomfortable questions, Mr. I Want to Know You?"

"I'm fucked, aren't I?"

Eyes dancing with mischief, Uriah is enjoying himself. "If you miss, you'll answer. If you don't, I'll answer."

Huffing with fake annoyance, I'm enjoying myself too. "You act as if you can't miss."

"RJ hated me when we were in high school– had to do all of my chores." Uriah stands in H position, and the ball sinks a second later. "Tell me, are you a registered republican?"

"Hey, I haven't taken my shot yet!" Retrieving the ball, I arc my arms, hoping the ball will follow through, just as Uriah lifts the edge of his t-shirt to wipe his brow.

Brick.

My grumbled, "Cheater," is met with smug laughter. "On my eighteenth birthday, the party wasn't because I reached the age of majority. All my high-profile family members were in attendance. Instead of cake and presents, we filed out my voter's registration as a republican."

"Dayum…" Uriah drawls out, already in the O position, ball sinking without him even aiming. "Are you a republican?"

I take my shot, and I'm sad to say Uriah doesn't try any sexy cheating tactics, thinking I suck.

Swoosh.

I answer anyway. "I'm middle leaning, thinking both sides are corrupt leeches sucking the American people dry. Ransom's the same– his birthday party is already in the works, and everyone is terrified he'll register as a democrat just to cause a stink."

"I cannot wait to meet your nephew." Uriah moves to the R position, but I stop him in his tracks.

"Nice try, sneaky snake, but I get a question." The question isn't about getting to know Uriah, but it's been one on the tip of my tongue all day long, nearly asking everyone I've met. "What do you suggest if you're fooling around with someone, and they're saving their ass for someone special."

"Butt plug," Uriah answers without hesitation. Staring me down, no expression on his face, he tosses the ball one-handed, never taking his eyes off me.

"Seriously, what the fuck?" erupts from my throat as the ball bounces twice before Uriah's picking it back up, after it made a perfect arc into the basket.

"Not my first game of Horse." Uriah is already standing in the S position. "Your shot, cowboy."

"This is so unfair– I don't have a snowball's chance in hell of duplicating that." Uriah laughs at me the entire time I stare him down and try to shoot the ball one-handed without aiming.

Air ball.

"How long have you been in love with your roommate?" Uriah turns, facing me with the hoop at his back, and then crouches down to toss the ball from between his knees. In a perfect arc, I watch in utter amazement as the ball sails over his head and swooshes through the net.

"Are you fucking kidding me?" Growling, I don't even duplicate the shot, I just lob it near the backboard, and miss it entirely.

"Poor sport!" Uriah's sadistic giggles fade in the distance as he chases the ball down through the field behind the court.

Retrieving my Gatorade, I pound half of it before Uriah makes it back with the basketball. "You did that on purpose," he accuses me, out of breath. "But I forgive you."

"Says the guy who doused me with a large fountain Coke," I mutter grumpily, not wanting to answer the question. "I've been enlightened recently against the heavy denial I've been living under."

"Better enlighten me before I take the last shot." Uriah stands in the E position, grin so wide it's glowing in the waning light as dusk settles around us. "Denial? I pegged you for a straight dude with your reputation on campus, but after the way you keep looking at me and flirting with me, and the expression on your face when you mention your roommate…" he trails off, hoping I'll fill in the blanks.

"How long have I been in love with my roommate?" I muse, allowing my tongue to blurt out the first thing that comes to mind. "Since the third email where he poured his heart out about being clingy, and his grandfather didn't know how to handle it without treating him like a girl."

"That triggers so many traps in my brain," Uriah growls, expression shuttering me from the heavy emotions he's really feeling.

"Not my words. Not Kade's words. Those are the words of an uneducated, illiterate eighty-year-old lumberjack in the hills of West Virginia. The words of a lonely old man who didn't know what to do with a gay grandson, and lost the kid to a foster family and a distant relative… But that's not what you asked, and I answered."

Shoulders slumping, confidence evaporating, "Why are we here?" The ball slips out of Uriah's hand to bounce repeatedly until coming to a stop near the edge of the court. "If you're in love with Kaden Marx– the elusive reclusive, in-the-closet cutter is what people say around campus, by the way –why are you here with me?"

"Because love is a choice you make every single day," I answer with Kaden's words, words I've heard more times than I can count from my father, the divorce lawyer who saves more marriages than mediates divorces.

"Because as much as I can admit Kaden will be a part of my life for the rest of my existence, he's not the one for me. That has nothing to do with what sex parts he has in his pants, and everything to do with compatibility and the ability to compromise. Kade loves to argue and I love to debate, but I couldn't handle the stress of always fighting to get through the day with him. I'm hoping Wynn– the kid Kade's saving his ass and mouth for, which is why I asked about plugging it up –is strong enough to stop Kaden from being self-destructive. I'm not– I compromise too easily to make Kaden happy, even at his expense."

"Wow!" Uriah just stares at me open-mouthed as I dump all my shit at his feet.

"I've thought of little else in the back of my mind since we started emailing each other three and a half years ago. The more I got to know Kade, the deeper I was hooked, the more I knew it couldn't work without one of us losing ourselves to the other… then I met you, was intrigued immediately, and all I wanted to do is get to know you. The more I know, the more intrigued I become."

Still stunned, I leave Uriah to mull over what I just said, and walk across the court to fetch the basketball. Returning, I press the ball to Uriah's chest, noting his nipples are still very prominent against his t-shirt. The sight turns me on, tripping all sorts of triggers in my body.

Standing with our toes touching, "Your turn," I breathe against Uriah's lips, then step away so he can take the shot.

Blinking out of it, hair flies wildly around Uriah's face as he shakes his head. "Did you have sex with him last night? Is that why your energy seems so different?"

Uriah turns and executes a perfect layup, ball bouncing off the backboard to swoosh through the net. Landing on his feet, Uriah retrieves the ball, then tosses it to me.

Knowing I have to answer Uriah, no matter what, I try to be as honest as possible before I even take the shot. "Yeah, Kade and I had sex last night, and it was eye-opening for me, how different it was. It had nothing to do with Kade being a guy, just how different it was being with someone who cares about me, someone I care about, someone I truly wanted to touch me back. It wasn't a conquest I had to conquer."

Turning, I dribble the ball as I try to get enough of a running start, then I do a layup, ball going into the basket. As I land, allowing the ball to go wherever the hell it wants to since the game is over, I finish answering Uriah.

"The energy difference isn't because I got laid– it's because I finally know who I am."

"Who are you?" Uriah asks, seeming to be as intrigued by me as I am by him, to the point I answer without reminding Uriah's he's out of questions.

"Demisexual." Shrugging like it doesn't still confuse the piss out of me, I blurt out the first question that comes to mind, knowing it may be insulting. "How'd the prostitution thing start?"

"I'd say you went in for the kill, but my *in love with your roommate* question was pretty harsh too." Chuckling without humor, Uriah retrieves the ball, then jogs across the court toward the kid he borrowed it from.

I don't move, simply stand, watching as Uriah animatedly talks to a kid who was eyeing him crosswise earlier. By the time Uriah is jogging back to me, the kid no longer looks confused by him.

Grabbing for his bottle of Coke on the edge of the court, "Let's go camp out in the grass." Uriah leads me into the mowed lawn situated between the basketball and tennis courts, where in warmer months, people are always picnicking and sunbathing.

Uriah folds to the ground, sitting crossed-legged, then unscrews the cap on his Coke. Joining him, I ask a question without thought. "Want to join me for dinner tomorrow night? If you're not busy, since I know you are tonight," I stammer, speaking too much but unable to stop myself. "My roommate wants to meet you."

"That's not awkward at all.. not at all." Lying back in the grass, Uriah stares up at the sky as dusk creeps in around us. "Sure– I'm free. Nothing expensive, but preferably has vegetables on the menu."

"Two things you need to know about Kaden Marx…" trailing off with a manic chuckle, I get comfortable next to Uriah, like it's easier talking if we're staring at the sky instead of each other. "He loves expensive things, and he loves junk food."

"I'm sure we'll get along swimmingly," Uriah mutters sarcastically. "If we don't end up pummeling each other out of pure jealousy."

"You'll get along." Rolling to my side to face Uriah, a sadistic giggle escapes my throat. "We'll go toy shopping after dinner. Kade is all theory and no practice, and I only have my nephew to bounce ideas off."

"So I'm your token gay guy?" Uriah snorts, the sound pure irony. "Why do you assume I'd know anything?"

"Because of the question you are clearly trying to evade."

Growling, but it's more amusement than anything, Uriah turns to face me. "I didn't forget, nor am I evading, but I don't have any experience in the toy department."

"Then we'll all learn together," I offer, intrigued by the idea. The blush blooming on Uriah's face, and the naughty outline straining at those jeans, is answer enough. Sighing, I close my eyes against the sight, relying on self-control to stop me from reaching out and outlining his hard cock with a fingertip.

"This is going to be an uncomfortable conversation– I don't know where to start."

"At the beginning?" Giving up on not touching Uriah, I show just how needy I can be. "May I touch your hair?" I figured it would be more polite than asking to touch his nipples or outline his cock.

Snorting at my lunacy, Uriah turns to capture me in his whiskey stare. "Creepy admission time… when we'd have lice-checks in elementary school, I used to shiver, every nerve in my body tightening my skin. Do you know what I mean?"

Never having a lice-check in my life, I can only guess.

Scooching closer, voice eager, "Like this?" I flutter my fingertips against Uriah's scalp, finding his hair coarser than it appears. Excellent for getting a good grip in many fun, sexual positions.

"That's perfect." Uriah presses into my touch. "But it's obvious I seem to make you one horny motherfucker."

Snorting at myself, I realize the sweatshirt bunched up and my package is in clear view. "I'm not the only one– those pants are driving me fucking insane– your nipples."

"I thought demisexuals weren't into casual sex?" The confusion in Uriah's voice clears my head some. "Or do you imprint on people hella quick, like a baby bird who's lost his mother?" My growl has Uriah chuckling against my shoulder.

"Just teasing– in a land far, far away... Bellefonte," Uriah mutters wryly. "There was this kid who confused everyone everywhere he went, but especially those dwelling in the high school. He had a crush on a guy who lived on his street– we'll call him Dick –but the guy was a few years older. Uriah would follow Dick around like a baby bird craving a worm–"

"Oh, my God!" Snorting, that turn of phrase has me thinking of Ransom.

"The baby bird would do anything for a taste of that worm. He never had a boyfriend, because he'd only met two other gay kids growing up– one became a good buddy who only wanted big, burly jocks, and the other was a girl... since this kid was tiny, liked the bright and shiny, and had an affinity for sundresses, no one developed romantic feelings for him."

"I'm looking forward to seeing you in a dress," I murmur in a husky voice, fingers slowly stroking Uriah's hair.

"So the boy grew into a man, spending half a day at high school and half a day at the community college, where he met older men who liked what they saw." Uriah pauses, sensing how my mood just shifted, or maybe because my fingers stilled in his hair. Trying to relax, I allow the inky strands to flow through my fingertips.

"These two men– professors –they respected the boy, helped him and gave him advice. They remained professional, mentoring him since he wasn't of age yet. At the same time, Bellefonte was all atwitter with the news of Dick's impending nuptials to his high school sweetheart –let's call her Barbie. Fiona's best friend, so

Uriah knew Barbie well –Dick and Barbie were getting married, and Barbie asked Uriah to help her plan it, since her theme colors were Uriah's favorite colors. This happy time brought Fiona and Uriah even closer together, especially in the absence of their big brother off to conquer NYU. Barbie was a nice girl– Uriah really liked her, and they got along well as they planned the wedding…

"But Uriah had to pick a gender, since gender-fluidness goes over everyone's heads. Uriah's sex is male, but his gender is fluid, finding it easier to go by *he*– which is Uriah's preference, by the way. In Bellefonte, Uriah's gender is seen as male, no matter what. So Uriah wasn't invited to the bachelorette party, even though he had a pretty new party dress he wanted to wear that coordinated with his sister's dress, and Barbie and her other girlfriends enjoyed Uriah's company too–"

The despondent tone in Uriah's voice has me blurting out, "I don't know if I can handle where this is going, Uriah." Heart hammering out of my chest, I tug Uriah to me, until his cheek is pressed against my neck with my arms cradling him.

"The bachelor and bachelorette parties were held at the same time. Barbie liked Uriah so much, she wanted him as a member in her wedding party, but this was Bellefonte. Uriah liked Barbie so much, he joined forces with the maid of honor and the bridesmaids and planned the bachelorette party for Barbie, so she could have the fabulous party she deserved…

"Barbie didn't want Uriah to sit home alone with his baby siblings pestering him all night, with his big sister at the party with Barbie, so she pushed Dick to invite him to the bachelor party. Barbie remembered how Dick used to hang with Uriah once in a blue moon around the neighborhood…

"Uriah was confused when he arrived at the venue– Dick's soon-to-be vacated apartment –when Barbie's party started at a salon for mani-pedis, moved to a liquor store to sample wines, involved a party bus, which made a quick detour to a bakery for cupcakes, and ended the night with pole dancing lessons–"

"You can plan our bachelor party," I breathe into Uriah's ear, loving the way he shudders against me.

"I caught that, my imprinting birdie." Uriah chuckles, snuggling closer. "The bachelor party was the usual shit Uriah avoided like the plague. Drinking, and the stupid games that go along with it, when Uriah isn't a fan of binge-drinking, thanks to a drunken mother. Secondhand smoking until Uriah's lungs hurt, when he suffers from asthma. Video games, which Uriah loves, but found out Dick's drunken groomsmen didn't appreciate the ego-bashing of losing to the girly guy wearing glitter nail polish…

"Porn. Porn. More porn. Gay porn used to taunt Uriah, with seven guys eyeing his crotch at all times to see if it made him hot or not. The gay porn turned into a drinking game, where if Uriah's dick twitched because the sound of a groaning guy got him hot, the groomsmen would make him drink–"

Freezing, "No," I groan in pain, terrified where this will lead.

"To put you out of my misery, I wasn't raped. I never got drunk enough where I could be taken advantage of, but my pride and rage got me into trouble. It was my own fault, at any time I could have walked out. I was trained to take down a man twice my size. I was just so angry, I did it to spite them and myself."

"Did what?" voice breaking, too many horrific scenarios are playing out in my head.

"Near the end of the night, where the groomsmen were bitching at Dick for not having any adult entertainment, Dick pulled out his dick and asked Uriah to suck it. He kept telling his groomsmen how Uriah had a crush on him, and would follow him around and check out his ass and shit. They kept calling Uriah a faggot and laughing at him…

"Uriah dropped to his knees, demanded a condom, and sucked Dick off in under two minutes. Uriah had never sucked a guy off before– fuck, he'd never touched a dick but his own. Uriah was a virgin. Never been kissed. Never been touched. A guy Uriah trusted wanted to take advantage of him, saw him as the poor as dirt Native American kid who was born in a trailer park to a drunken waste of space."

"Uriah, no– your mother is no reflection of you, and your heritage is intriguing and an amazing legacy."

"Sometimes I don't believe that," Uriah whispers against the side of my throat. "It took less than fifteen minutes for Uriah to give seven blowjobs as they stood side-by-side with their dicks out. Dick made Uriah do him again as soon as the line was finished. Then Dick tossed a wad of cash at Uriah while he was still crouching on his knees."

"What the fuck?" I seethe, hands curling into fists.

"The guys all cheered as Dick announced Uriah was the evening's surprise entertainment, and to give Uriah a tip if he did a good job. More money was flung at Uriah, as they called him dehumanizing names. Uriah was enraged, but a part of him felt he deserved it. Uriah got up, cash in hand, and left."

"That's it?" I demand, hoping there is a vengeance portion of this horrific story, since my story ended where it began with no justice sought. "What did you do after that?"

"Not me– *Uriah*," Uriah stresses. "Note the third-person narrative… Uriah knew where the bachelorette party was, a bachelorette party where all the wives, girlfriends, sisters, cousins, and friends of the groomsmen were, all in one handy location."

"That's my Uriah," I praise, a smile in my voice.

"Uriah waltzed into the pole dancing lesson, got on stage, learned a few pointers from the kind stripper lady, and then pulled out his cellphone. Uriah hooked his phone to the TV broadcasting a sexy pole dancer, and then pressed play."

"You!" Breathless, I sit up so I can look Uriah in the eyes. "Are. My. Hero!"

Chuckling, Uriah cracks a smile, looking pained but amused by my reaction. "To the background soundtrack of the groom and groomsmen calling Uriah a faggot, a cocksucker, a cum-dumpster, with the groom thanking God they used condoms, so they didn't get herpes from the virgin, the camera zooms downward to show Uriah wasn't aroused. Then it pans back up, where Uriah whispers into the camera–"

"Look at 'em– look at those hypocrite men calling me the cocksucker. But they were the ones who paid for it after demanding I do it. They're the ones who got hard for another guy– they're the ones who came in less than a minute with a guy's lips wrapped around their hard dicks. Ladies, the fag wasn't impressed by your guys, but your supposedly straight guys sure do love cheating on you with the fag, so imagine what they do behind your backs with those hot girls you call them out about all the time."

"Barbie dumped Dick. Three of the groomsmen were divorced by their wives or dumped by their girlfriends– one was my sister's boyfriend, who had been around me for years, treating me as a brother-in-law every single day except those three minutes where he demanded I blow him. I was terrified Fiona would hate me, but she thanked me for her future children. The girls didn't blame me, because they'd been there before, been treated like a hole used to extract cum from undeserving guys named Dick."

"I'm sorry you had to go through that, Uriah." Sitting in the grass, the park going quiet as the sun sets around us, my need to make sure Uriah is okay outweighs the insanity to hunt down those assholes and cut their dicks off.

"Mass humiliation at the hands of guys I've known my entire life, guys who might have joined my family, was just the gateway to prostitution. I'd made fifteen-hundred that night, so when my two professors asked me, I said yes."

"What. The. Fuck." I channel my rage into yanking grass out of the ground. "I will find them, and I will–"

"Do nothing." Uriah stops me with a hand to my chest, swirling in a comforting touch. "They are my first and regular clients. They are men past their primes, who no one looks at twice, even on online dating sites. They are good men, lonely men, who respect me, who have mentored me and given me advice, and helped me avoid the Dicks in this world."

"Do they… do they pimp you out?" I try to tread lightly, as I can hear the affection and adoration for these men in Uriah's voice.

"No… and, yes, I have thought about trying to hook them up together, but they aren't compatible, not finding the other attractive either." Uriah shifts, looking uncomfortable. "There's a twenty-year-old at my old college, they just introduced me to last month. They thought we'd hit it off, instead I'm mentoring him to take my place. Wade is more suited for it, willing to go beyond what I am. Plus, I'm never home."

"What do they– what do they have you do?" I fear the impact this will have on Uriah in the future. I now understand why I did what I did with those girls, and a big part of me feels guilty, like I'm one of Uriah's Dicks. But I made sure the girls got what they craved, at the expense of what I needed, not the other way around.

"It's not as horrific as you might think." Uriah busies himself by taking a gulp of Coke, no doubt ordering his thoughts. "One professor is retirement age– ought to have retired long ago. In the year we've had our arrangement, orgasm was only achieved twice. Once a week– last night –I give him a full-body massage. The two times he got aroused, I jerked him off. That's it. All humans need touch, just another hunger no different than food and water and oxygen."

"I don't think I could do it," blurts out my mouth, and Uriah stiffens next to me. "I'm not judging, and it's not what you think," I go on the defensive before he gets pissed at me. "Maybe it's that demisexual brain in my head, when I thought this is how everyone felt. But I just couldn't touch someone like that."

"All those girls?" Incredulous, Uriah's eyebrow raises high enough to almost reach his hairline. "Explain that, Casanova."

"That's a story similar to your bachelor party, Uriah– another time, because I'm too emotionally wrung out to do it tonight."

Uriah reaches through the grass, fingertips coming to rest on the top of my hand. "Understood." Slipping between my fingers, Uriah curls his until we're holding hands. The contact is nice, feels good, but it's comforting too.

"The other professor is middle-aged, but he's overweight and has zero confidence. His sex-drive is higher, alternating handjobs and blowjobs every other day. Almost like a sex addiction, I guess. He's kind and shy, and he's helping me break in Wade because he's wanting things against my rules, things Wade is willing to do for him."

"Do you think… is Wade okay with this?" Mind spinning, I think of ways to protect this kid from his professor.

"You should look in a mirror right now." Uriah struggles not to laugh, fingers tightening around mine. "You truly are a cowboy, aren't you? Riding in to save the day… Wade is a big boy, with a lot more experience than I have, getting a high off his professor paying him to fuck when everyone else thinks they ought to get it for free."

"I guess it makes sense when you put it that way." Now it's my turn to use my drink as an excuse to think for the few seconds it takes to open my Gatorade, have a gulp, and screw the cap back on. "How did you branch out to students?"

Smirking, Uriah has to bite his lip to stop himself from laughing outright. "First week I was on campus, another guy named Dick– they're the only ones I attract, the ones I can spot a mile away, and the ones I want nothing to do with. Dick was straight, attracted to my gender fluidness and my androgynous appearance. He asked me to blow him, never offering to date me, touch me, return the favor. So I told him to pay for it."

"And he did," I mutter, fury roiling in my veins.

"Nope," Uriah pops the P, amused by how enraged I've become so quickly. "A geeky queer kid overhead– he was a virgin. He asked me how much, and I just blurted out ten bucks, having no clue. Told him he had to wear a condom and not to touch me. I sucked him off in the bathroom, for all of thirty seconds… been sucking him off randomly ever since. He told a friend, his friend told another friend, and I've got a handful of regular clients, but I'm getting pickier about doing anyone else."

"Why?" I'm terrified, terrified something happened, terrified something will happen, terrified Uriah will be caught, arrested, and his future will go up in smoke.

"You saw that guy the other day, how entitled he was, how quick to anger he became– I can't do that anymore." Leaning back in the grass, Uriah sighs heavily. "Only my regulars from now on, as I wean them off me and onto other people… I'm sick of sucking cock and getting nothing out of it but some cash. I need more."

"I'm not going to tell you to stop–"

"I can read your mind, cowboy." Uriah rolls onto his side, stares at me with intensity, then rushes forward to kiss the tip of my nose. "I wouldn't do you like that, and I'm starting to think I deserve more than I've been giving myself."

Stunned, staring wide-eyed at Uriah, my nose tingles from the smallest of touches.

A beatific smile breaches Uriah's face, and then he sobers. "Duty calls." Rising to his feet, he brushes grass off his perfect ass. "Another client to dump tonight." After taking a few steps away from me, as if he can sense I'm on the verge of calling him back, "Text me a time and place, and we'll catch a meal and go toy shopping tomorrow night– I'm in class until four."

ICED TEA, BLACK COFFEE, KEEP THAT PEPSI

Kaden glares at me from Sybil's passenger seat, embarrassed over how I won the argument against driving the Durango, since Uriah wouldn't recognize it. Never argue with a pre-law student, just saying.

"You gonna pull my ass out of this contraption?" No one pouts or seethes better than Kaden Marx. "Half my ass is pressed up against the door. I'ma feel like a can of Pillsbury biscuits poppin' when you open the door."

Chuckling with a huge shit-eating grin on my face, I jump out of the car and quickly run around to the other side. Before Kaden can react, I've got his door swung open. His leg pops out first, Wolverine boot pounding on the pavement, with half an ass cheek overflowing the seat.

"Poppin' fresh," I taunt, hauling Kade up to his feet. Then, while he's still stunned, I poke him in the tummy. "Squee!"

"You fucking nut. Ugh!" Kaden is so prissy– he inspects the tail on his flannel. "It was hanging out the door, getting filthy." Voice dropping into a whine, "I wanted to impress your boyfriend."

"It was a three-minute drive." Biting my lip, I wipe road dust off his butt. "Suck it up. You're just grumpy because you're jealous."

"If you think your new man isn't jealous of me, you've got another think coming." Kaden arches an eyebrow while casting his gaze around the parking lot for a Subaru– what kind, Uriah never said. "I also think he's a virgin."

"No way," I scoff. "I told you everything about him, how the hell would you come to that conclusion?"

"Instinct." Being the tallest thing in the parking lot, outside of the sign and lamp posts, Kaden spots Uriah first. "Over there." Pointing at a Subaru Forester, "The car doesn't match the driver," is muttered begrudgingly while staring at Sybil with bitter hatred. "My Durango fits me to a T."

"It's a hand-me-down from Uriah's godmother– maybe it fits Rain to a T?"

"True," Kaden muses as he walks off with Uriah as his destination. "But that doesn't explain Sybil."

"What about Jack?" I ask of Ransom's car.

"Fits the driver," Kaden murmurs, not bothering to contain his smirk, because he knows he's pressing my buttons. "You're going to faint when you get a gander at your man." A low whistle sounds from between Kade's lips. "Jesus fucking Christ, this is gonna be interesting."

"Why are you getting your phone out?" Hurrying to catch up to Kade's larger stride, I already sound out of breath. Those butterflies are assaulting my guts with a vengeance– they've upgraded to a Gears of War Lancer, its chainsaw bayonet tearing into my guts. "Don't be rude– whatever texts you want to send, you can wait."

"Yeah, *texting…*" Kade snorts, one eye trained on me, one trained on Uriah, when I still can't see him over the other cars. The cellphone is raised, and I fear he's making fun of Uriah, but then I realize Kaden is recording me for some baffling reason.

…and then I see him.

From the shoulders up, Uriah is visible, with a pickup truck blocking the rest of the view. Feet stuttering as I attempt to walk forward, I almost end up ass-over-tea-kettle. "He dressed up for you." Kaden's words barely register. "Or maybe he's trying to impress me– jealous much?"

"Hi," I breathe softly, coming around the truck to get a better look at Uriah. "You look beautiful." Uriah fluffed up his stick-straight hair and outlined his eyes. The results are so striking, I notice little else.

"Hi," Uriah breathes back, eyes only on me.

Leaning down, "Virgin," Kaden whispers into my ear. "Look at his blush." As he straightens to his full height, Uriah's eyes are drawn upward. "You really are the most exotic thing I've ever seen," Kade admits with begrudging respect, thrusting his right hand out for a shake while still recording me with his left.

Releasing Kaden's hand, "Lumberjack?" Uriah swallows, throat muscles drawing my undivided attention. "You're not fronting, are you? That's not a costume."

Eyes held wide, Uriah gazes up and down Kaden's body, from his steel-toed boots, rugged denim, Hanes white t-shirt, plaid flannel, scruffy beard, and those thick curls bundled at the top of his head.

Uriah swallows again, and this time it's me who's jealous.

"A lumberjack who can't swing an axe is what my buddy loves to call me– Warren can be a bit of an ass, but he's like a brother to me."

"Future brother-in-law, right?" Uriah looks back and forth between us, asking if he got the connection correct. "Warren is Wynn's older brother?"

"Been talking about me, I see." Kaden pretends to be put out, but the blinding smile breaking across his face is answer enough– he loves being the center of attention.

"Why are you recording us?" is a furious whisper in Kade's direction, my voice breaking with mortification. "Stop it."

"Ransom demand." Kaden chuckles at his own joke.

Turning, I mouth over my shoulder at the camera, knowing Uriah can't see. *"I'm going to kill my nephew, and then I'm coming for you."* Stepping away, I'm drawn to Uriah. "Those jeans again– you're killing me."

Kaden and his cinematography fade into the background as I finally take in all of Uriah. With his poofed up hair, full makeup, a see-through blouse with half the buttons undone, nipples on full display, and those low-rise jeans– so low, there's a two-inch swath of pale, flawless skin showing. I'm dying. As another nail in my coffin, my eyes outline his dick, a noticeable ridge showing exactly where the head pushes at the denim.

Face a brilliant shade of red, Uriah's eyes flash away, like he's too embarrassed to look at me. "I have a confession." He presses up closer, driving me to the edge of insanity, and I notice we're no longer nose-to-nose. "I went all out as a test to see how you'd react to me looking like this in public."

"Did I pass?" Eyeing the short heels Uriah is wearing, I smile to myself. "Ainsley calls those kitten heels– very sexy."

Lips curling with unveiled pleasure, "You never fail to surprise me, Daniel Bishop."

"I'm hungry," Kaden whines, but he's still recording the moment. "We need to get a table before there's a mad-rush of hungry early birds."

Rolling my eyes at Kaden, my hand automatically curls around Uriah's waist, fingertips unable to stop themselves from playing with that enticing strip of bare skin. Heels or no heels, Uriah fits perfectly against my side.

Kaden picked IHOP of all places to share his first meal with Uriah. But, then again, I've eaten with Uriah at the dining hall and had Subway in the park– I'm making one helluva cheap impression on the guy.

In a haze, we're seated in a booth with Kaden smirking at us from the other side of the table. Kade and Uriah have been carrying on a conversation, but I'm completely oblivious because my mind is focused on the feel of Uriah's skin beneath my hand.

"Welcome to IHOP!" Our perky server must've just come on shift, because no way would anyone be that shiny after working here for more than five minutes. "What can I get you guys?"

"Coke." Uriah automatically goes first, which has a scowl on Kade's face– Kaden is the center of attention, remember?

"Pepsi okay, hun?" The server flashes a smile, already writing it down on the order pad.

Twisting his face up in detest, "Coffee," Uriah grumbles, annoyed because he's apparently addicted to Coke.

"Iced tea." Kaden says next, refusing to go last, causing Uriah to snort beside me.

"Sweet tea?" Perky server just stepped in a pile of shit by assuming the big guy with the West Virginian accent wanted sugar-laden tea.

"Black and strong, loads of ice," Kaden nearly growls. "If it's orange pekoe, I want coffee instead."

Stressed by our order already, with a bunch of scratches over the assumptions she made, the server turns to me with a tight smile. "What can I get you, hun?"

"Coffee would be great." I smile to take the sting away from her interactions with the picky, spoiled brats at the table. "Thanks."

"I'll go fetch your drinks and give you time to look over the menus."

"What's up with the tea?" Uriah is asking immediately.

Almost simultaneously, "What's up with the Pepsi?" Kaden is lobbing across the table.

As they engage in a staring contest of wills, I answer them both. "Uriah is addicted to Coke– Kaden's grandfather would only drink sweet tea, and it was syrupy and thick. Kaden rebelled by refusing to drink anything but unsweetened. It also pisses him off when people make assumptions about his accent."

"Nothing is better than tea brewing in an old gallon pickle jar out in the sun– no need to add anything but ice." Kade folds his arms over his chest, nodding to himself. "Two cups of sugar that man would dump into my jar of tea, thinking I wouldn't notice. The sediment was obvious. Yuck!"

"Pepsi and Coke taste nothing alike." Uriah folds his arms over his chest, mimicking Kaden, staring contest still in effect. "I hate when they try to pass one off as the other."

If it wasn't for the fact they are doing a pissing contest over me, I may get annoyed by their behavior. But it's a bit of an ego trip to see two hot people fighting over me, especially when I care about both of them.

Our drinks arrive, and we order quickly. No one is surprised at this point when Kaden orders half the menu with substitutions, Uriah wants a turkey sandwich, and I go for an appetizer platter.

How quickly we learn to operate without stepping on any toes, after a few insults are slung intentionally, and I have to intervene. The conversation flows seamlessly once I put firm boundaries down, since Uriah is known to toss his beverages, and hot coffee will hurt Kaden's broody face more than an ice-cold Coke would.

Smirking, I listen instead of join in, amused how the giant masculinity versus androgynous gender-fluidness can have similar personalities. Other than the outside packaging, I apparently have a type I hadn't realized existed.

High maintenance– I'm attracted to high maintenance.

"Journalism, huh?" Kaden eyes Uriah with suspicion. "You're nosy then, yeah?"

"I prefer inquisitive," Uriah volleys back, biting his lip against a smirk. "I'm a seeker of truths... elementary education? I take it you like kids."

"That sounded suspiciously like you're calling me a pervert," Kaden snarls, baring his crooked front tooth.

Eyes going wide, I shake my head at Uriah before he says anything else. Kaden has more landmines than Uriah and I do combined.

"Miriam– she went to college with my mom. Miriam is Kaden's cousin and guardian of sorts. Anyway, she's the school board president for the school district Kade went to–"

"Our schools are filled with ancients ready to retire, so there'll be a position for me when I want one," Kaden mutters with a shrug. "But what I'd rather do is become a school counselor."

"That's a lot more studying." Uriah's eyes dart in my direction, surprised. "I thought you were going back to your hometown…" he trails off, apparently wanting Kaden out of my orbit.

"There are colleges and universities in West Virginia, ya know?" Kaden narrows his eyes at Uriah, pissing contest renewing. "Communications degree, huh? That's a waste of paper and the ink it's printed on it."

"So…" Shifting on the padded booth bench, I rest a hand on Uriah's thigh to keep him seated, knowing he has a fiery temper. "Kaden's excited to get home after graduation. Wynn will be sixteen this December."

"Sixteen?" Uriah raises an eyebrow, looking directly across the table, baiting Kaden. "Like 'em young, dontcha? Isn't that statutory rape?"

Coughing into my cupped palm, "Not in West Virginia." I cough again.

"Didn't say I was gonna touch Wynn." Kade looks away quickly, but I know that look– Uriah's hits landed with wounding impact. Grumbling underneath his breath, Kade's words are almost inaudible. "He'll almost be seventeen by the time I move home. I'll behave. Fuck eighteen, I'll wait until he's twenty-one."

Kaden is stubborn and determined enough to do just that, and it terrifies me.

Face softening, Uriah reaches across the table to touch the back of Kaden's hand. "Sorry, I'm being a bitch." Eyes hitching in my direction, Uriah doesn't have to explain. "As long as you're going back home to Wynn, then I can deal with whatever you've got going on with Dan."

"I can share, if you can." Uriah's fingers clench against Kaden's hand. "I'm just lonely, and it's killing me."

Kade and Uriah make nice, and my smile couldn't get any wider. "What are you doing this weekend?" I turn to Uriah, not bothering to ask Kade first. His schedule is imprinted in my brain. "My family is having a gathering– Miriam and her son are going to be there," I say pointedly at Kaden, making sure he knows he's coming with me, no matter what. Kade loves to run away from Miriam, avoiding her at all costs, emotionally unable to handle her mothering him.

Turning back to Uriah, "You can meet my family."

"Imprinted baby birdie," Uriah whispers underneath his breath, but I hear it anyway. "You sure do move fast."

Mid-suck of his iced tea, Kaden nearly chokes to death as the act of drinking interferes with his snorting.

Standing, I reach over the table to pat Kade's back firmly while he tries to catch his breath. After batting me away, he sucks his ice dry.

Sitting back down, "Want me to slow up?" I ask Uriah, not wanting him to think me a nutjob. "Sorry if I'm being too forward."

In answer, Uriah rolls his eyes at me and Kaden snickers into his cup. "Word of advice..." Kaden points his straw at Uriah. "If you're not feeling Danny, let him know now. Otherwise, start planning the wedding, because our boy doesn't *date*."

"What do you mean, I don't date?" Scoffing, I grab the straw out of Kaden's hand.

"You never have, and I don't mean you didn't date your conquests." Reaching in, Kaden fishes out a small chunk of ice and then pops it into his mouth. "You're zero to wedding bands." Crunch. Crunch. Crunch. More ice. "It's like once you tuned into who you truly are, you're going strong. That denial saved your ass many a time, my friend."

"Says the guy who's waiting for a kid to grow up," blurts out before I can stop it. Eyes wide, I wait for Kaden to throw a temper tantrum in the middle of IHOP. It would be a classic Kaden Marx move.

Instead, I'm met with Kaden and Uriah sharing a laugh at my expense, bonding over my terror.

"How about those Cubs?" Uriah murmurs, grinning across the table at Kaden.

"Ha! Danny told you that story about Ainsley's prom too?"

"Do you guys want me to leave so you can be alone?" Jealous, annoyed, even I want to be the center of attention once in a while, not the butt of a joke.

Taking pity on me, Kaden catches the eye of our server. "I'm paying– don't even fuck with me, Uriah." Lifting his hips slightly, Kaden struggles to wedge his hand into his back pocket to pull out his wallet.

Uriah is too busy gawking at Kaden's package to give two shits about bitching about who's paying for our meal.

Kade tosses a few small bills on the table, and a handful of change. "Danny, don't even think of adding anything to that tip," he warns. "Never once checked in on us, and I'm so fucking thirsty, I had to suck my ice cubes. You bastards had to have coffee– ugh!"

"Now what?" Looking back and forth between them, I'm not ready to call it a night.

"Toys," they say in unison, sharing a naughty smirk.

Standing from the booth, Kaden turns into Demanda. "I'm commandeering your Subaru until we get back to campus– you and Danny can squeeze into that bullshit car of his."

HOW ABOUT THOSE CUBS?

Since Kade stole his vehicle, I tossed my keys to Uriah as consolation. It's a bit of a drive, and we're following behind Kade, who drives like a Crash Test Dummy.

"That guy has a death wish," Uriah hisses underneath his breath as Kade blows through yet another stop sign. "In my car."

"I let Kade drive us to Pittsburgh in his tank of an SUV, because we shave a good forty-five minutes off the trip."

"Plus–" Uriah turns to smirk at me. "Sybil can barely reach the posted speed limit."

"Ha-ha, not funny," I grumble, staring at the Forester's tail lights, fearing Kade is trying to lose us on purpose. "Can I ask you something objectively?"

"You have me intrigued, Daniel Bishop." Uriah pulls out my whole name when he's surprised by me– I like it, and I hope he never learns my middle name, because that would be a mouthful.

"I always figured how I felt was normal–"

"Your normal is your normal," Uriah cuts in, concentrating on keeping up with Kade.

"Yeah, but what I was getting at is how I never realized I was any different than anyone else. I obviously look at you and Kade a certain way– like I can't keep my hands off you, and I have this insane need to kiss Kade–"

"Don't go there. Please," Uriah begs, voice cracking.

I put him out of his misery, "No kissing Kade– that's a rule of ours. We haven't touched since, and to be honest, what I want, I'm not going to take. It's an exercise in self-restraint, but I'm behaving."

"You're saying you don't want to have sex with Kaden?" The incredulity in Uriah's voice almost has me laughing, because he's making my point for me.

"Kinda hard to have sex when you can't kiss, at least now that I'm not having straight sex."

"Confusion." Uriah gestures ahead of himself, out the windshield. "Confusion as far as the eye can see. You're gonna have to explain that shit, cowboy."

"When I was doing girls, I took them from behind, never kissing them. The only sex I've had with the same sex was much more intimate. I can't seem to wrap my mind around sex without the intimacy anymore."

"No kissing Kade means no having sex with Kade?" Uriah is catching on.

"Exactly– watching each other jerk off is hot and all, but not the same… I'm not complaining, I more than understand. But that's not what I'm getting at, not really."

"Get to the point before I experience a fit of road-rage and drive your car into the back of mine at the next red light, just so I can permanently harm the object of your affections."

"Jealousy is a good color on you." Laughing, I rest my hand on Uriah's thigh, loving how the muscles contract beneath my touch. "With girls, I pretty much took what they offered. I didn't feel this insanity, where I had to touch them. I thought that was how everyone felt. The orgasm wasn't my driving force. With you, I finally know what lust means, but that's only gotten stronger the more I'm around you."

"I'm liking where this is going." Uriah rests his hand over mine, pressing my palm harder against his thigh.

"But, as I was watching you and Kade do this lust-hate thing, I realized that's not how normal people–"

"There is no such thing as normal people, but if you mean people who aren't on the asexual spectrum, then yeah… a visual, a sound, a scent, a touch, a taste is all it takes to get our motors running."

"So I really don't think and feel like everyone else?" I'm glad I'm not the one driving, because I'm on a cusp of going off-line mentally to survive this gut-twisting sensation.

"Yeah, Kade and I were eye-fucking each other, liking the way the other looked, but that's where our morals and convictions kick in to keep us from acting like savages."

"That's how most people feel?" I think of Ransom, so goddamn horny, he gave one of his friends a blowjob today, having no desire to save that for someone who mattered. He was gloating on the phone after sending me a glowing selfie with two thumbs up.

"You needed to feel like a man with the women– I don't get why, but I understand. Emotional connection leads you to lust if the person trips one of your triggers. Being demisexual, faithfulness isn't so much of a concept than something that is hardwired into your personality, which is why I keep teasing you about being an imprinted baby bird. For the rest of us, being faithful is a difficult choice we have to make, similar to how you say love is a choice."

Pulling into the parking lot, Uriah parks and then pulls the keys out of the ignition. Turning to me, he can no doubt sense I'm losing my shit.

Slowly rolling my eyes up to look at Uriah, my voice warbles, "I'm a weirdo? You think I'm acting desperate and clingy?"

Flashing me a sad smile, Uriah leans toward me, then presses his lips to my cheek. "You have no idea what a prize you are, do you?" Pulling away, his hair tickles my forehead. "I don't feel like I deserve you, but that's not for me to decide."

"That's a bizarre thing to say." Mind spinning, I can't get heads or tails on what that could possibly mean.

"Kaden and I are a lot alike, so do me a favor." Uriah slips out of the car, shutting the door behind him softly. I follow, noticing Kade is giving us privacy, no doubt our expressions are giving us away.

"What favor?" I stop Uriah with a hand on his shoulder. "What do you mean?"

"We think alike." Uriah turns to me, smiling the most pitiful of smiles. "We like the same type of guys. We feel the same self-loathing." Chuckling without humor, Uriah knocks the wind out of me. "We're exactly your type... the favor– if this Wynn kid is anything like you, make sure Kade doesn't fuck it up because he doesn't think he deserves him."

"Like you're going to fuck us up?" I guess.

"No." Uriah grabs my hand, then pulls me to wrap my arm around his waist again, like when we were back at IHOP. "I like the way you look at me, the way you make me feel, the way you touch me and talk to me and open up to me, way too much to fuck it up and lose you. There wouldn't be lust-hate between Kade and me if I wasn't planning on fighting to keep you as mine."

Speechless, eyes-wide, I walk beside Uriah to the front of the store. Kaden falls into step beside me, cellphone in his hand.

"I'm starting to think your true passion lies in being a paparazzi," Uriah mutters wryly, and I have no idea what's he's talking about.

Kaden snickers sadistically, stowing his phone in his back pocket. "I'm going to make Danny look at the pics and videos later, because the guy never looks in a mirror when I tell him to."

"That expression…" Uriah trails off on a smug giggle.

"Stop talking about me like I'm not here." I sound grumpy, but I'm secretly ecstatic they're bonding through picking on me. "Lord, this place is something else, isn't it? It's a dinky pole barn in the middle of nowhere."

"It looks a helluva lot better than most of the buildings in Rusty Knob." Spoiled rotten Kaden looks perfectly at home, when I'm anxious we may get mugged by a dude hiding on the side building, while standing in the dark as night parking lot.

"Bob calls these places adult book stores–"

"Who's Bob?" Neither Kade nor Uriah makes a move to enter the establishment, dragging their feet because they're nervous– it's adorable.

"And Bob's my uncle." Chuckling at his own joke, Uriah is acting silly. "Nah, he's my dad, for all intents and purposes. Anyway, Pennsylvania is chock full of *adult book stores*. We make a few trips up to Seneca Falls a year–"

"Where the hell is Seneca Falls?"

"Upstate, New York." Uriah glares at Kaden for interrupting his story. "Every trip up there, there are less and less of the places open. Bob will whine about it, and Rain– my godmother –she'll start singing Video Killed the Radio Star."

"Oh, my God, I have to meet this woman." Realizing I interrupted, I zip my lips shut.

"What? I don't get it." Kaden pouts, looking beyond confused.

"Porno, as Bob calls it–" Uriah rolls his eyes. "Was killed off by the internet, taking away all the adult book stores."

Kaden laughs, shaking his head, catching onto the joke a minute or two too late. "The internet is killing off most stores, now that we can buy online. I would've bought toys online too, but I wanted to touch 'em first."

"I'll never forget this one place, about an hour or so from the New York State border." Uriah keeps speaking as if Kaden isn't interrupting him. "They had all this leather stuff, and American flags, and chainsaw carvings, and a bunch of motorcycles parked out front. RJ and I would whine, trying to get Bob to stop, and he'd always turn to Rain and say, *'Looks like one of those adult book stores, doesn't it?'*"

"Leather, eh?" My interest piques, instinctively knowing it was the leather drawing Uriah in.

Blushing, Uriah talks right over me, directing it at Kaden. "Maybe you ought to pick up a chainsaw and do some carvings? Rain would love a cuddly bear... maybe a garden gnome?"

"Ha-ha... ha!" Kaden mock laughs, glaring. "My hand-eye coordination is so bad, I'd probably cut someone's foot off in the next county... I always pretended to help with the manual labor."

A fond expression etches across Kaden's face. Oblivious to both Uriah and me, we share a look, waiting for Kaden to elaborate. When he doesn't, Kade receives a swat and a punch to the chest.

"Don't hold back on us, bro," I beg, hand stinging from his brawny chest.

"Asshat, give up the goods!" Uriah flings his hand, trying to get the blood flowing– the punch was from him.

The goofiest look crosses Kade's face, smile loaded with affection. "You know I'm a lazy bastard, Danny– not once have I cleaned our room." Moving to lean against the side of the store, his arms hanging loosely, Kade stares out into the distance.

"Okay, so this is totally embarrassing..." Kade covers his flaming face with his palms, hiding like he does under his blankies. "The last I spent any time with Wynn was *years* ago. I was pretending to help split wood– remember, I can't swing an axe to save my life. Anyway, Corbin– Warren and Wynn's alcoholic father –he's going off on me something fierce, and I had no idea why at the time...

"Warren drags Corbin back into the shack, leaving Wynn and me alone with a big pile of wood to stack. Something you need to know about Wynn– the kid has no modesty, no filter. He would run around in these Britney Spears cutoff shorts year-round, with the white pockets hanging down they were so short, and absolutely nothing else. Just those shorts, barely covering his junk, an angelic grin, and six feet of golden tan."

"I need a pic, or it isn't true," Uriah reminds me, flashing a naughty grin.

"For once, I wanted to pick up my own slack, hating how the kid worked so fucking hard and no one would help him, always with a smile on his face. I was protective of Wynn back then, trying to push those perverted thoughts from my head. Skinny, gangly, too dang tall, with zits and bad hair, and covered in scars. Grotesque–"

Uriah's eyes connect with mine, shocked Kaden could ever look that way. With a quick shake of my head, I try to communicate that Kaden has a problem with recognizing how he actually looks.

"I've always worn layers of clothing to cover the scars, but it was boiling hot out, and I was working for once. So I pulled up my shirt to wipe my brow, not realizing I exposed my hips and stomach, and when I pushed it back down, I noticed Wynn was freaking out– I was terrified that I'd somehow traumatized Wynn with how I looked.

"Wynn started hollering, *"War! Warren!"* In a panic, the kid was crying, face as white as a sheet, calling for his big brother to save him. I fell to my ass, thinking I'd hurt Wynn somehow– the unthinkable. Warren runs out, looking around Gillette Holler as if someone popped out of the aluminum piles to rob 'em of the rust.

"Wynn runs right up to Warren, hanging onto him for dear life. The kid was already a head taller and six inches wider than his big brother. Warren was trying to get him to calm down enough to explain…"

Uriah and I lean forward, trying to hear Kaden as his words get softer and softer, diction changing. The expression on his face goes from pained to amusement in a single heartbeat.

"War!" Kaden calls loudly, mimicking Wynn. *"War! War, help me! My dick done broke– Kaden broke my dick!"*

Bending at the waist, palms resting on his thighs, Kaden is laughing so hard he's rendered breathless. Head popping up, Kade catches both Uriah's and my gaze. "Here I was, sitting in a wood pile, getting splinters in my ass, eyes fucking huge, feeling like a goddamn pervert, because I was the cause of Wynn getting his first erection– and the boy was hung. H. U. N. G. HUNG!"

Kade parts his hands like he's telling a tall fish tale, and it's a motherfucking huge fish. "Warren comes running out after escorting Wynn into the shack, looking furious but he's laughing hysterically. My best friend– *my brother* –he hauls off and punches me so hard I see stars. It's a good thing I was already sitting on my ass, let me tell you, 'cuz Warren's built like a goddamn bull."

Speechless, all Uriah and I can do is stare at Kaden as that self-deprecating laugh reaches an all new pitch. Never once has he told me this story in the nearly four years we've been friends.

"Warren's laughing, because how was it possible Wynn didn't know what a hard-on was when he's from the Holler, when Warren bred coonhounds for cash, and Warren wasn't shy about fucking girls against the shed with Wynn nearby. Warren had shoved Wynn in the shower, and told the kid to jerk off… but the kid didn't know what that meant, and I highly doubt he's ever jerked off in his life to this day.

"Warren was seething, laughing, and crying, and begged me to lie to him– to tell him Wynn wasn't gay." Kaden sobers, staring me right in the eyes. "Couldn't do it– couldn't lie, even though we live in one of the most intolerant places in America… still innocent and embarrassed, the kid came out of the house fresh from the shower, still hard as a rock, eyes never leaving me as we finished stacking the wood pile… so I've stayed away."

"Oh, Kaden," Uriah and I cry out in unison, moving in tandem to rest our palms on his curled shoulders in comfort.

Looking up at us, Kaden rocks our worlds. "Wynn has one helluva work ethic– since sex isn't on his radar, he's on track to be valedictorian, all the while working a fulltime job, playing basketball, and taking care of his family. Wynn acts like a middle-aged guy in need of Viagra– and everyone back home knows I'm Wynn's Viagra."

"Jesus Christ," is hissed, and I don't know by who– maybe me, maybe not.

"When I go home, part of me makes sure Wynn catches sight of me, so he never forgets me. The Gillettes call me a pervert–

Warren too. Royce gets pissed at me, and Bren thinks it's hilarious. Wynn doesn't realize, the instant I get near him, he's walking around with a baseball bat in his pants, and that fucking terrifies Royce… so I stay away, and I wait and wait and wait. Because it has nothing to do with Wynn turning sixteen, or eighteen, or twenty-one, and everything to do with how I know Wynn will find me when he's ready… and when he does, I'm never letting him go."

Sniffling draws my attention, and I catch Uriah pulling his curled hand from his eyes, leaving smudged eyeliner behind.

Smiling at Kaden, "And you call me the romantic," I tease, heart squeezing with how fucking sweet yet insane that story was.

"You are." Kaden's eyes cut to a weepy Uriah, then back to me. "I'm not a romantic– I'm not living in a fantasy… I'm waiting for my reality." Kaden stands upright, then leans in to whisper in my ear so Uriah can't overhear. "Which is why we can never kiss again, because love is a choice, and I've made mine." Then he walks into the store as if he never said a word.

Swallowing, brushing renegade tears from his cheeks, I can tell Uriah heard what Kaden said in parting. "How about those Cubs?" he says with a weak smile, and this is the moment I fall in love with Uriah Crane.

A PROSTITUTE'S KISS

"Holy shit!" Kaden presses a jellylike phallus to the front of his jeans, and then pretends to jerk it off, really getting into it. Too bad Uriah and I are finding it erotic instead of comical. "It's got to be at least eighteen inches. Who the hell could take it all?"

"Wait a minute…" My brain is slow to process, I'm figuring it out, but Uriah beats me to it by stealing the dong from Kaden. "It has two heads," I point out, getting closer to understanding.

Wordlessly, Uriah handles the dong with care, positioning it horizontally, one head pointed at himself, the other at Kaden. I join the fray by putting my hand in the middle and moving it back and forth in example.

"I still don't get it." Kaden was never the quickest, truly struggling in his classes. He's not dim, but it takes hammering the knowledge into his thick skull. Repeatedly. With great patience.

"Somewhere, in the land of unicorns and sunshine," Uriah murmurs wryly. "There are these mythical beasts known as bottoms, and sometimes they fall in love with each other– or maybe they're just horny… they lie on their backs, butts touching, and hopefully a third party helps them insert their new butt-buddy, and then they wiggle around and jerk off."

"How do you know this?" Tone serious, Kaden is in interrogation mode. "Have you done it? Was this knowledge in your prostitute handbook?"

"Video Killed the Radio Star," Uriah replies with a straight face, and then wanders off in the land of sex toys, lubricants, prophylactics, and BDSM gear.

"I don't…" Kade puts the toy away, expression one of pure confusion, as I struggle not to laugh at him. "Oh! The internet!" Then he wanders away, and I give up on smothering my laughter.

I'm a social beast, and I'm out of my element, so instead of roaming aimlessly, I find the one person who knows what we need to know. The man just so happens to look like he used to own that leather-selling, American-flag-flying, chainsaw-carving, bike-riding adult book store near the New York State border.

Did I happen to mention Pennsylvania has more colleges and universities than most states? But we also have more adult book stores… and prisons. Major prisons.

My inner politician– those rat-bastard traits that come in handy in situations such as these –comes out to play. Smile friendly, I lean against the counter, praying to God this tattooed biker dude with the chain connecting his ear and nose piercings isn't a homophobe.

"I've never been in here before," I admit, laughing at myself.

Brows dipping over his deep-set eyes, a scar bisecting his forehead pulls at his skin. "You don't say…" he drawls out, thick southern accent north of the Mason-Dixon, nicotine-stained goatee long enough to French braid.

"That obvious, huh?"

In reply, the dude points at Kaden, who is testing dongs for size by jerking them off, then to Uriah, who is holding a frilly corset up to his chest, also for size.

Leaning over the counter, the guy whispers his menthol-fresh breath right into my face. "We won't have a problem unless you kids are doing some bullshit rite of passage by coming in here. If you're in here because you actually need something, but you're too innocent to know what that may be, I'll be more than happy to help."

"Thank you," I stammer, relieved. "We. Need. Help."

"Just floating this out there, 'cuz you look about ready to shit your preppy pants, you're so scared." With a wink, the guy shocks the hell out of me. "I'm bi, and I know how to use every item in this store, on both men and women– there is nothing you can tell me that will come off as a surprise. Hit me."

"That's a relief." My body sags to go along with my words. "I'm a pretty vanilla dude, myself… but my friend, he's in a long-distance relationship with his boyfriend." That sounds so much better than the truth. "And he's lonely. The boyfriend doesn't care if we jerk off together, but in the heat of the moment–"

"Big guy, right?" The sex-seller hits the nail on the head, lust sparking out his dark eyes in Kaden's direction. "He's ripe for the picking, isn't he? Yeah, we need to curtail that if we're going to keep him faithful, eh?"

"Precisely– anal is definitely his thing. We're thinking a butt-plug, maybe? Some masturbatory aids, because I don't think his own fingers will trip his trigger." A trigger I can't stop thinking about– Kaden went fucking insane when I found his prostate. What would Uriah do?

The dude flashes me a knowing smirk, no doubt my thoughts are being broadcast across my face. "Big guy is too tempting, and you're trying to keep yourself out of his honeypot, because you're into the little fella caressing my lingerie department."

"How did you–"

"Therapists use a sofa. Barbers a chair. Bartenders a stool... but the person selling sexual aids knows their clients' deepest and darkest desires– stay right where you are, I'll be right back."

Leaning against the counter, I find Kaden's interaction with the dude the most entertaining moment of my life. Uriah eventually finds his way over to me, falling into the same position I'm taking.

"This is so bizarre," Uriah drawls out. "I'm too innocent for this store– I'm motherfucking lost."

"Me too." I point down to my feet. "Notice I haven't moved an inch." Uriah laughs, which was what I was going for. Mutually amused, we watch Kaden turn the most animated I've ever seen him, which causes the clerk to become just as animated.

"Hope Kade brought his credit card," Uriah whispers near my ear, cuddling up against me. "Because this shit is expensive."

"Cheaper on the internet?" I ask as a trap to see if Uriah isn't as innocent as he says he is.

Whipping out his cellphone, "Don't know, but let's find out," Uriah begins scrolling through Amazon. "Ah, everything is waaaayyy marked up."

"Check this out, Danny!" Kade strides up to me, huge grin on his face while juggling toys. "This is perfect." A black butt-plug is slapped onto the counter, followed by a gigantic purple dong with visible veins. Giggling to himself, Kade suction-cups the dong to the front of the counter, then flicks it with a fingertip. "For fun in the shower!"

"Oh. My. God. This cannot be happening– I'm not here. This isn't real." Uriah turns crimson as all the blood in his body is split between two locations– his face and his cock. Those illegal jeans are about to split. Shuddering, he hides his face against my shoulder. "Can't get that image outta my mind– holy fuck, that's hot."

"How much?" Eager, Kade already has his wallet out and is rooting around for his credit card.

My hand immediately lands on Kade's wrist, stopping him. "That go to your trust fund?"

"You have a trust fund?!" Uriah practically shouts in outrage, eyeing Kaden. "How is that possible? You're foster kid from West Virginia, for shit's sake."

"Who said my foster dad was broke?" Kade isn't even insulted, just speaking matter-of-factly. Because even when he was poor, he never went without. Kade's father doted on him. His grandfather may have not known how to interact with him, but he still spoiled Kaden. Then there is Royce and Miriam… and me.

"If you pay with that card, Royce will know what you're buying," I remind Kade, because I know Royce keeps track of every shit Kaden takes. "You and Uriah go out to the cars and figure out who's driving what and where we're going next. Okay?"

"Thank you, Danny!" Kade kisses my cheek just to taunt Uriah, then takes the seething man by the hand like a giddy little kid would.

With the jingle of the bell over the door, the clerk starts in immediately, instinctively knowing his clients. I'm an easy mark who spoils Kaden, and finally gets to spoil Uriah too.

"The nipple clamps with the pink glittery crystals. The corset with the thick ribbons. The pink g-spot vibe, but it works great for prostate stimulation because of its wide base. The double-dong because having two guys at your disposal…"

The dude grabs the stuff in under two minutes, tossing in special lube made for anal, toy cleaner, and a douche bulb with instructional guide specifically for Kade.

By the time I leave, my bank account is half a grand lighter, my big bag is full, and my guys have worked out who's driving what and where we're going next.

"Umm… this doesn't look like any dorm room I've ever been in before." Uriah stops dead in his tracks as soon as I unlock our door and open it for him.

"What is this, Thermopylae?" Kaden complains, slipping past Uriah to get inside. "There are crazies on this hall– let's take it inside."

Lugging the big bag inside, I answer Uriah's unasked question. "It was a surprise to me too, when I came home from our date last night to find the room rearranged."

"I'm not always lazy." Kaden takes the bag from me, tossing it on our now full-sized bed, then begins rooting around in it.

"Your RA doesn't care?" Uriah spies a desk chair with his name written on it.

"I was making a lot of noise moving the beds to one side to create this big beauty." Kaden puffs his chest out with pride. "Jordan knocked, so I cracked the door open and thrust a fifty into his palm. He told me to have fun, and that was that… did you see I bought a memory foam mattress thingy so the crack between the beds wouldn't be noticeable, and I bungeed the legs together so it wouldn't crash apart."

"Ingenious," Uriah mutters, equally impressed and jealous.

"You're staying over, right?" Kaden is beyond perky right now, riding a high. "You have class in the morning here anyway, so why drive home when you can stay over and enjoy the benefits of our new Egyptian cotton sheets and plaid comforter? New cushy pillows too– Bed, Bath, and Beyond was a trip!"

In awe, Uriah and I watch as Kaden roots around in the bag, tossing his treasures to said plaid comforter. He reminds me of Ransom right now– how Ransom always steals the takeout bag from my hands, and then grabs whatever he wants, even if it was meant for me. Yeah, that's what Kaden is doing in the toy bag right now.

"Mine." He hugs that suction dong to his chest like Gollum and his precious. "Mine too." The butt-plug is set on the desk. "Ooooohhhh… smart thinking." The lube goes next to the plug.

I spot the instant Kaden finds the douche, because he hides it as he pulls it out of the bag, always modest, no matter what.

"I think I'm going to go shower." The douche and booklet are hidden in Kade's flannel as he strides over to his toiletry bag. "Behave while I'm gone– there's some awesome stuff in there for you, Uriah."

Leaning back in the desk chair, Uriah crosses his arms over his chest, one nipple visible because his blouse is unbuttoned partially. "Your roommate is something else."

Sitting on the bed, I can't help the satisfied smirk from splitting my lips. "Kade really is, he truly is something else. Everyday it's something else– never a dull moment."

Eyes flicking around the room, somehow noticing things that I hadn't yet. "He likes spending his foster dad's money, eh?" With the beds smooshed together in one corner, the layout changed. Whatever space was created is filled with Kade's newest creature comforts.

"Kaden likes to shop, and he likes new, nice things, but he does it to be kind. He wanted our environment to feel like home, so he kinda went overboard. But he did it for us, not just himself, so it's hard to stay mad at someone when he has good intentions for his bad behavior."

Biting his lip, Uriah stares at me, then he lets it fly. "I see why you said you two would be toxic together– you enable him."

"I do," I admit without hesitation. "I can't help it. I want Kade to be happy, even if it hurts him."

"That Wynn kid?"

"I've met Warren, and he really is built like a bull. Wynn will be as tall as Kade, if you can believe it. So, physically, they are a match. Mentally, Wynn is the town's golden boy– he's brilliant. Emotionally, he's got some fissures there. Mentality– eh, if Wynn can handle his father, he can handle anybody. He's a natural caregiver and a money-minder, and Kaden needs both."

Swirling in the chair, Uriah takes inventory of the desk. Inspecting a paperback, he cracks it open to a random page, then begins reading. While Uriah's distracted, I quickly put away the things I don't want him to see yet, saving them for later, because I know I'm moving too fast with him.

I turn to find Uriah watching me, paperback held open with a fingertip. "Why the bed?" It's a loaded question, but I don't know why it is.

"Truth?" Embarrassed, I blush so hard I feel lightheaded. "My parents did that co-sleeping thing, and I had my grandparents and older sister always cuddling me. Mom said for the first year of my life, I never once slept outside of someone's arms." Covering my face in my hands, I hide like Kade always does.

"I share a king-sized bed with my nephew– I need it," is a desperate admission. "Kaden did the beds for me, to make me feel safe."

In silence, Uriah stands from the chair. Walking over to me, he brings the book with him. Leaning down, he kisses my forehead, lips lingering until I'm left quivering with need. The book is rested open on my thigh.

"Thank you for telling me that." Uriah brushes a stray hair off my forehead, then steps away. "And I'm relieved that's the reason… not gonna lie, your history with Kaden terrifies me, but I'm trying to understand it."

"Just trust me, okay?"

"I do." Stepping away, Uriah pulls his phone from his back pocket. "Now I'm going to text my godmother and tell her I won't be home until tomorrow after class, and you're going to read the part where the book is open."

"I don't understand–"

"I own that book, Dan– just read that passage."

"Don't make me choose!" Todd shouts at Amy, the panic an angry storm cloud settling over their marriage. "It was so subtle– I didn't realize it was cheating until it was too late."

"You love him." Amy's accusation isn't a question, but a definitive statement. She's known her husband for decades, inside and out, and she's terrified of losing him. "I'm at a loss."

"We were just talking, and then we started hanging out while you were with your girls, and then it just progressed. Subtle. I didn't realize until he kissed me…"

Amy recognizes the warble in Todd's voice for what it truly is– terror. Todd's terrified to discover he's been emotionally cheating on Amy. Terrified to discover he wants a man. Terrified of losing Amy. Terrified of disappointing his kids, his wife, his parents, his boss, and his friends. Terrified of losing himself. Terrified of losing Ben.

Terrified.

As badly as Amy's heart is breaking, it's the terror that has compassion sparking. "Do you still love me?"

"Yes!" Todd rushes forward, grabbing Amy's shoulders, leaving fingertip bruises behind. She can sense he's on the verge of panicking because he doesn't want to lose her, doesn't want to hurt her too.

"I know you love me," Amy whispers, as if to say the words aloud hurts too much. "But are you in love with me still, after all these years?"

"Yes." This time Todd breathes the word, and it's filled with all the love he's had for Amy since they were in the fifth grade. But he's not that ten-year-old anymore, or the twenty-year-old, or the thirty-year-old, and the connection Todd has with Ben has nothing to do with Amy. Nothing to do with her failings or his misgivings, or about the love and passion they share, and all about evolving into a grown man who married young and didn't realize he'd change as he aged, while Amy essentially stayed the same.

"I can't explain it, Amy– it just happened. I don't understand it, and I don't know what to do about it. You're the one person I've always come to about these things, but it's about you and me ... and Ben."

Amy asks herself whether or not it's possible to be in love with more than one person. Everything she's ever known tells her the answer is no. How do you wedge another person into your lives? Doesn't the love you feel for another detract from the first.

But, then again, Amy has three beautiful children with Todd, and she fell in love with them while carrying them, never thinking she could love them any more than she did in the moment. Only, every day, she fell in love with them more and more, loving them as they grew up and changed, their idiosyncrasies. The love she felt for one, only strengthened the love she felt for the others, an infinite amount of love for her children.

Can romantic love be like that, Amy asks herself. What about pride, possessiveness, and jealousy? Insecurities? No way could that ever work.

"And Wesley... doesn't Ben have a boyfriend?" Todd and Ben were doubly cheating on both of their significant others.

Amy tries to tell herself it was just a kiss, and Todd immediately came clean, but the damage was already done.

Amy was taught cheating makes them bad people, but the pain radiating from Todd catches the breath in her throat. There are rules that govern betrayals, yet the emotions Amy and Todd are feeling contradict how Amy assumed they would feel in this situation.

Amy is the victim of Todd's betrayal, yet this is hurting Todd more than it's hurting Amy, even if society and the church tells Amy to blame Todd harshly and cast him out of her life.

"We'll figure out something, Amy." The desperation in Todd's voice has an edge of mourning. "For you, for me... for Ben and Wesley too. I can't let you go, but I can't let go of him either."

"I don't–"

"Just listen, okay?" Todd begs Amy, hands quivering where they grab her shoulders. "We'll be friends– all of us. You and I will live our lives separate from them, but spend time together occasionally. Maybe you'll enjoy Ben and Wesley's company, Amy. Just try. Please."

It's wrong of Todd to ask this of Amy. If Amy loved Todd as deeply as she says she does, she should hear his pain and listen to what it's telling her. Instead of being stuck in the victim role, with Todd cast as the villain, Amy needs to decide if she can live with hurting her husband, the best friend she's ever had, by leaving him when he's at his most vulnerable.

If Todd wasn't Amy's husband, but a lifelong friend, she wouldn't slap him in the face and scream and shout and cry and feel betrayed. Amy would swallow her pride and insecurity, and realize this isn't about her, then try to help Todd, even if that means Amy wasn't good for Todd anymore– even if that means finding out Todd isn't good for Amy anymore.

Or, maybe, Amy will find another lifelong friend in Ben, or Wesley, instead of destroying what she has with Todd over a kiss...

The book falls from my fingertips with a sharp clack on the floor. "What the hell am I reading, and why all the sudden do I feel like I need to throw up?" Feeling queasy, I glance up from the book to find Uriah lounging on my bed, scrolling an app on his cellphone.

Tossing his phone onto the mattress, Uriah slowly sits up, then tucks his hair behind his ears. "That was a brutal book to read, let me tell ya. Up and down. Up and down. Gutted me from page one until the end."

"I don't get it." Kicking the fucking thing like it personally offended me, the book flies underneath the bed. "What is that torture? Why read it?"

"It's narrated by all four impacted, Daniel." Uriah smoothly flows off the mattress, hand blindly reaching beneath the bed to retrieve the paperback. Then he tosses it back onto the desk where it came from in the first place.

"It's an in-depth journey of two couples struggling to understand polyamory. Amy and Todd love each other, are committed to each other, but Todd fell hard for Ben, while Ben was also in love with Wesley."

"Please tell me there was a happy ending," I plead, eyes stinging for some disbelieving reason.

Then Uriah's words hit with the force of a hammer to the skull. "It was a true story, Dan– a memoir, each part written by the one who lived through it. They wrote the book to understand each other, and it helped."

"So you're not going to tell me how it ended?" Lunging, I reach for the paperback off the desk, only to have Uriah tackle me to the bed.

Straddling me, in a position I hate with a passion, as it reminds me of Mrs. Turner rising above me, Uriah holds me down on the bed. "Amy and Todd stay married, nothing changing except for finally understanding each other as fellow human beings, not possessions or extensions of themselves. Todd and Ben forged a romantic and sexual relationship, no different than a true marriage. Ben marries Wesley, with an ease Amy and Todd didn't experience, since that possessive extension bullshit never had a chance to develop. Ben and Amy still struggle to not feel jealous of one another. However, the real surprise was the connection Amy and Wesley found– it slowly evolved over the years, similar to what happened between Todd and Ben, which helped them understand their spouses, until it no longer felt as a betrayal."

"And their statuses on Facebook all say *it's complicated*?" My words sound teasing, but the tone in my voice is anything but. "That is utterly terrifying."

"You're telling me," Uriah murmurs, fingertips clenching around my wrists. "Some things are inevitable, no matter how long and hard you fight it. Let's just say, this book on Kade's desk– a book I've read and just about died inside while reading –hits a little too close to home for me, making me contemplate what's best for me."

"I don't understand." Shaking my head side to side on the bed, I've never been more confused in my entire life.

"It's too soon, too many variables, so don't worry about it, cowboy." Straddling my hips, holding my wrists down to the bed, this position should be sexy, but it's about control, no different than Mrs. Turner. Only difference, I can tell Uriah is struggling, which calms my anxiety.

Voice sober, eyes intense, Uriah leans down until our noses touch. "When I'm ready, I'll be the one to kiss you first, and that's all you need to know." Breathing against my lips, as if it's physically killing him not to kiss me, "My kiss is the equivalent of signing a marriage license in blood, Daniel Bishop."

"Holy Christ!" Kade whispers from above us. "What did I just interrupt? A kiss from a prostitute means the same as a kiss from a demisexual... should I leave for the night?"

Rolling off me, Uriah releases all the tension with a bitter laugh. "Where would you possibly go, Kade? What other friends do you have on campus?"

"I was just offering, you don't have to be a piss-pot about it." Offended, all the light dims out of Kade's eyes, shoulders curling until he's that brooding sonofabitch again. Striding over to his dresser, he begins gathering up his clothes for tomorrow.

"Don't play games, Kade," Uriah warns, going after him. "Don't manipulate. Just don't play games with us, okay? I'm calling you out, because someone has to. You offered to leave, never planning on leaving, and knowing goddamn well no one was going to take you up on that offer. If we had, you would have sulked, and made sure Dan felt guilty, and held the grudge forever. So don't give empty, testing offers."

"You don't know me," Kade breathes as an accusation, and I'm torn as to when I should step in and stop this insanity.

"I know me," is all Uriah says, leaving it dangling to be interpreted however we see fit. "Did you douche?"

Kaden does the damnedest thing– he relaxes. While I felt Uriah was being harsh to him, Kaden seems to trust Uriah more now than he did. It's baffling.

"It was complicated." Heavy brows pinching in the center of his forehead, Kade is the epitome of confusion. "I don't know if I did it right."

"Did you follow the instructions?" Uriah reaches into Kade's toiletry kit and returns with a slightly damp instructional booklet. "If so, I'm sure you did it right."

"You ever use one?" Kade asks, and Uriah just shakes his head no in reply. "It's not very sexy." Sharing a laugh together, I just sit on the bed and watch them as they forget I'm even here. "I want… I want to use my new plug, but I'm gonna need some help. You okay if Danny helps me?"

Kade doesn't ask me, knowing what my answer would've been anyway. But it's amusing how Uriah reacts to being asked on my behalf– all the tension evaporates, leaving behind the slinky body that I find so intriguing.

"Dan's never done it. You've never done it–"

"You have?" Kade sounds shocked, when I'm not surprised.

"No–" now that's a surprise. "But, between the three of us, I'm sure we can figure it out."

"Okay!" Like a switch being thrown, Kade's that giddy, high, sex-up fool again. "We'll need to do this part with the lights on, but I won't get undressed until we turn 'em out… so–"

"Let me worry about that," Uriah murmurs smugly, like some type of negotiations took place, and the results are better than he expected, when I have no fucking clue what's going on.

I'm not an idiot– I know I was the item in negotiations.

Eyes darting around the room, annoyance and amusement warring inside me, I watch as Uriah and Kaden prepare for the *butt-plug ceremony*, as if it's a major undertaking. In a way, it is a big deal. It shows a lot of trust on Kaden's part, when he's so modest and shy.

I also learn something about Uriah too– he's shy too, but a natural teacher. Googling information, Uriah relays it to Kaden, figuring out quickly how Kaden has to experience something firsthand to learn it, versus be told how to do something. Uriah is patient and kind, and his need to help overshadows the shyness, leaving behind a blush that is a mix of arousal and embarrassment.

Kade is shoved face-first into the mattress, his ass in the air. "Just rub his back." Uriah has his own version of Kade's Demanda, and I'll have to name it some other time when I have a functioning braincell.

In a thermal and a pair of pajama pants he always wears when Ransom is around– since we share a bed, just like we are with Uriah tonight –Kaden gazes at me in a mix of terror and excitement.

"You gotta come up here with me." Uriah pulls me to my feet, both of us gazing down at the curve of Kaden's back. As shy as always, Kade yanks a pillow from the head of the bed and covers his face with it. "Kade might feel more comfortable if you do the honors."

"Do I just wiggle it in there?" Eyeing Kade's rounded ass still covered in plaid jammies, my dick is taking an intense interest in what comes next.

"Does Kade have much experience?" Uriah asks, voice holding a hint of amusement.

"No," comes muffled from behind the pillow. "I had a hard time with the douche too– maybe I'm scared."

"Or tight." Uriah covers his face with his upraised palms, scrubbing away the laughter. "We need to prep him." The cellphone comes back out again– Google seems to be Uriah's friend, which is baffling when he's the one with the most experience.

"Can we make it sexy please?" Kade begs, peeking out at me from beneath his pillow.

Not sure if I'm going to piss Uriah off, I leave him to his phone and take matters into my own hands. Crawling onto the bed to kneel beside Kaden, I lean down to flutter my lips against his ear.

"Remember how good it felt when I stroked you with my fingers?" Voice breathy, I cause a rolling shudder to wave up

Kaden's spine. "We're going to do that again, and we're all going to enjoy it."

"Yes," Kaden breathes back, instinctively knowing I need his permission.

Whispering a bunch of sexy stuff that spews out my mouth without checking in with my brain, I nuzzle Kaden's neck, peppering kisses everywhere but his lips. Hands rubbing along his back, I ruck up the bottom of his thermal to access the waistband of his pajamas.

The cool breeze on his exposed skin has Kaden freezing, but with a quick nod to Uriah, four hands begin massaging the rounded, fleshy ass, causing Kaden to not only relax, but to moan and thrust against the mattress.

Just as I did when I was doing the girls on my bed, with Kaden watching from his, I gaze into Uriah's eyes, connecting with him. But the similarities end there. It's like Uriah and I are jacked up together, experiencing Kaden together. What I feel, Uriah feels. What Uriah feels, I feel.

What Kaden feels is obvious by how he's rubbing his cheek against my crotch like a kitten scent marking its master. It takes all my self-control not to unzip my pants and give him what he's begging me for– my dick in his mouth.

There's only two hands rubbing the large muscles of Kade's thighs and buttocks, because there are four hands travelling everywhere else. Kaden rubs my ass, face rooting around to lift my shirt, then a tongue follows the line of my waistband. Uriah caresses my face, fingers coming too close to my mouth– capturing his fingertip, I suck deeply, then release it with a bite. While one of my hands is busy rubbing against Kade's hole, the other is slowly unbuttoning Uriah's blouse.

Panting, Uriah and I have a moment of perfect communion. Kaden is a hairsbreadth from coming inside his pajama pants. Uriah and I are both staring at Kade's exposed bud like it holds the secrets of the universe, and we're both curious to see what it feels like beneath our tongues.

"We need lube," Uriah pants breathlessly. "At this rate, we're all gonna end up popping off before the plug gets in there."

"Yes," Kade and I breathe in unison, both of us sounding starved.

Uriah squeezes lube onto the tips of my fingers, and then moves to put the bottle back on the desk. Moving quickly, I snatch it out of his hand with my dry one, flick the top with a fingertip, then dump a bunch into the palm of Uriah's hand. Before I toss it back onto the desk, I pour way too much down the crack of Kaden's ass.

Sucking in a sharp breath, Kaden shivers. "That's fucking freezing."

Uriah and I stare down in amazement as we watch Kade's asshole contract from the temperature difference. "That is…" Uriah trails off, voice cracking with hunger. Fingers curling, I can tell he's fighting the need to touch Kade, wondering if he's welcome.

"We'll do it together," is whispered, because I don't engage in possessive pissing-contests.

"Together." Nodding, Uriah looks at me in a way I cannot fathom, like he's on the verge of saying, *You never fail to surprise me, Daniel Bishop.*" I hear it directly from his head, and he smiles knowing I do.

The next few minutes are a test of our self-restraint. Kaden abandons touching me, because he's too busy moaning deep from his chest and thrusting his hips into the air, trying to get closer to our fingers.

Uriah and I switch between staring at Kaden's ass with hunger, and staring at each other with an even deeper need. It's in this moment where I wonder if Kaden is right, and Uriah is a virgin, because I can tell without a shadow of a doubt, this is the first time he's touched anyone like this, and I don't think anyone's touched him either.

Together, we slowly work the plug into Kaden, sharing a surprised giggle when his ass sucks it in tightly with a pop.

"Turn the lights off!" Kaden shouts in a panic, tearing off his clothing and jumping into bed in a matter of seconds, flashing Uriah more than he realizes. The blanket covers him up to his man-bun, not an inch showing. "I've gotta come– gonna jerk off now. You two can join in, if you want."

Uriah is stunned, Kaden's perfect naked body fused into his mind. "Lights off!" Kaden shouts at Uriah, but he's too gobsmacked to move.

Instead of jealous, I commiserate with Uriah, knowing exactly how he feels right now. I hit the switch, then make quick work of my clothing.

"Can I help you undress?" I ask Uriah, locating him in the dark. "Or is it too much?"

Fingertips light against my chest, quivering slightly as they caress me. "Yeah, but–"

"I understand," is said to the background soundtrack of Kaden really getting into it, moans pitching higher, the bed jiggling to hit me in the back of my knees. "Together, okay?"

Refusing to go too quickly, especially when our emotions are all over the place, I help Uriah out of his blouse as he strips off his jeans, leaving a pair of tiny panties on– I so wish Kaden wasn't so modest, because if the lights were on, I could see what Uriah looks like in his panties.

"You're beautiful," I murmur, voice breaking.

"You can't see me," flows from the dark, mere inches from my face.

"My fingers can," I whisper back, tugging Uriah onto the bed with me.

A foot slips underneath my calf for leverage, after I get situated on the bed. I can sense exactly what Kaden is doing– his knees drawn up, one hand pressing on the plug, the other jerking his cock roughly.

Completely naked, dick dripping profusely, I lie in between a man furiously masturbating and another curled up against my side, shivering with nervousness.

"Together?" I ask again, and I'm relieved Uriah understands. The whisper of sheets moving, he slips his hands inside his panties to touch his cock.

"Ah!" I grunt, shocked how amazing my own hand feels on me. Unbidden, my head flops to the side to bury against Uriah's neck, mouth open and panting to leave dampness behind on his skin.

Together, we all work ourselves, echoed moans lingering, and it's the most innocent yet intimate moment of my life. The trust. The feel of my face pressed against Uriah's throat– the puffs of hot breath scorching my forehead as Uriah comes into his own palm. Kaden, beside me, whimpering and laughing in elation.

▱▱▱

Uriah and I wake pretzeled together as light casts heavily across the dorm room, and I finally catch sight of the tiny pink panties with the bow riding over the base of his cock. Shuddering with how rapid and intense arousal hits me, my cock lengthens to poke Uriah in the belly.

"Definitely not morning wood." Laughing smugly, Uriah hands me a note.

You guys looked so beautiful together, I couldn't wake you. I turned off your alarms so you'd get some rest, but if you miss your afternoon classes, I'ma beat your asses.
TMI: I'm wearing my plug to class.
-Demanda

Time ceases to have meaning, not caring if I fail out of school at this point, as we caress and nuzzle with no expectation of release. Eventually I fall asleep again, waking to an empty bed, and it's my Groundhog Day moment, minus Uriah. If I hadn't found a note taped to my chest, a part of me would wonder if it was but a magnificent dream.

Cowboy,
Kade was right— you were too beautiful to wake. It was torture watching you sleep, but I had to tear myself away. I'm not a legacy like you, not a blink of an eye from graduation. Grants and work-study have rules I cannot break. I had to crawl out of your warm nest, stop kissing your neck, and drag my tired ass to class.
PS: I'll go to Pittsburgh.
FYI: I don't have a sassy drag name like Kade to end this note.
—yours

BISHOP'S CASTLE

Kade is doing his Crash Test Dummy routine in the driver's seat of the Durango, with Uriah manning the stereo from the passenger side. I've been relegated to the backseat with my laptop open and a stack of books and highlighters scattered along the seat, all because Tonya barged into our room last night and tattled about how I'm falling behind.

Friends, I'm glad I have ones who try to take care of me, even at the risk of pissing me off. But I really didn't want to be working on my first road trip with Uriah.

We were going to drive down three weekends ago, but Grandma fell ill with bronchitis. The Bishop gettogether was postponed until Grandma recuperated. The only problem with this was how it gave Grandma a ton of downtime to plan an even bigger event, especially with Uncle Edward home for the week.

"Don't be nervous." Kade is soothing my boyfriend, when that should be my job. "The Bishops are great– it's the extended family and their *"friends"* who are the problem." Kade takes his hands off the steering wheel long enough to make air-quotes, which is a terrifying prospect.

"The catered food is amazing, and the people-watching is entertaining." Kaden laughs to himself, an edge of mania echoing around the car. "Catty cocksuckers."

"Cocksuckers?" Uriah volleys back, grinning at me in the mirror on the visor. "Don't insult us, Demanda– I doubt they even lick pussy."

"Danny liked licking pussy." Kade digs me a bigger hole.

With Kade driving, we're closer to home than I realized, so I pack my shit up and join the conversation. It wasn't like I was getting any work done anyway.

"Nothing is more erotic than a woman coming all over your face. The wracking quivers. The way those shapely, smooth thighs clench so tightly your neck almost snaps." Shuddering, I use the heel of my palm to readjust my hard-on.

Kade laughs at me like I'm fucking insane, but Uriah's glare is filled with pure jealousy.

"Have you seen your thighs, Envy?" Kaden yet again engages Uriah before I can. Kade even gave Uriah a drag name. It may not be sassy, but it's accurate.

Envy.

Three weeks. Three weeks of nonstop obsessing over Uriah, getting closer to him and being sucked in until the trap is inescapable. I can't concentrate on my school work, thinking about what I want to say to Uriah, how I want to touch his skin and nuzzle his throat, and how I just want to laugh with him.

Three weeks of Uriah becoming more comfortable around Kaden, since we've returned to our usual selves around each other. Just one night of shared passion, kissing and sex, and now we're back to friends who jerk off together and hold a deep affection for one another. Kaden and I are showing great restraint and self-control. It's a struggle to not touch, to not kiss, but with time, I'm hoping it will get easier.

Three weeks of Uriah eyeing me when girls are in my vicinity, and I have no fucking clue what he's thinking in those moments, and it's driving me batty.

"What about my thighs?" Uriah is still glaring at me over my joys of cunnilingus commentary.

"They're hotter than any legs that have been wrapped around poor Danny's noggin, that's what." Three weeks of watching Kaden flirt with Uriah, perfecting it. Three weeks of Uriah blushing and soaking it up like a dying plant after water.

Three weeks with me enjoying how Kaden blooms into a confident man who will treat Wynn right.

Three weeks of almost platonic touches between Uriah and me, because I'm waiting for that kiss before I initiate anything else. The few times Uriah's stayed over, we've held each other all night, feathering fingertip touches on the safe places but avoiding the naughty ones. Kisses on cheeks, and tips of noses, and sucking marks against throats as we stroke ourselves to a fevered pitch.

Leaning forward, I grip the headrest of Uriah's seat, crossing a billion lines, but I'm too insane at this point to stop myself. Not even bothering to whisper, "When I jerk off, I dream of your legs wrapped around my face, your balls pressed against my nose, and your taint smothering me… deep in your bud as it clenches rhythmically around my tongue… coming on my face… jizz splattering my hair."

Whimpering, Uriah turns to face the window, hand out of sight, but he's moving around restlessly.

"Fuck, I think I just creamed my pants." Kaden releases uncomfortable laughter, hands clenching the steering wheel. "Lay off that dirty talk until you're in a room alone with Uriah– that wasn't cool, Danny. How the hell am I to hug your family while wearing sticky boxers?"

"Sorry." Sliding back to sit on the seat, I release the headrest. "Not sorry. Never doubt I want you, Uriah, and don't judge me on my past."

Still unable to speak, Uriah nods at me in the mirror, face sheened with sweat.

Envy– I learned pretty quickly what Uriah meant about knowing himself when Kaden accused him of not knowing who he was. Sometimes Uriah slips into a jealous monster, who thinks I should read his mind. He tests me. He baits me. He lays landmines in a field that was otherwise safe for me to travel.

There are no winners when Uriah gets like that, only losers.

Uriah knows Kaden inside and out, because they act just alike. Kaden understands Uriah in turn… and I'm just left confused as I try to figure out what I did wrong. It's the insanity of loving people who are high-maintenance.

"You need to hit the McDuck's drive-thru," I remind Kaden when we're a few minutes from my neighborhood.

"What's that about?" Uriah's back to normal, insecurities tucked away in a crate somewhere. "Are you hungry again?"

"I could always eat," Kaden announces as he pulls into McDonald's and gets in line with the other cars. "Usual?" he asks, knowing why we had to stop. "You want anything? Uriah?"

"Usual." Neither one of us answer Uriah's question, finding it hilarious to anticipate his reaction when we get to the house. "My usual too."

"Nuggets." Uriah looks back and forth between us, eyebrows scrunched together. "Large Coke. Barbeque sauce."

With every item Kaden adds to the order, Uriah's eyes get wider. "Oh, and a vanilla milkshake," Kaden adds, almost forgetting the last of my usual meal.

"Who are you feeding?" Uriah keeps looking at us, fuming because we refuse to answer. "Jesus Christ, you guys aren't going to eat all that, are you? Do I need to worry about bulimia?"

"You'll see," Kaden promises as he reaches out to grab our order, coming back with bag after bag of food, then a cup carrier and another. "You'll see."

Uriah forgets the food as soon as we enter my neighborhood, but my belly is growling so loudly Kaden is smirking at me in the rearview mirror. "Is your house as big as these?"

"No," I say with a straight face, part of me loathing how we have more than most, but another part is amused by Uriah's horrorstruck expression. His disgust is obvious from the rearview mirror.

"Bigger," Kaden ruins the surprise.

"But not as big as our neighbors," I make sure everyone knows that important bit of information, like it makes a difference in the grand scheme of things.

"The houses are getting bigger," Uriah growls, and there is no mind-reading necessary to understand where his anger is coming from. "And bigger... Jesus fucking Christ, how big can a house get?"

"My foster dad has the biggest house in all of Rusty Knob, and an even bigger barn too." I have no idea where Kaden is going with this, but he's no doubt picking up on my discomfort at Uriah's deep-seeded loathing of my family, sight unseen.

Uriah is openly glaring at me through the mirror, and his expression screams how he's not liking what he's seeing.

Yeah, I'm an entitled, white trust-fund brat from an affluent neighborhood, whose family is filled with republican devils. *I get it.* It's all I eat and breathe and sleep and shit, never escaping it.

That's not me.

How would Uriah like it if I turned everything into how he's a prostitute– at least those are his actions, whereas my family's political affiliations are not by my actions or decisions.

"Royce also owns half of all the properties in town, is the biggest contractor in the state, and buys up houses as they go on the market, only to rent them out–"

"Great," Uriah mutters snidely, expression warping with bitter loathing.

"Royce also buys up everything that is left at the end of estate sales." Kade pauses to make sure his point will be hammered home, and I finally catch on to what he's doing. "To the outside looking in, Royce looks greedy, right?"

"Exactly," is murmurs with a nasty twist of Uriah's lips, teeth bared.

"Pride. They feel as if they are providing for their families, not realizing Royce is helping them out. That's a good thing."

"Explain this to me–" Uriah challenges Kade, turning in his seat to stare at the side of Kade's face. "How exactly is Royce helping them?"

"Those buildings Royce owns, he puts motivated people in them to run their own businesses, with zero startup costs, to help our local economy. With the profits from his construction company, Royce is able to pay his employees for doing the work for free when someone truly needs it. Those houses Royce rents out, he makes sure people have a roof over their heads, at a monthly rate that fits into their means. He buys up the estate junk to make sure the families have enough money to pay for the final expenses of their deceased loved ones, with the stuff going to the donation centers.

"It's not the size of a man's bank account that should be judged, Uriah," Kaden chastises in a disappointed voice. "It's how he uses his money to benefit his people and his town. It's not the size of the home, it's about the people it houses."

Kaden turns slightly to pin Uriah with a frank look, then gazes back at the road. "Royce houses himself and his son, a gay orphaned kid he took in out of the kindness of his own heart, his twins who think he's their uncle, and Wynn, who'd otherwise be living in a goddamn shack up in the hollers .. and all of their friends and family when they need a place to rest their heads."

"I–"

"My point," Kaden doesn't let Uriah speak over him. "Don't judge a person until you actually meet them– otherwise, we may start judging you by where you come from, instead of how you act, and you've been acting like a snotty little cunt all day, Envy."

"I'm sorry." The tears in Uriah's voice has me reaching forward to comfort him, but Kaden lays on the brakes, causing me to jerk backward.

Uriah won't allow me to enable Kaden anymore, but Kaden won't let me enable Uriah either.

"Before we get out, I need you to realize there are four generations of folks living in this big house– multiple incomes, instead of spreading it over many separate homes. If you've taken five seconds of economics, you'll get where I'm headed with this… so stow your conservatives are evil, rich bastards rhetoric and behave until you know them enough to form a real opinion."

Chuckling to myself, I open Uriah's door while Kade runs up to the house like it's his family we're visiting. Uriah stands on shaking legs, tears in his eyes.

"And so the lone liberal walks into a den of evil right-wingers," I tease by breathing the words into Uriah's ear. "Never fear… Ransom, Kade, and I, we're on your side. Just don't ever insult a conservative to Kade's face, because those roots are strong in him, and it's like you're shitting at Royce Kennedy's feet."

"I–I–" Huge watery eyes gaze up at me, asking for help.

"But feel free to take a few cracks at my family around Ransom– he'll join in, and he can make fun of us like nobody's business."

"I'm sorry, Daniel." Uriah touches my arm, and I was never upset, nor was I angry. "It's like the first day we met, when I stuck my foot in it."

"You don't like being judged by stereotypes, and neither do I– other than that, we're good." Wrapping my arm around Uriah's waist like always, I encounter a starched shirt.

I didn't dare bring it up since Uriah was already tense and terrified of coming here this weekend. Uriah dressed by society's standards of a guy, wearing a pair of trousers and a dress shirt, with loafers, hair pulled back in a band at the nape of his neck. It hurts to see him dressed to fit in instead of like himself.

Uriah's shaking like a leaf at my side, teeth clattering, and I have a feeling no one has ever taken him home to meet the family. I'm a social beast, so the thought of meeting Uriah's godmother and their family actually intrigues me.

"Kade is such an attention whore," Uriah whispers in my ear, voice amused.

We have another Thermopylae situation on the front steps. "He loves it." A big grin splits across my face as Kaden is engulfed by the women in my family, oohing and awing over how he's a big, strapping boy. The men ask of Kade's grades and about his family. Ransom's asking for the takeout.

Then I'm spotted.

Like a rolling wave of shock, my family freezes mid-touch, mid-word, mid-movement, and they all look at me hugging Uriah to my side with my arm around his waist.

"Hi," I mutter smugly, trying very hard not to laugh. "Everyone, this is Uriah Crane." I gesture to the steps filled with my family. "Uriah, the salivating guy is my nephew, Ransom. The haggard old lady is my sister, Ainsley–"

"Hey!" Ainsley growls at me, looking amazing in her designer suit, obviously just making it home from Harrisburg a few minutes before us. Having her own apartment three hours away, her own life, working nonstop, it's a miracle when she makes it home on random weekends.

"I'm not going to complain," Ransom grumbles, hand on his belly. "I am salivating, but not for the reason you'd think." Swaggering forward, he juts his hand out to Uriah. "Why, hello there…" Voice deepening to comical levels, "I'm Ransom James Joel Talbot-Bishop."

"And you're only seventeen," Uriah says without missing a beat, expression smug because my nephew is eye-humping him.

If Uriah thinks Kaden is an attention whore, then he needs to look in a mirror. I find it cute on both of them, but let's call a spade a spade. Uriah loves it when someone flirts with him, looks at him, and wants him.

"And I like older men." Eyes going up and down, up and down, they drink in every inch of my boyfriend. "You're what, twenty?" Uriah nods in assent. "Too bad you're not dressed like you usually are– that's a disappointment."

"C'mon, you dipshit." Taller than all of us, Kaden wraps his arm around Ransom's neck and puts him in a headlock. "My Durango is filled with takeout." …and, just like that, Ransom forgets we all exist.

Other than my sister, everyone else is still frozen in shock. Ainsley parts her arms in welcome, a genuine smile on her face, as she walks toward us. I get the hug and kiss, and then she's kissing Uriah on the cheek.

"It's nice to finally meet you– I feel like I know you already." With that admission, Uriah relaxes, and I begin to wonder if he thought I was thrusting him on my family without their notice. I wouldn't do that. I didn't tell anyone but Ransom and Ainsley that Uriah and I are dating, but I knew they would figure it out immediately.

"Mom–" I try to get her attention. "Uriah Crane, this is Caroline Elizabeth Bishop– Libby."

"Mrs. Bishop." Uriah struggles, not knowing if he should shake her hand, but Mom comes to the rescue by embracing my boyfriend.

"Just call me Mom." Mom giggles, thinking it hilarious. "Even my grandson calls me Mom." Stepping to the side, she gestures to everyone else left on the stoop. "That's Grandpa, Grandma, and Dad, no matter who's saying it– that's what we're called. Only Ainsley, Daniel, and Ransom are called by name."

"She's not kidding," I whisper into Uriah's ear, causing him to snort. "Grandma can get prickly in a fight when her daughter-in-law is sneering Grandma at her."

"Oh, pish!" Mom swats my chest, which is where Ransom learned that trick. "Behave, sweetie."

"Does she really?" Ransom whispers furiously into my ear, voice breaking. "Does your mom actually call her mother-in-law Grandma?"

"Paintball," is all I have to say, causing Uriah to puff up and snarl like a feral cat.

"You're so precious." Ainsley is busting a gut, face redder than her lipstick. "No, really, call them Grandpa, Grandma, Dad, and Mom– leave it up to them to call each other by name. It's just how they want it."

"Welcome home, son." Grandpa is preoccupied with what's going down at the Durango, but he's too terrified of Grandma to make a beeline without greeting us first. "Nice to meet you, Uriah– Daniel never shuts up about you." With that duty done, we're no longer of interest. "I've got to go see where Ransom ran off to… that boy sure can get into trouble…" rambling bullshit for Grandma, Grandpa speed-walks to the car for his share of the loot.

"Where are you going, Edward?" Grandma waves at me, then acts as the warden of Bishop's Castle. "Come back here and talk to your grandson!"

"Hey, Grandma." Kaden pops out of nowhere. "These roses over here…" He leads her away. "Royce struggles with the flowers in the garden, can you give me any pointers to pass along."

"What the…" Uriah trails off, still not putting two and two together.

"Gimme my milkshake, Grandpa!" Ainsley gets into the action.

Giggling, Mom saves Kaden from himself, distracting Grandma with something in the kitchen… and then there is Dad, who is palming my forehead and shoving me down the front walk.

"Uriah!" I call, leaving him behind. "This angry man is Daniel James Bishop– he goes by James. My father."

Dad glares at me, mouth drawn in a tight line. "Welcome, Uriah– we'll speak once I'm done talking to my son." Realizing how that sounded, Dad's facial expression turns softer. "This has nothing to do with you, and everything to do with Daniel's adviser calling me yesterday afternoon."

"Oh, shit!" I gulp, finding it hard to swallow as Dad manhandles me to the side of the house, out of view and hearing range of the rest of the family.

You'd think a guy named Dad would be easy to escape, especially when he's the grandfather to an almost-adult grandson. But that's what happens when your daughter is an unwed teen mom, people assume you're decades older than you are.

James Bishop is fifty-one, hasn't even reached silver fox territory yet, and he's built like an old-timey boxer. But I'm not worried about him physically pounding me into submission– it's the cerebral assault that's going to be a problem.

I fucked up. Big time.

"Daniel." Dad tries very hard to calm himself as he releases my forehead. The divots from where his fingertips rested pound with every heartbeat. "Care to explain how you're about to fail out of your senior year of college?"

"I fucked up," blurts out before I can stop it.

"Preoccupied, are you?" Dad grins at me, and I'm rendered speechless. "By the little minx of a man you brought home– the one playing pretend in those clothes?"

"Dad, I can explain–"

"Do you ever ask yourself why there is such a large gap between you and your sister?" Dad floors me once again.

Don't get me wrong, I love the man– Dad's compassionate, understanding, and logical. It's that logic that terrifies me. Because after years of perfect attendance, I've barely understood a word in any of my classes in the past few weeks, and I deserve whatever comes my way.

"Ainsley and I are a decade apart– I figured you were doing some major family planning, or something. Then Ainsley comes along and fucks it up by popping out Ransom before you were ready to tackle another kid."

"Wrong." Dad chuckles, amused by how terrified he's making me. "I was distracted once–"

"Mom?" I guess. The woman is three years younger than him, and she was eighteen or so when they got married and had Ainsley. I always figured Ainsley was conceived before their wedding night.

"My preoccupation with Libby had me dropping out of college to get married and start a family–"

"What?!" I squawk, eyes narrowing with suspicion. "Bullshit."

"I get it, son– I do." Dad rests his palms on my shoulders, gazing directly into my eyes. "It's intoxicating. Freeing. Love makes you do the damnedest things. Until you realize you're in law school with a screaming toddler and a wife who doesn't understand how your education takes intense focus and dedication. Your mom felt I was choosing our future over the attention she wanted in the moment. Almost got a divorce... the only way we survived, I had to dump my young wife and our baby daughter on the doorstep of this house for my parents to handle, just so I could concentrate on our future."

"And they never left," I tease, because otherwise my head is going to explode.

"I get it– I do." Dad's fingers flex on my shoulders. "But don't focus so hard on today at the expense of your future. Because today turns into tomorrow, and before you know it, you have no future."

Without saying another word, Dad drops his hands from my shoulders and then walks away toward the Durango. After a quick search for Uriah, I realize he was probably drawn back into the fray by Kade, so I stalk after Dad in their direction.

"Is that?" Staring at Ransom as he shoves a Double Quarter Pounder into his wide mouth. "Is that my burger?"

"Sorry," Ransom tries to talk while chewing, almost choking on the big bite. "I was hungry."

"Where are my fries?" I accuse, looking around at my gluttonous family as they circle the Durango like it houses a crack dealer in the center of an upper middle class, affluent neighborhood outside of Pittsburgh, Pennsylvania.

The neighbors are used to it, knowing our house is devoid of processed sugars and trans fats.

"Sorry." Ransom got it from Grandpa. The eighty-year-old man is double fisting my French fries. "Grandma starves me with healthy shit." Voice warbling, looking pitiful as all get out. "I'm starving… wasting away, I am."

"My milkshake?" Then I remember hearing Ainsley earlier. Turning to the side, I catch my sister's guilty expression as she makes a mad-dash to the house, vanilla milkshake clenched in her paw.

Dad's munching on his Filet of Fish, confident in the knowledge none of us like the sandwich, which is why he always orders it.

Kade is guarding his Big Macs on the hood of the Durango, body language intimidating, with untouched French fries he's never going to part with.

"Savages," I hiss, belly letting out a loud grumble as I smell my food being shoved down their open gullets.

When I finally get married, I will have my own autonomy. I won't hide out on the sidewalk, because the lady of the manor lords over the cupboards and everyone within the household. We're all adults, with Ransom a hairsbreadth of joining us. The men in our family created monsters out of Grandma and Mom, by letting them get away with their unacceptable behavior.

I vow to myself how I won't be passive-aggressive, lie and hide, like a child who is being parented by their partner. I will respect my partner by not acting controlling, and I will expect that same respect in return.

"Cowboy?" Uriah calls out, face peering at me from the rear of the Durango. The rage and discomfort has been replaced by his normal, at rest expression, thank goodness. "Hungry?"

Uriah is sitting in the back, hatch open, feet swinging as he dips and munches on his nuggets, big-ass Coke safe and sound between his thighs. "Want one?" A nugget, with sauce already dripping off it, is held up to my lips. "Kaden ordered me a twenty-piece."

"Thank God." Starving, and mentally and physically exhausted, I sit next to Uriah as we share his meal. He even lets me have a sip of his Coke.

YOU DO YOU

"Does Uriah take forever in the bathroom?" Ransom's beneath me on the trundle bed, while I'm laying haphazardly across our bed, textbook in hand.

After a meal with too few fats and sugars, which made us susceptible to the inhibition-lowering effects of wine consumption, we played Cards Against Humanity.

Two gay guys.

A demisexual and his genderfluid boyfriend.

A thirty-year-old feminist, unwed mother.

An almost fifty-year-old stay-at-home humanitarian, with religious and political ties.

A fifty-year-old divorce lawyer from a republican political power-house family.

And a pair of eighty-year-old old coots, from another era, who are adorable racist, sexist, bigots by most standards, but they love us, so we didn't care.

We were all insulted, on many fronts, but eventually started laughing at ourselves.

Too many bottles of wine later, after we cleaned up the bloodshed… we had a grown-man slumber party, with Kade on one trundle and Ransom on the other, leaving the king-sized bed to Uriah and me. Our night featured an in-depth conversation on the ins and outs– or lack thereof –of gay sex. Since none of us would confess to doing the deed, Video Killed the Radio Star was projected from Ransom's laptop to the TV. It was an eye-opener to say the least.

It's the following afternoon, and we're sick to death of each other already, being locked in this house, waiting on this evening's party. The lack of caffeine and sugar is the real mood killer. Now it's the slow crawl as a household gets spiffy for the festivities.

"Okay, Grandpa," I taunt Ransom. "Are you pulling female stereotypes out on my boyfriend?" Eyes narrowed, I sling my upper half off the bed to glare down at my nephew. "If anyone is slow, it's Kade."

"Hey!" Kaden shouts from the other side of the bed, where he's reading yet another smutty novel he stole from Grandma. "Don't bring me into this bullshit– I have a lot of body to cover, of course it takes forever. Then there's all this hair–"

"Slow– Danny wasn't talking about how long you're in the shower, dippy." Wheezing, Ransom is laughing so hard, struggling to breathe from that intense verbal smackdown, he doesn't realize Kaden can move that uncoordinated, gigantic body of his pretty fucking fast when he's pissed. "Ugh! Goddamnit, that hurt– not the balls!"

Snickering, I just lie on my back, staring at the ceiling, listening to the battle song as Kaden beats the piss out of Ransom on the floor. "You ripped my shirt– I was wearing it to the party."

"Don't make insinuations that I'm an ignorant hillbilly, fuckface." Out of breath, Kaden is struggling to control himself.

"That fact that you used insinuations properly in a sentence negates the actual insinuation that I was calling you an ignorant hillbilly, doesn't it?" Ransom pops up, grab onto my leg for dear life, and tries to drag himself onto the bed to safety.

A large paw reaches up, palms the crown of Ransom's head, and slowly drags him back down to the floor.

Finding sick enjoyment, I'm laughing my nuts off when I glance up and notice Uriah standing in the doorway from our attached bath. He's staring at the mass of throttling arms and legs with confusion.

"What happened?" Uriah tries to sidestep the action, but then jumps back when one of them attempts to drag him into it. "Does this happen a lot?"

"Cabin fever– blowing off some steam." I get up, kick them apart, then drag Ransom away by the back of his collar. "Every time we come home, one of us gets into a fight."

Hopping to his feet like a Jack-in-the-box on crack, Kaden adjusts his dress shirt. "Ran's a little instigator." Then he leans down, tears the band out of his hair, and redoes his man-bun.

"Am not!" Proving Kaden right, my nephew runs through the room, slaps Kaden on the ass, then locks himself in the walk-in closet. "Need to change my shirt, fucker!" flows from behind the door. "It was my favorite too."

"My job here is done!" Kade brushes his palms together, like he's washing Ransom away. "You done in there?" he tilts his chin in the direction of the bathroom.

"Yeah." Uriah is in meek-mode, shy and sedate, not shining brightly like he does when he's comfortable. "I'm good." Wearing a tan dress shirt, brown slacks, and a pair of dark brown loafers, all of Uriah's sparkle is gone.

"You can't wear that." It's rude, and it's the wrong thing to say to anyone, man or woman, but I haven't been able to think straight since Uriah got into the Durango yesterday morning wearing clothing he took out of Bob or RJ's closet. "Did you bring any of your own clothing?"

"Daniel," Uriah barks sharply, his end of discussion tone. "Don't go there."

"I'm going there." Stalking from the bed, I use my presence to back Uriah up against the closed bathroom door– not to intimidate, but to make sure he doesn't run. Uriah's a runner, and I need him to listen for once.

My fingers slip behind Uriah's head to untie the length of leather holding his hair back at the nape of his neck. Pocketing the string, I use my fingers to comb Uriah's hair into his usual style. Then I begin unbuttoning the shirt that only an accountant would wear– which is why I assume it was pilfered from Bob's closet.

"I'm a quick study," I remind Uriah how I have to be if I plan on continuing on my career path. "You expect me to be a mind-reader, so I'm going to go ahead and tell you all the arguments you've got going on in your head, as to why you're dressed like Bob's personal assistant."

Trying to side step me, "Dan–"

With a hand to his chest, I gently push Uriah back against the door, making sure he can't get away from me. Wrong? Yes. But it needs to be done.

"In that beautiful mind of yours, you're being a martyr and thinking yourself lesser, just like the oaf in the bathroom does to me all the time too. You think you don't deserve me, that you're going to ruin my future as my own personal skeleton in the closet. You've twisted it around to how I don't truly want you– how I brought home the genderfluid queer kid to stick it to my rightwing family, as rebellion for them having a belief system I may not agree with on many points. You think I'm straight, waiting around to find a girl I want to marry and birth my babies. You think I'm parading you around, secretly making fun of you, wanting you to dress like yourself to get a rise out of tonight's high-profile guests. *Admit it*."

A tiny growl, teeth bared, and narrowed whiskey eyes are my answer.

"We've discussed this to death– the differences in our relationship versus mine with Kaden. How I enable him, but I refuse to enable you, because I care about our future, goddamn you." Now it's my turn to snarl, teeth bared. "This isn't a game. This isn't a test. I. Want. You. To. Do. You. Because I love you exactly as you are."

Stunned stupid, we both stare at the other, unable to blink from the shock of my admission.

Freaking out, I stalk away, muttering, "Jesus Christ," beneath my breath while tearing at my hair. Falling backward, I ass-plant on the mattress, my textbook jabbing me in the back.

"Sorry to interrupt, but I think we need a timeout." Ransom appears out of thin air to take Uriah by the hand. "I have some clothing from last year that are way too small for me to wear now. Trust me– my dad said he'd force me to live with his parents if I wore my purple pants in public."

"More republicans?" Uriah mutters wryly, one eye still trained on me.

"Worse." Ransom sounds so serious, even in my current state of crisis, I bark a sharp laugh. "Lutherans."

Both of them take another look at me as they enter the closet, leaving the door open. "These pants, they do amazing things for my junk–"

"If you fart in 'em, you'll split the seam right up your ass." Laughing, I remember Joel going postal the last time Ransom tried to leave the house in those pants. "They're obscene on your stocky frame."

"Hush!" Ransom chastises me, door slamming shut with a loud bang. "Get to studying, dummy, before you fail out of college– Uriah and I have some talking to do."

Sighing, struggling to dislodge the textbook from my back, I catch sight of Kaden standing in the open bathroom door. "Want me to eavesdrop?"

The only part of me that moves is my eyebrows and lips. "Like you were during my conversation with Uriah?"

"In all fairness, it's kinda hard to not listen in when you were inches from where I was trying to take a piss. Then I was trapped in there until you were done." Kade's got me there. "Bren taught me how to eavesdrop– I can do that for you, find out what they're saying."

"You taking pity on me because I'm a fucking idiot who just dropped the L-bomb in the middle of a fight, three and a half weeks into knowing one another? For shit's sake, we haven't even kissed yet."

Walking toward me, Kaden flashes me a sad curl of his lips. "You're not cornering the market on stupidity. I've been waiting for Wynn to grow up since he was twelve, and I'm five years older than he is, so it's been a long wait–"

"In the meantime..." I trail off, hinting at my own stupidity for unintentionally falling in love with Kaden during said wait.

"Your dad married your mom less than a week after they met–"

Jerking upright on the bed, "What?!"

"Ask James. It's true. He met your mom, and they got married less than a week later, terrified he'd knocked her up... and since Ainsley is on this earth, I'd say he was right."

"I *am* a romantic." Groaning, I hide my head in my hands.

"When you say romantic, you sound just like Uriah when he uses the R word, or like Ransom when he uses the L word."

"R word? Romantic? L word? I thought that was love."

"Republican," Kade deadpans, somehow managing to keep a straight face. "Lutheran... I'ma eavesdrop, even if you don't wanna know what they're saying."

"Do what you want to do, but I don't want to know." Grabbing my textbook, I hunt down my notebook and highlighter. "If Uriah wants me to know, he'll tell me."

"Yeah, that's not how I roll." Snickering, Kade darts over to take his smut novel with him as a prop, and then he leans against the wall near the closet door, pretending to read.

To the background soundtrack of Kade's under his breath commentary, I attempt to get some studying done for Monday's early morning class. Dad was right, of course. Whether or not Uriah and I go the long-haul, I still have to graduate and get a job someday. I can't just be obsessed with Uriah and expect to be a functioning adult.

Easier said than done, when I know Uriah is getting some sort of talk from my nephew. After a few minutes, I fall into the rhythm I created since I learned how to study in the second grade.

Kade landing heavily next to me on the mattress, bouncing three or more times until he goes still, knocks the pen out of my hand. "What are you doing?" I whisper in a harsh tone. "Leave me be."

Quickly tossing a pillow behind his head, Kaden cracks open the paperback and pretends to read. "Shh... they're coming out of the closet."

Ransom and Uriah eye Kade and me, finding us in the throes of a childish giggling fit. "Out of the closet..." Kaden chokes out on a laugh, always finding himself amusing. "I'm priceless."

"M'kay..." Ransom rolls his eyes at our antics, and I'm pleased to note he's wearing a pair of tailored trousers, instead of the obscene skinny jeans he loves to wear.

After a billion 'dress for your body shape' lectures from his mother, Ainsley took Ransom out to buy new clothes. He has on the only *sexy* shirt his mother allowed him to purchase, because it complemented his stocky frame. This doesn't mean our closet isn't loaded with shit Ransom should never, *ever* wear in public...

"You look stunning," rolls off my tongue as I catch sight of Uriah wearing all the things made to fit his lithe body. Those too-tight, purple skinny jeans– the very ones Joel threatened to incinerate in the fireplace while Ransom was still wearing them –fit Uriah perfectly. The white button-up that Ransom always looked like he was about to go full Hulk-mode and bust out of the seams is flowy on Uriah, with the cuffs unbuttoned and only partially tucked into the front of the waistband.

"Wow." Slowly, I stow my books, then lope off the foot of the bed. "You look like an imp who just crawled out of sexed-up sheets."

"Thanks." Blushing, Uriah tucks his hair behind his ear. Ducking his head, he hesitates, then darts forward to bury his face into the side of my neck. "Me too," is a soft whisper, followed by the brush of damp lips.

Stunned, confused, my arm wraps around Uriah's waist, where it plans to stay for the duration of the evening.

"Sure, nobody's said how magnificent I look," Ransom pouts, taking the attention off Uriah, and for once it's because Uriah is uncomfortable with the attention. "These pants were *literally* made for me– then look at you two, not giving a fuck."

"My wardrobe is like Garanimals." Snorting at the horrorstruck look on my nephew's face. "Everything matches. Underwear. Sleep clothes. Work clothes. Casual clothes. Dress clothes. Seasonal. I just yanks something out, depending on the situation, and I know it matches. Good to go."

Kade's, "I ain't high maintenance," has me choking on my own tongue. Face going bright red, he admits defeat. "Okay, so not when it comes to clothing. I really don't give a damn as long as I'm covered… let's get this shit show on the road."

<hr>

Curling up against my side, lips pressed directly to my ear, "Is it always this boring?" Uriah whispers, thinking Kade and Ransom can't overhear.

"Yes!" rings from three voices– Kade, Ransom, and me.

Leaning against the wall, with the entryway to the foyer at our backs, we're pretty much hiding from those who enter the room, because they can't see us until they are *inside* the room. The political movers and shakers are in the left-hand entertaining room, and their unmotivated dragged-along guests are sulking over here with us, draped all over the furniture with drinks and food in hand. One woman asked if we had any pets she could go hang out with for the evening. When I said no, she asked to wash dishes, just so she could hide out in the kitchen.

This is the introvert side of the house.

Ordinarily, I'd be more social, but I'm mentally, emotionally, and physically exhausted. Besides, they'll find me when they want something. My senator uncle is on the other side of this wall. After I introduced Uncle Edward to Uriah, where my uncle was cordial and genuine, Uriah made the sign of the cross when the man moved along. I decided it best to keep Uriah away from the rest of Uncle Edward's buddies after that.

The irony is how Uriah doesn't realize he's voted for several of the people milling around this house. Uriah has it in his head that liberals and conservatives don't mix nor mingle, barter nor negotiate, when that couldn't be farther from the truth. Neither could exist without the other.

We never use the front part of our home. We don't even use the front entrance for anything but a party. We park in the driveway or garage, come into the house through the garage door into the kitchen, using the back steps to the upper floor.

The front of the house is divided by a large foyer featuring a curved staircase. On each side of the foyer, there are two identical rooms used for entertaining. Behind the left-hand entertaining room is an entrance to the dining room, which is left open for overflow tonight, as we aren't serving a full meal. Behind the right-hand entertaining room is a hidden doorway to the family room and my grandparents' bedroom, both easily accessed from the kitchen.

Our personal rooms and the upstairs are off-limits during a party. Even the main staircase has a snazzy red velvet rope from banister to banister to cordon it off. The party guests mill around the two entertaining rooms, the dining room, and the guest bath located beneath the grand staircase. They are strongly deterred from entering the kitchen by Grandma.

"Hey, come back here with that." Kade flags down a server, then double-fists the appetizers. "These mushroom caps are delicious."

"Are you watching Netflix?" Uriah catches sight of Ransom binge-watching Shameless with one earbud hidden in his ear.

"It's either that, or I'm going to start a confrontation with Uncle Edward, and nobody wants to see that." The devious glint in my nephew's eye says otherwise.

"I'm just here for the food." Kade flags down another server, this time palming cream puffs. "Mmm… my favorite." An argument erupts from the other room, echoing across the foyer. "Oh, and that's the real reason I'm here."

We all flash Uriah Cheshire cat grins.

"Did you happen to vote in the last election?" I turn to Uriah, an innocent expression on my face.

"Of course, why?" Eyebrows knitted, he's adorably confused. "I did my civic duty."

"I don't vote," Kade admits, then pops another cream puff into his large mouth. "Neither does Danny."

"What?" Uriah looks at me like he's never seen me before. "Why?"

"Danny says once you're inside politics, you're close enough to realize everyone running makes your skin crawl," Kade answers for me. "That, and it's Danny's only way to rebel."

"Remember the man who hit on you?" We all snicker as it plays out in our heads. A congressman hit on Uriah, wasn't even subtle about it, with me standing right here. "You voted for him."

More eyebrow scrunching, "I did?"

"Yeah, and he's fighting over policy in the other room." Ransom plucks his earbud from his ear, then stows his phone in his pocket. "I think..." He palms his ear, pretending to listen. "I think Uncle Edward is calling me... in need of his pet instigator. Excuse me, gentlemen."

"Is he– is Ransom being serious?" Uriah's about to panic, voice warbling, hand gripping onto my arm.

"Relax." Kaden leans out the doorway, having an unimpeded view into the other room. "It's Ransom– he's going to debate Senator Edward Bishop Jr., not side with him... then he's going to flip it around, playing devil's advocate, and prove them both wrong."

"Why?" Uriah doesn't get it.

"Unlike me, Ransom plans on going into politics. Riding the center, he simultaneously pisses everyone off, while also siding with them. He becomes everyone's ally. They love and loathe the seventeen-year-old who may someday ruin them."

"Smart kid." Kade wanders off to go eavesdrop, as he usually does. Even the lady who wanted a pet or a dishpan scuttles out of the room to watch the show.

"Uncle Edward!" Ransom's voice rises in pitch. "You don't believe I have the right to marry whomever I wish?"

"Son." The strain in Uncle Edward's voice is obvious, even from rooms away. The consummate bachelor is rumored to enjoy male companionship from time to time himself. "That's not what I said."

"That's what it sounded like…" My attention span is cut short as Ransom's parents stride into the room, trying to blend into the surroundings as their son embarrasses the piss out of them in the other room.

"There's better food over there," Ainsley tells a couple taking up an entire sofa to themselves. "And champagne."

Walking past us, "Nice pants," Joel tells Uriah for the tenth time. "Please keep them," he begs, then moves on to try to bargain with the couple refusing to move.

"Why does Ransom's dad keep saying that to me?" Uriah stares at my would-be brother-in-law. "I have no idea if Joel's making fun of me for wearing them, thinks me poor for borrowing them, or is hitting on me."

"It's Joel," I offer as explanation. "His sense of humor is so dry and dark, it always goes right over our heads. He laughs during horror films and real-crime documentaries."

"You're kidding, right?"

"His son is currently pitting a republican senator and a democratic congressman against one another, with a quarter of Pennsylvania's higher government watching on. Do you honestly think it's not genetic?"

"Okay, but what's up with Joel's fascination with my pants?"

"Joel's making fun of himself– parental squabble with the instigator over those very pants. Joel truly means what he says. The pants suit you, and never give them back to Ransom." Smirking, I eye said pants with heated eyes. "They look great on your ass, but they are beyond obscene on Ransom's stocky frame. Obscene like the favorite jeans of mine you wear."

Turning to the side so no one can read my lips, I whisper, "I can see your juicy cockhead in those jeans, and it takes everything in me not to drop to my knees and bite it."

Whimpering, Uriah clenches my hand. "I should give these back for Ransom's future boyfriend to appreciate." Uriah turns teasing, blooming when given naughty attention. When it's unwanted attention, he clams up shy. When it's wanted attention, he blushes or becomes emboldened. It's fascinating to watch.

"Seriously, get your asses off my sofa." Ainsley's been short-tempered the past few days– Uriah keeps avoiding her, saying her chaotic energy is contagious. The couple mutters about how rude my sister's being, but at least they vacate the room.

"I need to get off my feet." Ainsley lands on the sofa with a heavy sigh.

"Oh, c'mon!" Joel throws his arms up in the air, voice projecting to the angry couple. "She said she was sorry."

"No, Ainsley didn't," Uriah mutters. "Your sister's energy is off the charts– it's suffocating."

"Well, she contributed to the other half of Ransom's genetics, and shares a close match to the man who had you making the sign of the cross to ward off his evil."

"You're right– I'm going to have to smudge myself with sage when I leave here." Uriah is dead serious, causing me to flinch with rejection. A moment later, he's chuckling underneath his breath. "Paintball."

"You... you ass!" Slapping Uriah's chest, I cop a feel as I pull away, swiping my fingertip across his nipple.

Uriah leans in to whisper in my ear. "What's up with them, anyway?" Joel is coddling Ainsley, talking her down from her recent shit-fit. "Are they, or aren't they, together?"

"Think about it... what man would stick around for eighteen years, all through his prime– Joel's only thirty-two, by the way – never dating anyone else... wouldn't it go to reason that Ainsley's been throwing him a bone on the regular?"

Eyebrows hitching high, *Really?* Uriah's voice pitches higher.

"We have theories– see, Joel's proposed six times, and Ainsley always starts shouting about how he's just asking because they share a son. She's terrified it's duty, not love, that has Joel asking her to marry him. He stopped asking about five years ago. We're now a few months shy of Ransom's eighteenth birthday, and Joel is around less and less, and Ainsley never comes home from Harrisburg."

"You think they're shacking up together now that Ransom's an adult?"

"That's my theory." Tilting my chin toward the sofa, we catch Ainsley nuzzling Joel's throat, giggling something into his ear.

"Joel's hand has been protectively on her belly since I met him," Uriah's points out, eyebrow raised wryly. "Rain and Bob did that nonstop when she was pregnant with the little ones. Ainsley's mood swings and bitching about getting off her feet– pregnant."

If I were Ransom, I'd crash across the room and demand answers. But I'm not, so I just stare at my sister with my mouth wide open in awe. "Good for her– good for Joel."

"Ransom is going to make this interesting," Uriah mutters with anticipation. "Babies are a blessing."

We share a look, and then both burst out laughing, because I've heard hours on end from Uriah about how his baby siblings drive him up a wall, sometimes quite literally.

A flash of blonde catches my eye– instinct has adrenaline flowing in my veins in an instant. My mouth waters profusely, unable to swallow it quickly enough. Gulping for air, my lungs don't work properly.

"I think I'm going to be sick," I warn, palm cupping over my mouth. Making a mad-dash for the foyer, it's a straight stretch to the kitchen, and then up the back staircase, taking two steps at a time. My panic has my stride wobbly, but I make it down the hallway in record time, banging into my bedroom, door colliding with the wall.

Lunging into my bathroom, I'm at the toilet, everything I've eaten and drank over the past few hours finding its way into the toilet, followed by a shit-load of bile. Dry-heaving, my stomach and throat muscles won't stop contracting.

With a shaking hand, I turn the knob to get water flowing from the tap. Sticking my entire head into the sink, I open my mouth and allow the cool water to flow into it, simultaneously rinsing away the foul taste and refilling my belly in case I need to throw up again.

Grabbing a hand towel, I wipe the sweat beaded on my brow and the water dripping off my chin as I re-enter my bedroom. I've got to go find Uriah and tell him what happened, fearing he'll worry.

Just as I'm about to step out into the hallway, a manicured hand presses against my chest, pushing me back into my bedroom by her very presence alone.

"What are you doing here?" I accuse, voice warbling. "No one is allowed in our personal rooms. Leave," I order, but with no authority backing it up.

In the face of a forty-something heiress, I'm no longer a twenty-year-old college senior on the cusp of adulthood. There's no such thing as a future or the present. No Uriah. No help. All I see is the past.

I'm transported back to how I felt that night. A dizzy drunk thirteen-year-old, terrified out of his mind, paralyzed on his bed while a woman stole his innocence. The room spins, back then and now– my eyes feel floaty, tears dripping down my cheeks.

Blonde hair trailing down to tickle my face. The heavy weight on my hips and thighs. The jarring movement of the bed. The feel of being inside another human being, before I even knew what that meant.

"Daniel," Mrs. Turner purrs, fingernails digging slightly into my chest, creating pulls in the weave of my shirt. "Didn't you want to greet me in front of your boyfriend? Or were you too worried the truth would be obvious?"

"The truth would be something to my advantage," I remind my rapist.

"The truth is subjective– thirteen or twenty, you can't prove when, sweetie, but I know you have a mole on your left testicle." Laughing a twinkling sound, Mrs. Turner flips her blonde hair over her shoulder, cold blue eyes regarding me with intense interest. "It would be easy to say I know because you took advantage of me. Overpowered me… *and I'm so very helpless*," she trails off, bottom lip quivering with false fear.

"Always reverse the truth to your advantage, just like your husband." Sneering, I hate myself for not saying anything back then, more worried about protecting my family than myself. "Attack your opponents with the very crime you committed."

Boys are never believed, especially when it's a beautiful, rich woman with a powerful husband.

We wanted it.

We're the aggressor.

Little boys are taught our dicks make us predators and vaginas make victims. As soon as an accusation is made, we're already tried and convicted. It's a form of manipulation evil has used since the dawn of time, because to not believe a victim makes a good person feel guilty, so they'll believe anything they hear in their quest to exact justice. Others jump in, thinking they are doing good by chastising those who want silly things such as evidence, until everyone is shamed to believe every accusation based on blind faith. But the real victims are those who lose their voice, both the innocently accused and the abused.

It's a witch-hunt, where the innocent is condemned and the evil thrives.

Rape doesn't have a gender, nor is it about sex. Power. Yet society lumps men of all ages into the same box, seeing women as delicate victims, even when they are older, bigger, and more powerful than the one they accused. Male victims are shamed, or discounted, when they come forward, so they don't, throwing off the very statistics used against us.

Equality means we have the ability to enact the same atrocities and shouldn't get a pass due to gender, no matter the statistics on who hurts who more. Men are raped. Every. Single. Day. By both men and women. Boys are molested. Every. Single. Day. By both men and women. It shouldn't be laughed off and ignored purely because it happens more to one gender than the other.

I knew it, and Ainsley was terrified of it when she found me– as a child, I would have been painted as a perverted rapist. Meanwhile, my rapist's husband would have gotten higher up in the food chain by stepping on our vulnerable backs, so I kept my goddamn mouth shut, felt powerless without justice sought, and had to look my rapist in the eyes during functions from that night forth.

"I like the adult version of you better." Purring again, more pulling at my shirt with her fingernails. "You've filled out."

"I've aged," I remind her, a few weeks shy of twenty-one. "Still not able to drink legally, among other things in most states. Still considered a child by the government, on my parents' insurances and needing their financial info for my student loans. With how old you are, you looking at me like that… it's gross."

"I think it's precious how you're saving yourself for me by dating that freak of nature downstairs." Mrs. Turner's words have rage igniting inside me, enough so I'm able to break out of the frozen trance she's placed me under.

Mrs. Turner is up here to get her rocks off. Power. There will be no sex, and not because I'd say no. She's furious Ransom is downstairs handing her husband his ass, so she's taking it out on me, getting off on the terror she inspires in me.

She wants me to snap and hit her.

I know it, she knows it, and we both know there's not a goddam thing I can do about it. Just as I can't physically remove her from this room, because she would struggle, and any marks left behind from said struggle will be used against me.

No one would believe me– the truth.

It would open up a pathway to the past, where Mrs. Turner would cry wolf about the rape she committed, but with me as the aggressor, saying it happened in the present.

Uriah thinks me wrong for refusing to vote– this is why. All power is corrupt. I've seen it from every side. Even my relatives got to where they are on the backs of others, by coercion and extortion, manipulation. Senator Edward Bishop Jr. is a criminal, I'm positive– on the other side of the coin, Congressmen Turner sicced his wife on me to hit Uncle Edward. This happens behind closed doors, away from the voting public, and there is no escaping it.

There are always people fighting the good fight, not realizing they are compromising their morals to get to where they need to be to make a real difference. But, by the time they get there, finally in the position to change the world, they are as corrupt as those they replaced.

It's a vicious cycle that infects the justice-minded souls. If they won't bend their ethical or moral code, they will be consumed by the system itself, unable to help anyone.

Stepping away, hands hanging loosely at my sides, I back toward the bathroom, where I plan to lock myself in until Mrs. Turner gives up and leaves. "I suggest you leave and never come back," I warn, pulling out my cellphone.

"Daniel," Turner purrs, advancing forward until she has me trapped by the edge of the bed. If I move a single inch, I'll either go directly into her or fall onto the bed, neither is a viable option of escape. "The way you felt inside me–" she leans in for a kiss, baiting me to either hit her or shove her away.

No matter what happens next, Mrs. Turner wins.

Locking every muscle in my body, I gulp down the urge to vomit all the water I swallowed. Mrs. Turner's gin-tinged breath flutters against my mouth, her lips turning upward in a victorious smirk.

A sharp intake of breath has Mrs. Turner swiveling with that evil smile locked in place, giving me a few inches of space to sidestep her, but my world crashes at my feet when I spot where the sound emanated.

Betrayal is etched across Uriah's features, lips drawn in a taut line and eyes narrowed with suspicion. "I knew I was right," is all he has to say, and I understand exactly what he means. All those negative thoughts swirling around in his head, what he wants to see confirms it. Validates his fears. Fears Uriah created.

It's exactly what anyone else would see if they walked in here. Me wanting it. Me asking for it. Me with Mrs. Turner pressed up against my bed in a romantic entanglement. No one would believe me, and Uriah's insecurities will never have him believing me either.

"This is not what it looks like," I stress, trying to walk around Mrs. Turner to get to my boyfriend. "Trust me—*please*," I beg, voice warping with rage and agony. "Please, Uriah, you have to listen to me."

"Daniel was the best I've ever had." Mrs. Turner will not quit trying to provoke me as my attention is drawn from her to Uriah. With Uriah in here, there's a good chance she'll get me to punch her to save my relationship with my boyfriend.

Snapping as I spot tears in Uriah's eyes. "Get out!" I scream, pointing at the door, glass reverberating from the force. "Get. The. Fuck. OUT!"

"Daniel's been waiting for me." Mrs. Turner advances on Uriah, and I freeze in terror. She runs her talons down his chest, smiling to herself. "Thank you for keeping him busy for me."

"I should have known," Uriah gasps, tears flooding his eyes. "Why would someone like me deserve someone faithful, right?"

"Hey, Danny?" Ransom's voice floods from the hallway. "You alright? I heard you shouting from downstairs." He skids to a stop, sees the tableau, and then immediately gets the gravity of the situation. "MOM!"

Throat open as loud as it could possible get, "MOM!" Ransom's shouting his head off. "MOM!" knowing every mother in this house will come running. "Get the fuck out, Gayle. Mom already told you to walk out of the room if Danny was in it."

"My husband was invited." Sober and confident, Mrs. Turner goes head-to-head with my nephew, who is infinitely stronger than I am when it comes to this woman. He's not terrified– he's enraged.

"That's only because we kept your fucking secret," Ransom snarls at the woman. "No one knows but us, knowing you're lying in wait to bring it out in hopes my uncle ever runs for office and you can twist his nuts to get him to do what your husband wants."

Gesturing to the six-foot tall blonde bitch, "This is my skeleton in the closet," flows despondently from my throat in a croaking sound. "Never you, Uriah."

Ainsley appears, gasping for breath from the run, with Joel at her side. To my utter shock, the man seems to know what's happening, immediately taking Mrs. Turner by the arm. "I'll escort you back down to your husband, and I'd suggest you give Daniel a wide-berth from now on, like I suggested the last hundred times you tried to pull this shit."

"I tried," Ainsley cries out, the agonized sound gutting me. "I got distracted. I always make sure you two are never in the same room." Following Joel and Mrs. Turner, "God, I'm so sorry, Danny," my sister says from the hallway.

With his parents and Mrs. Turner out of the room, Ransom looks between Uriah and me, getting the gist. "That was definitely *not* what it looked like," he warns.

"Who was that woman?" Uriah breathes, refusing to look at me.

"Ya know that congressman who hit on you in front of Danny? The very one I was engaging in battle with? The one you voted for?"

"Yeah," Uriah mouths, confused.

"That cunt is his wife." As soon as he drops that bomb, Ransom's yanking my frozen body into a quick hug, then he's over at the closet with my bag in his hand. "Let's get you two gone, yeah? I'll drive Kade home tomorrow, give you two some alone time, especially with that drive, yeah?"

"What's going on?" Uriah demands, voice tight with confusion and leftover betrayal.

"You two are never alone, are you?" Ransom begins bagging up my textbooks. "Always in the dorm room with Kade, or out in public because Uriah lives with his family, or stuck on a campus with a bazillion people. There's always someone or something wedging in there... you need to be alone, right? Danny?"

"Yes," I breathe, sounding like death warmed over. "We need to talk."

"Good." Ransom pats me on the shoulder on his way to the bathroom. "How about you help me pack your shit up, Uriah? Danny needs a minute to himself."

DIGNITY

Twenty minutes into the drive, Uriah hasn't said a word to me, and I wish I had his uncanny ability to read the energy weaving around somebody, because my mind-reading skills are offline.

My fingers are wrapped around the steering wheel, trying my damnedest to keep the shaking at bay. I'm chewing gum to help with the chattering teeth and to absorb my saliva. The air is cranked to combat the cold-sweats, and the radio is blaring to drown out the noises I'm making– maybe that's why Uriah's not talking, since I wouldn't be able to hear him anyway.

"Do we have any more water." It takes three tries, swallowing down all the saliva my body is creating, to get the words out. My salivary glands are on revolt, constantly pumping into my mouth– the more I swallow, the more I have bile rising in my throat. I've tried holding it in my mouth, because swallowing makes the contractions in my gag-reflex activate.

Not doing so good.

"Are you sure you're okay to drive?" Uriah twists the cap off a bottle of water, then holds it out for me to take.

"Yes," I squeak, water splashing everywhere because I can't focus the shaking on clenching the steering wheel if I'm grabbing the bottle so hard I squeeze it like a drink box. "Need something to concentrate on."

"There's a gas station coming up." Uriah points to a sign. "I need to take a leak."

Uriah's lying. I know he is and he knows I know, but he also knows I'll do anything if it's for him. He wants me to stop for me, so I stop.

I'm not entirely sure how, but I get the Durango off the road and into the parking lot, but it's a total fail on parking straight. After parking and turning off the ignition on autopilot, my neck refuses to support my head, falling against the headrest with an audible thump, eyes slipping shut.

The locks are hit, and a few seconds later, I startle as my door is being wrenched open. Uriah's hand slides across my belly, reaching to unhook my seatbelt. After that business is taken care of, he grabs my thigh to swirl me around to face him.

"Hey." Worrying his bottom lip, I hate how the glow in Uriah's eyes has dimmed to sad. "I'm going to help you into the passenger seat, okay?"

"Okay," I mutter limply, unsure if I can get my legs to carry me there.

Palms cup my face, warm and supportive. "We can talk about it if you want– you can trust me." Before I can respond, Uriah's brushing the flyaway hair off my forehead. "*I trust you*," he stresses. "So you need to trust me. It took me about thirty seconds to figure out something else was going down."

Eyes slipping shut, I rest my cheek in Uriah's palm, soaking up the attention. "It's complicated. Politics and other shit."

"Yeah, it's the *other shit* I'm worried about right now." Drawing me down to his lips, Uriah kisses my forehead, my cheeks, the tip of my nose, even my eyelids. "It's going to be okay– I'm here for you, just tell me what you need."

"Distract me, because I can't tell you why I'm upset, not while trapped in a car for the next few hours." What I don't tell Uriah, I might need a toilet to heave into, and copious amounts of water to pave the way. "Let's get home, and maybe I'll feel better once I explain."

"I have an idea." Uriah hooks his arm around my waist, and it's a good thing we're the same height for even weight distribution. For as thin as Uriah is, he's all wiry muscle and willpower. Pushing me into the passenger seat with a gentle shove, "Ugh, yeah… get settled in." Hands grip my thighs, swirling back into the seat, and then my seatbelt is hooked again.

With the slam of the driver's side door, Uriah's already talking. "How about we get a hotel room, huh?" He tries to be perky, smiling at me as he pulls out of the parking lot. "I saw a sign for a Holiday Inn Express about ten miles from here."

"That sounds wonderful." Swallowing nonstop, I really need to figure out how to get my body's involuntary reactions to knock that shit off. "Any idea how to get salivary glands to stop going nuts?"

"It's an anxiety reaction– same as the other things you're unsuccessfully trying to hide." Uriah hitches his eyes in my direction, flicking to my forehead, my mouth, then down to my hands. "Until you relax, you're not going to feel better."

"Christ." Closing my eyes, I bang my head backward repeatedly on the backrest.

"I... I-uh, recognize it because I felt like that after the bachelor party," Uriah admits hesitantly. "I love to sound strong and badass, but as soon as I told the girls, I kinda crashed and burned. Sad to say, it was my professor asking for services that gave me my power back."

"Trust me– I'm not discounting your journey –but that ain't gonna fucking work in this case."

"I know, but I'm just saying I get the physical manifestation of mental and emotional pain– the panic. Your head is foggy, but your body is just doing all this shit and you can't stop it. I get it, not that saying that helps any."

"It helps," I gulp out, then swallow a billion times.

"Shower. Food. Sleep. Distraction. Conversation. Distraction. Not necessarily in that order," is just what Dr. Uriah Crane orders as he pulls into the hotel parking lot. "Sit tight, I'll only be a few minutes."

What feels like a few seconds, my eyes are snapping wide as my door suddenly opens, arm falling to my side. The supportive hands are back, sure and strong.

"I got us a king room, and I paid extra for a late checkout tomorrow afternoon, since we're checking-in so late tonight– no need to rush back to campus on a Sunday." Mouth moving, I attempt to respond. "Don't worry, we can study in the morning in the quiet of the hotel, and we can switch off driving, quizzing each other."

"You're amazing," I breathe as my feet land on pavement.

"But wait– there's more," echoes like a gameshow host. Grinning, Uriah wraps his arm around my waist, but instead of how I always do it because I'm proud he's on my arm, he's doing it to support me. "We're in luck. They actually have room service."

"I don't know about food," I grumble, stomach revolting.

"Trust me." Uriah kicks the door shut, then hits the fob. "I'll get you up to the room, then I'll come back for our bags. Let's get your feet moving– you'll feel better. More human."

By the time we hit the elevator, I'm moving on autopilot but without the need of Uriah's support. His arm wrapped around me feels fantastic though, especially since I was terrified I was going to lose him because of Mrs. Turner.

"You're a good man, Daniel Bishop." Uriah's been singing my praises the entire walk. "You're a giver, a caretaker. You think being strong and taking care of your family is what it means to be a man. To be sensitive is to be weak, which translates into being feminine."

Uriah releases me, making sure the wall is there to catch me should my knees give out, then he inserts the keycard into the door. Once the door is open, his mouth is moving again.

"I will admit, that even gets to me sometimes– the need to be strong. Maybe it's my gender-fluidness, but I don't think being a caretaker is universally a male trait. Once you meet Rain, you'll see what I mean." Uriah's arm comes back around my waist, getting my feet moving again.

"Room's nice– anyway, it's a human trait in certain personalities. The need to be strong. The giver. The caretaker. The person who has to always be on and available to others. We attribute this to males, yet it more accurately describes the mothers of our species. Most mothers, anyway– sure as fuck not mine."

Hands smooth up my sides, hooking into my armpits, and then I'm slowly lowered to the bed. Uriah stands above me, eyes taking inventory of my person. "Something you need to know about me, Daniel Bishop…" he trails off.

Uriah's looking at me quizzically, so I return the look and ask at the same time, "What?"

"There are many reasons why I've held back when it comes to us." Uriah cups my cheek, lifting my face, forcing me to meet his gaze. "Kaden, for one. My past, but not because of my heritage or mother– *prostitution*," he twists out, smirking without humor.

"I feared that two givers. Two caretakers. How they couldn't find a happy medium without it essentially changing the other's personality. It's about balance, and if we're fighting who gives, both too stubborn to take, which one of us will turn into a narcissist to right the balance."

Stepping away, Uriah feathers his fingers through my hair, as if he doesn't want to stop touching me. "Think that over while I get the bags, if you can… it's your distraction."

Sitting on the bed, my mind is too blurry to focus on the task at hand. Instead, I concentrate on how the television is brand new and offset for better viewing on one side of the bed versus the other, instead of centered.

The room is mellow, with burnt orange accents and pictures of woodland creatures and hilly mountainsides from the region. The TV rests on a bureau, and I'd bet good money there is a mini-fridge and microwave behind the larger door opposite the drawers and open cubbyholes.

"Kade would love this piece of furniture in our dorm room— multipurpose, space-saver," I mutter to myself, no doubt losing it.

Uriah returns, breathing hard from carrying all the bags at once, and he picks right up where he left off. "We've been having a power-struggle, you and I. I've watched you with Kade, how he just takes what you're offering with a smile on his face, and you glow when he asks for more."

The bags are dropped on the floor, then Uriah goes about divvying them up to their rightful locations. The bookbags on the desk, the toiletry bags in the bathroom, and the weekender bags on the luggage stand.

"You always give into Kade." Uriah starts rooting around in his bag. "With me, I'm always struggling to give to you, but you won't take it— you're so worried about giving to me, you don't realize I'm trying to be generous and giving too. Like in the dining hall, or at Subway— I loved the switch the subs, getting to know you, by the way —buying me shit at the toy shop but not giving it to me once you realized that was a stupid move ...

"Emotionally, I get that I'm high-maintenance." A shirt is flung from the bag, making room for Uriah to find whatever he's looking for. "We all have flaws, and I'm working on it. As for the girly shit, I heard it asked whether or not I take forever in the bathroom—"

"I'm sorry," I mutter lamely, just now realizing how thin the door is from my bedroom to bathroom.

"I like to primp, and take bubble baths, and cook and do crafts with the kids, and be lazy and binge-watch TV, but that doesn't make me a girl. I love to study and take classes, and fix things around the house, and play basketball and video games, but that doesn't make me a boy."

Getting fired up, Uriah takes it out on the contents of his bag, mostly the clothing he borrowed from his family, because he had brought it trying to fit in to the very thing he is going off at the mouth about.

"There's no either/or with me, where little girls giggle and boys don't cry. I don't ascribe gender to emotions, to activities, to objects. Bows tie to hold back something– it's not masculine if made of leather or feminine if formed of silk. Chocolate is a food source, not an estrogen leveler. It's a bubble bath, not a feminine bathing ritual. It's a shower, not a masculine washing rite of passage. A Bic for Her writes exactly the same as a regular Bic pen. Pink is not a vagina and blue a penis. It's science-fiction, not a dick flick. It's a rom-com, not a *chick flick*." Uriah stands before me, pissed off again. "That doesn't make me high-maintenance."

"You're right." I follow James Bishop's rules of marriage and just agree.

"Growing up, I had to take care of my mother and me– I've heard Bob and Rain wondering if my gender-fluidness was due to me being the mother and father to myself, instead of just accepting I was born this way. I cooked and cleaned and bought the groceries and paid what bills I could get my hands on. But Mom wouldn't eat the food, because a drunk only drinks their meals. She messed the house back up, and sold the groceries. She bought booze and drugs and smokes with the bill money. It was an uphill battle to take care of a person who was working so hard to be negligent, and that meant no one was taking care of me.

"I'm not high-maintenance because I wanted to buy my own food on the day we met. I'm not stubborn– I've always taken care of myself, even when I moved in with Rain. To prove I appreciated it, I helped do the chores and take care of the little kids, doing more than Bob's kids because it was their house, and I had to prove I deserved to be in it with them."

"Oh, Ri!" I reach forward to grab his hand, but he sidesteps me.

"Ri? I like that." Uriah touches my chin, smiling down at me. "So I worry about us. I worry we won't find a balance of give and take. You'll think you should give no matter what, until you're drained dry and there's nothing left of you… and somehow, I'll look like a high-maintenance gold-digger, because I can't find my place in the power structure that is our relationship. Not gonna enable you, nor am I going to be enabled. I'm looking for something I've never had– not codependency, *equality*. Partnership."

Uriah digs in my bag, finding my pajama pants. Holding the swath in one hand, he grabs my wrist in the other. "Tonight, it's my turn. No ifs, ands, or buts, I'm taking care of you. All night. Tomorrow morning. Tomorrow afternoon, when we get back to campus, you can take the wheel again. Okay?"

"Okay," I gasp out in shock, relief so potent I almost lose my balance.

I was born into a family with a firm structure in place, where I just fell in line. I was only three when Ainsley got pregnant and all the family's focus was on her, then Ransom arrived. I was cuddled, and I was loved, but somewhere along the journey, I felt taking care of Ransom was my job, plus worrying about my grandparents as they aged, so Ainsley could get her education and Dad could focus on his cases as Grandpa got close to retiring. I turned into Mom's mini-me as she and Grandma kept the family in line. Then my education became my job, because I needed to walk in my father's footsteps to avoid stepping in the tracks the rest of my extended family laid down before me.

Then there was Kaden, where I've been terrified every single second of every day, in the back of my mind, worrying about his mental state and whether or not I'd find him cutting again, or worse– every time I open our dorm room door, I fear what I'll find on the other side. That level of stress takes a toll on a person.

All the while, I never worry about me, always too busy to fix what Mrs. Turner broke, and that's why tonight happened.

"Thank you," I whisper to Uriah as he helps me into the bathroom.

My brain switches back on, but in the place of panic is induced calm. Knowing this won't last, but it's too pleasant to take for granted, I try to be in the moment with Uriah.

We don't speak, a deeper intimacy growing between us as I allow Uriah to take control for once. All those questions in the beginning of our relationship, where Uriah was hesitant to answer, because I was making it one-sided in a quest to make it not about me. I was curious and intrigued, wanting to know all there was to know about Uriah Crane– what I failed to realize was, that perhaps, he felt the same way about me.

You never fail to surprise me, Daniel Bishop.

If I expect Uriah to trust me, then I need to trust him.

Holding my gaze, Uriah slowly unbuttons my shirt, his nimble fingers suddenly fascinating to watch as they pluck button after button. Warm palms snake underneath the fabric, then skate up the planes of my chest, curling around my shoulders, shirt falling to the ground.

Damp lips press against the center of my chest, hot breath causing a shiver to roll its way down my spine. I long to touch Uriah back, but this is a test he is giving, one that will leave us both as winners if I pass.

Breath hitches in both our throats, the hushed sound surprisingly loud in the tiled room, as Uriah slowly draws down my fly. Button still fastened on my trousers, Uriah flows down fluidly to crouch by my feet. Rolling his eyes to meet mine, they take on a golden note I've never noticed before, a color I hope to see gazing at me often.

This is the Uriah I first met, the commanding, in control, naughty Uriah who feels empowered on his knees. Smirking, no doubt Uriah's sensing the direction of my thoughts, or maybe it's the erection prodding out my unzipped fly, straining my black boxers for escape.

In silence, Uriah preforms the most basic of tasks, but it somehow feels new and exciting– the simple act of unlacing my shoes, something that hasn't been done for me since I learned to tie my shoes at age three.

With a funny little smile on his face, Uriah's voice is soft, sounding loud after all the silence. *"Build a teepee, come inside. Close it tight, so we can hide. Over the mountain and around we go... Here's my arrow, and here's my bow!"*

Instead of untying both shoes, Uriah sings a song from his childhood while he reties the laces, fingers going through the motions at the appropriate times.

Smiling up at me, Uriah presses on the back of my knee, the other hand going to the heel of my shoe to take it off. "Rain taught me that song, saying it was neat how folks used us for teaching aids instead of just Disney movies, Westerns, and Thanksgiving."

Smirking, he tosses my loafer across the bathroom. "Stubborn, refusing to learn, I've been teaching Winter to tie her shoes, and she thinks it's great, even if I find it rather ironic and tasteless."

"A kid's happiness should come first," I mutter, amused for both Uriah and his little sister.

"That they do." Uriah's expression turns sober, focused on me, as if he can somehow guess I was a child when I was harmed. "That it should." My second shoe lands next to the first, followed by my socks.

Kneeling before me, Uriah proves he's the one with all the power right now, even when he's physically beneath me. That mischievous glint is back, forcing my heart to start chugging faster and faster with every passing breath.

Palms run along my calves, curving around my knees, and run up my thighs, thumbs purposefully nudging my bulge on their way by. With a quick pop, the button on my trousers unfastens with practiced ease.

I've never felt this way, not even with Kade. The anticipation. The lust warring with intimacy. My wants competing with making sure Uriah's needs are met.

Always, I was the selfless one, thinking more of my lover's pleasure than my own. Tonight, I feel selfish, having a hunger that is trying to find its voice.

I don't know if this is a good thing or bad– is this where I turn into the narcissistic leech always taking? Or is this what it truly means to find a balance, where I have needs that should be met, just as Uriah does, and we make sure both happens?

Maybe Uriah's sensing the energy around me, or maybe my thoughts are broadcast across my face, or maybe it's my cock drooling through my boxers, but a satisfied chuckle rolls off Uriah's tongue, sounding positively smug.

Kaden created Uriah's drag name. Envy. But I never felt it suited him. Standing here, watching Uriah find pleasure and purpose in servicing me, with that devious little smirk flirting with his lips, his drag name whispers through my mind.

"Minx." I try it out for size, finding it perfect as it rolls off my tongue. "If I'm your cowboy, then you're my minx."

Biting his lip is a tactic I'm starting to wonder if it isn't a seductive tool used to look coy, be it highly calculated. Then the blush flows across Uriah's pale cheeks, flooding color in a deep wash, and I know without a shadow of a doubt, he's innocent and glowing from the attention.

Fingers slip beneath the waistband of my boxers, then slowly side downward, taking my pants along for the ride. My hard-on gives Uriah some difficulty, as he's trying very hard not to touch it or look at it, which is comical when he's blushing and side-eyeing it with interest. It's sweet though, how he's trying to respect me after the night I had, instead of giving me the impression this is only about sex.

Reaching into the shower stall, Uriah cranks the water, tests its temperature, and then shoves me inside. Immediately, my face seeks the spray, neck bowed upward as water cascades in a cleansing wash over my head, into my mouth, and down my body.

Curious, I wonder if Uriah will join me– not once have I seen him completely naked. I've never seen his cock, only the meaty outline in those illegal jeans of his that never fail to make my mouth water.

"Behave," is a whispered warning as Uriah slips into the shower behind me, hard cock nudging at my ass cheek, but I can't guess to its size or shape. "Let me take care of you tonight."

Continuing on from undressing me to washing me, Uriah is in caregiver-mode, with both of us desperately trying to ignore how it feeds into our lustier natures.

"Ah!" is a throaty moan as Uriah slips his arms beneath mine and reaches around me, naked front aligning perfectly with my back, cock pressed upward to wedge along my crack. Slick skin sliding along slick skin as he works a bar of soap between his hands to a rich lather.

Panting, Uriah tortures me as his soapy hands touch every inch of my body, from the roots of my hair to the bottoms of my feet, and all the naughty locations in between. The feel of Uriah's hot breath skating across my skin, as he washes me, is a transcendental experience… and then he passes me the soap.

"Jesus!" I'm on Uriah in a second. Hands everywhere, breathing in sharp gasps as I finally get to see all of him unimpeded by fabric or hidden by shadows. "Stunning."

I try, I try very hard, not to go straight to the spot I've never seen. It helps how Uriah's fleshy nipples are utterly fascinating, how they are larger than mine, more meaty and fleshy, aroused and suckable. I spend way too much time cleaning this area, earning me a few breathy moans and a chuckle for my efforts.

Leaving one of the best places for last, I do the opposite of how Uriah washed me. Whereas he pressed to my back, I press our fronts together, hands curving over the perfect handfuls of his ass. Only because I'm thorough, a fingertip sneaks down his smooth crack to swirl around his pucker. That's when I feel it, and that's when I need to greet it.

Uriah's cock bucks against my stomach, an inch or two too far left to align with mine. Instead of seeking instant gratification by shifting my hips slightly, I drop down into a crouch to wash his cock.

In the near silence, Uriah's panting breath hitches as I take him in hand for the first time. Long and thin, looking longer than it is because it's so thin. Pale with nary any visible veins, it's flawless with a blushed pink head.

I never thought I'd say this, because most cocks are just ugly– not grotesque, just ugly. Wrinkly. Grublike. Angry looking at times. Don't get me wrong, I love my cock, and I enjoyed touching Kade's in the dark, but Uriah's looks different to me.

"Your cock is the prettiest thing I've ever seen." Ignoring the ridiculous urge to coo at it. "I want to put a pink bow around the base, because it's like a present."

Laughing a giddy sound that rings in my ears, Uriah's body flushes in a visible wave from the center of his chest. "I'm naturally hairless, in case you're curious. It's sparse down there and doesn't grow anywhere else."

Smug.

Smug is a good color on Uriah.

"So pretty." I tap the head, never having been this close to a cock besides my own– not even then, since mini-Dan will forever be two and a half feet from my face, no matter what. It takes all my self-control not to take Uriah in my mouth or stroke him with my hand.

I was told to behave.

As I slide back to my feet, I quickly steal a kiss, lips feathering briefly across the tip of Uriah's cock. Flowing to my full height, I lick my bottom lip, tasting soap and something more exotic melt on my tongue.

"Ugh!" Hair gripped, I'm shoved up against the shower wall, five and a half feet of naked minx plastering himself to my body. Writhing waves go through us, our cocks getting into the action, trying to rut against one another, with getting off as the objective.

Uriah tugs my wet hair, struggling to get a grip, mouth so close to mine. Growling, teeth bared, those fingers tighten in my hair. "Not yet," is whispered across my lips. "Almost, but not yet." Pulling away with another growl, "Holy fuck, I want to kiss you." …and then he bites me in the neck. Hard. Leaving a mark, probably even bleeding me, but I can't tell with hot water cascading over us.

"Bed. Now." Confused as to why Uriah is placing so much weight into a kiss, I walk on wobbly legs to the bed area.

For me, kissing is an intimate experience, more so than sex even. I can't even remember who I shared my first kiss with, but after I realized I didn't enjoy it, I stopped doing it. Kade taught me that was because a kiss held importance for me. I needed to feel an emotional connection.

I could have kissed Uriah within seconds of meeting him, that's how jacked up to him I've been, so it confuses me as to why he's still holding out on something we both want.

We towel each other dry, and then Uriah helps me step into a pair of pajama bottoms, doing his damnedest to ignore my cock. However, testing my sanity, Uriah remains nude, walking before me into the bed area.

After all the salivary action, my mouth runs dry at the sight of Uriah's ass– toned and rounded, it's the surprising amount of jiggle that has a guttural groan escaping my lips. I envision myself lunging forward, dropping to my knees, grabbing Uriah by the hips to stop his onward movement, and then biting his ass harder than he bit my neck in the shower.

Smirking, no doubt laughing at me on the inside, a brightly blushing Uriah points at the bed after pulling back the sheet. "Lie on your stomach. I'll just be a minute– we're going to make sure you're relaxed."

Doing as Uriah bids, a laundry list of options, all ending with cum on these sheets, comes to mind on how to relax me. There's rustling in our bags, then the sharp metallic sound of a zipper being pulled shut. With a thump, the bags are put back into their rightful place.

With steady yet light pressure, Uriah settles onto the backs of my thighs, and I curse the person who created pajama bottoms, so badly wishing I could feel Uriah's naked flesh upon mine again. The scent of almond fills the air, then the telltale sound of something liquid being squeezed from a bottle has me tensing in an instant. But then comes another sound— the sound of Uriah being thoughtful and kind.

Uriah warms the lotion between his palms before pressing them to my back. Working in silence, he loosens my muscles with his sure but small hands, with a surprisingly firm grip. He's not gentle with me, going deep, but the slight edge of pain is almost a pleasure in and of itself.

Uriah knows exactly what he's doing, but somehow it goes straight over my head until the words starts spewing out. Uriah's trusting me. He's taking care of me. He's opening himself up to my rejection should I not return his trust.

Uriah's not testing me— he's proving he can be exactly what I need, if only I'd let him.

"I hate politics," I admit out loud for the first time. "I. Hate. IT. The pathway was opened to me because Uncle Edward never had children. My uncle loves me, respects my decision to avoid politics, and he is good to me. His allies and enemies all treat us as if Ransom and I are his heirs, and that has its own set of problems."

"I'm so fucking sorry I made the sign of the cross after Edward walked off," Uriah croaks out, causing me to laugh.

"Uncle Edward tried to push me toward politics, wishing to have me by his side. But it's not in my nature. He's always treated Ransom and me as his sons— technically, we're living in his home too, ya know? He just never put up a stink about Dad being clingy to their parents. Ransom fits with Uncle Edward, and I'm not jealous… their mock-debates feed some thrill in each of them. They love to debate, argue, and disagree, and I'm happy they have each other."

Sighing, I take what is freely being offered and use Uriah's touch to center me. "A part of me hates women too– not gonna lie, and I feel horrible saying it, as most of my favorite people are women."

"Why?" Uriah breathes softly, trying not to startle me, but needing me to answer before I move on and fail to explain myself.

"I'm not a misogynist– my sister is a feminist, and she raised me just as much as my own mother did. As soon as I said anything even remotely unbalanced, Ainsley would slap me upside the head with her words."

"Cut you down for size?" Uriah muses, amusement obvious. "I can see your sister doing that."

"Misandry isn't the polar opposite of misogyny, even though some of Ainsley's friends would love to say it doesn't exist." Turning, I look at Uriah over my shoulder. "I'm not saying misogyny isn't a big issue, but we're not talking about women right now. I'm telling you about me– *a man*, in both gender and physical sex, and this is my take on the world. I'll leave a woman to discuss her struggles in a misogynistic world as a woman. But she better allow me to discuss misandry without thinking I'm discounting her, all the while she discounts my journey. We're not mind-readers, and only those affected have a voice about a specific issue."

Sensing I'm getting defensive, having to explain myself, Uriah rests his hands on my shoulders, finding a pressure point with his thumbs to take the fight out of me. "I want to know what's going on inside that amazing mind of yours, cowboy. *Please?*"

"True feminism fights both misogyny and misandry, Ainsley taught me that. Two wrongs don't make a right– you don't cut anyone down to raise yourself higher… and I feel weird saying this to you, because sometimes I don't understand your gender-fluidness, but there are differences between the sexes that cannot be denied, at least in the majority of us. They should be embraced, not erased. I don't mean attributed to a specific gender, just not vilified."

"Believe me, I know that better than anyone." Uriah continues to touch me, evidently not offended by my commentary.

"As a kid, I had no autonomy, and I was raised by no less than three women at all times. I understand when you're very young, you have to be protected from yourself, since a child is incapable of predicting consequences. Don't touch the stove. Don't walk home alone. Don't play with matches. Take a shower. Eat. Sleep. Do your homework."

"I have Sunny and Winter hanging off me, remember?" Uriah's laughter eases me some.

"I think adults forget what it's like to be a kid, but it's stuck in my head all this time. The negatives. At some point, it stops being about boundaries and keeping your child safe, and turns into a power struggle. In their infinite wisdom– *bullshit!*" I cough loudly "–none of us know what the fuck we are doing, no matter how old we are. In their infinite wisdom, they pass on their knowledge– *bullshit!*" I cough again. "Baggage."

"Drunk mother, remember? I'm feeling ya on this topic, cowboy."

"I have no idea what it's like for a girl, or for someone who doesn't identify with a gender, but I can tell you how this little boy felt. Stifled. Silenced. If you don't like it, eat it anyway, even if it's about your taste buds, not because you're being picky. Don't be rude, give that hug to a distant family member you've never met before. Kiss that stranger on the cheek in thanks for saying you look cute and how you're going to grow up to be a heartbreaker– it's not disturbing to sexualize a toddler, or anything, is it?

"Don't be rude, talk to the nice lady you've never seen before. Don't be rude, let that stranger wash dirt off your face, zip your fly, or tie your shoe– don't forget to say thanks, even if you're creeped out to have their big hands on you. Don't be rude, share, as if it's not yours and you have no right to say what happens to it. Don't be rude, you can't hide in your room while your house is invaded by dozens of strangers more than two feet taller than you, who look at you like a trained pet and use condescending baby talk. Don't be rude... don't speak unless spoken to, do as you're told, and don't tell anyone you don't want to do it... don't say no."

"Oh, shit!" Uriah's hands still on my back, and I have a feeling he knows exactly where I'm going with this.

"Go to sleep at the same time as your nephew, when you're twelve and will lie in bed staring at the ceiling, finding it hard to fall asleep because you were forced in bed at seven in the evening, hours before your natural clock will allow you to drift off.

"My sister was verbally tearing me down for saying anything negative about a woman, even when it's not because of her gender, but because she was treating me poorly, and it wasn't fair. It was never fair. Ever. Treat people as you wish to be treated– I am, dammit! But they are *NOT* returning the respect. If I helped someone with their math problems, and then they made fun of me on the playground, I'd get in trouble for refusing to help them again, just because they were a girl."

Sighing, Uriah leans forward to kiss the nape of my neck, trying to soothe me as I lose my shit.

"I'm not discounting a female's journey, but I won't ignore my own because of some pissing-contest on who has it worse. This is my story, and I feel guilty voicing it, like I'm whining *what about me?!* But the problem is sitting in silence, always worrying about how others think and feel."

"Rain does that to me too, so I cannot imagine having three-generations of Bishop women doing it to you."

"Not just them– but teachers and my aunts and cousins. I appreciate it, I do, because I understand to the best of my ability what women go through, so I behave at all times… and before you scoff about the amount of women who have been on my cock, I'm getting to it."

"I will never judge you," Uriah promises, and I believe him, because he understands what it's like to be judged.

"At school, I was treated as if I was going to grow up as an entitled, little prick, treating me as one right then when I was a little boy. My teachers were hard on me, almost angry at me because I was a boy, because I was born into the family I was. At home, I learned by example, how men have no autonomy or else it's misogyny. Do as they say. All three women treated Dad and Grandpa no different than they did me and Ransom– to our faces, treated two grown men we saw as our heroes *as children*. They would laugh and mock them when out of earshot, thinking we couldn't hear, or we were too stupid to retain it. Grandpa and Dad were strong enough and smart enough to stand before a judge and battle, but too stupid to know how to take out the trash when ordered to do so."

Uriah's chuckling says it all.

"Ransom and I have discussed this a lot, because I only felt safe talking to him about it. I'd be verbally smacked if I said anything negative about a woman, when that negative was to bring to attention how it wasn't fair how they treated Dad like an idiot. My mind is built to see everything from the center– a wide scope with a large view. I'm justice-minded, no bringing emotion into the issue, so when Dad would tell me it was easier to agree with a woman instead of standing up for yourself, I began to resent them as a boy. Pick your battles– *they are right, and you are wrong* was hammered into my head…

"No autonomy. No privacy. No dignity. Reach over and use a fingernail to pop a zit on my forehead, or talk about the mortifying, confusing physical changes I was going through, in *public*, around people I didn't know. Around twelve, any of the women in my house would take me by the hand and tell me my boy-stink was driving them nuts. They would wrench my arm and toss my ass into the shower, and then scrub the piss out of me. I was going through puberty, and it was embarrassing. It was as if my body didn't belong to me, *but to them*. They told me what to eat, when to eat it, when to sleep, what to do every waking hour, and not because of boundaries, but because of a power-struggle as old as the test of time, and it had nothing to do with me."

"Jesus Christ, cowboy." Uriah shifts on my hips. "I see what you mean. I never thought about it before. But I see it with Sunny now. This has nothing to do with gender, but I have a feeling you're getting to why that matters. Sunny is independent and loves it when I watch her and Winter. When Rain is around, she's more worried about the girls doing as she says instead of listening to why they are doing it the way they are. Tell them to do their homework, but then interrupt them to take out the trash, and then pitch a fit if they don't take the trash out in the middle of working on their fractions. Call 'em lazy, and say they never do as asked."

"Exactly– *asked*, yet it's a demand. Now, or I'm going to ruin the rest of your day for not bowing to my demand when I wanted you to. My father chose his profession because he didn't want to go into politics. He saw how my grandmother treated my grandfather, and he wanted to give a voice to that type of marriage in mediation. The irony is how Dad drifted to allow it to happen in his own marriage. I love my mother. I love my grandmother. We all have flaws, and I accept them as they are, but what it taught me was to my detriment, and now I refuse to live in the imbalance."

"To be honest, I'm a little bit scared to see how this connects."

"You should be– and it makes little boys and girls susceptible because of it." Gulping, I swallow down the copious amounts of saliva that is firing again. "Stranger danger teaches us how men are bad. Our mothers teach us to run to a woman, because to tell us not to trust women would be tantamount to telling us not to trust our mothers. Women do bad things, but not as often as men, or so the flawed statistics say, so we'll just focus on the men being bad. But it leaves children open to stranger danger, and the way we are raised teaches us that one gender is to be feared and the other is safe. Stranger danger should be genderless, and it shouldn't just flow to strangers.

"I was thirteen, body maturing, emotionally the same with Ransom. Ransom's always been mature, going through puberty a year and half after me. I've always seen us as equals until recently, when that almost four-year gap widened because at twenty-one to his seventeen, our mentalities are finally different. But at nine and thirteen– I was still playing with toys, still sharing a bathtub because Ransom liked to use body paint. Innocent, naïve, and sheltered. Girls weren't on my radar– I kind of knew how babies were made, because Ransom exists. Thinking a boy and girl rubbed on each other, not knowing there was a hole, because Ransom was taken from Ainsley's belly, not between her legs."

Uriah's body is frozen above me, and I know he knows where I'm headed with this.

"Inside my home, in a quest to right the past wrongs done to women by men, the women in my family didn't realize they were harming the young men they were raising as they told us men were bad. I was taught to trust women, to give them what they wanted, because to say no meant I was a misogynistic prick. They are always right, never doing any wrong. I was taught my body didn't belong to me, but to my grandmother, mother, and sister, and someday it would belong to my wife. Even at eighty years old, Grandma controls Grandpa's diet and what time he goes to bed. I had no say in it if I was tossed into the tub and scrubbed, or hugged by strangers, or told to kiss a relative that gave me the creepy-crawlies. I was taught men were the danger– and I felt badly about myself because I was going to grow up to be a man. A bad man.

"With politics, I didn't know there were enemies and allies. As I said, this is Uncle Edward's family home too. We hosted parties every weekend when Uncle Edward was in town. I was so focused on the policies they were discussing, not tuned to the underlying words not being said. Enemies are allies, allies are enemies, and political lines mean nothing in the quest to get what you want to feel powerful. I'm of another mindset, where the policies mattered, but those are the fools who either turn to the dark side or get devoured."

"What do you mean?" Uriah's no doubt confused about the swift, conversational switch-up.

"You'll stab your ally in the back if you feel you're doing it for the greater good, but that's not how I view the world. Ethics are important to me, and to bend even a bit is to give up on who I am. The reason you're fighting so hard, it gets lost in the crimes and atrocities you commit to get that bill passed... I didn't know this at thirteen, thinking them all virtuous people, fighting hard for the people, not realizing I would be used as a pawn because Uncle Edward saw me as his heir.

"We were having a party, and I was listening to every word Uncle Edward was saying to Congressman Turner. They were frenemies, opposing parties, but in different parts of government. The hand that strikes you is not the hand that called the strike. They are always three or four people removed, so the motivations are always unclear, and the evidence trail leads to nowhere."

"You were hurt for political gain?" Uriah tests the words on his tongue, evidently finding them unsavory.

"Yes, by a woman." Swallowing a good dozen times, bile rises in my throat. "Uncle Edward and Turner love to debate. We were all standing around watching, even Ransom. Mrs. Turner kept refreshing everyone's glasses, as if she was the lady of the house. Ransom and I were having virgin versions of the drinks the adults were drinking, because we liked mimicking them, but mine tasted funny... I told Ransom I wasn't feeling so good, then ran up to our room."

"Exactly like tonight," Uriah notices the similarities as to why tonight hit me so hard, versus all the other times I've seen Mrs. Turner in public.

"The room was spinning, and I had cold sweats, and I thought if I went to bed, I'd feel better, because that was what I was taught to do. I struggled to get out of my clothing. A waistcoat. Tie. Dress shirt. Undershirt. Suspenders. Belt. Trousers. Briefs. Socks. Shoes. Because Ransom and I were dressed as dapper little gentlemen, which is why I refuse to dress that way now. What Kaden finds as armor, I find suffocating."

"I'd wondered why you didn't dress like the rest of your family," Uriah muses, voice barely audible.

"Ransom loves the very thing that put me in harm's way… I struggled to get changed. I was going to go into the bathroom after I got my pajamas on, but I took too long. Mrs. Turner walked into my room just as I was tugging my pajama pants up my legs, briefs still on."

"No!" is a harsh gasp, Uriah finally getting the full picture.

"When you're that age, knowing someone your whole life could literally mean a few months. If you've seen someone one time before, a kid doesn't see them as a stranger. That's what we're taught. Plus, Mrs. Turner was my mom's age, a woman, and not a creepy dude in a van passing out candy laced with drugs, and she wasn't a middle-aged man with a puppy. She wasn't a male relative being too handsy. She helped me as I struggled to pull my feet out of the pantlegs. After Grandma, and Mom, and Ainsley having total autonomy over me, I thought nothing of asking Mrs. Turner to help me.

"A part of me feels as if I asked for it, because I asked her for help, because I trusted her. Mrs. Turner didn't pull my pants up, she left them at my knees, pulling my briefs down, then pushed me on my bed. The room was spinning, even though my body wasn't moving. My eyes were floating in my head, blurry and unfocused. My arms and legs felt deadened with heavy weights. I'm sure I could move, but I was stunned and confused– I was taught to let women do as they wanted, because it was wrong to say no. I didn't know what was happening, I didn't like it, but I didn't like most of what my grandma and mom forced me to do… so I just laid there unmoving."

Uriah leans down, pressing his chest against my back, arms sliding between me and the mattress to hug me tightly. He doesn't speak, just kisses my exposed cheek and lends me the strength to continue.

"I'd say sex education isn't a thing in conservative schools, putting us in harm's way by keeping us innocent, but I have a feeling it's as inadequate in most schools. Boys aren't taught much of anything that we don't hear from our friends, because it deals with the mechanics of sex– *that's naughty!* –not the biology of it like girls discussing menstruation cycles. I didn't have friends my age, only Ransom and his friends, so I was utterly clueless…

"I'd been getting morning wood for a few months, but Dad said that was normal and to not worry about it. It happened all the time, but for no reason. Mrs. Turner used her mouth on me, and then I learned where babies actually come from… I have no idea how long it lasted, and I didn't finish because I didn't know what that meant back then. Mrs. Turner was spooked by a sound, and she got off me and left my bedroom."

"Why the fuck did she do that to you?" Uriah squeezes me tightly, his tone seething. "It wasn't to get her rocks off, so why?"

"Politics," I mutter in disgust. "I didn't understand until Ransom found me lying on the bed with my underpants down, unable to move, and moaning because my head was spinning, and my gut was twisting. A minute later, my sister was there to take care of me, like always."

"Politics? How the hell would molesting a child– *rape* –be considered good for politics?"

"Ainsley came into the room, with Ransom trying to tug my hand so I wasn't lying down on the bed. I remember she sniffed the air, a look of total disgust crossing her face, like she could literally smell what happened. It was a worse look than when she bitched about my boy-skink and grabbed my arm and put deodorant on me… I remember Ainsley was crying and panicking as she washed me, and Ransom was nowhere to be found."

"Where was he?"

"It was all a blur, because I spent some time with my head in the toilet. But the next thing I remembered was being tucked into Ainsley's bed and Joel was there… and this is the part that I go over and over, not what happened with Mrs. Turner. It's the aftermath, where they thought I couldn't hear, where Joel and Ainsley discussed what to do and why it happened, and it was Joel who was panicking the worst."

"To what end would this benefit Congressman Turner? Mrs. Turner would have been arrested for rape and his career would have been ruined."

"Uriah, maybe it's your gender-fluidness, or the fact that if someone looked at you, your androgyny is the first thing they see, so you're in a gray area where people don't know where to place you... women continuously fear being assaulted, and men have to fear being falsely accused and never being believed when they report an assault. Didn't you get the memo? Men can't be raped, and we can't be abused. Look at the statistics, right? It's the men who do the bad shit, so when it happens to a man, we deserve it to punish those who didn't get caught."

"I understand that *now*," Uriah stresses, "But at thirteen? And why?"

"I haven't grown more than two or three inches since then, Uriah," I point out that I looked older than I was, almost full-grown. "It wasn't for Turner, but I'm sure they were given a leg-up for it– it was three or four or more degrees of separation, a trump card held in a pocket for use when they could hurt Uncle Edward the worst, or me should I follow in his footsteps. A few months, or forty years, and I wouldn't have been believed, whether I was thirteen or fifty-three."

"No way," Uriah scoffs. "If someone hurt Sunny or Winter, they would be believed immediately."

"Note how I was targeted," I point out. "Not Ainsley. Ainsley would be believed, from birth to death. Ransom, being nine, he would've been believed– now he's the instigating little shit who understands the underlying words more so than the policy being discussed. Ransom will never be a target, because he is seen as a future ally or adversary– hard to say he assaulted a woman when he's publicly out as gay. I was the quiet kid, the one who followed the rules, and I was the easy target, the one who had Uncle Edward's affection. Do you get that?"

"I'm starting to, I guess."

"To an outside observer, it's nearly impossible to grasp... I was swaddled in Ainsley's bed with Ransom, my nephew sucking up every word his parents said as they discussed me. Ransom has a political mind– mine is justice, his is strategic. Ainsley and Joel were a similar balance, weighing the pros and cons about calling the police or ignoring it ever happened."

"Ignoring it won out?" Uriah sounds enraged for me, but he doesn't understand.

"They protected *me*," I stress. "They never once brought up our family or Uncle Edward except to figure out Mrs. Turner's motives. Joel was terrified I'd be labeled a perverted young man who preyed on Mrs. Turner, because any woman who would resort to that would resort to anything. It wasn't about sex, because I had nothing to offer. It was a political maneuver, with every angle already plotted out on a game board in their minds. If we made a move, I would be ruined forever, more so than dealing with being raped but also imprisoned. Whatever would happen to Uncle Edward wasn't even a factor, and they knew, knowing how we thought, this was the only play we could make. Wait in terror until they used the card. But we didn't tell anyone, especially Uncle Edward, because that ruined their plans for them."

"Do you really believe you would have been convicted?" Uriah slides off my back. Hand on my shoulder, he grips me firmly and rolls me onto my back. Staring down at me with equal parts compassion and frustration, "No way would you have gone to prison."

"It's not about the punishment– it's the accusation you can never escape." Sitting up slightly, I try to get Uriah to see if from my point-of-view. "The retraction on page-six is never seen, but the dirty gossip is always believed, even when proven innocent. It would have followed me for life… and, at any time, Mrs. Turner can pull the trigger on the accusation and destroy my life."

"How?" Twisting an expression, Uriah's eyebrows hitch high with incredulousness. "Just how?"

"How would a woman know where I have moles on my body if she hadn't seen me naked, especially when the moles are on my testicles and taint, or the birthmark on my inner thigh. She'll cry, make me sound brutal and violent, say she was too scared to tell anyone when it first happened. She will be believed. No matter what."

"That is so wrong," Uriah cries out, so frustrated he's pulling at his own hair. "What monsters!"

"But to not believe a victim makes us bad people, right? That's what we're taught, guilt-tripped into not waiting for proof. The allegation is the only proof we need to destroy a person, not realizing we may be doing someone else's dirty work for them– making ourselves the monster. As a victim, knowing I wouldn't be believed, I understand not coming forward out of fear. I get it from both the victim's side and that of the falsely accused. There is *NO* winning for me. No justice."

"There's nothing you can do…" Uriah trails off, sounding like a statement, but it's a question.

"Foil their plans by never telling Uncle Edward. You can't leverage someone when they don't know you have leverage. If they play their hand too soon, they look like the monsters they are. Right now, we're in a stalemate, where Mrs. Turner stalks me, hoping to get a rise out of me. If I lay a hand on her to protect myself, she'll flip it on me. So I'm continually assaulted because I can't have a voice in order to protect myself and my family."

"That bitch was using me to get to you tonight? She set us up?"

"You think?" A sharp bark of humorless laughter is torn from my throat. "I think you'll appreciate what I say next. Evil is not masculine. It's a facet of the human condition, and women are not immune to it. To be shocked over someone going to those lengths to ensure a victory, tells me you are too good for this world, and it's going to eat you alive."

"I know people do bad things." Uriah glares at me, and the swiftness of his anger directed at me is a comfort. He's still my fiery minx, even after knowing what happened to me.

"Trust me, everyday people have no clue what the true definition of bad is, not by comparison to children born into politics– it's gross. I hate it." Reaching over, I grab for Uriah's hand, needing the connection.

"The girls. That's what's making my salivary glands go nuts, playing out in my subconscious." Now, when I laugh, it's a mix of humor, dread, and pain.

"When I was seventeen, I tried to have sex with a friend after prom. Didn't go so well, never finished the act. I felt guilty and ashamed. At eighteen, after a party, I lost my virginity in my room at boarding school. A girl followed me and my roommates back to our room, and she wanted to have sex– I fucked her against the door while my roommates watched. I was taught not to tell a girl no, which is why I created the rules I have.

"No autonomy. To say no is to insult them, to reject them, to hurt them, then they will hurt you. To respect women is to give them what they want. Never once have I approached a woman. I'd try to befriend, and they would want sex, and I'd give them sex until I couldn't handle giving them any more sex, making sure to protect myself every step of the way. Without Kaden there, I doubt I would have ever got off at all."

"You enabled them, just like Kaden–"

"I do, and I wonder why?" Choking on the truth, I shake my head back and forth as if I can erase it.

"It's not healthy, Dan– it's not."

"I know," my voice drops into a whine. "Not for the enabled or the enabler. I was taught to do so, and it's also in my nature. Give people what they want, and they will be happy. Give people what they want, and they won't argue with you, be mad at you, be disappointed in you. Give people what they want, and I won't feel guilty, even at the expense of harming myself. No shouldn't be in my vocabulary, and I shouldn't feel betrayed or enraged when they have the audacity to ask things of me in which I don't wish to give."

"Everyone has the right to say no."

"As a child, it was hammered into me how I wasn't allowed. Then Mrs. Turner, and the aftermath, I was just supposed to get over it. Then I watched as everyone caved to everyone, doing things they didn't want to do, because love meant losing yourself to other's demands," I snarl in bitter resentment, thousands of interactions playing out in my head. "They're right, you're always wrong– in my justice-minded eyes, that's abuse, not love."

"After my mom, when I see Bob and Rain interact, or interact with the kids, I never thought about it that way. Because Mom was just so broken, it was a comfort to see a real relationship. But, you're right– they're still infected with that arrogance. If you loved me, you'd just shut up and do what I asked. On both sides."

"It's genderless, and it's disgusting," I mutter, still seeing it play out before my eyes. Our takeout game is because Grandma and

Mom control every ounce of food in the house, saying it's about health when it's not. "I won't live like that– couldn't survive it. So I understand your imbalance concerns, because that in and of itself is exactly why I'm going into the profession I am. Relationships shouldn't be enslavement, where you lose your voice to the stronger voice."

Sitting upright, I fold my legs beneath me, and just look at Uriah as he struggles to understand. "I think I was supposed to meet you, supposed to find you intriguing, and was supposed to never let you get away. There's a reason I figured out I was demisexual, so I could fall for you... because a part of me hates who I am as a man, and another part hates women for who they made me become, and you are neither."

Uriah is stunned silent, staring at me with huge eyes, eyes that have that golden spark, as what I'm saying is truly hitting him hard.

"You're Uriah... as I've gotten to know you, I've realize none of this has to do with gender at all, and everything with requiring people to treat me with dignity and respect, and making sure they do the same with others."

FIRST KISS

"Argh!" whooshes out of my chest as a firm body careens into mine, knocking us both backward onto the mattress. Our arms and legs tangle, but it's the unexpected gift of our lips finally meeting that has me rendered speechless.

Uriah pulls us to our sides, somehow instinctively knowing a body on top of mine triggers the memories. The hard kiss, lips pressed tightly together, shifts to a flutter, going softer and softer, and ending on a sigh.

Laughing in delight, "You shocked me– trust me when I say I wanted to kiss you back, but I was totally floored by you." Fingers curling, I cup the side of Uriah's face, loving how his pupils are blown and his face is flushed, lips damp and rosy.

Drawing my hands upward, I pull my fingertips through Uriah's hair, exposing every inch of his face to my hungry gaze. Everything about him is utterly unique, and I could spend every second of my life looking at him, forever finding it new and fascinating.

"I could sense you holding back, and I wasn't about to kiss you, or do anything else, until it wasn't wedged between us anymore." Uriah leans forward slowly, almost seeming unsure, mouth slightly open, and then he presses his lips to mine. "This is me saying yes, telling you how you can do anything you want to me, because I'm not going to pressure you into anything, fearing you'll never say no."

"You can do anything you want," I offer, eagerly pressing closer.

"That's what I'm afraid of," Uriah mutters wryly, rolling his eyes. "I'll follow your lead. Once I figure you out, I'll initiate in the future. But not tonight– I'm giving you the reins. You're in charge, and I'm game for anything. Bear in mind, if I don't like it, I won't think twice on telling you no."

"But I don't know what I'm doing," I nearly whine, fingers tightening in Uriah's hair, and he rolls his eyes at how preposterous I sound. I know he's talking about sex. Real sex. Sex by society's definition– penetration. "I'll fuck it up."

Uriah's lips curl into a knowing smirk, like he's keeping a juicy secret and he's going to make me figure it out. "Use your instincts, cowboy– I won't know the difference."

My confused, "Huh?" is cut off by a pair of pouty lips descending. Uriah always calls me the eager one, but he's different tonight. Even after saying I was the one in charge, he's assertive and demanding, and I feed off the energy swirling around us.

Mouth opening wider, I angle my jaw for better access to Uriah. The instant my tongue darts into his mouth, for the very first time, giving a playful lick to his, he writhes against me, releasing sounds I've never heard him make.

A part of my mind is chanting Kaden's words. *Uriah's a virgin. Uriah's a virgin.* Yet I can't even contemplate that by Uriah's ex-profession. But, as we kiss, and Uriah is soaking up everything I'm showing him, I can tell he's untried yet eager. I'm not sure what he has and hasn't done, so I'm going to assume it's all as new to him as it is to me. We were both learning from helping Kaden, and now it's time to put it into practice.

With a playful nip, I capture Uriah's tongue, sucking it into my mouth, showing him how to kiss me back. Uriah shudders, muscles clenching, an obvious precursor he's getting into it too quickly, so I back off.

I could kiss all night, finding it to be one of the most erotically intimate experiences when with someone I feel a connection– for Uriah, it's ramping up his need for release, the more tongue-action, the harder it will be for him to last.

"Holy fuck." Panting into my mouth, Uriah pulls away, neck arching in silent invitation. "I didn't think it could feel like this– don't stop." Voice warbling, his fingertips shake against the nape of my neck as he pulls me closer. "*Please.* God, don't you dare fucking stop."

Kaden once asked me how you know if someone is into it, probably worried about how unsexy it would be to ask every thirty seconds if what you're doing is okay before moving onto the next leg of the journey, and I answered with body language. Sex is filled with unspoken communication, every touch and moan signaling consent. This is obviously a big deal for me.

Uriah already gave me permission to do whatever I wanted, saying he'd have no issue stopping me if I crossed an unvoiced line. I'm not a mind-reader, and no one should have to be. Right now, Uriah's praise spurs me on, but it's his body language screaming the loudest. Writhing, rubbing against me all needy and greedy, he ready for more.

Mouth sucking marks along the narrow column of Uriah's throat, I roll him onto his back, gaining access to all of him. Uriah bathed me, and then gave me a massage, and it isn't the need to return the favor that has me exploring his body– I want to touch Uriah. Need it as much as the air I breathe.

I'm an unselfish lover, getting off on getting my partner off. Never before was the need for release part of the equation. The longer I've known Uriah, the more that has become a factor. I now want to get off with Uriah. The biggest difference, I know Uriah is of a similar mindset, unselfish and wishing to fulfill my fantasies, not just his own.

While my hands rove Uriah's lithe body, fingertips skating lightly and nails scratching to enliven nerves, the objects of my fascination draw all my attention. "I think you wear those shirts on purpose, trying to drive me fucking nuts with these."

Eyes rolled up to connect to Uriah's wild gaze, I slowly lower my mouth to suck his nipple. Uriah's confirming laughter is cut off with a deep moan, as my tongue flicks the tightly bound nub. Pulling slightly away, I breathe on his saliva-slickened nipple, chuckling as it contracts even tighter.

"For nearly a month, you've driven me mad." Licking and kissing and sucking a path down Uriah's body, I taste his skin, savoring how utterly unique it is. "Wearing shirts that flash your nipples, those goddamn pants showing off your pretty dick, and the way you bury your face into the side of my neck and suck as you paint your hand with cum... driving me insane, because you wouldn't let me watch you get off, not your facial expression or your dick."

Sucking Uriah's nipple and the surrounding tissue, I marvel how his body is so different than mine. Smooth and flat, without any raised muscles, even though I know he's wiry and strong. No hair anywhere on his body, except for the long, black hairs at the base of his cock. Completely androgynous, the only truly fleshy parts are his bubble butt, puffy nipples, and the juicy bits dangling between his legs.

"Jerking off beside you for the past few weeks has been an exercise in sanity... how badly I wanted to see you come– to be the one to make you come."

Skating my mouth down to Uriah's belly button, I nip every inch in a straight line from one hip to the other, curving around where his cock lays on his belly. "You're not escaping me tonight– you're going to look me in the eyes, and you're going to moan my name as I make you come."

There's no hesitation, and I feared there would be, which is why Kade and I fooled around that night– we both needed an education to make it good for our future partners, and I was terrified after always being with girls, I didn't know what to expect as a reaction when I was with a guy.

None of that matters now, because this feels natural and right. Brushing kisses turn to lingering nips as I work my way along each of Uriah's hips, ignoring the one part I want to taste the most.

"You're killing me, cowboy." Uriah whines, hips thrusting into the air and twisting to the side, trying to make contact with my lips. "Driving me fucking crazy."

"I know the feeling," I mutter wryly, smirking against the top of Uriah's thigh. "Consider this payback for rubbing your body against the side of me while we jerked off in bed, but not allowing me to touch you."

"Ramped up the anticipation, didn't it?" Uriah teases me back, smirk evolving into a full-out, smug laugh. "Don't think it wasn't driving me batshit, cowboy. I've been jerking off nonstop when I'm not around you, so fucking distracted, I burn supper for the kids or phase out during lectures."

"Good." Now it's my turn to sound smug. "Glad I'm not the only one."

Licking along the inside of Uriah's smooth thigh, the scent is muskier down here, and it goes straight to the head of my cock. Pounding, dampening the hair on my leg, my cock isn't going to be able to tolerate this for too long before he demands his own attention.

With my nose nuzzling against Uriah's sack, he eagerly helps make more room by spreading his legs on the mattress. Nudging the dangly bits out of the way, I fasten my mouth deep between his legs– not quite the taint, not quite the thigh –and I bite down, sucking at the same time.

"FUCK!" Uriah shouts, writhing all over the place, and I fear I might have given him too much, too soon and made him pop. A pleading, "More, gimme more," answers that.

A quarter of the girls, I went down on. I'm not going to lie, I enjoyed every second of it, because there is nothing as erotic as knowing you're making another person so insane, they orgasm. Sometimes the oral was enough, and we didn't do anything else. When I had sex with them, most of the time I didn't come, because it wasn't about that. A few times, and truly not many, the girls would go down on me. I enjoy blowjobs, but it was usually just a means to get me turned on enough, so I'd make them come instead– I've only come a handful of times with a girl when Kade wasn't around as the conduit. It felt too intimate for me.

As I stare down at Uriah's junk, I have no idea what to do. The girls sucked my nob for a few minutes, and then we moved along to other fun things for them. I don't know what I like when it comes to oral, other than knowing I love it, so I can't use that as a guide as I touch Uriah.

Without a roadmap, I do whatever the hell I want, and figure Uriah will tell me one way or another if I'm mucking it up. Just to toy with him, I leave his cock for last.

"You really don't wax?" My awed tone has Uriah laughing in delight, getting off on how turned on he's making me. "Your balls are so fucking smooth, I'm going to gobble 'em up."

"There are theories," Uriah stops me before I go down on him. "Maybe I have more estrogen than testosterone, which explains the differences between you and me. Rain and Bob begged me to go to the doctor and have my hormones checked, but I like who I am and how I look. I don't want to find out it's hormonal, then have to take meds that will change the shape of my body. All I know, I'm just as horny as everyone else, and everything functions, so that's good enough for me."

"It's more than perfect for me." Shifting downward, I shut Uriah up with my mouth on his balls. Warm, heavy, and musky, I'm tempted to be too rough because of the squishy texture, but I try to be careful.

Uriah doesn't make being careful easy on me, as he wiggles around the bed, making enticing noises, so I move on to darker places, a place my cock is going crazy to enter. This activity doesn't freak me out, because I know what I'm doing after the two times with Kaden, but what I'm doing is a new adventure of me.

Hands locked behind Uriah's thighs, I lift to open him up, and then bow down to a feast. Smooth and flawless, I could do this for hours. The high-pitched moaning spurs me on to keep licking and kissing and prodding with my tongue, but my needs are getting impatient.

Using my saliva, Uriah is so goddamn tight I fear I'll hurt him. "Here!" is shouted, voice eager and hungry, then I'm hit upside the head with a bottle of lube. "I came prepared."

Chuckling beneath my breath, "All boy scouts do," I pour more than I need into my palm. I never thought tonight would be happening, but I guess Uriah is more calculating than I am. No doubt that lube was with the lotion he used during my massage.

A niggling of unease pops into my mind when I realize why Uriah's probably prepared. Then I realize I ought to thank that ancient professor, because I loved the way Uriah touched me, and I'm sure the mentor taught him touch more than academics.

As I work a fingertip into Uriah, I know without a shadow of a doubt I've seen all of the tricks Uriah was taught, and everything else will be new to the both of us.

"Whoa… every hair on my body is standing on end, and I've got goosebumps." Uriah's wild laughter is infectious. "Didn't realize."

"What's so funny, huh?" Smirking against his thigh, I work him until I can slip two fingers in easily. "Hmm?"

"Nothing!" Uriah shouts, laughing louder, taking on a manic edge. "Just something I thought when we were helping Kade with the butt-plug, but it's too embarrassing… don't ask."

"Oh, like that will make me any less curious," I mutter sarcastically. "I could always make you," I threaten, breathing on Uriah's cock.

"Don't you dare!" Jackknifing up off the mattress, Uriah's movements force my fingers in deeper. His protests die off on a guttural groan. "Jesus fucking Christ, that's insane!"

"What's insane?" Getting closer, breath getting hotter, I extend my tongue to drip saliva along the tip of his cock. "What was so funny about Kade?"

"Zipping my lips!" Uriah arches, jerking his hips closer to my face, trying to get me to take him into my mouth. "Not telling ya."

"Look at you, acting like a naughty, little minx, refusing to answer me." Preparing to rock Uriah's world, I chuckle sinisterly. "I'll make you tell me, to the point you'll beg me to fuck you."

"No, never." Head rocking side to side, Uriah's living in his own personal world of ecstasy. "Never gonna happen, cowboy."

Nipping at his thigh, "I guarantee it, minx," I threaten, and then I move in for the kill. Swallowing Uriah's thin cock, I angle my fingers to hit his gland. The guttural sounds flowing out of his throat is music to my ears, making me forget about my lack of confidence when it comes to sucking dick.

Uriah's not the only one making noises, nor is his cock the only one going insane— jerking and dripping precum, it takes everything in me not to rut against the side of the mattress.

"Tell me," I order breathlessly. After waiting a few heartbeats, I suck on Uriah's cockhead, knowing that will do the trick.

"Goddamnit!" Uriah gulps, hips moving to where he's fucking my face instead of me sucking his cock. "The only thing I could think of, when we were helping Kade, is how badly I wished I was in his place. I wanted to know what it felt like, and seeing Kade go nuts made me envious… now fuck me."

"Not yet." Chuckling, I pull off Uriah's cock before he spills down my throat, fingers working frantically inside him. "Tell me, did you play with yourself to see if you liked it too?"

"No," Uriah pants breathlessly, nearly gasping in need. "I was saving that for you." Hips jerking, self-possessed Uriah turns into a greedy, needy little minx, just for me. "Daniel Bishop, get in me. Now."

Pulling from Uriah's body, "Demanding," I chastise, with a tap to his ass. "I like." Falling to land on top of him, I smile down at the frustrated expression he's tossing my way. "Told ya, I'd make ya beg."

"High maintenance, remember?" Uriah gives me no warning, grabbing for my cock where it rests between us. A second later, he puts it against his entrance and thrusts downward on it. I register wet heat and deep pressure, and the threat of my balls readying to erupt.

Intense pleasure rolls down my spine, a hand lashing out to press against Uriah's chest. "Gimme a minute." Panting, I don't dare move. "I cannot believe you just fucked yourself on my dick… that's so hot. Shit!"

Giggling naughtily, Uriah hooks a palm across my nape, and then draws me down to him. Bodies pressed tightly together, my cock deep inside his ass, his cock trapped against my belly, we spend long minutes kissing, our lower halves staying stationary until I'm firmly under control.

"I could kiss you forever," I warn, simultaneously fearing it and looking forward to it. My arms slip beneath Uriah's back to draw him closer to me. The wet press of lips, the teasing licks, I cannot get enough, to the point I don't realize my body has a mind of its own until it's almost too late.

We're moving together, bodies slick, and it feels natural and right, as if this is what I've been waiting my whole life to find. All those other times were just conquests. With Kaden, it was pure connection. With Uriah, it's also about the intimacy, but there is an undercurrent of thrilling intrigue that bites its hooks into me and will never let me go.

"I was your first kiss, wasn't I? That's why you held off– I was your first. You were a virgin." Laughing in Uriah's ear, I bury my face against the side of his neck. "I just broke every rule I've ever made."

"Blame me." Kissing my forehead, Uriah teases his fingernails down my back. "I'm a bad influence."

"I don't know if I broke the rules, or if I finally found the exception to the rule." I think back to a month ago, to the last time I had sex with Manda– the last time I had sex with a girl. I remember spewing my rules, hoping to incite her enough to get her to leave me alone. She wanted to fuck, so we fucked until she didn't want me anymore.

The only person I'd ever ride raw, the only person I'd ever, not only come with, but cum inside, will be the person I spend the rest of my life with– I broke some of those rules with Kaden, but not all of them.

"I'm going to marry you someday, Uriah Crane," I vow, confident with how the words sound rolling off my tongue.

"I know," Uriah volleys back, and damn if the minx doesn't sound smug about it too.

· PRESENT ·
· PITTSBURGH, PENNSYLVANIA ·

COWBOY AND MINX
Daniel Bishop

Unable to eavesdrop anymore, I slip inside the bedroom to find Uriah curled into himself on the bed, with Wynn prowling between the foot of the bed and the bureau like a pissed off predatory cat– blond, majestic, and toned with coiled strength. If Wynn had a tufted tail, it'd be flicking with frustration because we're not doing as he wants.

"I would like to speak to my husband alone, please." Voice soft, I can't look away from Wynn, because I'm too terrified to see a Uriah I don't recognize.

"I think that is a good idea." Wynn looks at me pointedly, arching a challenging brow.

I've known *of* Wynn for nearly a decade, hearing it all from Royce and Kade, but I've known him personally for close to half a year, and he only gets stronger by the day. A few months back, Wynn started calling me. The calls started progressively getting closer and closer together, until he began calling me two times a day, to talk about nothing and everything.

"I suggest you're honest with one another." This time the comment is not directed at me. Wynn steps around me, then turns to clasp my shoulder in solidarity. With a firm squeeze, Wynn warns, "I think it's high time my own husband is honest with me."

The sound of bootsteps fleeing down the hallway has Uriah sparking to life– an almost evil sounding laugh flows from my husband's throat. Wynn joins in, his chuckle anticipatory. Meanwhile, I know exactly how Kade is feeling right now.

Terrified.

"Let this be a comfort." Wynn's hand squeezes my shoulder again. "It's Uriah who should be running like Kade just did… we'll be on your balcony– it's time we polished the rough edges off our marriages."

Uriah stares at me from the bed, holding onto himself. As I step forward, Wynn's voice echoes down the hallway from the bedroom to the kitchen. "Find us when you're ready!" Another predatory laugh has a shudder roiling along my spine. "KADEN MARX– my teacher man. Your period of denial comes to an end. Right. Now."

"Wynn's no enabler. Any clue what that's about?" I hitch a thumb over my shoulder, willing to do anything, talk about anything, other than what's happening inside this room.

"Besides you, you mean?" Unbracing his arms, Uriah unfolds his knees from his chest, and then sits crossed-legged at the head of the bed. He reaches for a pillow, hugging it to his chest. I remember a time when it was me Uriah reached for, the one Uriah turned to for comfort, the one Uriah held onto for dear life.

I miss it– I miss us.

"Fair enough," I croak out, voice warbling with fear as I approach the bed. I gingerly sit on the edge, feeling uncomfortable in my own home, with my own husband.

"Wynn and I talk," is all Uriah says in reply.

"Huh," I grunt, mulling that over. "Seems like Wynn would have no time to do anything else but talk on the phone… how does he go to school, go to work, spend time with Kade, and help his family?"

"You too?" Uriah squeaks, sounding surprised Wynn calls me at all.

"Yeah, a good twice a day, most days," I muse, still unsure what that's all about. "I talk to Wynn more than Kade."

"Shocking!" Uriah whispers in a hiss, sounding hella sarcastic.

Sighing, I slump to curl my shoulders. "What's going on with us, Ri?" Turning to the side, I make sure Uriah can't see anything but me. "I need a little help here– I'm no mind-reader. If it's Kade, I thought we understood each other before we made a commitment. It hasn't changed since. So color me confused now."

Uriah turns animated, relaxing against the headboard. "It's handy having a lawyer for a husband. No Is left undotted or Ts uncrossed."

"I thought that you needed the security?" Confused, all I can do is look at my husband, and miss the chaotic spitfire I met crouching in a bathroom stall after giving another man a blowjob for ten bucks.

Uriah and I shared everything, making sure both our needs were met, never making demands– the balance of power had to be preserved. Uriah naturally fell into the role of the man of the house, working from home, while I focused on finishing school and then building my career. Our life fit us, I thought.

"How could I not make sure we were good when I'm a divorce lawyer, Ri?" Leaning forward, I yearn to touch Uriah's hand, but I curl my fingers into fists instead, unsure if I'd be welcome while we battle. "I asked those questions for *you*, not because I'm uptight and boring."

"I know!" Uriah yanks at his hair, pulling it away from his face, and I realize he'd been using it as a shield to hide the tears in his eyes. "You're perfect, Dan. *Perfect*, and I'm not."

"I don't want perfect," I blurt out immediately, and no one could mistake the desperation in my voice for a denial. "You're not feeling me anymore?"

"Oh, my God." Uriah scrambles forward, nearly toppling me to get at me. "Not *that*– God, Dan. This has absolutely *nothing* to do with you. Don't you get that?"

"I'm not a narcissist, but if something's going on, and you won't tell me about it, I'm going to assume one of two things. Either you don't trust me enough to confide in me, or it's about me. Otherwise, it makes no sense to hide it from me, when all I want to do is help you."

"You're so goddamn perfect," Uriah hisses, slipping off my lap. He doesn't sound as if that bothers him, so much as it makes him sound guilty. Guilty of what, I have no idea. "I can't even– you truly are, and I'm a goddamn mess."

"Let me help you, okay?"

"The only way you can help me is to not judge me as I clear my conscience." Uriah's words have terror lighting in my veins. "There's nothing you're not willing to give me, to do for me... except for this."

"Anything," I gasp out, so desperate to keep Uriah happy and healthy. "Please tell me, and you can have it."

Laughing without humor, Uriah's hair flies around his head as he shakes it aggressively, the sound so painful and ashamed. "That's the thing, *you can't*... and I can't even give it to myself. I'm a broken, cosmic joke."

"Let's just talk it out, okay?" Tugging Uriah, I position him on the bed until he's facing me, even going as far as to cross his legs for him. Then I mirror his position.

Uriah raises an eyebrow, small smirk playing along his lips. "Mediation technique, Mr. Bishop?" voice breathy, surprisingly flirty. "If so, it's working."

"Good." I smirk back. "Because usually I save this as a last resort. After my clients don't behave at the conference table, I drag their asses to the floor for acting like children, and we have a little timeout. Eventually they start talking to one another from their respective corners."

"I love you, cowboy." Uriah's heart is bleeding out his eyes.

"I love you too, minx... and I want you just as badly."

"That's what I'm counting on." Guilty, Uriah's gaze flicks away from mine to light on where he's wringing his hands. "You know how everyone preaches how happiness and validation comes from within? How it's self-confidence, self-respect, self-esteem, self-love?"

"Yeah," I whisper, fearing where this is headed. "You've been with me through thick and thin for the past six years. It's been rocky, but we can get through anything, and I can forgive as long as you forgive yourself."

"Too perfect," Uriah says like it's a curse. "I went to a therapist to talk about what's happening with me, and they preached all that self-horseshit, so I found another therapist. One who got it."

"Got what?" I almost beg, far too eager to help.

"Maybe I'm vapid. Maybe I'm high maintenance. Maybe I'm just a slut–"

"Ri, you've only ever been with *me*," I remind him, never once seeing those blowjobs as anything but a transaction.

Uriah winces, and I lock all my muscles to keep myself from flinching.

Realizing how that sounded, Uriah grabs my hand, squeezing with all his might. "Not what you think, okay? When I say this has nothing to do with you, I mean it. I'm not trying to soothe ruffled feathers, or not hurt your feelings, I mean it. There is nothing I want to change in our marriage."

"Are you sure?" Mind going back months, where Uriah froze up after Wynn and Kade left their living room, leaving Uriah to experiment on me, and he freaked out on me instead.

Knowing the direction of my thoughts, "We'll get back around to that." Eyeing me with heat in his eyes, intrigued terror has my cock hardening in my pants. "I like to flirt. I love the way people look at me, like they're wondering what my lips would feel like wrapped around their cocks."

"Oh, Jesus." Grabbing at my own cock, I give it a tight crank to punish it into behaving.

"That reaction makes me feel hopeful... the first therapist slut-shamed me, the guy who has only ever been with his husband. Shamed me for these thoughts rolling around my brain, telling me validation is from within and all that happy, delusional horseshit. How if my husband was so perfect, then it should be enough. But it wasn't, and I fucked up... My therapist now, she understands how I tick. I've never met Beth in person, but Wynn found her for me."

"Really?" Shocked, all I can do is stare at Uriah with my mouth catching flies.

"Yeah." Uriah flashes me a shy smile, and I see the boy I first fell in love with– the flirty yet innocent guy who glowed with confidence when he was on his knees.

"Maybe it was the bachelor party, or maybe it was my professors, or maybe it was selling my mouth, or maybe it's just how I was born. I love the way you want me, but I also like it when someone *other than you* looks at me, like they're thinking about bending me over and fucking me senseless. That's not something you can give me. That's not something I can give myself... and it's not something that can be written away if I want to be happy."

"Just looking?" I venture into a dark territory, terrified of what I'll learn.

"I like random strangers lusting after me, but I don't want them." Uriah cups my face, trying to ease my fears. "I almost cheated on you," Uriah admits, eyes slipping shut. "I guess I did cheat on you."

Leaning out of Uriah's touch, it's an involuntary reaction, not an act of judgement or rejection. "You almost? Or you did?"

"I interviewed a guy a few times for an article I was working on– we met at the bar in his hotel." Uriah refuses to look at me, and my mind wars between my self-respect and the ability to forgive, and whether or not they are mutually exclusive notions.

"He hit on me, and I liked how it felt. It never crossed my mind to actually go through with it– I didn't want him, I only wanted him to want me. It fed something in me."

Relieved, all the oxygen in my lungs gushes out at once, causing me to slump forward. "This guy was the almost, I take it?" After so many years, I can read Uriah. The guilt was with the *almost*, not the *I guess I did*.

"He asked me up to his room, touching my thigh while he asked. I said no thanks, because I had you waiting for me at home. But that doesn't mean it didn't make for some hot fantasies I lived out in the shower."

"Yeah, no shit– that's normal."

I may not conjure up random people for my fantasies, but that doesn't mean Kaden doesn't star in my spank-bank, even if I feel guilty during and afterward. The first time Wynn popped into my head, mid-jerk-session, all bossy and ordering me around, I freaked the hell out. My dick's been rubbed a bit raw as of late.

Uriah looks at me, expression twisted with guilt and shame. "It's hard having someone so perfect, ya know? You're demisexual, so I never have to fear you physically cheating on me unless you're emotionally cheating on me first. If that's the case, I know I'm fucked, because you'll leave me."

"No." Resting a finger over Uriah's lips, I erase an old fear that is always cropping up. "Love is a choice. I refuse to put myself in that situation, knowing how painful it is." Now it's my turn to tell the truth, for once. "Do you know why I'm always fisting my palms when Kaden is around?"

"No," Uriah whispers, never realizing how painful what he suggested is for me.

"It's a struggle to be near someone I love and not touch him, to not kiss him. I chose you, and it's a choice I'll make every day for the rest of my life. I'm faithful, not because I'm perfect, or demisexual, or because you are so fucking awesome I couldn't live without you, or because of Kaden… I'm faithful, because I couldn't handle having another person hurt me as much as Kaden does."

"Kaden hurts you?" The tears in Uriah's eyes guts me.

"Of course, he does," I fling out, too emotional to stop myself. Uriah brushing my cheek has me realizing I'm crying to. "No way in hell would I do that to myself again. Just like you said, your problems have nothing to do with me, my faithfulness has nothing to do with you. Why torture myself? I know it's possible to love someone else while I'm in love with you, so I can understand why you being attracted to other people is an involuntary thought, something inborn in you, and it cannot be erased because you're in love with me. I get it."

Crying outright, Uriah gazes at me, suffocating on guilt, I suspect. "I cheated on you. It had nothing to do with you, and everything to do with what's wrong with me–"

"Nothing is wrong with you," I bite out, trying so very badly to be understanding and compassionate, without fracturing to bits. If I clench my muscles any tighter, to keep myself from moving, they'll cramp and spasm. "We'll figure it out."

"I found Beth after I cheated on you– Wynn found her for me."

"You said that already," I mutter, still not getting it, because the shock of Uriah's admission has my mind incapacitated, emotions rearing up to take control of my body systems.

"I cheated with Wynn– I sucked his dick."

Falling back to the mattress, I laugh so loudly, there's no way Kade and Wynn aren't hearing it all the way out on the balcony. Holding my belly, the laughter continues to spill, almost as hard as the tears of relief from my eyes.

Uriah sounded so guilty, ashamed, heartbroken really, I assumed it was someone in our daily life that would be a horrible betrayal. Ransom even crossed my mind for a split-second, then I immediately discounted it. The fact that it was Wynn– the guy who walks up to me, every single time he sees me, and says he's going to tear my husband a new asshole –well, that's just icing on the cake.

Tugging at my arm, "It's not funny," Uriah is wicked pissed at my reaction. "Last time we were at their house, I was freaking out over what happened with the guy I was interviewing, and how my therapist shamed me for it, and I just snapped. I told Wynn, and he made me suck his dick."

Picking my head up slightly, "Made?" I arch a brow in challenge, knowing Uriah's been wanting on that big dick since before we even met Wynn in person.

The Kade and Uriah rivalry has been a decade-long drama, with me being tugged back and forth in the middle. Then there's Wynn, charging right into the fray, buck-ass naked with his giant cock bobbing in our faces– Wynn doesn't cut the rope pulling me apart, he yanks us all toward him.

"Made you? I'm calling paintball on that– *wanted to*. Even I couldn't resist if Wynn told me to suck his dick."

Laughing at the expression on my face, Uriah cups my cheek, staring down at me as if he wants to kiss me to death. "Actually, yeah… *made me*, not that I didn't want to anyway. After I was done, cum in my mouth and all over my pants, Wynn zipped up, looked down at me, and asked, *"Feel better?"* and then he left the bathroom as if nothing happened."

"What the fuck?" Try as I might, I cannot wrap my mind around Wynn's behavior most days– it only makes sense after he explains the punchline. But I do know there's something I can do for Uriah. "You didn't cheat on me, Ri. It was only Wynn."

"It doesn't matter who it was, or why I did it." Uriah's actually going to argue with me over this– how precious. "It only matters that I did it."

Sitting up, I yank Uriah into my lap, curl him against my chest, then rest my chin on top of his head. "If you really want to feel guilty, have at it. But I don't see it as cheating, especially when one day you might have to forgive me for fucking up and touching Kade when I said I wouldn't."

"Actually… you never said you wouldn't," Uriah points out, picking up so much from his lawyer husband.

"Exactly," I mutter smugly, always leaving that loophole open just in case I do something I can't take back with Kade. "Wynn can be your loophole."

"Or…" Uriah turns his head, dislodging my chin, so we can connect by looking into each other's eyes. "We can find a solution to both of our problems, including the only problem in our marital bed."

"Oh, yeah? What problem is that?" rolls off my tongue with a flirty lilt, so relieved to have the truth out, to have Uriah's guilt evaporate, to know we're moving forward instead of the stagnant bullshit for the past few months.

"You can't say no to me," Uriah reminds me of our first time. "I couldn't go through with penetrating you, knowing you wouldn't say no, even if you didn't want it. Not added on top of me not knowing what I was doing. If I hurt you, you wouldn't have stopped me."

Uriah is always a mix of confidence and shyness. When it comes to things he's never done, the shyness pretty much makes him immobile. I thought that was why he was freaking out, forgetting his fears that I'll never say no to him, giving him what he wants no matter what.

"My therapist– Beth suggested a mutually beneficial solution, and it fits all of our problems. Your inability to say no to me–"

"You realize that probably extends to this solution too, right?" I turn Uriah in my lap, fighting the urge to kiss the shit out of him, and then fuck him into the mattress.

"I'm counting on that fact," Uriah volleys back smugly.

"Of course, you are," I whisper, trying hard not to smirk.

"My lack of confidence when it comes to anything anal on you… my vapid need to seek outside validation, seeing you as an extension of me, so you don't count. The fact that you're in love with Kaden, and he pretends he's not in love with you."

Amused, I have no idea where my husband could possibly be going with this. "What did this twisted therapist of yours suggest?"

"Polyamory," Uriah drops as a bomb. "With Kaden and Wynn."

TEACHER MAN AND HIS LITTLE SHIT
Kaden Marx

As soon as Wynn announced how he was going to interrogate me, I ran off to the fridge to grab as many beers as I could handle, and hightailed it out to the balcony. Slumping into a chair, Wynn finds me as I pound my second beer.

"I'll haul the contents of the fridge out here if you promise not to lie to me," Wynn mutters wryly, eyeing the bottles at my feet.

I'd managed to carry seven bottles at once, knowing it would piss Wynn off. We've had some knock-down, drag-out fights over alcohol, to the point I used to have a stash hidden at Bren's. Wynn has a bloodhound's uncanny ability to scent out hops and yeast, loathing beer because his daddy is a recovering drunk.

Ever since Cain came into our lives, Wynn's a different guy. He drinks anything but beer, but only in moderation– if I try to drink more than two, he takes it away. He smokes, pot on occasion, or a menthol now and again. He's a force to be reckoned with, willing to try anything twice, and sometimes scares the piss out of me because he's fearless.

"There's only a bottle of wine left in there." Feeling stupid, I arrange the beer bottles in a row, empties at the end, and then select a fresh one. Popping the cap, "Sit, or are you trying to lord over me from on high?"

Smirking as if he has a secret– or a better analogy is that Wynn knows all the secrets –he produces a bottle from behind his back. Watching as my husband takes a sip of wine, eyes never leaving mine, Wynn terrifies the piss out of me.

If Wynn is drinking, one of two things are about to happen. He's either going to hand me my ass, and needed fortification, or he's toying with me, and thought it would be fun to be buzzed while doing it.

Shit!

Leaning on the door to the kitchen, only one foot on the balcony, Wynn looks like a dirty magazine ad, featuring a perfect pretty boy who's willing be naughty just for you.

"I love lording over you." Blue eyes sparking, Wynn's entire being glows, eclipsing all darkness surrounding him. "I'll sit once you stop lying."

"You're so mean to me– abusive." Sipping on my beer, I lean back in the cushy chair, instinctively knowing it's Dan's seat. Instead of looking at my devastatingly gorgeous husband, I gaze out over Pittsburgh and its many bridges and orange lights. So different than the view of Warren's house from my front porch, or the tree-filled, hilly view from my empty property in the hollers.

"I bought you a new gnome yesterday." Wynn kicks my foot, wanting my sole attention. "I spoil you rotten."

"You called me stupid– Gnome Saggy Pants was an apology." Pouting, I show Wynn how much that hurt my feelings.

Laughing, Wynn takes another sip of wine, places his bottle safely by the other chair, and then leans down to steal all of my unopened beers. "You'll get these back once you stop lying to yourself." The beer is gone, the fridge door opens then closes, and Wynn is back in less than ten seconds.

"I said you were *acting* stupid for calling yourself stupid." Wynn sits down in the colorful moon chair on the balcony– there's little doubt who it belongs to. "I gave you the new gnome because you were sad, not as an apology for calling you out on your bullshit. You kept calling yourself stupid, so I told you how stupid it was to do that to yourself."

"Fine," I growl, hating how Wynn has to be so goddamn logical all the time.

"I'm not going to let you get away with anything, you know?" Wynn kicks his shoes off, propping his socked-feet onto the railing. "You love that about me… Nice view– couldn't handle it every day, but once in a blue moon, it's a nice change of pace."

Wynn's not going there, and the longer he doesn't go there, the more pressure I feel to go there for him. Wynn is nothing if not patient. He's overflowing Uriah's chair, feet on the railing, eyes gazing out over the city, wine bottle finding his lips every few minutes.

Staring down at the empty soldiers at my feet, I'm not patient, and my curiosity gets the better of me. "What?"

"What *what*?" Wynn teases me, grinning– the little shit. "I'm not going to tell you which lies you're in denial about. That's up to you to decide. I'm just here for when you need a listening ear."

"Bullshit," I growl, reaching for Wynn's wine bottle. After a tussle, we're too evenly matched, I'm leaning back into my seat empty-handed. "Really, give me a starting point."

"Why'd you hold back on kissing Dan?"

"I didn't," is a lie before I can stop it.

"Liar." Another sip is gone, Wynn's lips stained red. "If you answer truthfully– for *yourself*, not me –I'll share." Wynn rattles the bottle, nearly a third already gone. "If you wait too long, the less there will be left to share."

"I don't know…" I trail off, smirking. "A drunk Wynn is a fun Wynn. It's win-win for me either way."

Wynn leans forward, hand poised to dump the bottle into a large planter filled with fake greenery. Holding my gaze, my husband is challenging me, proving there is no win-win unless I do as he asks first.

"I'm not a child," I remind Wynn. "I can get up and go to the fridge, or I can head to the store."

"I'm treating you as a kid because you're acting like one." Wynn takes another sip, eyes still holding mine. Man doesn't blink until I do.

"At least you're not calling me a kid like you called me stupid," I grumble just to annoy Wynn. His satisfied laughter pisses me off. "You couldn't handle it if I really kissed Danny."

"Bullshit– *you* couldn't handle it."

"Danny couldn't handle it," I admit the truth, and the bottle is pressed into my palm as a reward. Wynn's gaze turns from a challenge to a soothing wash of compassion. "You don't understand."

"Instead of lying to yourself, which leads to you lying to me, how about you let me in, yeah?" Wynn takes the bottle back, since I'm holding it limply, not once taking a sip from it. "You know goddamn well I'll never judge you, stupid kid that you are."

"Fucker!" I kick Wynn's foot off the railing, then go back to being pissed at myself and the universe. "Danny's demisexual."

"Dan lies, saying he's straight with girls and demisexual with guys, but that's a lie too– y'all fucking lie nonstop." Now Wynn's pissed, West Virginian diction popping out when we've all tried to lose the vocabulary while keeping the accent.

"He has a reason," I mutter lamely. "And I'm not lyin' or evadin' by not tellin' ya." Shit, now I'm doing it too. Heavy emotions always make me revert back to how I used to speak. "Danny didn't even tell me, Wynn. I just know."

"Dan's demi-pan, by the way– in case anyone gives a shit about the truth of the matter." Wynn props his foot back on the railing, getting cozy with his bottle of wine. "Ain't no straight. Ain't no gay. Ain't got nothing to do with gender at all... and I know what happened to Dan, because he told me."

"What?!" I squawk, insulted on so many levels.

I only found out because Ransom refused to tell me why Danny and Uriah took off from Bishop's Castle, in my Durango, without me. The kid was so upset at the time, the truth flowed like water. Danny knew Ransom ratted him out, and seemed relieved I knew without having the fanfare of telling me himself. Danny and I've talked about it since, but there was never the big, emotional reveal between us.

"Yeah..." Wynn laughs, all confidence and a small trace of arrogance I've never heard before. He's gloating. "I asked, Dan told me. I used my knowledge of his orientation to my advantage."

Eyeing my husband, it's like Wynn's a different person– an intriguing and hot as fuck person, but a stranger nonetheless. "What are you talking about?"

"I've been seducing your boyfriend since I met him in person," Wynn admits, chuckling underneath his breath. "For your benefit, dummy– so stop looking so betrayed. Ain't feeling a bit of guilt."

"Do I know you?" I reach for the bottle, and Wynn lets me have it. Tilting my head back, I open my throat and drain the bottle dry.

"Impressive." For once, Wynn actually sounds impressed with what he calls latent alcoholism. "Your tongue gets loose when you drink."

"Shit. Fuck. Damn." Snarling a string of curses, I wish I could take back the three beers I pounded and the quarter bottle of wine.

"See..." Wynn drops his feet to the balcony floor, then leans to get closer to me, bringing our faces inches apart. "My entire family lied to me from the time I was born. Royce lying about the twins broke my trust in more than just him… but Cain–"

The rage and sorrow on Wynn's face murders a part of me. No one with such light shining should ever look so dark. I love Cain like the brother-in-law he is. Wynn doesn't hate Cain– he refuses to get to know him, because Wynn resents the lies that are wedged between them.

"Life's short," Wynn says with finality. "I'ma be selfless and selfish. I'ma be brave, not reckless. I'ma be firm, not ruthless. No guilt. No shame. I'm never going to apologize for something I'm not sorry for doing. I'ma own it, not allow it to own me."

"I'm not as brave as you, Wynn," I breathe the truth of it all.

"We're married– we're partners –that's the point. I'll lend you the strength, and you can lean on me when you're not brave enough to face the truth." Wynn reaches out to take my hand, fingers entwining with mine. "Let it out, and let it go, Kade."

"I wasn't a virgin!" I blurt out before I can stop myself, the guilt always riding shotgun. "I lied to you. I lied to myself. I made up stories, and thought them over and over again, until I believed they actually happened, because the guilt was killing me… no amount of cutting could change the past. Bleeding didn't release the pressure. I'm sorry."

Chuckling with satisfaction, Wynn surprises the shit out of me. Large hands wrap around the back of my skull and yank me to his mouth. The kiss is messy, a mashing of lips, teeth bashing together– it's uncomfortable and awkward, exactly like our first kiss, which was exactly the point.

"Thank you," Wynn whispers against my damp lips as he pulls away. "'Bout time you admitted that, 'cuz I didn't believe you when you said you were."

"What?!" I gasp in shock. "I was awkward as fuck with you, popping in seconds!"

"Yeah, but that's normal when you get overexcited," Wynn teases me, smirking like he loves that about me. "You knew things no one could know without experiencing them, and I don't mean by experimental and exploratory masturbation with your toybox. No way, no how, were you a virgin, and it didn't matter to me none."

"It was a fantasy, and if I believed it enough, I could make it reality."

"I don't need a fantasy, Kade– I just need honesty, and that means inside your head too. No more of this bullshit, where you hate on yourself, call yourself names, and then turn it around on me when I call you out on it. I love you, inside and out, and I'm not asking you to change. I'm only asking for you to be honest."

"Uriah never gave me a lap dance– that whole story I told you about how Uriah and Danny hooked up was a lie."

"*I know*," Wynn stresses, chuckling at me. "Kinda hard to keep a lie going when Uriah told me about his first time– his first time with Dan, and you were not in the story."

"Dan was my first–"

"No shit." Wynn laughs like I'm being ridiculous. "We weren't dating. You weren't even on my radar. I don't blame you for being with either of them. Just so we're clear, I know you fucked 'em both."

Hearing those words from Wynn's mouth, I startle, the guilt overpowering me.

"I don't care, Kade." Wynn shakes me. "Knock your shit off, and get the fuck outta your head. The limo story you told me, the one the night before their wedding, that was bullshit too, because I twisted Uriah's arm into telling me."

"Literally?" I squeak out, embarrassed.

Wynn rolls his eyes, and growls, "The saying, you freakin' idiot. Uriah gave no details, but the guy is easy to coerce into pointing out your lies."

"Fucking perfect," I snarl, needing more booze for this conversation. "Dan's in love with me–"

"No shit, and you're in denial if you think the rest of us don't know you're in love with him too."

"*I* was their bachelor party," I stress, blushing, cock going hard in an instant. To be helpful, or evil, Wynn reaches over to squeeze my bulge, doing the same to his own, knowing I pop off sometimes when I get overexcited. Like now, how I buck up into Wynn's hand before he has time to pull away.

"That's hot as fuck, you get that, right?" Wynn chuckles, the sexual sound taking on an edge of discomfort. He jacks his pantleg up, then adjusts his crotch. "And apropos, since they were our bachelor party too."

"You don't get it—"

"The point is I want to get it, but this little fantasy in your head has you locking me out and lying to yourself."

"Fair enough," I allow, relenting. "Dan knew I was waitin' on you, and I thought he was straight, and it just sort of happened— the sexual and romantic connection. Then Uriah showed up, and I was jealous but relieved, because the tension broke between us enough for me to breathe and not fear fucking you and me up... but that tension never truly *ever* goes away, no matter what."

Pulling away, I can't look at Wynn while I tell him the truth— admit the truth to myself. "For a semester and a half, Dan and I shared a bed. We never kissed, it was too much for both of us. But we'd jerk off together— jerk each other off when Uriah was in bed with us. They'd have sex with me in the bed with them. I'd kiss Uriah— we'd have sex too, frotting. He loved the attention, and I wanted to be near Danny. They were my lovers..."

"I was excited to go home after graduation, missing my family and hungry to be near you, but I was sad too. Sad because we had to say goodbye, finish it, and never do it again. It was our ending, because it was their beginning— yours and my beginning too."

Turning around, I lean my hip on the railing, facing Wynn. "I got certified, and then started teaching first grade. I avoided you until I couldn't handle it anymore... it took me a good month to get the courage to enter the Circle K while you were working. It was teaching the twins, seeing you reflected in them, that made the temptation too much."

"I was so pissed at you when you came in the store and handed me my ass." Wynn laughs, staring at me with all the love and lust a person could ever feel for another. "I didn't understand it, but I think I was angry because I wanted you so goddamn much."

Eyes slipping shut, guilt nearly suffocating me, "What you don't understand is what I did a month earlier... It had been almost a year and a half since we were together. Dan was in Connecticut— Yale. Uriah was still in Bellefonte. I hadn't seen Danny since our goodbye, but Uriah and I met once a month, still visiting Danny's family as if we were a part of them. All of us were a motherfucking wreck. Lonely, miserable, losing it."

"Why not give in?" Wynn interrupts me, not understanding what it's like to love someone you cannot have. He's brave. He's a fighter. There's no such thing as a temptation too great to reach out and take.

"Danny's dad gave him advice. See, James met Libby in college, and he had to take a year off because of it. Ended up married with a kid, and he had to beg his parents to take care of them in order for him to finish school. Bishops are romantics– all-in type of guys. Danny almost failed out our first semester, senior year, so we agreed with James. Uriah needed to finish up at PSU, with Danny at Yale. But after Uriah graduated, Danny was a wreck. He had two more years ahead of him, and he couldn't face them without Uriah. That aching need was more of a distraction than having Uriah with him."

Closing my eyes, all those desperate phone calls and emails from Danny, and how broken Uriah looked when I saw him face-to-face. Without someone riding my ass, emotionally supporting me, I was living in a house by myself, cutting the shit out of my sides, and it took adopting Perty to momentarily snap me out of it.

"We had been each other's companion, day-in and day-out, for four years, and it was hard to lose that companionship, the friendship, the affection and intimacy. Then there was a year of that as lovers with both of them, and I was just on the periphery of their relationship. I was living in a house alone, but they had the states between them– all miserable. I convinced Danny to ask Uriah to marry him immediately."

"The closure– you thought that would stop you from loving Dan?" Wynn's a billion times smarter than I am. "Never gonna happen, Kade."

"Yeah, I figured that out, since I felt worse." Laughing without humor, it's strange yet freeing to be this open with Wynn, and realizing he truly won't judge me or punish me for feeling the way I do. "I was now the wreck– the happy couple, Danny had something to look forward to and Uriah got to plan a wedding with Danny's family's blessing."

"Oh, I wish I could have seen that." Wynn's smirk is telling. How often has my little shit been meddling in their lives these past few months? "Get to you being the bachelor party, and I want the dirty details."

"A hotel room, Uriah willing for anything, a free-pass to Danny's kiss, and a very horny, emotionally starved me." Pulling a Wynn, "And the details belong to me."

"Oh!" Wynn kicks me in the shin, sadistic chuckle echoing into the night. "You bastard. I'm not gonna tell you my juicy shit unless you give me something," he nearly whines, eyes begging me.

"Uriah wouldn't let me break my promise about no oral or anal. But it was a goddamn close call, Wynn." The sincerity in my voice is enough for Wynn. With a nod, he understands. "Having Dan touch me was a relief and a curse, but having him kiss me nearly killed me. We both concentrated on Uriah, unable to handle the emotional fallout to do anything else… and then I came home and stalked you, and once you noticed me, I never let you get away from me."

"Having Dan's affection is intoxicating." Wynn drags me back down to my chair, and it isn't until I'm seated that I comprehend what he said. That secretive smirk is back, baiting me to ask, but knowing I'm not brave enough to do it.

"Since we're doing a confessional." Wynn leans back in his chair, totally relaxed, a satisfied curl to his lips. "I don't feel guilt anymore. If I do something by accident, then I should feel compassion for who I hurt, but not guilt since I didn't mean to do it. If I do something on purpose, then I need to own it. Full stop."

"I'm not going to like where this is headed, am I?" Eyeing the empty soldiers by my chair, I wish Wynn hadn't taken the other bottles away. Wynn is completely shameless, no modesty, and terrifyingly in control of every situation he finds himself in.

"You won't need any more beer to get through it, if that helps any," Wynn murmurs, lips curling into a taunting smirk. "Remember when you sat Jack and me down and told us to jerk off together?"

"Yeah." Now it's my turn to smile, remembering it like yesterday. Fond of Danny's and my experiences, I wanted Wynn and Jack to share the same.

"We jerked each other off, and I feel absolutely no guilt about it." Wynn looks me dead in the eyes, challenging me to call him a cheater. "Not only that, we licked each other's hands clean, and then I manipulated Jack into begging for blowjobs."

"I knew it!" I shout, face glowing with amazement. Wynn expects me to be outraged, betrayed even, but the awe I feel for my husband knows no bounds. "Why, though? Not the handy-jays, but the coercion?"

"I want what I want, I know it will help us, and I needed to know if it would work or not. So I picked Jack. Harmless, loveable Jack. Who would want to hurt him, or be mad at him? Plus, I really wanted to blow him."

"What would work?" Filtering out all the irrelevant bullshit, I home in on the one important detail.

"How we'd feel sharing someone we trust," Wynn admits with a shrug, completely shameless. "Would we be jealous? Would we be totally in it and lose our heads–" Wynn looks deep into me, then laughs. "It was a total win in all columns. Sharing was a goal. My only issue was how you wouldn't fuck me, but Jack made that happen."

"You... you– little shit," I snarl, realizing now I was played by the both of them. I lost my head, almost fucking Jack, to the point I literally lost it in the shower with Wynn afterward, fucking him without a directive from my brain.

"Then I needed to meet your *friends*," Wynn twists out, suddenly annoyed. "*Years*. I begged for four years before you'd let me see Dan and Uriah."

"I wonder why," I muse sarcastically. "I'm a liar, and they had my truths. Plus, I didn't honestly think you'd share. I thought you were saying that naughty shit to get a rise outta my dick. I was terrified, on the verge of pissing myself, when we walked into the restaurant to meet them that very first time."

"I married you right then and there, because I knew what I wanted, and what you wanted, and what they wanted, all matched up. It took less than three minutes, and I had plans... short-term and long-term plans, and I've been keeping on schedule."

Wynn gestures around the balcony and to the city beyond, as if to say, *look where we're sitting.* "Uriah sucked my dick," he drops out of nowhere, catching the breath in my throat. "Nope, I've tried to feel guilty about that, but I can't force it."

"Are you a sociopath now?" I squeak out, amazed yet terrified. "If I touched Danny, I'd be bleeding over it."

"Because you get off on feeling guilty, Kade– I don't." Shrugging, Wynn looks totally unrepentant. "I'm not Rusty Knob's

Golden Boy anymore. I'm not an apologist, nor a martyr." Leaning forward, Wynn gets into my face, then pokes me in the temple. "One life, Kaden. One. Life. We get one life to live, why ruin it with this bullshit."

"What bullshit?" It's like something clicks in me all the sudden. The more Wynn talks, the more I buy into what he's selling. No, not buy into it– *believe it.*

"Guilt. Shame. Fear. Worry. Jealousy. Envy." Wynn leans back, never more sincere in his life. "Other than being a pathological liar– *to yourself* –you've never hurt anybody. So why the mental, emotional, and physical self-flagellation routine?"

"Because that's just me, I guess," I mutter lamely, now seeing how ridiculous I behave.

I can't even go on the internet anymore, unless it's Amazon, and I have to be babysat so I don't look at the product reviews, because it creates a visceral reaction in me, where I hate myself and everyone else, thinking very bad things.

"There's no sense to it, Kade. None. Should I feel guilty over Jack? Should I be apologizing to Bren? No, and I'll tell you why." Wynn shifts in the chair, finding it too small to be comfortable. "Jack's a person, not an object, and Bren doesn't get a say in it. Same reason I feel no guilt or shame for having Uriah suck *my* dick. My. Dick. My. Choice. If you know me, trust me, then you know it would never go past that... not gonna make me feel guilty."

"I don't know how you stop worrying or feeling guilty, or not be jealous," I nearly whine, half the time unable to look in the mirror without wanting to punch it, or break down and cry when I see my daddy's reflection gazing back at me.

"I love you. I want you. I don't love you more or less than I did two seconds after Uriah's mouth was on my cock– wasn't about you. It wasn't even about me. It was what Uriah needed. If the neighbors get a new pool, I ain't paying for it, or maintaining it, or even swimming in it–"

"I'd love a pool," I cut in real quick, and Wynn's laughter has a smile splitting my face.

"Of course, you would," he purrs, voice filled with indulgent affection. "If the guy we spot on the street is hotter than me, I don't suddenly get uglier. So envy and jealousy are the most irrational responses, even if it's human nature. Dan's family being rich doesn't take money out of our bank account."

"I wish there was more in it, though."

"Of course, you do." Same tone, same indulgent expression etched on Wynn's face. "One life. I'm living mine in drive, not reverse or neutral. Just like the internet, you could post *Have a Nice Day*, and people would tell you to go shoot yourself. So why bother with their judgments– I'm just gonna live that one life, feel no guilt or shame about it, and leave the worrying to those in neutral."

"I'm gonna need to be in the passenger seat, because I'm not brave enough to drive," I breathe, voice barely audible.

"That's exactly why people get married, Kade." Wynn leans closer, stealing a quick kiss. "Sometimes one driver has to pull over and let the passenger drive for a while, 'cuz they get exhausted. That's a part of life too."

"Uriah really sucked you off?" No anger, all awe. "I've only had you, but you've now blown Jack and got sucked by Uriah. I'm jealous."

"Ain't no need to be, Kade." Wynn flashes me that *I've got a secret and you're about to get the surprise of your life* smirk. "I don't own your dick–" he gestures into the kitchen and beyond. "Use it."

"I-I–"

"How I feel about you won't change, and I can promise how you feel about me won't change, either." Wynn shrugs, like it's no big deal. "Because pretending you don't love Dan doesn't make it go away. Those feelings exist, and they are permanent."

"Yeah, but–"

"I've been talking to someone." Wynn knocks the breath out of me– I've been to countless therapists and doctors and group sessions, and he's always refused. "About our situation."

"How? Who?"

"Franny first, actually." Now Wynn has the grace to look sheepish. "I needed an impartial party. When Franny was up for the wedding, Sage overheard us talking, and then Sage jumped in to help."

"Our situation?" the upward inflection in my voice has me flinching. "Is Sage who you're talking to?"

"Our situation– the fact that you and Dan are in love with each other, and fighting it every step of the way. You should have seen yourselves the last time we watched TV together. Both of ya leaning on each other, hands fisted on your thighs to keep from cuddling. Just fucking cuddle, Kade– ain't nobody stopping ya, ain't no shame."

"Dan's not my husband–"

"Yeah, *that!* Jesus, just fucking cuddling while watching a movie ain't gonna hurt anyone, but not cuddling is hurting all four of us... That's what had me talking to Franny and Sage, hoping their views from California would be wider... Kade, Uriah is on the verge of cheating on Dan to feed his need for attention– that's why I had him suck me off, and he was so relaxed and happy afterward. Uriah needs it."

"I kinda really want those details," I admit, blushing.

"Yeah, when you supply me with the details of you being their bachelor party, I'll tell you about how great Uriah is at sucking dick."

"I'm sure he is– he used to sell his mouth, ya know?"

"*I know.*" Wynn arches a brow in challenge. "I bet I know more than you do... I said I was seducing Dan the demi-pan, and to do that, I needed to form a connection and bond over heavy, emotionally charged conversations."

Eyes wide, mouth gaping, all I can do is stare at Wynn in awe. "You wouldn't."

"I would," Wynn states matter-of-factly.

"You didn't!"

"I did." Wynn's confidence has definitely entered arrogance territory, not something I ever thought I'd see. "I can be very charming when I want to be... I told you I talked to Franny and Sage, but what I didn't get to explain yet was how they told me who I really needed to talk to... and that person said the quickest solution was to ally with Uriah, bond slowly with Dan, and then tell you when I was done."

"You're done?"

"We're here, ain't we? In their apartment?" Wynn bugs his eyes out, looking at me like he truly believes me to be stupid now. "What conversation do you think they're having in there, Kaden? They're having the same conversation we're having out here, because I told Uriah to have it."

"What's going on?" Maybe I am stupid, because I'm not getting it. I was always slower than others, needing to learn things other than out of a book. Needed hands-on experience. Practical, not book-learning or theory. College was an uphill battle I had to conquer, and my four degrees prove it.

"Sage got me in contact with someone. His stepmother's nephew. The middle one plays video games with Bren, Jack, and Sage. Karen? No, that ain't right. Kieran plays online with 'em. Weston is Sage's *one who got away but I'm too spineless to go after him*. Devon's the oldest, and that's who Sage hooked me up with. Franny and Sage just moved up near them in Massachusetts."

"Why? I don't get it."

"Dev is a demisexual, Kade." Wynn pauses, making sure I'm following along, knowing how my mind operates. "Right now, Uriah's convincing Dan to talk to him. Dev's a cop, and he's married to Uriah's instant best friend– Essie. She owns a salon, and she loves to gossip– well, you can see why Uriah would connect to her."

"That's nice, and I'm all for making new friends, but I'm still not getting it." Terrified, I fear Wynn's trying to hook us up, not make new long-distance buddies. I'm okay with sharing with each other, but I'm not down with that.

"I met Rory through Dev– that's my counterpart."

"Your counterpart?" I mutter slowly, hoping it will sink in and make sense the slower I say it. "Do I have one too?"

"A man's man. Blond, blue-eyed, and built like me but muscular, Rory is bisexual, loves cars, runs a bar, and is a bro–"

"Are you giving me his dating profile?" I snarl, getting jealous.

"Rory's *wife*," Wynn stresses, rolling his eyes at me. "Beth is an incredible woman, who saved Uriah from himself. She's a therapist, specializing in sexuality–"

"Oh, *my counterpart*," I mumble, feeling like an idiot. "The person you're going to try to get me to talk to, right?"

Smirking, Wynn's eyes narrow and cut away. "Not exactly. See, you're missing the bigger picture here... they're together. See? Two couples. *Together*. They were best friends, got married, some heavy shit happened, and the two guys hit it off. They struggled, and they offered to help us with our journey, so we don't fall into the same pitfalls."

"I'm missing something, aren't I?"

"You are, but I still love you anyway." Wynn pats my head, trying his damnedest not to laugh. "I love our life, and I don't want to change it, except for the one thing that is always riding shotgun— it's getting harder to ignore it, exhausting us all. Pretty soon, I'm going to have to pull over, and once I do, it's going to be in the driver's seat. But, I'd rather be ready for it, instead of one day having Uriah cheat on Dan, you finally realize you can't live without Dan, and me following my live life to the fullest attitude and experiencing something I'll truly feel guilty about and regret forever."

"Us?" I'm slow, but not a friggin' idiot. "*Together?*"

"Polyamory, Kade," Wynn drops the bomb, exploding all over us until we aren't who we were five minutes ago. "Not like the Masons and Essexes, but similar. They're navigating this right now. Two couples intersecting into a third, with the girls as best friends. Different relationships combined into one big relationship. They're moving in with each other, gonna raise kids together as one family. That's not what I want."

"Thank God." I deflate, looking out over the city. "Because I can't live in this rat-race, and they won't live in hillbilly-infested West Virginia, and I love our life just the way it is."

"Me too." Wynn's lips brush over mine, curled into a relieved smile. "Me too. Fidelity, not monogamy between two husbands. Commitment. Boundaries. Companionship. Friendship. Intimacy. Sexual exploration. Two partnerships meeting in a bigger relationship, each of us having a different connection to the others."

"It sounds complicated," I breathe in wonder, voice warbling. "Are you sure?"

"Yeah, I am." Wynn's confidence calms me, takes the nervous shaking from my muscles. "Years, Kade. I've been thinking about this for years. I've been actively working on it since I met them face-to-face, talking with the Masons and Essexes for advice, and talking to both Uriah and Dan to get a handle on how they feel."

"You're in the driver's seat," I say with certainty, and it melts all the stress away. "I won't always have to be on edge, worrying about hurting your feelings, or Uriah's, or feeling jealous, or envious, or having to hold myself back, and the hollow ache I've felt since I was eighteen years old over Danny would go away?"

"*That*," Wynn stresses, leaning in to rest his forehead against mine, lips so close I can feel his breathe fluttering against my skin. "For you. For me. For Dan. For Uriah… we need this, and we'll make it work, but all of you have to trust me."

"Trust the baby alpha of our ragtag group," hits my ears and has me jerking in shock. Dan stands in the doorway to the kitchen, hand holding the door open in a similar pose Wynn used earlier, with Uriah standing at his back. "Raise of hands– anybody else terrified?"

MISADVENTURES IN POLYAMORY
Wynn Gillette

Snorting, I find it beyond hilarious as Uriah raises his hand slightly, as if he can't help himself, when he's been my partner in crime from the get-go. If Kaden's finger so much as twitches, I'm going to punch him in the nads.

Staring me down, because that's Dan for ya, always challenging me because I'm six years younger than him and he sees that as too much life experience I haven't lived yet. Holding steady, Dan raises his hand like a little school kid asking permission to go to the potty, then the bastard waves it high over his head.

For the past three or four months, I've had to study, and work on commissioned pieces, around everyone else's schedule, because I've had to create bonds out of nothing but other's opinions of me. Dan and Uriah didn't know me– they knew me through Kade, and we can all agree Kaden's view on anything is always skewed.

I've packed more conversations in a few months than I have in my entire life, and it's emotionally exhausting.

"You don't trust me?" I lob at Dan, unable to disguise the hurt in my voice.

The downside of being calculating is that it tends to hit a person threefold in return. Bethany Essex wasn't the one to come up with seducing Dan– Devon Mason said Rory and he were shoved together by their wives, and nature took its course, and I should just shove myself up Dan's ass until he couldn't imagine me not being there. Only one problem with that, I like being there now, and that's terrifying.

Now I understand how Kade feels around Dan, because I have a whisper of it in me too– there's nothing on earth as intoxicatingly painful as love.

"I didn't say that." Dan stares at me, no doubt his mind is making lists, balancing the pros and cons, and the rest of us don't run on logic. Logic is great when it comes to responsibilities, then I have it in spades, but not when it comes to following your heart, in which I toss logic to the curb and do what I want without feeling a shred of guilt.

Life's short.

Sometimes you learn your daddy is an altruistic, hired killer, and not the drunk deadbeat you thought him to be– I'd really like to hug that motherfucker, if only I could find him. Your adoptive dad lied to you by saying you shared a niece and nephew, when they were his own kids– that broke something in me, because Royce Kennedy was my hero, and now I realize he's just a man. Then there is the goddamn dinky Gillette ghosting around Rusty Knob, making me love him against my will– it's hard to hold onto the rage when Cain is giving me beaten puppy dog eyes, eccentric oddities and baffling behavior, when looking at my brother is like gazing at my own condemning reflection in a tarnished mirror.

Life's too short to not live in the now, learning from where you've been, and looking forward to the future. The three men standing around me, they're stuck in the past and worrying about the future– if they never live in the present, what's to look back on in the future?

I'ma make us some memories.

"I need to see something real quick," I warn, coming up out of Uriah's saucer chair as quickly as it will allow. "Nobody punch me."

Listing to the side slightly, I try to hide it by patting Kaden's shoulder in mock comfort. Draining that bottle of wine was stupid of me, being the light-weight that I am, but I needed to tempt Kaden into drinking it to loosen his tongue. Now I'm on my way passed buzzed, and that's a scary position when I'm the one in charge.

Kade looks confused, Uriah looks guiltier than a dog who just shit on his master's shoes, and Dan's looking leery of me. We're gonna change all that.

Striking faster than a snake, I palm the back of Dan's skull, and trap him with my other hand, fingers splaying along his jawline to keep firm control on the situation. "This is our final– let's see if we passed."

"Huh?" Dan grunts, jerking his head backward, trying to dislodge me. But the fuss he puts up doesn't matter none, not with me being so much bigger and stronger, and the fact that as soon as my lips touch his, all the fight runs right outta him.

Even stunned, Dan responds with an open mouth and a questing tongue– all slick spit and breathy moans, with strong man hands no longer trying to push me away, but rather pull me closer.

I'm a sexual guy, and I can be affectionate if the mood strikes– the only lips that matter to me belong to Kaden, unless they're wrapped around my dick. But the threefold rule comes back to bite me in the ass, because my control is only physical in nature.

Dan's in control when it comes to the intimate nature of kissing. Yanking back, we're both breathing heavy, and no doubt my face is just as flushed as his.

"That's part one," I pretend I'm unaffected, voice hoarse. "Now for the extra-credit."

One hand still palming the back of Dan's noggin, the other reaches down to grab his crotch. No need to check myself out, since my dick is ready for anything I toss his way. But Dan's dick operates on a different wavelength, needing an emotional connection to join the party. All those girls, it was an emotional connection– a negative one. Since, Dan hasn't had the desire to touch anyone but Uriah and Kade.

As the one in charge, there was no way in hell I was standing on the sidelines– it's all of us, or we're staying as two separate couples. Dan's dick needs to be in agreement.

Leaning into Dan, I playact the menace, whispering into his ear, when what I'm actually doing is hiding how my eyelashes flutter shut at the feel of the hard bulge filling my palm. "You liked kissing me." Not a question, a statement, and I ignore how breathy and needy I suddenly sound. "We passed."

With a thrust upward into my palm, Dan suddenly goes from lusty to enraged, finding the strength to push me off. "Fuck you, Wynn!" Palms connect to my chest and shove me back onto the balcony, as Dan steps backward into the kitchen. "Don't toy with my emotions like that– was none of that real?"

If the threat of tears escaped my knowledge, the thickness in Dan's voice would clue me in. "It's not like that," I warn, already in damage-control mode. "I wasn't playing you– it was real. You didn't know me, so I took it upon myself to force you to know me."

"You were seducing me." Dan walks deeper into the kitchen, causing me to follow, and I realize this isn't going to be as easy as I thought it was. Coercion and seduction are against Dan's moral and ethical codes, and I did both to get us to where we are right now.

Dealing with Kaden is hard, but worth it. We fight, and we both get off on it. Uriah is the easiest for me– he's submissive, until he ain't, then I back off and reassess. Dan doesn't like to argue, doesn't like drama, and is a martyr. The only way to get to Dan is by meeting him on his level, where logic and honesty rules.

The nonstop sex and companionship of polyamory sounds amazing, until I realize having three lovers is going to be like herding feral cats in an enclosed space filled with juicy mice. They're not going to listen to a word I say if they're distracted.

"Dan." I reach for his shoulder, stopping him from fleeing down the hallway. It's a good thing this apartment is small. "Wait up– lemme explain, okay?"

Scowling, Dan turns to face me, arms folded over his chest in a defensive position. Behind me, Kade and Uriah are playacting ghosts, their worry polluting the air.

"I don't lie," I point out, hoping our trust isn't broken. "Can't do it– so everything we said to one another, I meant my part. It wasn't a game, and I wanted to get to know you, but those facts don't erase how it was necessary for you and me to connect, or this won't work."

This is Dan, so I know I don't have to suffer through any irrational bullshit, crying jags, fist fights, and being frozen out and ignored, like I would with Kade or Uriah.

Putting my life at risk, I step forward and press my lips to Dan's, not touching him with any other body part.

The expert kisser forgives me, or so I assume when Dan opens his lips and sucks my tongue halfway down his throat. Leaning forward on a desperate moan, I try to get closer to Dan just as he sidesteps me.

"Whoa…" I gasp, hand reaching out blindly before I take a header into the hallway wall. It's Kade who catches me from behind before I faceplant, but my eyes are too busy following Dan's backside as he steps into his bedroom… he doesn't close the door, so I take that as an invitation.

Dan's a hard taskmaster, teaching me a lesson and laying down boundaries– I can respect that, once my head stops spinning and my feet regain feeling.

Kade pulls me to lean back against his chest, arms wrapped around me securely. "Remember when you asked why I didn't give it my all when I kissed Danny?"

Uriah releases a sadistic chuckle as he swaggers by, round ass jiggling enticingly– no longer in charge, suddenly I feel like the cat chasing after the mice, distracted and confused. *Hungry.* "I believe that's what romance novelists describe as a swoon."

"It was the wine," I lie, regaining my footing.

"I thought you didn't lie?" Dan shouts from the bedroom. "Get in here, you little shit."

"I'm thinking Wynn needs to graduate to big shit," Uriah taunts me, and that has my feet carrying me into their bedroom. Holding Kaden's hand, I lie to myself again, saying it's for his benefit, not my own.

We find the other couple milling around their small bedroom– I really don't understand city-dwellers. There's no space to wander and breathe. The old shack in the hollers had more square-footage than this apartment. Makes our tiny house feel like a mansion. You have to hunt down grass to rest your feet, but don't step too far left or right, or you'll be on pavement again. Pittsburgh is a beautiful city to *visit.*

In Rusty Knob, I find it oppressive living in town, where you step out onto your porch and look at other houses, with too many watching eyes peering out every window. I dream of how it used to feel to step out the backdoor of the shack, buck-ass naked to take a leak, and there was only trees and woodland creatures as far as the eye could see.

As my mind takes a mini-vacation to Gillette Holler, I fail to notice how all three of my companions are looking at me for what to do next. "I was learning algebra while you guys were fucking each other, remember?"

Three pairs of eyes land on me– confused, guilty, and challenging, and you can guess whose is whose. That guilt must go away, so my decision is made.

"By society's standards, Uriah and I cheated on you both." I drop Kade's hand, then stalk deeper into the bedroom, finding a small slice of empty space near the side of the bed, with their dresser breathing down my neck. "I'm sure you both asked for details, so how about a reenactment?"

"Holy fuck." Uriah's legs give way, dropping his ass onto the edge of the mattress.

"I do believe that's a swoon," Kaden taunts Uriah back, always baiting each other in a lust-hate competition over Dan. In truth, they just really want to fuck the living daylights out of the other, but they're both too squirrely to admit it.

I own my shit.

Hooking my arm around Uriah's neck, I pull him up on wobbly legs, pressing my bulge against the small of his back. Eyes connecting with Dan's, I slowly lean down to press my lips to Uriah's ear, speaking loud enough for the words to carry.

"Here's what we're gonna do…" I trail off, licking a line down the side of Uriah's throat. The guy would sink to his knees before me if it wasn't for my arm wrapped tightly around his chest, keeping him on his feet. "You're gonna suck my dick–"

Dan didn't like that, how baiting I'm being, not realizing this is another test. Kade steps between us, but not enough to break our alpha stare-down.

"Tell your husband the truth– tell him you want to suck my cock," is an order issued from lips currently sucking a pathway along Uriah's sharp jaw, eyes still locked on Dan's enraged, possessive glare. "Tell him."

"I want to suck Wynn's cock!" Uriah releases, voice all breathy but taking on an edge of desperation.

"Good. It's your mouth, and only you get to say who uses it," I mutter pointedly to his husband. Reaching up, I cup Uriah's jaw, turning his head to the side, far enough to peck a kiss on his lips. "I'ma fuck you before Dan fucks me… fuck you so hard, you'll be feeling me for the next week. Gonna come inside ya too, so whoever comes after me, their dick will be sliding through my cum."

With a bite to his pouty bottom lip, I twirl Uriah around, then press my hand on top of his head, applying steady pressure until he kneels before me, just as we did in my half-bath last month.

In near silence– the only sound filling the air is the anticipatory panting –my zipper has Dan flinching, Kade leaning forward for a better view, and Uriah licking his chops like a starving dog after my bone.

Not bothering to pop the button on my jeans, I wedge my dick out my fly, keeping the rest of me under wraps. After learning Uriah's past, I knew he'd appreciate me simulating a sexual transaction.

Dan is the first to break the silence. "Jesus," is a breathy hiss, probably because the last time he saw my dick, he wasn't interested in it. We haven't fooled around since Kade's and my wedding night. All the days since, I've been seducing Dan into wanting my cock as badly as his husband wants it.

Turning slightly, I make sure Dan and Kade are standing to the side, where my back and Uriah's head aren't blocking their view.

Stroking my cock from base to tip, I add a swirl when I get to the head, eyes shuttering with pleasure. As my eyes flutter open, I catch sight of Uriah wiggling around with anticipation, just like last time.

"Open," is an order, one in which Uriah obeys immediately—lips widening, tongue darting out to lick them wet in anticipation. Reaching forward, I grip Uriah's lower jaw, fingers splaying along his neck, "Don't move," I warn as I tap the head of my cock to his damp lips. "Open wider."

Cock slipping inside, I have to warn again. "Don't move. Don't suck." Using my hand to guide my dick, I press in until the back of Uriah's throat stops me. Wet heat, a tongue fighting where my cock is pressing it down, "Open wider, let me do all the work– don't move, or I'll end up hurting you."

The breath catching in someone's throat beside me– whether it's Kade's, or Dan's, I have no idea –has me being too eager, too impatient. Hips snapping forward, I barely catch myself before I harm Uriah.

"Arch your neck, tilt your head back." Lifting on my toes slightly, I use our height differences to my advantage, finding the perfect angle to fuck Uriah's throat. I ignore our husbands, all my attention on the man at my feet with the trusting brown eyes that never leave mine.

Rubbing my hand along Uriah's neck, I can feel my cock moving beneath, inside the tight sheath of his throat. Curses are said beside me, but I'm too hyper-focused on Uriah to understand anything but the fact that Dan and Kade can see my dick moving beneath Uriah's skin.

The wet suction creates a garbling sound on the exit, and a sharp inhalation on the entrance. Uriah grunts, wiggling his knees on the floor, hands pressing against the ever-widening damp spot in his jeans.

Uriah needed this. Dan and Kade needed to see it. This isn't for me, so I don't take my release, no matter how badly I wish I could.

There's no guilt here– I won't allow it.

As I slowly pull out, dick hard and covered with strings of saliva, I tilt Uriah's head back down to a comfortable angle. "You didn't come like last time." The disappointment in Uriah's voice has me chuckling with satisfaction.

"If I'm gonna fuck you, I need to be hard," I remind Uriah, using my words as a threat and a promise to my husband and his. "My fucking you will get you hard– I'll make you come again."

"I don't think I could do that," Dan's whispering to Kade, thinking I'm too far gone to hear it. Dan slumps to the bed, and Kade follows, both looking exhausted but out of their minds with lust. "I don't think I could take it either."

"We tried it once, and never again…" Kade trails off, and the quiver in his voice has me grinning. Kade's the one who wanted to try it– *on me* –and the one who regretted it when I excelled at doing it *to him*.

"Dick too big," Dan murmurs, clearly been checking me out, no longer able to play pretend.

"Yeah," Kade huffs out, laughing with pride. "It's great for everything but whatever you call that shit."

"I thought I knew how to deep-throat–"

"Whatever that was, that's a whole 'nother level of cocksucking."

As Uriah kneels before me, we don't move, eavesdropping on the idiots who think we aren't listening. Sharing a wry smile, Uriah thumbs spit off his lower lip, then licks it off. Shuddering, I barely shove my hand down my pants in time to grab my balls roughly before I pop.

"You'll pay for that," I warn, chuckling down at the seductive little brat. "Crawl over there and get to sucking– vanilla, no cranking them too high. Their dicks are for me after I'm done with you, no milking them dry."

Eyes wide, Uriah looks at me as if he can't believe his ears. After a second to make sure I'm not fucking around, he zeroes in on Kade.

Scuttling back on the mattress, "Oh, shit!" Dan finally breaks a sweat, no longer as composed as he pretends to be. Kneeling near Kade, Dan tries to get a bird's-eye view.

"Change of plans," I murmur underneath my breath to Uriah. "You take mine and I'll take yours."

Chuckling evilly, Uriah flows to his full height, and then runs his hand up Kade's chest, flicking Kade in the chin. "Let's get you naked, yeah? It's time I got orally acquainted with that dick I've cranked more times than I can count."

The real test is watching my husband kiss Uriah, while Dan watches me from the bed, tapping directly into my thoughts. The guy loves to say he's no mind-reader, but more often than not, Dan knows exactly what we're all thinking.

Dan's seen the show, had both my husband and his in bed with him for nearly a year. I've always known this in theory, but never in practice. I've been so focused on how they felt, I never checked in with how I truly feel, always seeing Dan as the one I needed to worry about taking me from Kade's heart.

Uriah crawls up my husband's body, fingers tugging Kade's shirt out of the way as he goes, then settles on straddling his lap. As they kiss slowly, I stand three feet away in this dinky bedroom, able to see the peek of pink as tongues mingle inside Kade's mouth, even the glisten of saliva.

Investigating how I feel from every angle, I realize I'm trying to force myself to feel how I think I should be feeling. Kade's my husband, and some hot fucking piece of ass has his hand shoved down Kade's pants, tongue thrusting into his mouth, and I should feel jealous– betrayed even.

A heartbeat later, I see it for what it is. Kade is having the time of his life, finally getting to do things with Uriah they've always avoided, and they look gorgeous and ecstatic while doing it. Their mingled moans are doing wicked things to my exposed cock, but my mind is still swirling in chaos.

"Hey." Dan tugs me to the bed, always too compassionate and considerate to be anything but perfect. "You okay?"

Sitting next to him, I try to get a handle on my emotions. "Yeah, I think I am– it's just a lot to take in."

"When you're not the one driving the action, you mean?" Reaching over hesitantly, Dan rub my back in soothing circles, and that threefold problem rears its ugly head again.

Dan's all about the intimacy, and this is as intimate as it comes, and what Uriah and Kade are doing right now is about lust and need.

"I've been where you are, Wynn." One hand becomes two, and a rub becomes a massage. My shirt is pulled over my head, and suddenly I'm not the one in charge anymore. "Uriah's been where you are– Kade's always been where you are."

"Paying my dues?" Laughing without humor, I stare down at my cock as he kicks in response to the throaty moans echoing around the bedroom.

Kade's down to his boxers, with Uriah's hand still shoved down the front, obviously working his cock. They're kissing, with Kade's hands yanking Uriah's clothing off in a rush. As always, I'm impressed with Uriah's lithe body, especially in juxtaposition to Kade's muscular one.

Seeing Uriah's hands roaming over Kade's masterpiece of tattoos, jealousy and possession kick me in the teeth. Those are our tattoos, and Uriah's touching them. Tattoos Jesse designed for Kaden to feel empowered to have survived his history of cuts. From wrists, up his arms, across his shoulders, dipping to create a scoop neck, Kade's entire back to the crack of his ass, and his chest and torso too, all the way down to the tops of his thighs, are a canvas of tattoos telling *our* history. Not to cover where Kaden's bled, but to accentuate it.

"See… that's the downfall for anyone who's trying to reach a goal." Dan uses my shoulders to pull himself up to his knees. Kneeling behind me, he uses the leverage his height offers to get my muscles deep. Now it's my turn to add a guttural groan to the mix.

"Once you reach your goal, it's then what? You're always hyper-focused on what everyone else needs and wants, you forget you can't give yourself what you need and want– that's what we're for." Dan kisses the side of my neck, and it's like a switch flips in my head. Falling limp, I let Dan drive for a while, knowing I can easily wrench control back.

"Tell us what you want," Dan coaxes, nimble fingers unbuttoning my fly, then hands are working my jeans off my hips, while other hands are attacking my socks. "We've perfected playing with each other, while skating along boundary lines–"

"No more boundaries." Lifting my head, unsure when I laid down in the first place, I catch the eyes of all three of them as they kneel around me. Kade and Uriah each have a leg, taking off my socks, and Dan is leaning over me, hands tugging my jeans down.

"What you don't seem to get..." Dan turns over the duty of unclothing me to Kade, who knows how to get me out of my clothing with a single look. *Poof!* I'm naked.

"You're new to us, so you're feeling out of place– maybe like a fourth wheel. For us–" Dan gestures to Uriah. "It's like someone plucked the hottest fucking god of a man out of the ether, and ceremoniously dropped him into our bed with a *you're welcome...* we don't want to do each other, we want to do *you*."

"Jesus!" hissing, I grab for my cock, squeezing my balls tight, regretting those deep-throating shenanigans with Uriah.

"You just relax and let us explore you." Dan communicates with Uriah and Kade with a single look, and I'm not surprised how they easily shift from taking my orders to taking his. "What's on Wynn's bucket list?"

"I never thought my little shit was serious." Kade talks like I'm not even here, but his hands are reassuring him I am, touch sparking flickers of need along my thighs.

"He was serious," Dan and Uriah mutter in unison, using the same cadence. All three of them share a sex-loaded chuckle, causing a shudder to roll along my spine, making it impossible to stay still beneath their exploring hands.

"Number one on Wynn's list–" Kade points at Uriah. "His ass."

Now it's my turn to laugh, belly contracting as I try to sit up. "No matter what, that's happening tonight." Eyes flicking to Uriah as he gets dangerously close to my dangly bits, fingertips feathering along my thighs. "I'm going to bend you over the foot of this bed and plough you from behind– don't plan on walking tomorrow."

Reaching for the nightstand, Uriah roots around in the drawer, and comes back out with a half-gallon, wholesale-sized, pump bottle. "Good thing we've got enough lube." Uriah's not laughing, but his tone sure sounds like he is.

"What else?" Dan's fingertips sneak beneath my head, digging into my scalp, and we find a new erogenous zone of mine. Toes curling, every nerve in my body lights up, tingling and leaving goose bumps behind. "Besides being touched, that is," he mutters wryly, satisfaction in his voice.

"I–" Kade looks at me, too cowardly to say it.

My bravery is just a line of shit I feed myself on a daily basis, so I don't break down and lash out at those who keep breaking their promises and betraying my trust. I adopted this new way of life, pretending I feel no guilt, no shame, and just grab what I want by the balls. It's true, but it takes a bit of convincing myself from time to time to go through with it.

My bravery is not bullshit tonight.

"I want…" I trail off, making sure I have their attention, feeling more in control now, even though I'm lying flat on my back with six hands rubbing various parts of my body. All intimate touches, not sexual– I'm gonna change that.

"After I fuck Uriah into the mattress, while he's still writhing beneath me, I want you both to fuck me. At. The. Same. Time."

Dan blinks, thinking he didn't hear me right. "You mean one in your mouth, one in your ass? I've always wanted to do that." Then Kaden's head hitches backward, a disbelieving laugh echoing around the room. "Oh, I take it that's not what you meant."

Smirking up at them, eyes connecting with Kade's. "That sounds fun too… *but–*"

"Wynn want both our dicks in his ass at the same time, Danny." Kade slaps Dan on the back, because the man just lost all higher thinking. "He wants to get off on knowing our dicks are sliding against one another inside him."

"Oh." Dan slumps to the mattress, body giving out on him, nearly toppling over me. "That sounds fun, but won't that hurt?"

"You don't look like it's going to take much convincing," I tease, turning my head slightly, lips grazing the edge of Dan's jaw. "I take it you're keen on the idea?" With a dreamy expression crossing his face, eyes slipping shut, Dan nuzzles closer to me in answer. "Yeah, that's exactly what I thought."

Leaning closer, I steal a kiss, knowing better than to fully open myself up to the intoxicating powers of Daniel Bishop's kiss. "How we doing this? Who wants to do what and when?" I try to take control, since Dan looks like someone flipped his switch to off when all the blood in his body flowed straight to his dick.

"I think we should all suck Wynn's dick... and prepare him." Uriah gets vocal, since Kade and Dan are still stuck on the fact that they'll be double-penetrating me. Not waiting for permission, Uriah shuffles closer, then bends at the waist to lick my dick.

"Ri!" Jackknifing upward, it takes all my concentration not to pop on contact. "What about everybody else?"

"We all have to take our turn being selfish in a bed of givers." Dan rolls to his knees, looking unsure for once. Talking to Uriah while gesturing to me, "May I... may I– um... may I taste Wynn?"

"Anything goes with Kade and Wynn, remember?" Uriah looks pointedly at Dan, and I wonder how in-depth of a conversation they had. I'd worried, fearing Uriah wouldn't say the bullet points I laid out for him without me there to supervise. But then what Dan said finally sinks into my lust-fogged brain, and I snap.

Rolling to my knees, I accidently knock Uriah off my hips. "You have too many clothes on, Dan." On my cue, the man is stripped of his clothes in a matter of seconds, with a few near misses with elbows thrown and heads butting as we yank and tear Dan's shirt over his head. It's a struggle, and the shirt's destination is the trash, but finally Dan's stocky, furred chest is bare.

"Oh!" Breath hitching in my throat, awed as my eyes flick back and forth between three naked men. "Best of both worlds in this bed– smooth and furry. Tan and pale, tattooed and virgin skin. Tall and short. Lithe and stocky. Lean and muscular. Blond and black and brown– long and short –straight and curly hair. Brown eyes, and hazel, and blue. Huge dicks. Thick dicks. Perfect dicks. And pretty dicks... God, Kade, what should we do to them? What are we going to do to you?"

Kade looks at me, and then that goddamn Teacher Man smirk tugs at his lips, the very one that made me lose my shit over five years ago. It's a bratty, baiting smirk meant to aggravate me as much as it arouses me.

With a slow blink, that smile hitches high. "Anything," is Kaden's answer to my many chaotic questions. "I love you."

"Ha!" is huffed from my chest. "Prove it."

In a heartbeat, I'm flipped to the mattress, with Kade's hands pressing my shoulders down. "You forgot to ask a question, little shit." Eyes rolling to look at either Dan or Uriah, "Why don't we show him."

Uriah's hands look tiny as he hooks my knees, drawing them up against my chest. "Um… guys? What are we doing?" voice cracking, I begin to worry.

Smirking, Uriah presses against my legs, putting all his weight into it, drawing my ass off the bed. "You pulled the car over, because the kids in the backseat were being naughty, so we stole the keys."

"Huh?" I grunt, then my husband adds to my confusion. Kade takes over for Uriah, kneeling behind my head, balls tickling my hair, he grabs for my legs. I find myself in a precarious situation, as Kaden draws my knees nearly to my shoulders, spreading them wide until all my junk and everything beyond is on full display.

"You didn't ask what we were going to do to you," Dan whispers, eyes hungrily roaming the dips and valleys of my body.

"Welcome to my playground," Kaden mutters wryly. "No fighting. Biting is welcome. Sharing is enforced. If you pick something up, please feel free to stick it in your mouth. If you make a mess, lick it clean… Upon your exit, I suggest you leave the playground in the excellent condition it was when you entered."

Eyes wide in shock, I witness Dan gulping for air and Uriah licking his lips, both of them sporting wood that has my hungry asshole clenching in need. Then Dan's serious gaze connects with mine, and I know I'm in trouble.

"My turn." Dan slides to his belly, face descending between my thighs, hot breath scorching me. Rolling his eyes up to look at me, "I've only done this to one person, so there may be a learning curve."

Arching backward, I'm thankful Kaden is holding me tight, because I lose control over every system in my body as Dan alternates between sucking on my dick, mouthing my balls, and rimming my ass.

"Quality over quantity," I gasp, marveling over Dan's oral skills. "In your case, quality and quantity with the same guy–

fuck…" colors burst behind my eyes as Dan sets his teeth into my taint, just this side of pain.

"Be forewarned." Kade leans down to rub his cheek against my forehead, somehow noticing a lock of hair was tickling me. "Wynn can come outta nowhere when he's being rimmed… check him out– he's probably already relaxed enough for us."

"Go take care of Uriah," Dan orders, hot breath tickling my sack. "Get him ready for Wynn, because nobody's going to last to the main event at this rate."

Two things happen within seconds of each other. One, I'm released, legs springing out, head conking on the mattress. Two, Uriah is squealing as Kade flips him over the end of the bed, then dives head-first between the fleshy globes of that jiggly ass.

I try very hard to enjoy the view, but Dan distracts me with a sneaky fingertip slowly slipping inside me. "Kade wasn't joking, I have a hair-trigger when it comes to this."

"Hey, Wynn?" Kade calls, top of his head barely visible from below the arch of Uriah's back. Popping up from where he was kneeling on the floor, he grabs for the lube bottle, lips damp and rosy red from the feast.

"Yeah?" is a breathy moan, hand reaching down to cup my sack, fingertips squeezing. "Not gonna last long… oh, God– deeper. Hook your fingers."

Half my attention on Kade, the other half floating around somewhere, waiting on an orgasm, I watch as Kade pumps several palmfuls of lube down the crack of Uriah's ass.

"If you don't get over here soon…" Kade trails off, standing to his full height. Cock in hand, a few stroking twists has him shuddering. "I'ma fuck Uriah for ya."

I've never moved so fast in my life, lust washing over my brain.
Blink.

Dan's knocked out of the way, fingers slipping out of me. My cock bobs so hard against my stomach, I almost come from the friction of it.
Blink.

My feet are planted on the floor with Uriah bent over the foot of the bed, luscious ass right in front of me. Kade's taunting laughter flutters against my ear.

Blink.

My dick is in hand, poised to enter the licked and lubed pink bud. Knowing that's my husband's spit slicking that asshole, I swirl my cockhead around in it.

Blink.

I'm shoving inside Uriah with a single, hard thrust.

Blink.

Uriah's sharp holler has me sparking back to cognizance. "Oh, shit!" Scorching flesh is molded around my cock, muscles contracting. "I didn't mean that literally– the tearing you a new asshole."

My hands automatically reach for Uriah's back, feeling his skin quivering beneath my touch, then I draw my palms downward, curving over his ass to hold his hips.

I'm about to apologize, but then I realize Uriah's jerking movements, the guttural groaning, and the way his ass is spasming around my cock, signal something he should be thanking me over instead.

Grabbing a handful of that long, black hair, I force Uriah's back to arch, pulling him deeper on my cock, bottoming out with my balls pressed against his body. "Yeah… you like that, Ri? You like me fucking your ass?" The echoing moan is answer enough, but I'm not even certain it came from Uriah. "Want me to fuck you harder? Wanna feel it for days?"

Uriah tries to roll his narrow hips back into me, but I control his movements by twisting his hair in my fist. Pulling tightly, I force Uriah to arch his back even more, legs spreading, ass rearing up, and then I pound him so hard, our balls are slapping together.

"God, Ri– your skin is flawless, I'ma mark it red." One hand in Uriah's hair, the other leaving dimpled fingertip bruises on his hip, I'm close to falling over the edge. "I don't know if you're super tight, or if it's because I have such a big dick, but I'm gonna be fucking you forever."

"Jesus fucking Christ!" Uriah collapses, snapping a few hairs off in the process. Hips gyrating against the mattress, the little brat tries to rut himself off on the blankets. "You're so fucking huge, it motherfucking hurts, but I'm loving every second of it."

Shuddering, I no longer know if I'm fucking Uriah, or if he's fucking me, but all I know, I'm not going to last much longer. Leaning into him, hoping his lithe body can support us both, I hammer as deeply as possible, bottoming out until my pelvis slams into a firm body.

"I can feel you... so fucking big– I can feel you pulsing..."

Dan and Kaden attack at once. Kade grabbing my hips to stop me from thrusting, and Dan grabbing Uriah's hair, yanking a lot harder than I had been. "Don't move," Dan warns. "Neither one of you– don't come."

A series of animalistic snarls fill the air, and hell if I know whether they come from me or Uriah– both of us, I suspect. I'm jerking inside Uriah, and his ass is greedily trying to suck the cum outta my dick, and these two assholes call a timeout on us.

"We're not waiting for you two to finish," Dan warns, and my mind is so foggy, I don't comprehend what he's saying. "If you weren't screwing Uriah while we did this, it would be easier. One on the bottom, one on top. But since all four of us are involved... I'll go first because I'm smaller, all around. Then Kade will try to wedge in next to me, since his cock is thicker and a bit longer, okay?"

"Okay," Uriah answers, but I think the question was meant for me. "But if you don't hurry up, I swear to Christ, I'm going to fuck your ass while you sleep."

"Okay, that's really kinky," I mutter confused, since Dan's ass is the last virgin sacrifice in this room. A second later, Dan's palming the crown of my head, pushing me forward, and it all clicks at once. "Holy shit, you're going to fuck me. Right. Now."

"I'm a patient man, Wynn, but I'm not a goddamn saint," is my three-second warning. Kade steps back, and then Dan is standing behind me. "Demisexual doesn't mean I'm a cuddly teddy bear, who doesn't get insatiably horny, to the point I have precum dripping on the carpet."

Squishing Uriah beneath me, but he doesn't seem to mind, my head's doing this floaty thing, similar to when I drink or smoke too much. "I'm going to regret seducing you, aren't I?"

Dan's cock presses into me, sure and steady, just like the man himself. "No, you won't," is the last he says, with a shift snap of his hips forward.

Stacked, Uriah and I grunt in unison– anything Dan does to me, flows through me into Uriah, in an endless cycle of suspending on the edge of release.

"I can't believe Dan's fucking you." Uriah grabs my hand, tugging it far enough so he can twine his fingers with mine. On the next sharp thrust, our grunt ends with Uriah sinking his teeth into my forearm.

"Jesus Christ!" I hiss in a combination of pleasure and pain, coming from all ends. Uriah's ass wrapped around my cock is incredible, his teeth in my arm hurts like a sonofabitch, but it's Dan's cock that's driving me to a fevered pitch. "I can't believe he's fucking me either." No longer in control– hell, I'm not even a passenger anymore –Dan is in charge.

"I can believe I'm fucking you, Wynn– you should see how gorgeous your asshole looks stretched around my dick. Everything on you is pale pink." Panting breathlessly, Dan finds the most bizarre of rhythms. I'd ask Uriah if it's the norm, but I can't catch my breath.

Dan pounds me, causing me to pound Uriah, causing Uriah to sink his teeth deeper. Then Dan pauses long enough for the edge to wear off, with no threat of any of us coming. Then he thrusts again, only harder than the time before, exponentially harder than the first thrust.

"Huh?" Kade's voice is soft, contemplative. "Interesting." Then his heavy hands are caressing my back. "Bet Wynn's not sure if this is the best sex of his life, or the most traumatic." Chuckling, Kade leans down to kiss my shoulder, and then brushes his lips over Uriah's hair. "Who knew? Wynn is a sadist when it comes to cock-swallowing, and Dan's picked up a brutal trick of his own."

"I never said I was boring," Dan deadpans, then thrusts the hardest he has, causing two sharp grunts to fill the air. "I'm feeling better now." The next roll of Dan's hips is slow and smooth, causing every nerve in my body to spark at once. "Had some aggression to get out, that's all. Care to join us?"

"Punishing Wynn for how he took Uriah at first, eh?" Kade calls Dan out on his bullshit, a smile in his voice. "Trust me– I've been on the business end of that monster cock, and nothing is as magnificent as Wynn losing his shit and going nuts. Uriah was in heaven, no need to put them in hell."

The only consolation, and miscalculation on Dan's part, is how it was the thrust itself that was punishing, not Dan's perfect cock– it was built for optimum gland stimulation, not thick or long enough to hurt anyone. But, even with the position we're in, my cock is big enough to punish if not careful, and it's Uriah's ass getting plowed with the force of Dan's movements.

"Fair enough." A series of apologetic kisses are peppered over my shoulders and down my spine, all the while Dan is slow and smooth, rhythm never fracturing. I sense this is his usual pace, and if he keeps it up much longer, we're all going to be coming unglued, judging by the mewing sounds spilling against my damp, ravaged arm.

"Let's see if this is possible." Kaden sounds doubtful. I try to raise my head to have a gander, but I'm too exhausted to move an inch.

Dan stops thrusting, dick pulling out of me slightly as he moves to the side to allow Kaden to stand next to him.

The fact that I'm an enormous dude is to our advantage. If we tried to double-team Uriah or Dan, in this same position, there wouldn't be room behind them. Me, my ass and thigh spread are proportionate with my height. My insides have got to be larger too– no way in hell would I allow anyone to try to double-penetrate the guy currently wrapped around my cock. I'd kill them for even suggesting it.

Somehow sensing my warm and fuzzy, ultra-protective thoughts, Uriah nuzzles into my ravaged forearm, rolling his hips in a perfect circle beneath me– the little slut is working my dick, a fraction of an inch at a time, earning a prostate massage for his efforts, all the while gaining friction between the blankets and his cock.

"You're killing me," I warn, cock threatening to erupt, spasms lighting along my shaft. "Slow your roll," I tease, causing Uriah to giggle. As punishment, I nip his ear between my front teeth, only that makes him thrust up into me harder. "Shit... so close."

...and then I feel it, Kaden fighting for space next to Dan.

I don't know where the fantasy came from. It wasn't a book, or a movie, or even internet porn. One day, I was staring down into the toybox, intrigued by this double-dong. Kade found me fondling it, and a weird expression came over his face– now I realize that Kade most certainly used it with Uriah. But, back then, I was intrigued.

The next time I was alone, I tried to bend the dong in half while masturbating with it, trying to see if I could get both heads in me at the same time. I wasn't coordinated enough, and ended up using two toys at once. I engaged in many exploratory masturbation sessions after that, so I know I can take 'em both. It's just a matter of getting them in there at the same time.

The thought alone has me a heartbeat away from coming inside Uriah's ass.

The stretch. The burn. The fight for space. I know in another position, this will work easier, but I wanted all four of us together this first try.

Body igniting, as every nerve-ending sparks to life, skin suddenly feeling too tight. It's the fullness for me, but it's also cerebral, because I can't feel much of what's truly going on, except for the tandem movements inside me. It's also the kinky factor of two men using my ass, their cocks sliding slickly next to one another, precum mixing.

For Kade and Dan, it means a helluva lot more than it does for me. Trembling fingertips rest on the small of my back, furry thighs wobble with every tentative thrust. Hungry whimpers echo around the room, and it's not coming from Uriah or me.

"Since we probably won't recover until we plan the next trip," Uriah whispers against my arm, and I know no one but me can hear it. "It'll be our turn– which one of them will be our victim?"

"Probably Kade," I whisper, grinning against the side of Uriah's face. "Since Dan's ass won't be ready for the likes of me."

"You get him ready for me, and I'll finally take it." The surety and hunger in Uriah's tone surprises me. If Dan's ass is a virgin, so is Uriah's cock, never having been inside anything but Dan's mouth.

"I'm going to wake you up with my lips wrapped around your cock," I breathlessly muse more to myself. "You're too selfless in the cocksucking department. It's high time we return the favor."

"Coming!" Uriah shouts, ass going fucking nuts around my dick, starting a chain-reaction. The sounds and scents of sex filling the air, create the most erotic moment of our lives.

After separate showers, meal and drink, and privacy, I wasn't sure what our sleeping arrangements would be. Every other time we've gotten together for a weekend, Dan and Uriah came to us, or we just met in the middle for a few hours at a restaurant, with drinks at a hole-in-the-wall bar afterward.

Instinct had me contemplating when Kade and Dan would break out of their pretend mode, even doing the business as usual routine on the sofa as we caught a few minutes of news. When it came time to hit the sack, my questions were answered as we were led back into their bedroom, with the cleaning gnomes having magically changed the bedclothes.

Emotionally and physically exhausted, after months– hell, *years* –of buildup, I crashed.

Maybe it was the fact that it's never dark here, not with all the lights smothering the darkness outside. No matter how thick the draperies may be, my rural nature can't sleep in the lights. Maybe it was just time for me to naturally wake, after only a few hours of rest.

Maybe it was the bed rumbling underneath us, and it ain't seismic activity, that finally answered the one question that had been on the tip of my tongue all night, but always went unasked.

In the light cast from the window, I finally witness what Dan's true kiss looks like. My husband is unhinged beside me, writhing all over the mattress, legs spread wide with Dan on top of him. There's no mistaking what's happening. Dan's *inside* Kaden, for the very first time.

Using that same smooth, rolling thrust he implemented on me, Dan is taking his time, more into the kissing than the actual sex, and Kaden is into it all.

I'd love to lie and say a part of me isn't jealous. Not so much the fucking, even though there is no way anyone could mistake this as anything other than making love. The frantic, needy, greedy, hungry whimpers spilling out of Kaden's mouth, only I've ever made him sound like that... until tonight... until Dan.

I'm not going to lie. I'm totally and completely, straight down to the marrow, jealous.

It's not the dick in Kade making him sound so crazed– it's the kiss.

Eyes cutting across their backs, I notice how Kade's thick fingers are grasping Dan's hair, desperately yanking him closer, and the other hand is grabbing Dan's meaty, furry ass, trying to get him to go deeper– hell, if it was lighter in here, I bet I could spot fingers thrusting deep inside Dan.

I'm jealous.

My biggest problem is that I love Kaden so goddamn much, I'm thrilled for him right now. Thrilled he's getting to experience something so intimate, so intense, something so long in the making, that he's disconnected from his brain long enough to be jacked up to his own heart.

I love Kaden so much, that I wouldn't take that from him, no matter who's giving it to him.

Am I jealous because it's not me who's making Kaden forget everything but love? Yes and no. Am I jealous that I'm not experiencing it right now? Yes. Yeah, I am– not gonna lie.

A part of me, that threefold part I knew was going to get trampled after the seduction coercion, is jealous because Dan doesn't feel for me, even a sliver of what he's feeling for Kade… and if that doesn't make me a rat-bastard, I don't know what does.

Sensing someone's attention on me, my eyes sight the source instantly. Leaning against the headboard, Uriah isn't watching them– he's watching me, as if he's plucking every individual thought straight outta my noggin. Sympathy reflects back at me, and it makes me feel even shittier for feeling as I do.

A satisfied chuckle startles me out of our staring contest, but it doesn't seem to take Uriah by surprise. "Wynn, what am I gonna do with you?" Dan sounds and looks equally thrilled that I'm upset.

That chuckle moves closer in the dark, and ends up spilling between my lips as an insistent mouth descends. This kiss isn't like the other two we shared, and it's nothing like the punishing fuck Dan delivered earlier– it's more thorough than the rim-job he gave me, and that's saying something.

Leaning into Dan, I'm embarrassed to admit a soft mew escapes my mouth, causing Dan to laugh outright in delight. "You stupid boy," he whispers against my mouth, lips curling into a smirk. "If you think I wasn't on to you, then you've got another think coming."

"You knew?" Confused, all I can do is gape up at Dan, as he never breaks that rolling motion inside my husband.

Kade doesn't register we're communicating, judging by his nonstop wiggling and clutching, knees raising higher as his thighs move uncontrollably– roving hand now digging fingertips into a meaty shoulder.

"I'm a social beast…" Dan pauses to kiss my husband again, and the Jeopardy theme song begins playing in my head as I wait. Uriah flashes me a sympathetic look, evidently having experienced this same impatience game.

Lips catch mine again, but only for a split-second. "But I don't let anyone get to know the real me." Dan picks up where he left off. "So, if you think I didn't notice how you were doing to me, exactly as I did to catch Uriah–"

"Then I've got another think coming?" blurts out before I can stop it.

"Exactly." Those lips are back, tasting like my husband, and I know they were wrapped around Kade's cock long before Uriah and I were awakened. Longing for their own slice of privacy, Dan and Kade had the decency to wait until we were asleep before they let their emotions fly.

"You can touch us, but behave until we're done– won't be long now."

"They're lasting longer than I expected," Uriah whispers in the dark. "Kade's been suspended on the edge of orgasm for the past five minutes, and Dan has never lasted this long before."

"I was fucked out, quite literally," Dan murmurs wryly to Uriah. It finally dawns on me, Dan's been kissing all three of us in turn. Impressive.

Since I was invited, and this vulnerable sensation is only getting more powerful as I lie in this bed, the need to be close to someone overpowers me. I snuggle closer, butting up against Kade's side, and then begin petting Dan's back, enjoying the interplay of his muscles at work with every rolling thrust.

The hand that was gripping Dan's shoulder unlatches itself to clutch onto me instead, letting me know Kade was, not only listening, but hearing everything we said.

As our husbands make love to one another, Uriah and I keep sharing bumping touches, as we skate our fingertips along Dan's back and Kaden's arm. The naughty glint in the brown eyes across from me, followed by the white flash of bared teeth, signals Uriah's patience has come to an end.

A sharp bite sinks into Dan's shoulder, and the man comes instantly, bucking so hard we all nearly bounce off the mattress. Kade's never been a quiet one, but this time Dan eclipses everything audible within the apartment and beyond.

"You don't play fair, minx." Dan's annoyance is feigned, as pride swells in his voice.

Leaning down to whisper in Kade's ear, the breathy sound is so soft, I can't be sure, but the syllables and pauses sounded a helluva lot like *I love you*. Receiving the same reply from my husband, slurred but audible this time, Dan rolls off Kade to tackle the minx on the other side of the bed.

Kade immediately curls into me, seeming more vulnerable than I feel. Arms clutching me tightly, those same three words are whispered in my ear, only in a tone specifically reserved for me.

"Tell the truth," I bait, pretending that's not what I'm doing, as I'm a man who doesn't engage in cerebral warfare or catty fishing expeditions. Our companions are having a similar, baiting conversation, in a similar position, with the same results. "Was that everything you hoped it would be?"

Pulling away slightly, Kade looks at me, tears glistening in his eyes. "Thank you."

My husband's response is the very reason I'll forever give him what he wants, and exactly why I'll love him as fiercely as anyone can love another human being.

"Thank you."

• EPILOGUE • SPOILER-WARNING •

Due to an intersecting storyline, Wager (Blended #7) & Polished (Rusty Knob #4) share the same Happily Ever After epilogue. If you read both series, or plan to read both series, I'd suggest not reading farther unless/until you read both books first.

If you don't read both series, continue onward, knowing there may be slight confusion as four characters are shown (characters briefly mentioned in the later chapters of Polished, but not in Wager due to the timeline). Their story has no direct impact on this journey, just characters from another series lending an ear while discussing the pitfalls of living in a polyamorous relationship.

If you read both series, never fear– this message, and the following epilogue, will be word-for-word in both books. Whichever book you read first, you don't have to go back to it to read the epilogue, just continue forth to read the Happily Ever After for both sets of characters.

Thank you for being patient and understanding… with the flip of the page, enjoy the epilogue.

· THE FUTURE·
· FAIRPORT, MASSACHUSETTS ·

FRANCIS 'FRANNY' PARKER'S WEDDING

EPILOGUE- A REAL ONE, NOT JUST THE LAST CHAPTER
3rd Person Narrative
(Yeah, Erica Chilson's going there for once)

Rusty Knob meets Blended in the final of finales. **In the distant future**, the Blended series has just met its end, with readers wondering if Ms. Chilson will ever revisit for the next generation, and the Rusty Knob series has probably been concluded many books ago. M&M of Restraint is probably still kicking, with the 100+ characters the author accidentally created.

Readers will never know, because this is Erica Chilson, and she does what she wants, when she wants, but this is the outcome she has envisioned since the beginning… Will it change? Doubtful. Maybe. Quite possibly… you'll have to wait and see.

Some of Rusty Knob's cast came out in support of Francis Parker, forgoing quick flights for a road trip. Bren and Jack, with Jesse and Libby, loaded the kids into a minivan, and wanted to murder each other somewhere in the middle of Pennsylvania. Honor pulled the van over, told everyone to get out, and forced them to have a time-out on the side of the road. When the adults were behaving– no longer baiting each other –the kids let them back in the van.

A first honeymoon of their own, Penny and Warren will regret leaving their teen children alone for a week, learning Copper is just as conniving and intelligent as Grandpa Corbin, and Ginger is just like her parents when it comes to keeping her panties on. Never fear, Aunt Willa is scary when the neighbors seek her out in hopes of shaming her for letting her kin run wild.

The grooms from the double-wedding are flying high in the sky toward destinations Erica has yet to decide on. Francis Parker and Sage Fischer, best friends forever, but they surely aren't marrying each other– their grooms are also best friends forever, popular even outside of Fairport's circles, but you'll have to wait until the final book in the Blended series to find out… oh, and in case you fear Ms. Chilson is creating a trend– never fear, they don't share.

Dan and Uriah were hanging out in their larger apartment, right in the heart of Pittsburgh, exhausted after Ransom and his husband thankfully gathered their children after their special day with the uncles. Neither man has ever wanted to procreate, not with Ainsley and Ransom filling the world with more Bishops, and Uriah's siblings via his godmother are quite randy. Their rest was short-lived, because Wynn and Kade showed up to stuff them into a very large, and equally expensive, SUV, maxed out with the latest tech and all the creature comforts of home.

Their road trip was amazing, filled with many touristy stops along the way. Wynn was waylaid in Amish Country by woodcraft. But once they hit New England, every stop promising *real* maple syrup had Kade, Dan, and Uriah groaning like little kids asking, *are we there yet?*

Wynn and Kade are smarter than the average bear (Warren and Penny), and had the good sense to drop their kids off with the grandparents. Royce and Willa were happy to have some snuggles, since the twins have flown the coop and Brynn is lonely without siblings to harass. No fear, a broody Copper was dragged in by his ear, complaining he's an adult by Rusty Knob standards, and Penny's locked herself in Hailey's bedroom after Willa lit into her on the virtues of being a lady.

All's good in Rusty Knob, with Willa playing sheriff and Royce as her deputy.

Here, in Fairport, agreeable kids are tucked in beds, with the older Mason, Prynne, and Kline spawn roaming the streets as a gang of artists and misfits. The adults are also tucked in bed, either fast asleep or having a second honeymoon of their own.

Bren and Jack lied to Libby– the more gullible and agreeable of the mothers –saying they were going out with the boys, sticking Jesse and Libby with the kids for the night. Hiding out in a hotel room, Bren and Jack put the **Do Not Disturb** sign on the door, and plan to not come out until late tomorrow morning.

Clustered around the living room, in a rehabbed drug den, across the street from Rush, Polyamory Not-Anonymous meets face-to-face for the first time. After years upon years of online communications, and random phone calls, they finally meet those who offered comfort and support from afar.

"I wish we had people like us when we were younger." Essie's in a plush recliner, rocking a chubby baby. "Well, we had Robin."

"Robin!" Beth and Rory huff out in a laugh on the loveseat, with Devon's, "Tweety!" echoing from near their feet.

The wine is flowing, so Devon found a place on the floor– the grown man is kneeling by the coffee table, putting together a 500-Piece puzzle Maeve wants to hang in her bedroom –confusing the four men dominating the sofa.

Kade and Dan are cuddled in the center of the sofa, with Wynn and Uriah butted up closely to their sides, holding their hands. They may be confused, but they are also amused by how this house is run.

No surprise, Devon is obsessive, to the point he bought the house that changed his, Tina, Tom, and Taryn's lives. Devon bought the house and the lot next to it, Willow's company renovated it with several additions and an at-home practice for Beth, and Essie flawlessly planned to move eight people into it. Rory was pleased with the commute, a thirty-second jog across the street to get to work at Rush.

Devon and Essie, and Rory and Beth, and their four children haven't lived here long, but it's been a struggle to adapt, especially socially.

"At some point, you just have to go with your gut and not give a shit anymore when the townsfolk try to shame you." Devon looks up from his puzzle, pinning the four guys on the sofa. "I've broken most laws I was sworn to uphold. I've repented, but our relationship is the one thing the town holds against me. Do you see how ridiculous that is?"

"Gay!" Kade, Wynn, and Uriah blurt out, raising their hands, with Uriah finishing it out. "Even in today's day and age, gay is all people see. Especially allies, believe it or not. *I'm going to support Uriah's magazine because he's gay*, not because it's a great publication spreading information on LGBTQ issues. Like I have a handicap attached because of my sexual orientation and my nonbinary gender. I want my work to stand beside all the rest and be judged on its content– sometimes they toss in my ethnicity too."

"Woman!" Beth and Essie chirp at the same time, then giggle at one another.

"I understand, Uriah– I do." Beth reaches across the coffee table to pat the man's thin thigh. "Certain men are allowed to accomplish things without a disclaimer attached, and the rest of us aren't. Female and gay Olympiads– *the wife and mother won the gold medal*," Beth twists out in a commentator's voice. "Sometimes going as far as to give the husband's name first. *The gay diver broke a world record*. When just a man wins, his name is the subject of the announcement, and his achievement is the predicate, and there is no mention of his sexual orientation, ethnicity, gender, his relationships, or his children. He owns his accomplishments, not a large grouping of people or the husband and kids in his life."

"Oh, my God." Essie leans forward, adjusting the baby in her arms. "Remember when I won an award from the Fairport County Chamber of Commerce?"

Rory leans forward to take the little fella from his mother's arms. As the youngest of the children– Essie's last baby, since she had a tubal to ward off Devon's incessant need to procreate– Devon Junior is fair of hair and eyes, the spirit and image of the man holding him.

Incidentally, there is another little boy sleeping soundly in his bed upstairs. Rory Junior. Beth's only child is dark of hair with the darkest of blue eyes, and isn't the spirit and image of his namesake or his mother's husband.

The children's origins cause much speculation and censure among the pitchfork carrying townsfolk.

"Instead of the article being about Primp and Essie, it started off with the Mason legacy of law enforcement, listing John, Malcolm, Devon, Ozzy, all the way down to Violet, and mentioned the future generations they hoped to join the force." Cradling the baby to his chest, Rory looks down at Devon for a split-second before continuing with what he was saying.

"Then Weston was brought up, listing his entire football career– but it did add he was the *gay* co-head of Fairport School District's athletics department," Rory mutters wryly, squeezing his son to his chest.

"Oh, my God!" Essie throws her hand up in the air, causing everyone in the room to grin at her theatrics. "Then the article talked about Lucky Clover's, and all the foodservices it provides, never saying Clover's name at all. Then Ren and Wreck & Ruin–"

"My favorite was how they said your parents were wintering in Florida," Beth taunts Essie, earning a feminine growl in response. "Then they mentioned the kids, how Will is on the honor roll–"

"They never mentioned Essie until the last line of the article." Devon places a puzzle piece, focused and concentrating on the task at hand, not how there are too many people invading his personal space and the scent of alcohol riding the air. "Essie won an award for her mentoring and scholarship programs, and that was never once mentioned in the article. Essie's accomplishment was connected to everyone but her, as if she didn't do it– earn it herself."

"You're shitting me." Uriah leans forward, eyes narrowed with a glare, enraged for not only Essie, but the industry he loves so much. "Does this press have a physical location? Because this is the first time I've wanted to commit an act of vandalism."

"Cop!" Everyone but Uriah shouts, pointing at a grinning Devon.

"Don't worry about me– I'm sure my son has some spray paint somewhere." Another piece is set. "Colin caught Will, John, Opie, and Avi in the act last week. Crime spree for the untouchables. They were spray-painting a poem, of all things, on the basketball court at the little school. They were wooing Ian."

"Ah," Beth coos, an expression of pure happiness on her face. "That is so sweet, following in their parents' footsteps."

"Little too incestuous for my liking," Essie interjects, seeming terrified for her oldest child and baby brother-in-law. "Ian's a complication we don't need."

Beth's still advocating, "Ian and Opie are trying to get to know each other–"

"But wherever Penelope is, Will and John are sure to follow. I love Opie, and I want her to get to know Ian, but I don't want those boys around him."

"Lord knows what they're up to tonight," Rory mutters underneath his breath, looking proud of the mischievous new generation of Masons, Prynnes, and Klines. "Maybe they found a boombox at Revamped, and they're camped out in Ian's front lawn, reenacting a 1980s teen flick."

The newcomers on the sofa are leaning forward, soaking in every word, not knowing what any of it means, but are simultaneously relieved their lives are simpler, yet entertained by the drama playing out.

"And they say incest is a West Virginia thing," Wynn breathes into Kaden's ear, and a booming laugh filters through the living room.

"Yeah, this is deeply skirting incest, especially considering Ian's paternal line, *but the lines don't cross*," is directed at Essie in a tone that brooks no room for argument. "Our oldest son and my youngest brother, they're only a few weeks apart in age." Devon continues working his puzzle, able to be focused on one task while engaging in another, using it to keep his mind from spiraling out of control and the anxiety from rising.

"They spend every second together– it's not gross." Devon levels another look at his wife. "It's emotional, nothing sexual or romantic. After growing up around and in polyamory, they don't have the same views on relationships as everyone else. Opie and Avi's parents are in a triad. Our children in polyamory. My baby brother, John doesn't view the world like most do, even if his upbringing is traditional... so when this kid popped up on everyone's radar– I'm not going to get into the hows and whys – Will and John don't fight over him, and Ian's more confused than the rest of us."

"They're just wooing Ian into their gang– welcoming him into the fold and into the family." Rory puts his large paws over his son's ears. "They aren't trying to screw him."

"*Yet*," Essie bites out in a mother lion voice, not having it one bit.

Uriah bends forward to look across Dan and Kade at Wynn. "Remember when you laughed in our faces for saying we didn't want kids–"

"Yeah, but–"

"No, buts," Uriah stresses, gaze never disconnecting from Wynn's. "We have your kids, and our nieces and nephews– that's plenty... don't give me any more bullshit about being lonely in our old age without grandkids."

"We'll just spoil yours," Dan mutters wryly, eyes flicking to Kade. "Share in their accomplishments. Less drama, less cost, all the benefits."

"Yeah, but…" Wynn flashes Kade a pleading look. "Don't you want to see yourself in them?" Gesturing at Rory holding Devon Junior, son a miniature version of his father.

"You don't have any biological kids," Dan points out. "You only wanted Kade's, remember?"

"Well, maybe I want yours too," Wynn blurts out, and a second later he looks horrified. "Shit! I mean, look at Uriah– who wouldn't be interested in what his child would look like." Wynn backpaddles, face a wash of embarrassment. "I didn't just mean Dan's kids, by the way, even though that's how it sounded. I've been pressuring both of them. It's like I have a biological clock ticking down, but it ain't mine."

"Welcome to our world." Rory sings, voice filled with amusement. "You came to us for advice, and that's the most important we can give."

"What's your dynamic?" Beth interjects before things get dicey. "We have very clear lines in our relationship, and I'm curious about yours. No one ever wants to be honest when I ask."

"It's not something easy to talk about." Wynn's face turns to the side, refusing to meet anyone's gaze. "We're too worried about hurting anyone's feelings, or being rejected."

"I always knew I'd marry Essie someday." Devon stops sorting pieces to sit upright and stare at everyone on the sofa. "I was in the husband and wife mindset, where you've only bedded each other and no one else ever. It was society's picture of family and morality. But it didn't fit, no matter how hard we were forcing it– I don't mean our marriage. The mindset. When Rory and I first fit together, it was a struggle to come to terms with it."

"I was an insecure wreck, not gonna lie." Essie reaches for her son, needing a comfort object. "But then I realized, I had my best friends with me, and my husband was happy instead of hurting, and I let those insecurities go."

"I felt guilty," Rory pipes in, hand landing to rest on Devon's shoulder, fingers squeezing lightly. "I felt like I had to choose between my wife and my best friend, fearing it would destroy all four of us."

"It took *years*," Beth stresses. "We were living separately, struggling to find our place in the lives of the children we didn't bear, as if we weren't in one relationship. We eventually figured out we have several relationships inside a large partnership. The house, the kids, the accomplishments, the hurts and joys, they belong to *all* of us."

"About those several relationships…" Kade trails off, hand wavering to-and-fro, guilt obvious to anyone with eyes and ears. "What's yours?"

"You gonna tell us yours?" Beth volleys back, smirk flirting with her lips. "It's a romantic and sexual relationship between Rory and me, Devon and Essie, and Devon and Rory. Essie and I are best friends, and any girl out there will tell you that's a bond that no one can tear apart– it matters, and it's important."

"What about between you and Dev?" Uriah tries and fails to keep the tumultuous emotions out of his voice. "Rory and Essie?"

"Devon and I, we're best friends," Beth admits without hesitation. "Always will be– have each other's backs. But we're too much alike to forge a romantic connection. Not gonna happen."

"Do you have sex?" Dan's more than curious. "With Devon being demisexual?"

"We fuck, and it's good," Devon says outright, not caring there is a baby with impressionable ears in the room. "I love Beth, would never hurt her, and see her as my partner, but I'm never going to be in love with her, and I refuse to force it."

"Same!" Beth swats Devon upside the head, smirking down at him. "Don't force it."

Chill, Devon doesn't retaliate. "I was an atheist, but it was the kids that changed that for me. We'll get to Beth and Rory's struggles in a bit… but it was realizing God had a plan for us, that the four of us needed to come together, or my son sleeping upstairs wouldn't exist, and the baby in his mother's arms wouldn't either. Rory and Beth wouldn't be parents. No matter what society says, we were supposed to be together."

"I would like to know the struggles now, if you don't mind." Wynn is hyper-focused on children, and will do anything to avoid admitting feelings.

It's Beth's turn to be uncomfortable, face turning away, a sniffle echoing around the room. "I had a goal, and nothing would stop me. After I got my master's degree, I kept going for my PhD. I started my practice– we have a small garage in the back lot for me, but back then we didn't. I work with patients, but also with clients in our private club. I didn't realize fertility and age go hand-in-hand. I'm an educated woman, *obviously I knew*, but it didn't hit until it was too late."

"Even if we had tried when we first got married, it wouldn't have mattered, little pup." Rory pulls his wife into his arms, comforting her. While feathering kisses against her hair, he explains. "By the time Dev and Ess were pregnant with their second, we decided we wanted to try."

"Best friends, remember?" Beth's watery eyes and quivering smile has Rory holding her tighter. "I wanted to carry a baby at the same time as Essie, do all of that together, have our kids grow up together. That's a best friend thing. By the time Maeve was born, I still hadn't gotten pregnant."

"We did fertility testing, and Beth took hormones." Rory hides his face against the top of his wife's head, tears obvious in his voice. "By the time Will was eight or nine, and Maeve was four, we still couldn't get pregnant."

"It was *us*," Beth stresses. "Together. My body was attacking his sperm, no matter what meds I took to combat it. Fertilization was impossible. We tried IVF, and my body rejected the embryo."

"I always knew I'd put a kid in Beth's gut." Dev's words are harsh, almost unforgiving, but he takes over because Rory and Beth are too upset to continue. "Always knew it. Beth and I didn't have sex together for all those years they were trying– didn't want an oops. Maybe it was frustration, or anger at the world, but Beth didn't turn me away when I came to her in bed, and it took a long time to get pregnant, especially for a Mason."

Varying reactions of amusement and irony echo throughout the living room, with Beth's snort the loudest.

"I get it, Wynn." Devon looks across the room and connects with the other man. "You want biological children with the ones you love. Rory and Beth can understand how bittersweet it is to not share that. I feel it too, wanting children with Rory, and knowing it's a biological impossibility. So I gave my son Rory's name, a son grown inside his wife, and we did the same for the baby in my wife's arms right now... I get it."

"It's romantic between Essie and me." Rory continues to massage Devon's shoulders, sensing his emotions are going off the charts. "We're just built softer, I guess. It's hard to be with someone day-in and day-out, share a bed and children, and not be in love with them."

"So it doesn't bother any of you how everyone is in love with Rory, Devon and Beth aren't in love with each other, and Beth and Essie are just platonic?" Uriah's like a dog after a bone, clearly upset about the dynamic in his own relationship.

"I think it's time you're honest with each other," Beth orders knowingly, voice slipping into the one she uses during counseling sessions. "Wynn, I think it's best to come from you, judging by Uriah's questions."

"Do you guys see other people outside of the relationship?" Wynn is refusing to go there, terrified of Uriah's reaction to how he feels.

"You will stop evading me before this night is out, Wynn." Beth is confident, knowing she is slowly chipping away at Wynn's reluctance. "I'll answer this, but you will owe me my answer. Fair?"

"I promise," Wynn whispers, voice cracking.

"I trust your word." Beth looks at Essie, then Rory, finally settling on Devon. Beth and Devon hold a silent conversation for several suspended seconds. Nodding, Beth continues. "Rory and Essie are happy within our home, with no need to look outside of it. However, my profession is a sticky situation."

"A therapist?" Kade drawls out, eyebrows hitching high. "We're committed to each other."

"To have sex outside of a relationship doesn't mean we're not committed or faithful," Beth chastises, tone calm enough to make you open your mind, not get defensive.

"My patients have firm boundaries. However, the work I do in our private club is more hands-on. I'm helping others, teaching them about sex, and it involves sexual contact on my part. It has nothing to do with my partners, or even me, and everything to do with the gift I was given to help those who need my help."

"You have sex with other people, but no one else does?" There's no judgment in Uriah's voice, only curiosity. "I get how with Devon it's about an emotional connection. Are you guys okay with it?"

"That's funny you should say that…" Devon trails off, with a chorus of laughter from Beth, Rory, and Essie. "I have a pass– I'll probably never use it, but I have it just in case."

"One of our friends," Essie sneaks in, amused. "It's a game Devon and Kurt play, and none of us will be mad if it happens. There's a history there, but it's private. With Beth and the Playroom, it's our life and it makes sense to us. Someone did that for us once, pushed Rory and Dev together, and Beth's returning the favor."

"We have boundaries, just like everyone else." Rory's still chuckling at Devon, who's blushing and trying to sink into the floor. "I have no desire to go after anyone else, when I have everything I need at home, and then some."

"I go with Beth." Essie glances at her best friend. "She's never alone. Sometimes the guys go too. There's a risk emotionally, since Beth is tapped into their emotions. Physically, sexually, that's another issue."

"Most of my Playroom clients are women," Beth picks it back up. "When men are involved, Rory or Dev comes with me, and Essie stays home. Safety first. It's also in a family member's home. It's not about me getting off with other people."

"Devon, on the other hand…" Rory drawls, looking simultaneously amused and jealous.

"If Kurt would give me two seconds, I'd let you join." Devon snickers sinisterly. "Besides, we got to watch Beth fuck him."

"Whoa…" Essie reaches down to slap a palm over Devon's mouth. "Private."

"*Client.*" Beth shrugs it off, knowing Devon only said that because he's the jealous one. "We answered your questions, Wynn. You answer mine. What's the *actual* dynamic in your relationship."

"Obviously we're in love with our husbands." Sheepish for once, Wynn's having trouble pretending to be brave, fearing rejection himself. "Dan and Kade fell for each other first, starting with emails before their first day at college. I fucked up, and knew the only way this would work is if Dan wanted me, but that backfired."

"I wouldn't call that a backfire." Dan leans around Kade to cup Wynn's face. "It's mutual, you get that, right? I love you too, Wynn."

Breath hitching in his throat, it's evident Wynn didn't realize that, but it's Uriah's reaction that draws everyone's notice. A mournful sob is painful to hear, especially combined with the way Uriah slides down the sofa, away from everyone else. His partners stare at him, feeling utterly powerless and confused.

"Uriah," is a command from Beth. After years of conversations with all four of them, Beth is the only person who knows their fears and miscommunications, but is dutybound not to share their innermost truths, even if it was used as a means to heal. "Explain why that bothered you so much."

Sucking in a deep breath, Uriah is comforted by the firm hand Beth is using with him. "We're all in love with Dan, like Rory is with you guys." Sheepish, insecurities pounding him in all directions, Uriah refuses to look anyone in the eye.

"Everyone loves Dan, and Dan loves everyone." Hand lashing out, Uriah slips his fingers to lace with Dan's. "I'm happy about that, *honest*. Kade and Wynn love each other. But…" he stammers, unable to continue.

"But where does that leave you?" Beth coaxes, everyone else in the living room falling away for Uriah. "Are you on the outside looking in? Are you only included because of Dan? If you weren't around, would it matter?"

"Yes," Uriah breathes, expression so shattered, the men in the room grimace, and Essie clutches at her chest in pain. "I know how I feel about them, but Kade doesn't like me most of the time–"

"Stop!" Kade orders, voice whipping out to slap Uriah. "Our fighting all the time isn't because we don't like each other. It's because you're a brat who plays the martyr, and I'm a spoiled-rotten headcase. We butt heads, but that doesn't mean I don't love you, Ri."

"You love me?" Uriah perks up, seemingly shocked. "I love you too, and it hurts because we don't spend any time alone together, like we did when Dan was in Connecticut. I miss that– I miss us. We all find alone time with Dan, butnotwithme…" Uriah trails off quickly, words barely audible and scrunched together.

"It's hard to find any time for anything right now," Wynn growls, clearly as upset as Uriah. "Between work, our families, our kids, our friends, and the fucking drive, I spend most of my time either missing you, or on the phone with you."

"You miss me?" Uriah's voice pitches high, only to turn into a squeal of shock as a very large hand grabs him by the front of his shirt and hauls him over both Dan and Kaden. At seventy-pounds heavier and half a foot taller, Wynn easily manhandles Uriah onto his lap.

A flurry of whispered words is thrust into Uriah's ear, only loud enough for those on the sofa to hear. Wynn pours his heart out– the fear of rejection dissipating in the face of Uriah's misery. As the words slow, Uriah melts into Wynn's arms.

"I hear it," Wynn speaks to everyone in the room. "I hear the ignorant shit everyone says, and I know it's just the tip of the iceberg. We don't flaunt it, and being visible shouldn't be considered flaunting. We've had parents protest Kade and me working with kids, saying our lifestyle is morally reprehensible. They're the perverts, getting off on spreading how it's all about sex. Why are they even thinking about what we're doing in bed?"

"I'm no machine." Kaden releases a self-deprecating laugh. "Until this road trip, it had been months since we shared a bed together." Kaden reaches over to rub Uriah's back in comfort, then laces his fingers through Wynn's resting on Uriah's hip. "I hear it too, the condemnation."

"For me, it's about the intimacy and companionship." Dan's hand joins the party, trying to erase Uriah's pain through touch. "I spend the majority of my time either anticipating when I can see them again, or missing them desperately... I never feel satisfied or happy, like something is missing."

"It's a hollow ache that never goes away, even when we're together." Wynn glances across the room, comforted in the fact that understanding is reflected back at him– Devon, Essie, Beth, and Rory walked this rocky path before they did.

"When we're together, I'm praying time slows down, so I end up spending those precious hours fearing the ache when they're gone." Wynn closes his eyes, resting the side of his face against

Uriah's hair. "It has nothing to do with sex. Empty, that's how I feel most of the time, but it's how gutted I feel the instant they walk out our door that plagues me the most."

"So why do they?" Devon asks from his position on the floor, head cocked with confusion.

"Why do they what?" Wynn sounds even more confused.

"So why do they leave?" Rory answers, always jacked up to what's playing out in Devon's head. "Why do you let them leave your house? Stop them. Tell them to stay."

"Rusty Knob is our home," Kade tries to get everyone to understand. "We have roots. It's different for us, and I don't mean our families, or our children growing up where we did. The land is in our blood. We grew up poor, generations struggling to survive. The land was the only thing we had of any worth, and you never sell it, because the financial profit would be an emotional loss. Those seventy acres are all I have left of my father and grandfather– at least five generations of Marx men. We built our home on the land for Darien and Lydia– our children."

"Have you asked them?" Beth looks at Dan as she speaks to Kade. "Have you asked them if their roots in Pittsburgh matter more than their connection to you? It's understandable how you feel about your inheritance– your home."

"We're not selfish enough to ask that," Wynn butts in before Kade can answer. "I don't want the responsibility of being the one to ask, the one who caused them to resent us, knowing they wouldn't say no because it's not in their nature, not because they want to join us."

Uriah shifts off Wynn's lap to sit on the sofa cushion. "If you think it feels any different to us–"

"Then you've got another think coming," Dan mutters their private joke.

"You came here for our advice." Rory sits up farther on the loveseat, clearing his throat. "We grew up in the same town, lived blocks from each other, and felt that hollow ache you're talking about. I cannot imagine being a couple hours apart, having to drive to see each other a few times a month."

"I think we're missing the bigger picture here." Beth knows everyone in this room, inside and out, their secret fears and wants, and she's not going to tiptoe around it any longer. "We moved in together, had kids together, even though we have a platonic relationship between Ess and me, and a sexual one between Dev and me."

Always slower on the uptake, "I don't understand," Kade whispers, but it's obvious his partners are clued in.

Devon puts his puzzle pieces aside, then gazes at the occupants on his sofa with compassion. "Who cares what everyone else wants you to do? You're not broke, you're all educated, so location means squat. Stop making excuses. Stop living in stasis. Stop getting off by being in pain."

"What my husband is trying to say," Essie jumps in, because Devon is being his usual harsh self. "We're not all in love with each other, but we make it work. You guys have an advantage."

Looking around for some help, "What's that?" Kade asks, still confused.

Dan relaxes in relief, as Uriah and Wynn wear a shocked expression, looking enlivened by the revelation.

It's Dan who puts Kade out of his misery. "All four of us are in love with each other."

Thank you for reading POLISHED. Don't miss out on what's to come…

RUSTY KNOB– Wynn Gillette

TARNISHED– Royce Kennedy

STAINLESS– Brennan Kennedy & Kaden Marx

POLISHED– Daniel Bishop, Kaden Marx, & Wynn Gillette

COMING SOON:

CORRODED– Cain Probst & Jeb Franklin

Acknowledgements

A lot of work goes into writing a novel, and it isn't just by the writer herself. **My parents:** for their unconditional support. **My readers**: thank you for reading my twisted words and spreading my books to the masses. For without you, no one would've ever heard of my stories. My readers are my lifeblood. A shout out to the members of the **M&M of Restraint Group on Facebook**: thanks for the endless entertainment and inspiration. **Wicked Reads**: (in all its incarnations) **Angela G.**, thank you for taking over and making Wicked Reads better than I could have done by myself. & thank you for helping promote my work and the work of other authors. Angela? Have I told you lately how much I appreciate you? A huge thank you to the **Wicked Writer's Betas** for keeping me grounded and encouraging me to keep trudging along when I get frustrated. Your thoughts and observations are invaluable. ((Hugs)) Beta readers who helped with Polished: **Kris | Angela | Linsey | Tassie |** Someday I'd love to meet you all in real life– it would be the experience of a lifetime.

ABOUT THE AUTHOR

Erica Chilson does not write in the 3rd person, wanting her readers to *be* her characters. Therefore, writing a bio about herself, is uncomfortable in the extreme.

Born, raised, and here to stay, the Wicked Writer is a stump-jumper, a ridge-runner. Hailing from North Central Pennsylvania, directly on the New York State border; she loves the changes in seasons, the humid air, all the mountainous forest, and the gloomy atmosphere.

Introverted, but not socially awkward, Erica prides herself on thinking first and filtering her speech. There are days she doesn't speak at all. If it wasn't for the fact that she lives with her parents, giving her a sense of reality, she would be a hermit, where the delivery man finds her months after expiration.

Reading was an escape, a way to leave a not-so pleasant reality behind. Reading lent Erica the courage she gathered from the characters between the pages to long for a different life. Writing was an instrument of change, evolving Erica into the woman she is today– a better, more mature, more at peace thinker.

Erica has a wicked mind, one she pours out into her creations. Her filter doesn't allow all of it to erupt, much to her relief. Sarcastic, with a very dark, perverse sense of humor, Erica puts a bit of herself into every character she writes.

I love hearing from readers. If you would like more information on release dates, works in progress, teaser chapters, and random bits of madness, please visit my Facebook Fan Page:
https://www.facebook.com/thewickedwriter my website:
ericachilson.com or please contact me via email:
wickedwriter.ericachilson@gmail.com
DEVIANTS ONLY, if you'd like to join Erica Chilson's closed Facebook group, M&M of Restraint:
https://www.facebook.com/groups/MistressandMaster/

www.ingramcontent.com/pod-product-compliance
Lightning Source LLC
Chambersburg PA
CBHW070158260626
47160CB00002B/378